PERFORMING WHITELY IN THE POSTCOLONY

Performing **WHITELY**

STUDIES IN

THEATRE HISTORY

AND CULTURE

Edited by Heather S. Nathans

in the Postcolony

AFRIKANERS IN SOUTH AFRICAN
THEATRICAL AND PUBLIC LIFE

MEGAN LEWIS

UNIVERSITY OF IOWA PRESS Iowa City

University of Iowa Press, Iowa City 52242
Copyright © 2016 by the University of Iowa Press
www.uiowapress.org
Printed in the United States of America

Design by Richard Hendel

The University of Iowa Press is a member of Green Press Initiative and is committed to preserving natural resources.

Printed on acid-free paper

Library of Congress Cataloging-in-Publication Data
Names: Lewis, Megan, 1968– author.
Title: Performing whitely in the postcolony : Afrikaners in South African theatrical and public life / Megan Lewis.
Description: Iowa City : University of Iowa Press, [2016] |
Series: Studies in theatre history and culture | Includes bibliographical references and index.
Identifiers: LCCN 2016007770 | ISBN 978-1-60938-447-0 (pbk) | ISBN 978-1-60938-448-7 (ebk)
Subjects: LCSH: Theater—South Africa. | Performing arts—South Africa. | Afrikaners in literature. | Whites in literature. | Race relations in literature. | Afrikaners—Race identity—South Africa. | Whites—Race identity—South Africa. | South Africa—Social conditions—21st century.
Classification: LCC PN2984.2 .L49 2016 | DDC 792.0968—dc23
LC record available at https://lccn.loc.gov/2016007770

For Tristan

CONTENTS

ACKNOWLEDGMENTS

No life of the mind is possible without material support. This book was made possible by the generosity and support of two institutions: the University of Massachusetts Amherst and the University of Minnesota. At UMass, I am thankful for the unflagging support of my Chair, Penny Remsen, Dean, Julie Hayes, and my colleagues in the Department of Theater; and for research funds from the College of Humanities and Fine Arts, Massachusetts Society of Professors, and Publication Subvention Program. At Minnesota, I was supported by an Imagine Grant, Faculty Travel Grants, International Travel Grant from the Office of International Programs and Institute of Global Studies, and a UMN Scholarly Events Fund Grant to sponsor Peter Van Heerden's residency in 2010. A Targeted Research Grant from the American Society for Theatre Research also made this scholarship possible. I thank the Five College Performance Studies Seminar and Gibson Cima at Tufts University and Grinnell College for the space to work through chapters in progress. I am eternally grateful to my expert editors, Heather Nathans and Catherine Cocks, for their faith in me and support of this work; to Susan Hill Newton at University of Iowa Press, and Christi Stanforth, my freelance copyeditor; and to my peer review interlocutors.

For intellectual and emotional support, I thank my villages of colleagues, mentors, and friends, from North America to South Africa: Judyie Al-Bilali, Robin Back, Lou Bellamy, Jenna Blum, Marcia Blumberg, Joye Bowman, Lisa Channer, Gibson Cima, Stephen Clingman, Catherine Cole, Clifton Crais, Laura Edmondson, Harley Erdman, Mark Fleishman, John Fletcher, James Graham, Viveca Greene, Chris Grobe, John Higginson, Tim Huisamen, Talya Kingston, Michal Kobialka, Anton Krueger, Sonja Kuftinec, Stephanie Lein-Walseth, Alex Lewis, Chet Longo, the MN Mafia, Priscilla Page, Chris Perry, James Plugh, Malcolm Purkey, Penny Remsen, Jennie Reznek, Daniel Sack, Eric Severson, Amilcar Shabazz, Demetria Shabazz, Jenny Spencer, Charlie Sugnet, Maggi Tocci, Pabalelo Tshane, Tamara Underiner, and Shannon Walsh. I thank all the undergraduates who continue to join me in working through whiteness, performance, and African theatre in my classes and my graduate students, from whom I have learned more than I ever could teach them, particularly my fellow Global South minds: Ryan Hartigan, Elliot Leffler, and Paul Adolphsen. My deepest thanks goes to the artists who have opened their minds, hearts, homes, and archives to me for this book: Deon Opperman, Peter Van Heerden, and Pieter-Dirk Uys. I thank my pioneering English adventurer father, Clive Lewis, for inspiring me to take risks and encouraging the art of writing. I thank my Afrikaner artist and iconoclast mother, Majak Bredell, for keeping the Afrikaans language alive for me all these years in America and for teaching me how to speak truth to power. And finally, I could not have written this book without my husband, Michael, who nourishes me body, mind, and soul, and our son, Tristan, for whom I do the work I do.

Please forgive any errors; they are, of course, my own.

PREFACE

STAKES OF PERFORMANCE AND RACE,

NORTH AND SOUTH

I wrote this book in Amherst, Massachusetts, seven thousand miles away from my birthplace of Johannesburg, South Africa. Several potent images have framed my writing, connecting North and South in a social choreography of racialized impressions. They are iconic images embedded in deeply troubled histories, and they express the complex, imbalanced matrices of power of the cultures that engendered them. Circulated repeatedly by global media, these images enact rehearsed scenarios[1] that culture circulates, consumes, and internalizes. They perform, at least partially, the racial dynamics of their societies. I begin by connecting images, North and South, because this work, a study of South African whiteness and performance, is in constant conversation with the racialized dynamics of my current home in America. And because whiteness needs serious attention in the United States, now more than ever.

The first image crystallized during the revision of this manuscript, when protests erupted in Ferguson, Missouri, after Darren Wilson, a white police officer, shot and killed an unarmed black teenager named Michael Brown on August 9, 2014, and left his body in the street for hours. On November 24, a grand jury decided not to prosecute Wilson. Protestors in Ferguson carried signs and walked with their hands in the air, shouting, "Don't shoot!" The fallout from Ferguson was coupled with the fatal shooting of another unarmed teenager, Trayvon Martin, by another white man, George Zimmerman, on February 26, 2012, in Sanford, Florida. The Black Lives Matter movement, which has taken up the "Hands Up, Don't Shoot" gesture, coalesced following Martin's death as "a call to action and a response to the virulent anti-Black racism that permeates our society" (blacklivesmatter .com) and has gained greater momentum following Brown's death, as well as the choke-hold death of Eric Garner in Staten Island on July 17, 2014.[2] Thus, the image of an unarmed black man with his hands raised above his head haunts our contemporary landscape and, for me, conjures up images of black Africans being dehumanized by white policemen in another part of the world. The racialized dynamics of these global choreographies, from South to North, are my focus.

I grew up in one of the world's most blatantly racist societies—apartheid South Africa—where hideous atrocities were inflicted on black South Africans in the name of protecting little white girls like me. The South African Police (SAP) and South African Defense Force (SADF)—the joint civil and military arms that enforced the apartheid regime—routinely dehumanized black South Africans to quell unrest in the townships. The second set of images I consider here are of SAP officers whipping black bodies with truncheons and *sjamboks* (bullwhips) and unleashing snarling dogs on fleeing protestors, scenarios that permeated the apartheid era. They pair in an uneasily familiar way with the representations circulating in the American media of 2014 and 2015, which in turn cite images from the American civil rights era.

Undergirding these iconic images of police brutality in both my home and adopted country are systems of white supremacy that privilege portions of the population over others, enforce racism under the name of peacekeeping, law, and order, and allow white authorities to enact violence on black and brown bodies[3] with impunity. Under apartheid, black South Africans were brutalized while white authority reigned supreme. Police officers fudged paperwork and circulated misinformation, assaulted and tortured prisoners to coerce confessions, and threatened and intimidated black people (Duncan 1964; J. D. Brewer 1994; Brogden and Nijhar 1998; Shear 2012). In the US context, predominantly white juries agree not to press charges against white officers (Associated Press 2014), and white officers are mostly unconscious of their own implicit bias (Semien, Meek, and Cole 2015). Police departments are often given incentives to increase arrests in poorer neighborhoods where blacks and Latinos reside, effectively creating an "artificially criminalized underclass" (King 2015; Davey 2015; Shapiro 2014). Finally, law enforcement is increasingly militarized (Edwards 2015), thereby justifying what Tim Wise (2014) calls modern lynching, "the extrajudicial killing of [black] people without a trial for their real or perceived crimes." Whiteness—that invisible yet ubiquitous structure of privilege and power that has undergirded and continues to define culture in both South Africa and the United States—is at the core of both these scenarios; both my homes are haunted by whiteness. This book is my attempt to wrestle with whiteness, to make visible — using the language of performance — the "machine" (Martinot 2010) of whiteness that is designed to perpetuate itself uncritically.

For my third image, I'd like to juxtapose the iconic figure that haunts the American imaginary at the moment — a black man with his hands up in surrender — with a South African analog: a white hero fallen from grace, his face buried in his hands, sobbing for his sins. The heroic rise and tragic fall of Olympian and Paralympian sprinter Oscar Pistorius has fed into the global imaginary around whiteness. Celebrated for overcoming his disability as the "Blade Runner," he was knocked from his heroic pedestal when he shot and killed his girlfriend, Reeva Steenkamp, whom he mistook for an intruder, on February 14, 2013, in his home in Pretoria (Tolsi 2013). In 2014, Judge Thokozile Masipa found him guilty of culpable homicide (akin to manslaughter) and sentenced him to five years imprisonment, only ten months of which he served before being released on house arrest in October 2015 (de Wet 2014). His trial held the world's attention for almost a year as it rehearsed narratives of fearful white (Afrikaner) men living in laagers (gated communities in Centurion near Pretoria) who shoot first and ask questions later, who are gun-happy and entitled, and who ultimately "get away with murder" (Kelto 2014; Sinha 2014). But Pistorius's drama is also a story of remorse. In court he cried distinctly unmanly tears (in South African terms), and he has reached out to Reeva's family financially and to apologize. One might say that Pistorius stands as the metonym for white masculinity in contemporary South Africa: caught between his horrific past actions and his attempts to negotiate a better future, an entitled man deprived of his privilege. Pistorius as metonym also marks how shame is triggered when whiteness fails to live up to its ideal. News stories paint him as a hero fallen from grace, an abhorrent self who has crossed a line and become othered (Steinberg 2013).

Yet although he has been made to face his demons, to pay for his crime, he also remains in a position of advantage compared to black or brown prisoners in his same situation.[4] Pistorius, as a white Afrikaner man, remains cocooned by his wealth, his maleness, and his whiteness. First, his wealth afforded him the best legal representation money could buy. It also allowed him to offer significant financial compensation to Steenkamp's family. Second, his maleness eclipsed Reeva Steenkamp and her family behind what Brad Cibane calls "the skyline of Oscar's privilege" (2014). Overshadowed by his spotlight, Reeva's tragic death as a victim of domestic violence (a reality for multitudes of women in South Africa; Faul 2013) retreats into the shadows. And third, Pistorius benefited from an entrenched system of white privilege that assumed him to be innocent until proven guilty and that argued for preferential treatment in his sentencing. The defense's argument for leniency and the judge's decision to allow him to serve all but ten months of his sentence under house arrest all drew on his status as a first-time offender, his remorse, and the likelihood of his rehabilitation, all considerations that he was afforded due to his racial, gender, and social status (Dixon 2014; Dlanga 2014).

Pistorius's identity is also complicated by his disability. He was perceived as a hero for defying the limitations of his body, excelling not only in the Paralympics but also in the "regular" Olympics. He became superhuman, an imperfect body who, through willpower and talent, overcame his limitations. Imagined as a superman, with all its Aryan supremacist logic, he also defied perceptions about disabled people as asexual: having a fashion model girlfriend affirmed his masculinity despite his disability. But after his fall, the apartheid-era perceptions about disabled people as deformed, twisted, or cursed returned; his actions were a sign that he and his Afrikaner masculinity were inherently cruel, depraved, and evil. Disabled by his history as a white Afrikaner male, and unable to perform his white masculinity competently, he was caught in an impossible bind.

Pairing the black man with his hands raised in defense with the white man, his head in his hands sobbing, sets out the stakes of my investigation into whiteness and performance, tying whiteness always to the violent, repressive regimes that enforce its privilege. In the following pages, I will tease out the tensions surrounding a population of white Africans known as Afrikaners as they register in the global imaginary and perform themselves across their 360-year history on the southern tip of Africa. What are the performance dynamics of this population, who occupy a contested position in South Africa culture as European settlers, outsiders and invaders, yet who hold a deep and abiding sense of belonging in Africa? How have they leveraged performance to stage themselves into, around, and out of power over the past century? And what can their scenarios contribute to our larger understanding of whiteness in our postcolonial moment? Following Sarah Nuttall, my hope is that this study will reveal "what South Africa can contribute to global debates about identity, power, and race" (2009, 12). As I

trace the history and performances of Afrikaners within and outside the laager or circle of wagons, I will reveal, through my own subject position as a
South African–born American, the potentials and pitfalls, tensions and fault
lines of what it means to perform as a white subject in what Achille Mbembe
(2001) calls the postcolony[5] and which Mark Fleishman describes as the
"multiple, contradictory moments in everyday life in Africa read against
the persistent accretions of slavery, colonialism, apartheid, and neoliberal
forms of democracy" (2011, 8).

Amherst, MA

2015

PERFORMING WHITELY IN THE POSTCOLONY

INTRODUCTION

I begin by defining who Afrikaners are and mapping their representation in the global imaginary. Then, as I theorize whiteness and the way it intersects with performance, I clarify my own positionality and methodological approach and explicate the book's title, *Performing Whitely in the Postcolony*. After locating my book in the literature on whiteness and situating whiteness's reliance on performance, I illuminate how South Africa is located within the global colonial context, then I place this work within the fields of Theater and Whiteness Studies and briefly summarize each chapter. As I chart various scenarios of South African whiteness, I suggest what they offer to our global understanding of how whiteness is imagined, staged, perpetuated, and resisted, and what options white subjects have to perform their whiteness in the postcolony. Throughout this introduction, I make reference to the 2013 Whitewash Conference, which I use to unearth many of the stakes around studying whiteness in South Africa.

WHITE AFRICANS IN THE GLOBAL IMAGINARY

"*Kaffir* lover," spits the silver-haired old white man with the heavy South African accent (Joss Ackland) at the white detective (Riggs, played by Mel Gibson) about his black partner (Murtaugh, played by Danny Glover) in the 1989 sequel to *Lethal Weapon*. In the same year that President F. W. de Klerk began negotiations with imprisoned African National Congress (ANC) leader Nelson Mandela, Ackland's character disavowed moral responsibility, saying to Riggs that he had "diplomatic im-*mun*-ity," ejecting every word from his mouth as if the syllables were arrows. Ackland plays Arjen Rudd, the minister of diplomatic affairs for the South African consulate in Los Angeles, and he and his enforcer, Pieter Vorstedt, are using their diplomatic immunity to launder millions in krugerrands (then illegal in the United States) and run a drug ring. "My dear officer," Rudd chuckles, flaunting his immunity, "you could not even give me a *pah-king tickit!*"

Rudd and Vorstedt are marked as Afrikaners, South Africa's white settlers of Dutch and French Huguenot descent who colonized and then dominated the southern tip of Africa starting in the seventeenth century, became the architects of apartheid in the twentieth century, and since 1994 have been part of a multicultural, polyglossic democracy.[1] Depicted as cutthroat racists, these characters are emblematic of the way that Afrikaners are frequently portrayed in popular culture, particularly outside South Africa. With his thick accent, marked by its rolling r's and guttural tone, Ackland's Afrikaner is thuggish and simple-minded. The physical brutality of Vorstedt and the racist epithets he and Rudd use so easily draw on common practices of, and assumptions about, Afrikaners, who created and commanded the apartheid system in South Africa from 1948 to 1994. This image of the Afrikaner portrayed outside South Africa is a product of discursive practices aimed at assuaging American white guilt and making us[2] (Americans) feel better about ourselves by positioning the racist Afrikaner claiming immunity from moral responsibility as our abhorred Other.

Lethal Weapon 2's depiction of Afrikaners is not uncommon. Whenever Western media report on Afrikaners, common tropes frame their storytelling, and they fall into easy use of stock characters: evil racists, insular whites, and heroes fallen from grace. First, there are the Afrikaners as what poet and author Antjie Krog calls "bad racists on the rise" (2009), ugly bigots whose whiteness defines their every move. Rudd and Vorstedt are openly racist, unabashedly using the word *kaffir* (the South African analog for the N-word) and treating black characters with loathing and disdain.[3] When Afrikaners are covered by the international media, the stories are about right-wing splinter groups like the AWB, the Afrikaner Weerstandsbeweging (Afrikaner Resistance Movement), and its leader, Eugène Terre'Blanche,[4] who was murdered by laborers on his farm in 2010. Or they are stories about the Kommandokorps, an extreme right-wing group that trains young men to defend their *volk* (nation) (van Gelder 2011). Or they are narratives about racist white university students who made a degrading video about abusing black janitorial staff at the University of the Orange Free State in 2008 in reaction to the university's efforts to integrate its residences ("Outcry in South Africa" 2008).

Second, there are the wagon-circling supremacists, anxious white Africans enclosing themselves in gated communities, whites-only areas, or wagon laagers. As I will argue, the laager of wagons that Dutch pioneers used in the nineteenth century to protect themselves from the African wilderness and its inhabitants is a founding organizational metaphor for Afrikaner self-representation. Western media draw on this "laager mentality" in their storytelling about Afrikaners, highlighting gated, whites-only communities such as Orania and Kleinfontein ("Orania" 1991).[5]

And third, there are Afrikaners as once-exalted people now fallen from grace. Oscar Pistorius is one example, as I discussed in the preface. There are also stories of poor Afrikaners, the Rainbow Nation's new underclass. In July 2008, Peter Biles reported for the BBC on "South Africa's hidden white poverty," framing poor Afrikaners as victims of the new political dispensation.[6] Retrenched as part of the Black Economic Empowerment (BEE) efforts of the new democracy, "poor whites are joining poor blacks in poverty," claims Biles. And a piece produced by ABC Australia in 2007 features images of a white Afrikaner man begging at a busy intersection, making a gesture with his fingers to his mouth at each passing driver. Then, holding his hands in a prayer pose and clearly exasperated, he pinches back tears with his dirt-covered hands (ABC Australia and Journeyman Pictures 2006). In contrast to the finger-wagging, entitled white supremacist embodied by former prime minister P. W. Botha during the 1980s, the new image of Afrikaners is a portrait of a suffering population victimized by democracy.

Suffice it to say, the narratives of racist South African whites engaging in deplorable acts with immunity, enclosing themselves in gated communities, or claiming abjection after losing the privilege apartheid afforded them permeates our popular imaginary. This "laager mentality" draws from a long history of the concepts of enclosure and exclusion that began on the frontier of the Cape Colony and were popularized as part of the Afrikaner nationalist project—the cultural, religious, and political movement of Afrikaner ascendancy that led up to the formation of the apartheid state in 1948. These early twentieth-century efforts aimed to galvanize and unify a decidedly "Afrikaner"—white, Calvinist, patriarchal—volk, by leveraging cultural capital, nation-building theatrics, and public performance.

POSITIONAL ENTANGLEMENTS

I remember my own feelings of shame at the lack of remorse of Joss Ackland's character and his goon, and at the ugly portrayal of "my people," when I saw Lethal Weapon 2 in New York in 1989. I was appalled at their racism and ashamed that we shared ancestry. I was also outraged at the glib way that an entire people was depicted as unabashed racists. This shame and outrage catalyzed a deep and abiding need to understand the matrix of whiteness and privilege I was born into as a white South African of mixed British and Afrikaner ancestry.[7]

As such, and living and working in the United States as a naturalized American citizen, I have a strong scholarly and personal relation to this subject matter. Inhabiting multiple cultural borderlands, mine is an entangled, hybrid identity. I am an English-speaking South African American, daughter of an English father and an Afrikaner mother. An Anglicized name masks my Afrikaner roots. And hard Americanized r's obscure my flattened South African vowels. In 1981 I emigrated from South Africa to the United States, where I eventually earned my doctorate and where I have lived for the past three decades. As Jonathan Jansen suggests, "Outsider status, the stance of not-being-at-home, yields valuable analytical advantage" (2009, 21). My "outsider stance" allows me the critical distance necessary to tackle this topic as an object of scholarly inquiry, just as my insider situatedness means I bring a unique and intimate perspective to it. My positionality as insider-outsider, or what Sarah Nuttall (2009) would call entanglements, is also central to this work. At times, I place myself in the first person; at others, I assume the distanced third person. Wherever possible, I note such shifts in address and point to the split such shifts indicate.

Afrikaners continue to occupy a complex political, social, and imagined position in South African culture. As a settler culture[8] with a 360-year history on the African continent, "we" call ourselves "of Africa" (Afrikaners) and claim deep ties to South African soil, seeking, as J. M. Coetzee claims in *White Writing*, "a dialogue with Africa, a reciprocity with Africa that will allow [us] an identity better than that of visitor, stranger, transient" (1988, 8). Afrikaners have also been responsible for the longest-standing, openly white supremacist, minority-dominated state in recent history. Their leadership also relinquished power in the historic period of the early 1990s, and Afrikaners are negotiating new ways of participating as one ethnic group among many in the twenty-year-old democracy. While the media portrayals I have just described present a narrow vision of Afrikaners as racists, most today are living in a space where racism lives side by side with progress, where tolerance and intolerance, old and new, historically disenfranchised and newly enfranchised coexist. It is no longer a world where, as Eusebius McKaiser claims, "South African whites [can be] unconsciously habituated into an uncritical white way of being" (2012, 2); rather, it is space in which white privilege is being called to task and made to answer for its sins. It is a world of conflicting coexistence, at once looking nostalgically to the past, struggling with a fluid present, and moving uncertainly toward the future.

When I saw *Lethal Weapon 2* in 1989, I had yet to begin my formal education in theatre and performance studies, or to have the language of postcolonial and critical theory with which to name the discourses this film was circulating and circulating within. But I knew that something about the way Ackland spat out "diplomatic immunity" was deeply troubling. I knew I could not remain immune to his ugly racism and patriarchal entitlement, nor could I sit idly by as this version of Afrikaners dominated the popular imaginary of my adopted country. What I registered then were the stakes of my insider-outsider position, suspended between critiquing my country's racist past and hoping for my family's future. In my work, I strive toward what I call a compassionate position of critique—what Vincent Crapanzano, in his book *Waiting: The Whites of South Africa*, called having "a certain sympathy even for people whose values one finds reprehensible" (1985).

METHODOLOGY

My task in this study is to find a way to write about Afrikaner theatre and performance that neither patriotically deifies it nor glibly demonizes it. I draw great inspiration from John Fletcher, who has written eloquently on the stakes of writing activist theatre history (2012). How, as theatre and performance scholars, he asks, are we to engage with work that does not follow or support left-progressive agendas? As critic-historians, he suggests, we often write from a space of "avowed sympathy with the causes of our subjects" (2012, 110), but "you can't afford to treat communities and groups that you politically oppose, however fiercely, as if their motivations and habitus aren't as complex and historically intricate as any other community or group" (2012, 8). Theorizing through thick description, I demonstrate the intricacies of Afrikaner performance at multiple positions on the political spectrum. I follow Fletcher in espousing "good-faith criticism" that urges us to approach non-left-leaning subjects not with what Eve Kosofsky Sedgwick (2002, 126) identifies as the "paranoid stance"—a scholarly attitude that takes as its starting point the certainty of large, oppressive systems that operate behind the scenes—but rather with "critical envy," what Fletcher describes as being "open to finding something in the other's position or methods that you find admirable, that you wished your own side had in greater abundance" (2012, 9). Such an approach, according to Fletcher, "can make our theatrical histories of activism more careful, more effective, and more curious" (2012, 9).

Yet I remain acutely aware that any study that explores the dramatic matrix of whiteness, history, and performance—and Afrikaners specifi-cally—enters into risky territory. I risk being conflated with my subject mat-ter, especially because of my ethnicity, deemed a supporter of the worst sides of white supremacist identity and behavior. I also want to avoid falling into the facile Afrikaner-as-pariah trope that writes off an entire population of "white people" as right-wing racists without any redeeming value. Such are my challenges as I embark on this study of a population who claim white-ness explicitly and cannot escape their notorious history of minority rule. My aim is to interrogate Afrikaner performances and to *trouble whiteness*. I put Afrikaners in the spotlight, not to extol their position, but to better under-stand something about how whiteness and hegemony are created, enacted, and contested.

The study of whiteness is also tricky territory. Recently I participated in the first-ever academic conference on whiteness at the University of Johan-nesburg (UJ). The goal of the two-day conference, titled "Whitewash" and held in March 2013, was to address Critical Whiteness Studies' lacunae within the South African academy and to "critically rethink, renegotiate and reframe whiteness within the global South" (Farber and Falkof 2013). The first morning of the conference was fraught. Passionate critiques were flung across the room: that by studying whiteness we were simply recenter-ing white privilege, or that our efforts (as a gathering of white scholars) were acts of "navel-gazing" that ultimately reified whiteness and the privileged positions of white scholars, or that to study whiteness was "impossible." These comments were made by the few people of color in the room as well as some members of the invited plenary panel.[9] Anxiety was palpable, and the threat that the conference would be canceled before it had even started loomed large.

As a US-based scholar working in Whiteness Studies, I had felt these anxi-eties before. I understood the critique weighed at the conference (particu-larly by people of color) and the stench of privilege that marred its very in-ception (especially at UJ, which used to be the conservative Rand Afrikaans University). I witnessed the anxiety and shame of the mainly white scholars who did not want to be seen as asserting their privilege and who simultaneously wanted to share their critical work on whiteness as a first step as *allies*, toward dismantling the privilege of whiteness. Who if not white people, we argued, should undertake the study of whiteness and begin the labor of dismantling white supremacy from within? Eventually, there was consensus to move ahead with the conference and to focus on articulating the "critical" in the discipline and practice of Critical Race Studies.

Because of its implications with power, whiteness is difficult to discuss, as it triggers anxiety from multiple sides. For many people of color, for instance, the mention of whiteness triggers outrage because of their personal experiences on the receiving end of that power structure. For many of those who benefit from white privilege, discussing whiteness is an endeavor riddled with guilt and discomfort. Louise Bethlehem, for example, in her plenary remarks at the 2013 Whitewash Conference, described Whiteness Studies as a "guilt-etched endeavor," and the self-critique and nervousness with which that conference began is an indication of such an epistemology.

The facts that such tension surrounded the conference, and that it took until 2013 for such a conference to be held in South Africa in the first place, inform my need to write this book, which represents my scholarly and pedagogical labor over the past two decades. In all of the literature about whiteness (which is heavily weighted toward the American situation) cursory mention may be given to the Global South, and to South Africa particularly, but very few scholars have taken on whiteness in this racially charged nation. Melissa Steyn has long been one of the few.[10] My study intervenes where others have not, especially in the United States, as I believe that by bringing whiteness into closer focus, by examining how and in what manners it operates and is performed in culture, we do not risk recentering its power and privilege, but accomplish the exact opposite. By putting whiteness "under erasure" as Bethlehem (2013) suggests[11]—by critiquing its existence as it remains legible and examining its paradoxes, inadequacies, and ambiguities—we can begin to dismantle its power.

EMPIRES OF WHITENESS

As settler colonies, Canada, the United States, Australia, New Zealand, and South Africa are all former sites of European colonization, all nations that have settler populations who permanently relocated to each colony and became entangled (Nuttall 2009) in its culture and history. Under the logic of "Anglosphere" empire (Yancy and Chomsky 2015), these spaces were framed and shaped by white privilege and supremacy, as two recent studies demonstrate. Lake and Reynolds (2008) trace the formation of these five so-called White Men's Countries from the mid-nineteenth century to the early twentieth. They trace how white European men sought to secure their political and economic interests across the globe using whiteness as a "transnational form of racial identification" (3). And Boucher, Carey, and Ellinghaus (2009, 3) argue for "read[ing] the colonial back into whiteness" by demonstrating how this racial category traveled around the routes of empire.

In the United States, white supremacy undergirds the culture but whiteness remains largely invisible, requiring obscurity in order to remain in power. Unlike the United States, where whites hold a majority, South Africa has a majority indigenous population and whites have been a minority ever since colonization, comprising about 10 percent of the population. Yet while South African whiteness was explicitly foregrounded under apartheid (as it was in Jim Crow America), it still requires amnesia to function. South Africa, which Jansen describes as "the last of the former colonies and the last of the settler states to yield on white minority rule" (2009, 24), is a new democracy that offers a compelling site in which to explore *how the once-privileged perform once that privilege is deflated.* I use South Africa's Afrikaners to examine how whiteness and nation function not simply to focus on an esoteric site but, rather, to ask what this case study can reveal about some of the ways in which whiteness operates and how performance functions within and against it. I imagine the Afrikaner case study to be a provocation to understand the lingering desire for national belonging in our historical moment, when the nation-state is no longer the singular defining structure of communal identity and in a space and time where historic baggage and personal truths collide. As a global lesson in our postcolonial moment, this study looks to Afrikaners to see both the potentials and pitfalls, the nostalgic acts that regress toward the past, as well as bold new performance negotiations of national identity. I don't claim Afrikaners are unique in their use of performance to articulate their nationhood; rather, they exemplify such practices, which may be instructive to contexts outside South Africa, particularly the United States.

THEORIZING WHITE(LI)NESS
I will now tease out how race, power, and performance cofunction and what South African whiteness, particularly Afrikaner whiteness, can contribute

to our understanding of theories of whiteness. Below I outline several such theories, key concepts I have gleaned from the significant body of scholarship on the subject.

First, whiteness is interdisciplinary, as it is always embedded in multiple discourses. Fundamentally, I understand whiteness to be the pivotal concept around which the very idea of race is constructed. Boucher, Carey, and Ellinghaus, in *Re-Orienting Whiteness*, describe whiteness as "the sovereign — if sometimes silent — social, legal, cultural, and experiential category that the very idea of race functions to privilege" (2009, 5). The hegemony of whiteness functions when it is juxtaposed against an imagined less powerful opposite: blackness. Toni Morrison, in her seminal work on literary whiteness, articulates how the Self (the white writer's assumed sense of Americanness) requires an Other (a real or fabricated Africanist presence) in order to exist (1992, 6). Morrison notes how blackness becomes for whiteness "an extraordinary meditation on the self" (1992, 17). For Morrison, racism not only impacts the non-white subject, but "equally valuable is a serious intellectual effort to see what racial ideology does to the mind, imagination, and behavior of masters" (1992, 12).

My whiteness in South Africa afforded me privileges not available to black citizens because of the politicized fiction of difference on which the apartheid state was based. I understand whiteness to be an imagined category of identity, based on the fiction of racial difference, but one that nonetheless has material consequences both for those within its sphere of privilege and for those who are excluded from it. As Alfred Lopez suggests, "Whiteness is not, yet we continue for many reasons to act as though it is" (2005, 1). When W. E. B. Du Bois claims, in *The Souls of White Folk* (1920), that "whiteness is the ownership of the earth forever and ever, Amen!," he marks the vast reach, the huge swath of entitlement and power, that whiteness claims.

As a "machine" designed to perpetuate itself (Martinot 2010), whiteness is supported by cultural systems at every level. For Richard Dyer, "whiteness reproduces itself in all texts all of the time" (1997, 13). It consists of what Steyn calls "an ideologically supported social positionality" (2005), which Alistair Bonnett argues is "structured upon a varying set of supremacist assumptions (sometimes cultural, sometimes biological, sometimes moral, sometimes all three)" (1999, 140). This "systemic supremacy" maintains itself by sustaining "norms, cultural capital, and contingent hierarchies" of a culture that privilege not only white people, but white values and white ways of being (Garner 2007). Since the moment of encounter, South African culture has been shaped by white supremacist logic: outsiders from Europe claimed the African continent for themselves and fashioned social and political structures that privileged Caucasian bodies and European cultural attributes and advanced white values at the expense of the indigenous black and brown population.[12] Such "white values" were made explicit through the machine of apartheid. All facets of South African life—from religious dogma of the Dutch Reformed Church to the legislative power of the apartheid government, from the nationalized educational system to social norms, behaviors, and mind-sets—were designed to sustain white privilege and supremacy.

As a racialized system of imbalanced power that often refuses to acknowledge its own construction, whiteness functions predominantly as an invisible, unmarked norm that has been naturalized as the default category of existence; it is equated with being human, the assumed universal position, "the Greenwich Mean Time of Identity" (Garner 2007, 47). This is particularly true in the Global North—particularly the United States and Europe—where whiteness requires forgetting in order to maintain its power. In South Africa, however, whiteness doesn't hide in the shadows; rather, it has historically been explicitly visible, the dominant, most powerful, often most desirable, category of being on the social hierarchy. In his opening remarks to the Whitewash Conference, Dean F. Freschi of the University of Johannesburg affirmed that while northern whiteness was invisible, "hidden in plain sight" as he put it, and thrived on its own invisibility, South African whiteness had always been explicitly foregrounded, front and center.

While I agree, I take issue with any claim that argues that South African whiteness is more conscious of itself or less blind to its own construction. We still require much critical unpacking to tease out the ways that it functions as an internalized practice even when identified openly as a category of power to be suspicious of in the new democracy. For Rita Barnard and Samantha Vice, "whiteness in South Africa is both visible (in the lived and undeniable hierarchies of daily life) and invisible (in its powerful normativity and purported universality)" (Barnard 2012, 160). Vice describes the lingering ubiquity of whiteness as an "epistemic position of seeing the world 'whitely'" (2010, 324),[13] and it is from her formulation that I draw the title of this book. As an adverb, the term whitely describes the gerund state of being, the doing of actions or the performing of self. Whitely modifies acts of behavior and, because action is the building block of theatre, whitely is an apt descriptor of the performance of whiteness. As well, as an adjective, whitely describes the South African habitus I discuss in this book; it can refer to a state of being, an ideology, a set of behaviors or habits, or an enactment, performance or staging with distinctly white attributes. Thus when I speak of a *whitely nation*, I mean it both adjectively and adverbially: what the nation is and how it performs. And when I refer to Afrikaners as a nation, I mean the Andersonian imagined community that they, as white settlers, have cultivated over time to distinguish themselves from White English-Speaking South Africans, or WESSAs, and black and brown Africans. An explicit whiteness is central to their self-definition as a volk, and thus race and nation are often interchangeable when discussing this population.

"Whiteliness" permeates South African culture, its everyday spaces, its academy, and its theatre.[14] Despite major contributions by black and brown artists and theatre-makers over the past twenty years of democracy (and prior to 1994, of course), South African theatre is still predominantly white-faced in terms of the real power brokers.[15] The people who control its production are, for the most part, still white.[16] Its power structures (and infra-structures) privilege certain ways of making theatre: traditional, Western, Aristotelian, text-based, logocentric. One could say that South African theatre is often still trapped in its own "white-sight."[17] For Alfred Lopez these dynamics are a product of postcolonial whiteness. He writes that "whiteness remains behind in the new postcolonial state, in the form of both actual white subjects . . . and the cultural and ideological apparatuses that continue to reflect the values of the colonial regime—a national language or religion, educational system, government infrastructure and so on" (2005, 13). So, despite all the scholarship that has critiqued whiteness as constructed, an imagined figment rather than an a priori truth, the material power and the cultural practices supporting its perpetuation have very real consequences for people who benefit from its power as well as those who do not. In other words, *whiteness matters*. It is still—and especially—necessary to unpack, understand, and expose the "epistemologies of ignorance" (Steyn 2013) that lubricate the machine of whiteness. Even though Critical Race and Whiteness Studies are several decades old, the work of dismantling white power is far from done.

WHITENESS AND PERFORMANCE

In his 2008 essay, "Looking at *The Heart of Whiteness* in South Africa Today," Thomas Blaser argues that whiteness in contemporary South Africa is "perceptual, contingent, and situational" (82) and that "whiteness is thus less about skin colour and far more about how 'white' South Africans *present themselves publicly* (and are seen) and engage with some of the aspects of power, privilege, and advantage that previously shaped their notions of themselves and the ways they interacted with other members of South African society" (82–83, emphasis mine). In other words, whiteness—as a discursive category and a lived practice in South Africa—is about public presentation, or staging, of identity; whiteness is about its *performance*. Or, as Mary F. Brewer suggests, there is something "inherently theatrical" about whiteness (2005, xiv).

I maintain that whiteness is perpetuated and maintained through performance and enactment.[18] If, as Henry Giroux suggests, race is "a set of attitudes, values, lived experiences, and affective identifications" (1997), then it is only logical that the language of performance—of enactment, embodiment, staging, affect and attitude—is a useful frame through which to examine the iteration and maintenance of whiteness. The theatre, from the Greek *theatron* or "seeing place," offers us a chance to make visible the systemic nature of whiteness's power. Theatre—as a mimetic endeavor that can mirror or reimagine reality—marks something "as performance" and hence is a useful frame through which to bring the invisible construction of whiteness into the spotlight. Following Jill Dolan, I imagine theatre/performance as "a place to experiment with the production of cultural meanings, on bodies willing to try a range of different significations for spectators willing to read them ... a pedagogically inflected field of play at which culture is liminal or liminoid and available for intervention" (1993, 431–432).

Joseph and Fink pick up on this notion of liminality, claiming that as a space in which performances happen iteratively and where cultural norms are enacted—and contested—theatre is a "liminal, negotiating arena of social efficaciousness" (1999, 7). Thus while whiteness is maintained through the actions and behaviors of individuals and groups in everyday life, performance becomes a *space in which to mark and negotiate whiteness*. If, as Bruce Wilshire suggests, "theatre is the art of imitation that reveals imitation" (1982, ix), then it is through theatre/performance that we can examine whiteness, even if only for an ephemeral moment, and "give pause to its unreflective reiteration" (Warren and Heuman 2008, 222). Often theatrical works directly address whiteness, like those of performance artist Peter Van Heerden or satirist Pieter-Dirk Uys, but just as often, performance as a methodology allows us to analyze whiteness in performances in public life. As cultural signifiers, performances within and outside the proscenium arch present windows into how a culture constructs narratives about itself as well as about others. On the one hand, since the language of performance is useful in describing how identity functions, as Judith Butler suggests (1990, 1993),[19] then it is only fitting that theatre and performance practices are deployed in the maintenance of communal identities such as nationhood. On the other hand, performance as a critical framework can be useful in unpacking those stagings. As twice-performed human behaviors (Schechner 2013), theatre acts/performances are marked as constructions (something staged) and therefore can be useful spaces in which to mark the constructed nature of whiteness. Theatre and Performance Studies are fruitful frameworks through which to articulate the formation, internalization, and public expression of our identity as national—as well as raced and gendered—subjects.

To overcome the white-sighted dynamics I described above, we need to *make whiteness strange*, to use a Brechtian notion. We need to resingularize its defaultness, unmask its secretive mechanisms, and reveal its fictions. We need to be able to critically examine whiteness as a performed set of practices to be able to begin to disassemble it. Alastair Bonnett suggests that the "racist construction" of whiteness should be "permanently caged between two inverted commas" in order to confront its ubiquity and power while simultaneously "denying its essentialist pretentions" (1999, 140). So, I ask, how might performance and theatre—human practices that mark behavior *in inverted commas* as constructed—be ways of knowledge-making that allow us to better see the construction of whiteness and work toward its dismantling? And if we seek to dismantle whiteness, then what are the options for white subjects in the postcolony? In what ways can/do white subjects negotiate performance in our contemporary world? What are their possible performance repertoires?

I imagine South Africa as a nation organized around the principle of the museum, "constantly staging itself for itself" (Chaudhuri 1995, 249) and for others. Patricia Davidson argues that museums "give material form to authorized versions of the past, which in time become institutionalized as public memory" (1998, 145). Thus, Afrikaners, a marginalized population who sought to establish themselves as powerful, engaged in acts of "re-membering and forgetting, inclusion and exclusion" (Davidson 1998, 145) as they imagined their national community into being. The Afrikaner nation architects, like the museum curators Davidson discusses, "determine[d] cri-teria of significance, define[d] cultural hierarchies, and shape[d] historical consciousness" (1998, 145) as they performed a singular script or narrative of Afrikaner national identity.

Throughout their history, Afrikaners, like many Western nationalists, have used performance and theatrical practices to stage themselves into national cohesion, creating a socially constructed, imagined community of people who perceive themselves as part of such a group. For example, in 1904, they performed themselves *as* an underdog nation for America after their defeat in the Second Anglo-Boer War (as I will demonstrate in chap-ter 2). They performed themselves *into* a nation in 1938 with the Centenary Trek reenactments that formed part of the nation-building enterprise and culminated in the apartheid state (chapter 1). Under apartheid, theatre art-ists like Pieter-Dirk Uys used their position as performers to mark the per-formed nature of the state, its falsehoods, and its flawed rhetoric and logic (chapter 4). In the new millennium, several successful Afrikaans language musicals have tapped into nostalgia for the past at a time when Afrikaners are now *out of* power, one minority among many in a multicultural democ-racy (chapter 3). And in post-1994 South Africa, artists are engaged in per-formances of what it means to be a South African citizen today, confronting and exorcising the past and imagining new possibilities for whiteness and being *for the future* (chapters 5 and 6).

Afrikaner politicians have long engaged in performances of their politi-cal and social power and whiteness. Dramatic political rhetoric in the apart-heid era frequently simplified complex social matrices into easily recog-nizable stock characters or types, usually along black/white binaries. For instance, Prime Minister P. W. Botha warned his Cabinet at the height of the State of Emergency in 1985 in his infamous "Rubicon" speech: "Destroy White South Africa and our influence, and this country will drift into faction strife, chaos and poverty" (Giliomee 2008). Botha's brand of whiteness was aggressive, abrasive and easily defensive. Known as Die Groot Krokodil (The Big Crocodile), Botha was renowned for licking his lips while talking and shaking his index finger emphatically at his audience.[20] He had an "irascible temper" (Engelbrecht 2006), did not tolerate being questioned by the press, and clung doggedly to the Afrikaner laager.

In comparison, earlier in apartheid history, in a speech filmed by British Pathé in 1961, Prime Minister Hendrik Verwoerd performed a far more genteel version of Afrikaner whiteness, one coded in "royal we" appeals to sister Commonwealth nations. Filmed against a wall of books in the regal study of his white-walled Cape Dutch mansion, Verwoerd begins by claiming that "the Republic of South Africa is the only sure and stable friend the Western nations have in Africa." Then, dismissing the "sensational journalism" reporting oppression in the country, he offers a highly coded spin on apartheid: "Certain restricted measures had to be taken recently, mainly to ensure the protection of the masses, of all races, who seek peace and order" (Verwoerd 1961). Between Verwoerd's gentlemanly appeal to the British, his former archenemies, and Botha's entrenched finger-wagging, political rhetoric under apartheid was always a performance, aimed at justifying the regime, convincing the rest of the world of the logic of apartheid, and minimizing the realities of the racist system.

Afrikaners have also written and produced many Afrikaans-language[21] plays and staged them in traditional theatre spaces and at festivals. They have made films about their history and screened them on significant holidays in commemoration of that history.[22] They have also deployed nation-building theatrics like large-scale reenactments and pageants, with compelling and dramatic narratives of loss, oppression, and rising underdogs, sometimes even starring famous Boer War generals, for crowds of thousands of onlookers. These include the 1904 Boer War Circus in St. Louis, Missouri (which I discuss in detail in chapter 2); the 1910 Union celebrations; the Eeufees (Great Trek Centenary) reenactments in 1938 (which I discuss in chapter 1), and the 1952 van Riebeeck Tercentenary Festival.[23]

More often than not, these performances—which spanned the nation-building era—follow a common narrative arc and remain faithful to stock character types. Afrikaner national scripts are predicated on the notion of a small or outnumbered volk fighting to bring the light of (white/Western) civilization to darkest (black/savage) Africa and finding protection against the uncivilized hordes within the safety of their laager, or circle of wagons. Because Afrikaner whiteness is an extension of its patriarchy, these scenarios reinforce a particular brand of rugged masculinity and docile femininity. In these scenarios, Afrikaner women are stoic keepers of the hearth and engenderesses of volk and culture. The Voortrekker[24] woman in her large-brimmed hat, or *kappie*, and long skirts is iconic. The male Voortrekker, or *trekboer*, is entrepreneurial and resourceful, rugged and manly, bravely defending his land, his family, and his volk with the limited materials at his disposal. This can-do attitude is exemplified in a common Afrikaans saying, "'n Boer maak 'n plan" (a Boer always makes a plan). Both male and female characters are intensely devout and justify their political, personal, and racial actions with Calvinist scripture. Fierce and plucky, these Afrikaner characters reiterate the narrative of fighting against empire (Britain) to the bitter end;[25] even when wounded and downtrodden, their pioneering spirit triumphs through adversity.

MAPPING THE SCHOLARLY TERRAIN

The scholarship of whiteness simultaneously omits South Africa as a site of inquiry in its predominantly US-centric approach and overlooks performance—both as *sites* and *practices* of identity formation/reformation. My work addresses these omissions. Boucher, Carey, and Ellinghaus perform a very important intervention in "transnationalizing whiteness studies—and thus bringing it into contact with colonial history," and expanding the narrative of whiteness beyond its US-centric birthplace "across the times and spaces of empire" (2009, 3). It is notable that in this important work, South Africa (decidedly a colonial space and most certainly an appropriate place to study whiteness) is given only cursory mention.

Even though the racial, political, and social category of whiteness relies on *iterative enactment*, very few scholars of whiteness explicitly address its performance. Two notable exceptions are Gwendolyn Audrey Foster's *Performing Whiteness: Postmodern Re/Constructions in the Cinema* (2003), a study of the cultural construction of whiteness in American films, and Mary F. Brewer's *Staging Whiteness* (2005), a study of the construction of multiple whitenesses in select British and American playtexts and their shifting sociopolitical contexts from the colonial period to the postmodern. My study joins their conversation by offering an African case study. This book also contributes to the conversation around Afrikaners as a population.[26] My study would not have been possible had it not been for my predecessors and their astute and well-researched contributions. I draw from Moodie (1975) and Templin's (1984) studies chronicling the rise of Afrikanerdom from the late nineteenth to mid-twentieth centuries, paying particular attention to the role of Calvinism in the nation-building project. Bloomberg and Dubow's (1989) work explores the secret Broederbond (Brother Bond) society and its connections to Calvinism and Afrikaner nationalism.[27] Patterson (1957) and Isabel Hofmeyr's (1987) work on the Language Movements and the cultural mobilization of the volk have also been invaluable. Giliomee (2003, 2010), considered one of the foremost historians on Afrikaners in the world, is my go-to encyclopedic reference. And in his ethnographical study of Afrikaners, Crapanzano (1985) established the notion that Afrikaners are caught in limbo, perpetually "waiting" for the world to see their point of view. *Waiting: The Whites of South Africa* also underscores the importance of the historical myths on which Afrikaner culture is based and the practices of self-deception that this population engages in to maintain that mythology. From De Villiers's (1990) personal and reflective apologia comes the notion of Afrikaners as a "white tribe" who throughout their history have excluded and oppressed others out of fear, which he laments and attempts to explain.[28] Jansen's (2009) nuanced and generous study involves his deep, committed research into whiteness as it unpacks how, as well as the reasons why, Afrikaners define themselves and behave as they do, especially after 1994. Jansen affirms Afrikaners as a group driven by fear and anxiety whose experience of trauma (at the hands of the British Empire) and constant loss (of power, visibility, approval) inform their ethnomythology. Guided by a faith in "a hitherto uncomplicated, straightforward, and uncontested knowledge of the past [that] has governed their lives" (2009, 46), Afrikaners, Jansen argues, are struggling to come to terms with a new reality that has left them embittered and aggressive, in denial or silent, and unable to process the guilt and shame they feel, or are made to feel, in the new democracy.

My study also joins those of several important scholars of South African whiteness, including Melissa Steyn, Christi van der Westhuizen, Liese Van Der Watt, and Nicky Falkof. Steyn's excellent sociological work at the Wits Centre for Diversity Studies addresses the changing position of South African whiteness after apartheid, particularly what she terms "white talk," or the discourses resistant to change. Van der Westhuizen's sociological work focuses on the intersections of whiteness and the middle-class heterosexuality of Afrikaans women. Van Der Watt, an art historian, examines whiteness in postapartheid visual culture. Falkof explores the pathologies of whiteness in late and postapartheid South Africa through a Media Studies lens.

What sets my study apart is my focus on performance as both site of investigation and as the critical framework through which to understand Afrikaner identity. As a part of my larger critique of race and empire, I attempt to resingularize the discourse on Afrikaners through a detailed unpacking of the ways in which they have performed and continue to perform themselves *into*, *around*, and *out of* power. I locate my analysis in several dynamic and discrete historic and contemporary performance sites. Unpacking the nuances and contradictions of what it means to *perform whiteness* and the stakes of performance as *white Africans*, I focus on multiple speech acts, political acts, and theatrical acts of the Afrikaner volk in theatrical as well as public life. As such, this study includes traditional performances that occur under the proscenium arch, as well as performances that take place in public pageants, museum sites, and popular music and film. While the moments I chose to unpack are loosely ordered chronologically—performances in the early twentieth century during the rise of Afrikaner nationalism; counter-mythic performances during the apartheid era; and performances after the 1994 power transition that ended white minority rule—this is by no means an exhaustive survey of all Afrikaans-language theatre; many others have done this work and are better equipped to accomplish such labors.[29]

I tackle this productive, if fraught, subject in order to make a case for the study of Afrikaners within a larger global, postcolonial conversation that asks how privileged populations perform themselves into power. And then again, once their privilege is deflated? How are the "commanding narratives" (Bank 2002, 590) of a nation interiorized by individual members of the group and then enacted as communal identity? How does whiteness play out, to use a theatrical term, within culture? And what are the possibilities for whiteness, and white subjects, performing in the postcolony? In our postcolonial moment at the beginning of the twenty-first century, after the heyday of colonial delusions and explicit white supremacist nation-states like South Africa and America, when whiteness as a category is being called to answer for its historical sins, and when our understandings of whiteness are moving out of the confines of the academy and into public discourse, what can the Afrikaner scenario offer us? How might our global understanding of whiteness, its longings and aspirations, flaws and failures, be informed by this population of white Africans? The six chapters that follow reflect on these questions.

The first three chapters concern historical performances prior to 1994; the fourth chapter covers the apartheid era and moves into the new democracy; and the final two chapters are dedicated to contemporary Afrikaner performance. In chapter 1, I trace how Afrikaners leveraged performance tactics and media to stage themselves into a cohesive nation, or volk, during the period of Afrikaner ascendency in the first decades of the twentieth century. A history of Afrikaner mobilization during this period and the ideologies that framed it maps the ethnomythology of the nascent Afrikaner nation and establishes the laager as an organizing principle for Afrikaner identity, teasing out what such an imagining makes possible and what it impedes. I also theorize the intersections between race (whiteness) and nation (Afrikaner volk). I pinpoint my analysis in three distinct yet complementary performance media: early film representations of Afrikaners, including *De Voortrekkers* (1916), *Bou van 'n nasie* (1938), and *'n Nasie hou koers* (1940); the public pageantry of the 1938 centenary commemoration of the Great Trek; and the Voortrekker Monument in Pretoria.

Next, I dedicate two chapters to the work of Deon Opperman, as he is the most popular playwright working in Afrikaans today, and his work demonstrates the nuanced potentials and pitfalls of staging whiteness in contemporary South Africa. In chapter 2, I explore the tenuousness and rehearsability of the laager, taking as my point of departure a moment in Deon Opperman's 2008–2009 Boer War musical *Ons vir Jou* (*We for Thee*), when the entire audience of the State Theatre in Pretoria was moved to tears. I map the genealogy of *Ons vir Jou* by refracting it through a prior performance of Afrikaner selfhood: the 1904–1905 Boer War Circus (or Transvaal Spectacle) in St. Louis, Missouri. The public performances in St. Louis at the Louisiana Purchase Exhibition (and in 1905 at Coney Island) point to a particular moment in history when Afrikaner identity was tenuously being negotiated in South Africa and the desire to perform "Afrikaner-ness" spilled outside the country's borders. The 2009 show, a *Les Miserables*–style musical about the Boer War focused on the Afrikaner hero General de la Rey, indexes continued anxieties about the Afrikaners' place as a settler culture within the South African socialscape.

In chapter 3, I discuss two of Opperman's other plays: *Donkerland* (*Dark Land*, 1996) and *Tree aan* (*Roll Call*, 2010). Here I tease out his theatrical and larger social labors, which combine a complex amalgam of national pride, nostalgia, political positioning, entrepreneurism, and attempts to (re)member and (re)define Afrikaner identity. *Donkerland* was a five-and-a-half-hour epic play that traced the history of Afrikaners from the colonial encounter in 1652 to the contemporary moment in 1996, only two years after the historic transition of power and official end of apartheid. And *Tree aan* (2010) brought to the stage the taboo stories of the young white boys recruited to fight for an ideology during the so-called Border Wars (1966–1989). I argue that Opperman's work indexes Afrikaner (white) anxiety at moments in time when their ethnic identity or political position is in question and that his work can be read as simultaneously reactionary and culturally relevant.

In the fourth chapter, I explore a possible option for the performance of whiteness and the gendered nature of Afrikaner *volkseie* (national identity). I focus on the binary gender construction that emphasizes Woman as the Mother of the Nation and propagates a hypermasculine identity for the nation as a whole. These gender positions were codified in such performance artifacts as the 1938 film *Bou van 'n nasie* (*Building of a Nation*) and the Voortrekker Monument in Pretoria, which was completed in 1949 just as the National Party came to power. Then, as a counterpoint, I turn my analysis to Afrikaner satirist and drag performer Pieter-Dirk Uys, who interrogates these gender constructions through his various theatrical personae, most particularly the character of Evita Bezuidenhout. For three decades, Uys has been giving new meaning to the role of the Mother of the Nation and has been questioning the logic of the apartheid regime in the faces of the apartheid censors. Since the country's historic shift in power in 1994, he has remained an active critic and continues to perform his satirical acts, this time to, and for, the current ANC government. I argue that Uys explodes the mythology of Afrikanerdom, radically critiquing conservative, narrow definitions of (white, heteronormative, patriarchal) power, and contesting gender norms by performing his alternative masculinity, in drag, as Mother of the Nation, Evita Bezuidenhout.[30]

If Opperman works within the world of nostalgia and historic reenactment, then iconoclastic performance artist Peter Van Heerden makes it his work to interrogate and deconstruct Afrikaner history and the logic that supports it. In chapter 5, I investigate another performance repertoire for whiteness, examining how, taking the Afrikaner male as his object of study, Van Heerden creates provocative performance installations around taboo subjects that involve visceral abjections of his own body. These performances ask his audiences to reflect upon outdated narratives of the past while imagining new ways of being in a multicultural democracy. Weaving together Julia Kristeva's work on abjection (1982), and my own formulation of betrayal, I examine how Van Heerden's iconoclastic interventions offer critiques of Afrikanerdom in contemporary South Africa. I unpack several of his major pieces, including *So is 'n os gemaak* (*Thus Is an Ox Made*, 2004), *Bok* (*Ram/Goat*, 2006), *Totanderkuntuit* (*Throughtheothercuntout*, 2008), and a one-man piece about white masculinity he performed (and I helped produce) in the United States called *Ubuntu* (2010).

In chapter 6, I focus on popular music, examining two Afrikaans rap artists. Both Jack Parow and Die Antwoord (The Answer) are part of what is known as *zef kultcha*, a contemporary counterculture movement of Afrikaner heterodoxy and self-deprecation. Deliberately positioning themselves as low-class, ill-bred, and boorish (Krueger 2012), these artists use the hip-hop practices of sampling and remixing, combined with rave hooks and beats, as they question orthodox Afrikaner (white) values and the logic of the apartheid past. They offer one possible answer for white subjects in the postcolony: to resist the past logic of white supremacy in favor of a slippery, foul-mouthed sampling of identity that dares to offend rather than complies with political correctness, is opportunistic rather than outcast from power, and stirs up controversy in order to remain visible. In my analysis of these white-trash-chic performances, I unpack several of Die Antwoord's music videos, including "Enter the Ninja," "I Fink U Freeky," "Baby's on Fire," and "Rich Bitch," and Jack Parow's music videos "Afrikaans is dood" ("Afrikaans Is Dead") and "Ons behoort mos saam" ("We Belong Together").

I conclude my study with a return to the 2013 Whitewash Conference. Considering where whiteness is currently positioned in South African culture—somewhere between its historic position of power and a new dispensation in which whiteness is being taken to task—I discuss the practice of what I call *boerekitsch* that has been proliferating recently. At Pieter-Dirk Uys's Boere Museum/Nauseum in Darling outside Cape Town, at the 2007 annual Klein Karoo National Arts Festival, or in a Pretoria restaurant called Boer'geoisie, the Afrikaner nationalist past is being staged—with irony. How do the privileged perform themselves once their privilege is deflated? Kitsch, or ironic framing, could be yet another possible answer for the white postcolony subject.

Laagers of Whiteness

AFRIKANER ASCENDENCY AND

THE STAGING OF A NATION

To open this study, I trace how Afrikaners leveraged performance tactics and media to stage themselves into a cohesive nation, or volk, during the Afrikaner ascendency in the first decades of the twentieth century. I explore several questions: How did Afrikaners become a volk in the first place? How did the divinely sanctioned ethnomythology at the core of the apartheid state develop? How did they perform themselves into power? And in what manners did they leverage theatrics to engender and reinforce their identity as a volk? First, I map the ethnomythology of the nascent Afrikaner nation in the early years of the twentieth century. Next, I establish the laager as an organizing principle for Afrikaner identity, teasing out what the concept makes possible and what it impedes, and theorizing the intersections between race and nation. To illustrate the laager's imaginative hold on Afrikaner culture, I analyze its earliest film representation: *De Voortrekkers* (1916). Then I focus on the large-scale nationalistic pageantry of the 1938 centenary commemoration of the Great Trek and the films *Bou van 'n nasie* (1938) and *'n Nasie hou koers* (1940). And finally, I explore the performative nature of the Voortrekker Monument in Pretoria.

AFRIKANER NATION-BUILDING ROUTES

Afrikaner identity is a rooted construction that often denies its own routes. Like its intimate bedfellow, whiteness, Afrikanerdom required that its constructedness remain invisible in order for the system to maintain its power. Isabel Hofmeyr argues that class formation in the early twentieth century among white Afrikaans-speakers became hitched to notions of ethnic identity (Afrikanerdom) which were disseminated through performative mechanisms, the most central of which was language. She traces the "invention" of Afrikaner nationalism to the years between 1902 and 1924, illuminating a series of inventive acts by which an educated elite socialized a population of poor disenfranchised Afrikaans-speakers from both rural and urban spaces into a "working class" (Hofmeyr 1987, 115). A secondary desire in this socialization process was to "make Afrikaans respectable" (Hofmeyr 1987, 104), and with this notion came moral and racial coding that would form the foundation of the Afrikaner nationalist project, the complex machinery that would secure the National Party political victory in 1948. This triumph inaugurated the apartheid state and placed Afrikaners in power at the expense of all others.

Afrikaner history is a singular narrative amid many competing claims to South Africa.[1] Despite apartheid-era history books that claimed otherwise, the Dutch settlers who colonized the Cape of Good Hope in the seventeenth century did not arrive into uninhabited territory; African space was already territorialized and not a blank slate.[2] Nor did the settlers remain untouched by the African habitus; their social, political, personal, and sexual interactions with black and brown Africans influenced their language, their politics, and their everyday lives.[3] As the original *uitlanders* (foreigners, literally "those from outside the land"), they imposed themselves upon African space but were also impacted by it. Ever conscious of the precariousness of their existence as European settlers in black Africa, or as colonials in conflict with other colonials (the British), the Dutch settlers performed themselves into and onto the space.[4]

Homi Bhabha has articulated the role of marginalized populations within the nation. He asserts that the margins disarticulate the nation and then rearticulate it; the margins address and thereby re-form the center (1990, 320–322). The iteratively performed Afrikaner script emphasized a divinely sanctioned history that justified their colonization of South Africa and reinforced their marginalization and oppression by British imperialism.[5] It was from this position of *marginalization* that Afrikaners were able to articulate their own kind of *center* in the form of apartheid, which itself became the center until the 1990s, when another marginalized group (the nonwhite *majority* of the population) disarticulated that nation and articulated a new South African landscape once again.

For Benedict Anderson, the appeal of nationalism lies in its religious quality, its ability to comfort its constituents in the face of suffering and death (1991, 10–11). With its messianic rhetoric, extreme claims of racial and ethnic purity, and fervent performance of belonging, the Afrikaner nationalist project skillfully manipulated this sacralized dimension of nationhood. A common refrain was the notion of Afrikaners being God's Chosen People,[6] driven by a colonial myth akin to Manifest Destiny,[7] to tame and colonize "savage black Africa" as the bearers of "white European civilization." As with any colonial encounter,[8] the reterritorialization of indigenous space by European settler-invaders was physically and symbolically violent. Internal conflicts existed between indigenous populations, and thus the space into which white settlers inserted their own scripts was already contested. For European settlers in the seventeenth century, exposure to tropical diseases and parasites, the rugged terrain and scorching sun, and indigenous peoples defending their territories, had to have been (in reality or perception) highly dramatic. Travelogues and accounts of Africa by missionaries, explorers, and settlers often reveal that they struggled to reconcile the exotic with the familiar. Entering the space of the Other, the European Self was forced to recognize its own historicity (De Certeau 1988), and when that self failed to make a neat match between the known and unknown, these accounts either wrote over the indigenous or shaped it to conform to a European lens. Such perceptive acts on the part of European Self produced an internal anxiety that in turn was articulated outward—back at the African Other—as violence, mistrust, and misunderstanding.

THE INVENTION OF AFRIKANER TRADITION

The Afrikaner volk is largely a product of the nation-building project[9] that began in the 1870s and culminated in 1948 with the victory of D. F. Malan's Herenigde Nasionale Party (Reunited National Party).[10] In the wake of the devastation of the Second Anglo-Boer War (1899–1902), Die Genootskap van Regte Afrikaners (the Fellowship of True Afrikaners)[11] set about codifying the Boers' common cultural capital under the name of "Afrikaner." This nationalist project drew on events of the previous century—especially the Great Trek of the 1830s and its romanticized pioneer life—in writing a particularly Afrikaner history of South Africa.[12]

Prior to 1994, official histories maintained that "Afrikaners" existed as a cohesive entity since they first landed at the Cape of Good Hope in 1652; in reality, the term *Afrikaner* only came into use much later. The first time that a white (European, Caucasian) person claimed a word hitherto used to describe locally born slaves, free blacks, and the Khoikhoi was in March 1707, when a seventeen-year-old Dutch settler named Hendrik Biebouw, who was born in the Cape, shouted at the local *landdros* (chief magistrate), "Ek ben een Africaander" (Giliomee and Mbenga 2007). Claiming "I am from Africa," Biebouw articulated his status as a native-born settler, distinguishing himself from European-born settlers. Afrikaners' sense of belonging to/in Africa is thus manifested in their name. The word made its way gradually into its current usage as the population of mainly Dutch settlers expanded its physical presence at the tip of Africa and developed a psychological and ideological presence.

Since Jan van Riebeeck's settlement of the Cape of Good Hope on behalf of the Dutch East India Company in 1652, Afrikaners have been negotiating their identity as European settlers on African soil. The words used by others to describe these colonial Europeans and by members of the volk to self-identify have shifted over time. A brief mapping of these shifts is helpful: At first, Dutch *settlers* colonized the Cape of Good Hope in 1652 and were joined by French Protestant refugees known as Huguenots in 1688. These settlers self-identified as *burghers*, or citizens, and were distinct from, and superior to various black tribes, the San, and the Khoikhoi.[13] After the British, whom Afrikaners refer to as *rooineke* (rednecks) or *khakis* (for the color of their military uniforms), took over the Cape in 1795, the Dutch settlers moved eastward to maintain their independence. *Trekboere* (nomadic farmers) eventually moved into the hinterland in the 1830s in a mass exodus known as the Great Trek in order to establish separate independent states.[14] A loosely organized group of Afrikaans-speakers known as Boers (*boere*, or "farmers") fought two major wars against the British: the Transvaal War (also known as the First War of Freedom, 1880–1881), which gained the Transvaal Boers self-governance; and the Anglo-Boer War or Second War of Freedom (1899–1902), which led to the Union of South Africa in 1910 and marked the consolidation of British hegemony and Boer defeat.

Drawing on the First and Second Language Movements[15] of the late nineteenth century and the nation-building project of the early twentieth, in 1948 Afrikaner nationalists formed a repressive and well-oiled political machine known as apartheid (separateness). Apartheid lasted until 1994, when Nelson Mandela, the white nation's most feared "terrorist," became the celebrated first black president of the new democratic, pluralist republic. As these various naming practices suggest, Afrikaner identity has always been a state of becoming. This ever-evolving population continues to reinvent and reimagine itself after 1994 in the new democracy.

The Boers were, until the 1930s, loosely defined groups of urban intellectuals and rural farming communities, as well as British sympathizers and religious groups of varying affiliations and degrees of fervor. They were far more heterogeneous than monolithic. Their history had not yet been codified. They had no clear political unity, nor did they organize themselves as a unified cultural or ethnic group. Instead, they were among the competing forces (including African nationalists and laborers, British royalists and business interests, and Calvinist religious leaders) all vying for access and power. Prior to 1876, "Afrikaans" did not exist as a language; rather, it was a dialect spoken predominantly by coloureds and called *kombuistaal* (kitchen language).[16]

The first signs of Boer mobilization, of deliberate attempts to unify the population, came decades after the Great Trek, in 1875, when Die Genootskap van Regte Afrikaners began gathering information for the express purpose of defining their volk. The task of unifying Afrikaans-speakers into a coherent political group was not easy. The breakup of the fabric of rural Boer families by industrialism, the declining role of religion, poverty, and disempowerment under British rule, all undermined the unity sought by the Fellowship. Therefore, a conscientious effort was made to create a united volk identity. In this process, cultural ideals were marketed as specifically "Afrikaans." Through the practice of Andersonian print capitalism, using newspapers, pamphlets, and literature to define and articulate a national identity, the idea of Afrikaner *volkseie* became standardized and disseminated. By the turn of the twentieth century, coffeehouses, reading circles, and drama societies were popular venues for the circulation of Afrikaner literature, cultural values, and ideology. These forms of media inspired pride and a sense of belonging in their audiences. The cultural capital of what it meant to be an Afrikaner—which was now distinctly marked as European in origin, white, male, "civilized," and Calvinist—gained value and was welcomed by an eager market now self-identified as members of this "nation."[17] Thus what Doris Sommer would term a "foundational fiction" was circulated, reinscribing "for each future citizen the (natural and irresistible) foundational desires for/of the government [that would be in] power" (1991, 31).[18]

A LAAGERED NATION

The Dutch and French Huguenot settlers' desire to seek comfort in the face of Africa's unfamiliarity took its particular form in the drive toward their nationalist identity. The principal metaphor of the Afrikaner volk became the laager, a purportedly impregnable, protective fortress of encircled wagons (figure 1). Circling the wagons was a historic practice on the frontier but is also a philosophical and ideological blueprint for how Afrikaners write—and perform—their own etiological myths; it is the symbolic image to which they return repeatedly. Principally designed for protection, the laager kept out undesirables (wild animals, enemy forces, black Africa). Simultaneously, the circle of wagons was a site of containment, a literal and figurative hearth around which families gathered to cook, eat, pray, communicate, sleep, and guard desirables (particularly white women). The laager served as a temporary home while on trek and once the Boer Republics were formed in the 1840s, the homestead replaced it as the site of belonging. In Afrikaner ethnomythology, the farm (*plaas*) is an extension of the frontier laager. "Located on the imaginary frontier, even if in fact in the midst of settlement," Loren Kruger suggests, "the family farm marks the colonial penetration of the hinterland and dispossession of the Africans, even as it claims to represent the natural rights of the Afrikaner" (1999b, 32). And during the Afrikaner ascendancy, the laager became a metaphoric anchor used to galvanize a communal volk around a national identity.

However, the laager is a Janus-faced metaphor. Imagined as impenetrable, self-contained, and exclusive, not unlike the logic of the Afrikaner nationalist project—or the system of whiteness, for that matter—the laager has two main zones of activity: the central core and the spaces in between. The physical space created within the wagon circle, around the central fire pit, is the safety zone, the space of daily domestic interaction (and thus the sphere of women) and nightly male vigilance. But the space between the wagons, the penetrable and porous interstices, close to the sleeping bodies of women and children inside the wagons (protected only by thorny branches and male vigilance), is a site of potential transgressions, unspoken crossings, and external threats. Thus, because the laager cannot ever be hermetically sealed, it is a fatal strategy; it is more porous and more tenuous than it is monolithic. Like whiteness, the laager must maintain a belief in its infallibility to remain intact and powerful and, like whiteness, it becomes vulnerable to anxiety when its porousness is revealed.

Figure 1.
Ceremonial
laager at the
Blood River
Monument in
Kwazulu-Natal.
© 2005 Renier
Martiz.

When contemporary news reports talk of white Africans circling their wagons against the blackness of Africa, they are drawing on the concept of the laager imprinted into the psyches of Afrikaners since the beginning of their organized nationhood. Scholarship on Afrikaner culture, politics, and psychology evidences how they have organized themselves into social, economic, and political laagers that exclude others and are vehemently protected in the name of the volk. For June Goodwin and Ben Schiff, for example, Afrikaners are exclusive members of a closed society, "reluctant to deviate from the official line, monolithic in their views, xenophobic, paranoid, narcissistic" (1995, 14). For Kruger, Afrikaners are committed to a "nationalist resistance to British hegemony, marked by linguistic exclusivity, the mythology of autochthony, and a chauvinist attitude to other, even more marginalized groups, whether indigenous or immigrant" (1999b, n37). For Johannesburg *Sunday Times* editor Ken Owen, the "perpetual insecur[ity]" of Afrikaners, the "children of an open frontier" (1996b), lends itself to the protective metaphor of the laager, a maternal enclosure that safeguards them and maintains them in a perpetual state of psychological dependency on the enclosure. Christina Landman terms it a "fantasy of innocence" whereby Afrikaners deify their heroic frontier adventures while simultaneously "ignoring the past and their culpability in and for it" (Daley 1998, 11).

Apartheid was the laager made manifest. A small minority of whites — comprising only 10 percent of the population and including WESSAs, as well as Afrikaners—reigned over the black majority for five decades. Nestled safely within the laager of privilege, in big houses with expansive lawns and swimming pools, whites could turn a blind eye to the poverty, dehumanization, and violence perpetrated on the bodies of black South Africans in the neighboring townships. White South Africans enjoyed (and still do) one of the highest standards of living in the world;[19] however, there was an ugly price to be paid for the wealth, security, and privilege that the white laager offered. The apartheid state was designed to benefit whites within the laager of privilege and discriminate against the majority of the population outside it. This insider/outsider topology defined—and was reproduced by—the political, legal, and economic machine of apartheid.[20]

The iconography of the laager and the insider/outsider trope were first performed cinematically in the 1916 film directed by Kentucky-born filmmaker Harold Shaw (1877–1926)[21] called De Voortrekkers, which was widely seen in South Africa. Advertised as "South Africa's National Film," De Voortrekkers is, in Jacqueline Maingard's assessment, "the first appropriation of the cinema as an instrument for presenting nation in South Africa" (2007, 16). It premiered in Krugersdorp in 1916 and was played annually thereafter every December 16 in commemoration of the annual Afrikaner sabbath known as Covenant Day.[22] With a screenplay by historian Gustav Preller, whom Edwin Hees describes as "a zealous champion of Afrikaans" (2003, 49), the film depicts the Great Trek of the 1830s—the Boers' migration northward from the Cape Colony to claim independence from British imperialism. Framed from the perspective of the Boers, the film is often compared to D. W. Griffith's 1915 American white supremacist feature, Birth of a Nation. As a popular "cultural signifier" (Maingard 2007, 18), De Voortrekkers effectively brought history to life, engendering a visual record of not only the content, but also the ideological framing, of Afrikaner history. As Hees suggests, the film was part of the "developing discourse on segregation" in South Africa in the early twentieth century (2003, 63).

This melodramatic fifty-four-minute silent film is narrated by intertitles (in English and Afrikaans) that describe the action and introduce characters, along with the actors—that is, the white actors—playing them, before each major scene. The black actors, including the two men who play the major black characters—the Zulu king Dingane and Sobuza, the noble Zulu who leaves his own people to fight alongside the Boers (and who is, arguably, the character with the greatest arc and depth in the film) — remain uncredited and unnamed, despite their significant on-camera presence.[23]

Two specific scenes encode the laager as central to Afrikaner ethnomythology and make its borders visually explicit. First, at the center of the film's narrative is the legendary clash between the Boers and the Zulus known as the Battle of Blood River.[24] In these battle sequences, the logic of the laager becomes most clear. After a title card informs the viewer that it is "Early morning of December 16, 1838," we see hundreds of Zulus streaming down a mountainside, carrying their *assegais* (spears) and *isihlangu* (shields). Cut to rows of prone Boers, aiming their muskets against the approaching warriors from inside the laager. This back-and-forth cutting, between Boers inside the laager and Zulu *impis* (warriors) outside it (i.e., in the wilderness), continues through the battle scene. When inside the laager, the camera is positioned centrally and slightly above the action, as if an omniscient witness. The shots of attacking Zulus outside the laager are taken from various points of view: long shots of hordes of Zulus streaming down mountains and across river beds combined with shots from within the melee. At one point, Zulus stream toward the camera and as they approach, they gesture wildly with their assegais directly at the camera lens, so that the viewer's experience is one of direct attack. The framing and the camera angles betray the ideological perspective of the storytellers: blackness is foreign and aggressive, while whiteness is the privileged, omniscient point of view.

The film connects the heroes (the Boers) with the *internal*, desirable, safety of the laager and the villains (the Zulus) with the aggressive, dangerous, undesirable *exterior*, feeding a discourse on racial difference and black threats to whiteness. There are literally thousands of black bodies in this battle scene, giving the sense that an endless horde of blackness is perpetually coming to attack; as one line of warriors is felled, another one appears. After the Boers hold off the first and second waves of the Zulus' attack, a title card explains, "The Boers have again driven the blacks to cover and they re-form their broken regiments." At this point in the film the term *Blacks* (in Afrikaans, *Die Kaffers*) is deployed, not the word *Zulus* (in Afrikaans, *Soeloes*) — as it has been in every previous intertitle. The hordes of anonymous "black kaffirs," actors who do not get named like their white counterparts, become the perpetual threat assaulting the safety of the (white) laager; they are *die swart gevaar* (the black peril or danger), a derogatory term used to justify police repression in the townships under apartheid and military action during the Border Wars. And this trope would be repeated years later in Cy Endfield's worldwide hit, *Zulu* (1964) and Douglas Hickox's 1979 follow-up, *Zulu Dawn*.

During this intense battle scene, two images depict the essence of this racial imaginary. The first shows the (anonymous) Zulu warrior stabbing his assegai directly at the camera (figure 2). The second is a shot of two Boer women (the characters Johanna Landman and her mother), holding each other tightly with looks of terror on their faces at the impending black attack (figure 3). The two images bookend one another as the film sutures the audience into a narrative about aggressive blackness and threatened whiteness.

Toni Morrison and Frantz Fanon have written on the dialectics of such racial constructions: for Fanon (1991), constructions of the other imply and rely on the construction of the self; whiteness (Self) exists always in relation to blackness (Other). In her 1992 essay on whiteness, Morrison posits that white identity becomes realized when it is "backgrounded by savagery" (44). Thus, the terror-stricken women that the laager is designed to protect become white in relation to the black hordes that attack them, the aggressive heathens to the women's civilized Christian selves. The fear of contamination and penetration of the white laager by the dark unknown beyond its borders — confirmed by the women's expressions of abject terror — is central to the Afrikaner (white) psyche.

The second scene I will unpack is at the end of the film, when, in the church that Sarel Cilliers promised would be built at Blood River, the white Boers sit in the pews and listen to the preacher's words (written on the title card): "And in keeping our covenant (*Heilige Verbond*) we shall, on every Sixteenth Day of December, render thanks to Thee, Almighty God, for our safe return and the preservation of our *Volk* and Country (*Ons Volk en Ons Land*)." The word *volk* here suggests both "people" and "race." The scene is racially coded: as the whites inside the church pledge their sacred covenant, outside on the porch steps sits Sobuza, who is attentively listening through the door as he, as a black man, is not allowed inside the building. Inspired by the holy words he hears, he points to the heavens, a gesture he makes throughout the film to indicate the presence of the Christian God. As he points, the film cuts to an image of a dark wooden cross, illuminated in a halo of bright, white light. Sobuza's salvation lies in his acceptance of white, Christian values. Unified with the Boer cause through his acceptance of their religion, he remains separated by his race. And the race that separates him from the

Figure 2.
Zulu warrior points assegai directly at the camera in *De Voortrekkers*.
© 1916 African Film Productions.

Figure 3.
Voortrekker women recoil in horror in *De Voortrekkers*.
© 1916 African Film Productions.

Boers inside is explicitly articulated in the first-person plural possessive of the covenant: *the preservation of our Race and Country*. This positioning of black against white, subservience and mastery, prefigures the apartheid system that will take effect a few decades later. For Maingard, "Without Sobuza's position as a servant, the white 'nation' and its hegemony cannot survive" (2007, 22). Thus, Shaw and Preller's film fixed a version of Afrikaner colonial history within a melodramatic visual register steeped in racist ideology. The film circulated widely in South Africa, screened annually on Dingane's Day, and as a cultural signifier influenced the formation of the apartheid state.

For a small group of white settlers in Africa to define themselves through the containment/exclusion binary of the laager was to become caught in a fatal strategy that would ultimately fail them. As a minority settler culture, Afrikaners would always remain trapped by the desire to distinguish themselves from both black indigenes and white Britons. They perpetually placed themselves in opposition to others—as bringers of the light of civilization to darkest Africa or plucky underdogs under the heels of Britain's mighty empire—and wrote narratives that set them apart. Their small numbers— their minority status—remained both the impetus for theses narratives as well as their ultimate undoing.

With the support of organizations such as Die Broederbond, the Voortrekker Movement[25] set out to "stitch together an 'Afrikaner' history" (I. Hofmeyr 1987, 109), which would become a myth of national origin, selecting historical events and weaving them into a coherent Afrikaner nationalist ideology whose goal was a white-controlled Afrikaner state. A particularly good way of capturing this audience was to appeal to the romantic, adventuresome mythology of the Great Trek. It became the Afrikaner's ritornello,[26] the refrain to which they kept coming back, the fabricated glue with which they attempted to hold their identity together. Prior to the 1880s, the term *landverhuiser* (emigrant) had been used to describe Boers who moved into the interior. But now, the term *Voortrekker* (literally, "one who moves forward") entered the vocabulary, helping to usher in an entire cult industry of Voortrekker mythology that would later form the foundation of Afrikaner nationalism.

The nationalist project's paramount performance was the public pageant known as the 1938 Centenary Trek, or Eeufees. On December 16, 1938, fifteen-year-old Johannes Meintjes,[27] dressed as a Voortrekker in khakis and a red paisley neckerchief, stood before the crowd of onlookers in Pretoria and recited a poem titled "Voorwaarts" ("Forwards"). It began, "Forward, young South Africa. From the ashes of the Past, we build our Future, our Present, we who carry the torches of Freedom" (Meintjes 1973, vii). In referring to the ashes of the past, Meintjes was indexing several factors from which nationalists aimed to build a united Afrikaner nation: the long legacy of Anglo-Boer hostility, and particularly the horrific treatment of Afrikaans-speaking women and children in British prisoner of war camps during the

Anglo-Boer War (1899–1902); the increased competition from blacks and *uitlanders* (foreigners) for work after the war (1900s–1920s); and the desire among Afrikaners to regain political control from the British.

Meintje's recital was part of the Eeufees, a four-month-long public pageant organized by the ATKV, the Afrikaner Taal-en Kultuurvereeniging (Afrikaner Language and Culture Association),[28] and inspired by Gustav Preller's writings on the Great Trek, as well as Shaw's film *De Voortrekkers* (1916). The ox-wagon trek was reenacted between August and December of 1938, passing through villages and towns on its way from Cape Town to Pretoria, retracing the steps taken a century earlier by the Boers who wanted to establish independence from British colonial rule. This restaging culminated at the site of the proposed Voortrekker Monument, which would be inaugurated in Pretoria on December 16, 1949, shortly after the National Party won its historic victory. The Centenary Trek, and the monument itself, enshrined December 16 as the cornerstone of Afrikaner ethnomythology, commemorating that date, one hundred years earlier, when Cilliers allegedly made that covenant with God before the Battle of Blood River. December 16, 1938, marked the date when documents, as Foucault (1972) describes them, were converted into monuments. The loosely affiliated "documents" of Boer society became a unified Afrikaner "monument" and a literal monument—the Voortrekker Monument—was erected in the Chosen People's name. A carefully orchestrated series of events was enacted before a largely decentralized public to rally support for an idea of national (Afrikaner) unity by a group of politicians and leaders who, building on religious and racist doctrines, sought to claim South Africa as their own.

The original plan was for a single ox-wagon to carry messages of celebration to Pretoria for the December laying of the cornerstone of the Voortrekker Monument. However, nationalistic fever caught on, and eventually *nine* ox-wagons left Cape Town on August 8, 1938, to begin what McClintock calls an "orgy of national pageantry" and a four-month spectacle of "invented tradition and fetish ritual" (1995, 371). The wagons were named after key figures of the original Great Trek, such as the *Piet Retief* (after the martyr who was murdered by Zulu Chief Dingane (ca. 1795–1840); the *Sarel Cilliers*; the *Dirkie Uys* (after the boy hero who died defending his nation by his father's side); and the *Vrou en Moeder* (Wife and Mother, a generic appellation in honor of the women who gave their lives during the Trek).[29]

By the time the wagons reached Pretoria in December, a national identity

Figure 4. The ox-wagon *Johanna van der Merwe* enters the arena at the Voortrekker Monument inauguration, December 16, 1949. © 1949 African Film Productions.

Figure 5. A family in pioneer dress at the Voortrekker Monument inauguration, December 16, 1949. © 1949 African Film Productions.

was solidifying among Afrikaners. In August 1938, Henning Klopper, Trek organizer and member of the Broederbond-supported ATKV, offered the following words of encouragement to several reenactors as they left Cape Town, effectively writing the script of a nation about to be born: "May this simple trek bind together in love those Afrikaner hearts which do not yet beat together" (Harrison 1981, 104). A "simple" event would later be construed as the "central" event of the Afrikaner nation's history. The implication that Afrikaner unity did not yet exist is clear in his statement; Klopper's aim was to articulate national cohesion and to begin to write its narrative. At this point, in August 1938, mass national unity was still a goal rather than a reality. The symbolic capital was not yet fully circulating among the majority of the Afrikaans-speaking population as it would be only four months later. The role of the symbolic—what Pierre Bourdieu calls the dialectic between the internalization of externalities and the externalization of internalities (Harker, Mahar, and Wilkes 1990)—was instrumental in transforming loose social ties into national cohesion. And the power of the symbolic "to maintain social relations in a state of coexistence and cohesion" (Lefebvre 1991, 32) was crucial. It took a performative event, replete with its symbolic accoutrements, restaging of history, and the involvement of a large audience and many acting participants, to gel Afrikaner identity en masse, and to accomplish what the coffeehouses and magazines had started years earlier.

Each wagon set out on a different route through the villages and towns of rural South Africa, making special pilgrimages to sites where important battles were fought, and laying commemorative wreaths and creating "shrines" to Afrikaner history. They became pageant wagons of a sort, stages beside which children were baptized with patriotic names such as Eeufesia (Centennia) and Ossewania or Kakebenia (Oxwagonia). Young people wiped their handkerchiefs in the wagons' axle grease, thus capturing a material piece of the symbolism for themselves. Couples performed their Afrikaner identity as they were married beside the wagons, their wedding vows resounding with Voortrekker terminology. The symbolic capital of Afrikanerdom was personalized as individuals enacted their life's rituals through a nationalist framing; once internalized, capital was made visible and disseminated, reinforcing the volk's cohesion.

The 1938 reenactments helped build a nation on the exchange and interiorization of symbolic capital in Bourdieu's sense. Symbolic systems involve instruments of knowledge and domination, the symbolic form of which (comprised of the intangible yet culturally significant attributes of a social group) is the most valuable currency a social world can employ. The exchange of symbolic capital functions on two levels: to make possible a consensus within a community about the significance of the social world, and to contribute to the reproduction of that social order. The political function of symbolic capital is its imposition of "legitimate" definitions of the social world. This particular set of performative practices exposes the broader field in which it operated; through the events of August to December 1938, it is possible to see how the past was recorded, made meaningful, and established as historical fact.

And one of the most powerful mechanisms for disseminating this history was film. In 1940, the film 'n Nasie hou koers (A Nation on Course) premiered. Dr. Hans Rompel and his crew filmed the 1938 reenactments. Rompel headed the revolutionary Reddingsdaadbond Amateur Rolprent Organisasie (Amateur Film Rescue Action League), a conservative group aimed at promoting Afrikaner filmmaking, in reaction to the British domination of the early South African film industry (Martin Botha 2006a). When it premiered in 1940, the film offered the chance for Afrikaner audiences to relive the events and nation-building theatrics of the previous year. It is divided into sixteen parts, tracing eight of the nine ox-wagons. Rompel documented the overall journey and also filmed the ancillary performances that occurred as the wagons reached small towns and communities. These included mass christenings, group weddings beside the ox-wagons, and the laying of various commemorative plaques along the way. For Maingard, this film is "an extraordinary record of the interface between broad nationalist idealism and locally based historical, cultural and religious ritual involving 'ordinary' people in building the Afrikaner 'nation'" (2007, 62). She also asserts that themes of heteronormativity and reproduction of the nation feature strongly in the film (Maingard 2007, 62). 'n Nasie hou koers was also the first cinematic reference to the Boer War concentration camps; in two scenes, plaques are laid at sites in Harrismith and Krugerdorp.

In addition to being captured on celluloid for posterity, the symbolic 1938 trek also reinscribed history onto spaces and people in material ways. Wet blocks of cement were prepared, through which the oxen walked and wagon wheels cut, leaving their imprints at each site they visited, "petrifying history as an urban fossil" (McClintock 1995, 377). A new history was being branded on each space they entered. Streets in small towns were renamed with Afrikaans names, reterritorializing the space of British colonial rule, writing over what had come before them, and thereby "solidif[ying] myths . . . into dogma" (Goodwin and Schiff 1995, 188).[30] As they approached Pretoria in December, the performative elements of the Centenary Trek became visible nationally. The choreography of human actors, flaming torches, wagons, empassioned speech-making, and a physical location at the site of the future Voortrekker Monument created a dramaturgy of nationalist cohesion.

A human chain of runners carrying a flaming *fakkel* (torch), Olympic style, from Cape Town met up with the wagons in Pretoria. (These torchbearers featured prominently in Rompel's film.) The final runner was joined by several hundred other scouts with torches. The runners lit the torches of onlookers, and women burned the edges of their hankies in the flames as mementos. The individual torches were then thrown into a huge bonfire atop the hill at Roberts Heights (later renamed Voortrekker Heights). The eternal flame of the bonfire was preserved and later placed within the walls of the monument when it opened in 1949, a year after the Nationalist Party gained its historic victory in Parliament.

In 'n Nasie hou koers (1940) there's a striking image where a man holds up a small ox-wagon replica over the crowd at Roberts Heights. Maingard suggests that this moment of nationalist "costume drama," inspired by the Voortrekker mythology popularized by Gustav Preller, continued the "'work' of entrenching nationalist ideals in the Afrikaner 'community'" (2007, 63). "We never had a symbol before," said Henning Klopper. "The ox-wagon became that symbol" (Harrison 1981, 106). With this symbol as a beacon, the Afrikaners had begun to identify as a volk. Maingard's remark that the event was a costume drama is quite apt. Women costumed themselves in traditional Voortrekker dress and bonnet, and children in khaki suits with red neckerchiefs sang Voortrekker songs. The film also solidified the icons of the Volksmoeder and the kappiekommando (bonnet brigade). Maingard describes two images in the film where a woman in a kappie is silhouetted against flying flags or a plaque commemorating the December 16, 1838 covenant at Blood River (2007, 63), tying the idea of Woman and Nation together symbolically.

Other symbols became much sought-after as souvenirs: postcards, tapestries, and stamps. A commemorative set of china was designed and to this day forms part of many Afrikaner households' heirlooms (including my own). The official program provided special pages on which to stick stamps or to place family photos in Voortrekker costume, and even included an official Certificate of Attendance for families to document their participation (or performance) in this significant occasion. Communal activities such as braaivleis (barbecue), volkspele (folkdancing and game-playing), and boeremusiek (traditional folk music) accompanied the festival. In Pretoria, historical representations of key events of the Great Trek and Voortrekker dioramas were staged in the main festival house by the People's Theatre Association of Pretoria, and special children's programs were organized to inspire a sense of nationhood in the young attendees. In subtle and obvious ways, Afrikaners purchased cultural currency—as well as literal currency, in the form of a commemorative set of coins—eagerly and abundantly during the centenary celebrations.

That same year, Joseph Albrecht released his film *Bou van 'n nasie (Building of a Nation*; 1938). It traces the history of white colonization of southern Africa from Bartolomeu Dias's rounding of the Cape in 1488 to the joining of Dutch and British rule in the Union of South Africa in 1910. The two-hour epic chronicles the Boers' constant desire for independence. Billed in the opening credits as "the saga of dogged endurance & high ideals. A story of the taming of a savage country, the conquest of savage people and the building of a nation," *Bou van 'n nasie* frames South African history as Afrikaner history. Throughout the film, an instrumental version of "Die Stem" plays. The old national anthem was based on C. J. Langenhoven's 1918 poem of the same name, which was set to music in 1921 by Reverend Marthinus Lourens de Villiers. The second verse of the song explicitly frames the nation's citizens as "waar en trou as Afrikaners, Kinders van Suid-Afrika" (dedicated and true as Afrikaners, Children of South Africa).[31]

In describing Portuguese mariner Dias's (ca. 1451–1500) rounding of the Cape in "the Romantic middle ages" in 1488, the film shows viewers a scene of white Europeans erecting the Padrão de São Gregório, a land claim cross, at Mosselbaai, on the southern coast of South Africa. The scene is intercut with images of San people (described as "relics of the stone age, living like baboons in their rock caves") fishing an octopus from the ocean as the narrator explains, "Thus the savagery of this land was first touched by a symbol of our civilization."[32] Whiteness is framed as the civilized state of being as Dias's sailors plant their phallic marker into African soil. Then the narrator explains how French Huguenots fled religious persecution in Holland and "from them and the early Dutch settlers sprang the race of *pioneer warrior farmers* that become the advance guard of civilization in the hinterland of South Africa" (emphasis mine). These pioneer warrior farmers would then fight for their right to exist against the British, the Zulu, and the British again during the rest of the film. The final image, as South Africa becomes a Union under white control, is of a Voortrekker woman sowing seeds across an open field: the seeds of nationalism. Also, it affirms Woman as a central icon of the nation, a trope that the Voortrekker Movement capitalized on. This historical film presents the heteronormative couple as a metonym for the budding nation (Maingard 2007). *Bou van 'n nasie*, like *De Voortrekkers* (1916) before it, helped secure in celluloid the history—complete with its logic of exclusivity and whiteness—that the Afrikaner ascendency sought to codify and disseminate.

A WHITELY NATION

The symbolic and racial coding of the Afrikaner nation, and the history that was being stitched together to support it, were decidedly white. Or, one could say, the Afrikaner volk imagined themselves *whitely*. For example, on December 16, 1938, at the centenary commemorations at Blood River, Dr. D. F. Malan—who would become prime minister from 1948 to 1954, and who, along with his Purified Nationalist Party, would actively work to create the apartheid state—waxed nostalgic on the Voortrekkers and their sacrifices, calling for a Second Great Trek, this time to the cities, which were largely controlled by English-speakers and staffed by a predominantly black labor force. He said: "Afrikanerdom is once again trekking, on his new Great Trek. . . . It's not, like a hundred years ago, a trek away from the center of civilization, but a trek back—back from the city to the country" (Mulholland 1997, my translation). The spirit of the Voortrekkers continued for Afrikaners, he said, and "their freedom was also, and above all, the freedom to preserve themselves as a White Race." He asked his audience, "Have you the patriotism and sufficient power in this year of celebration to use this God-given opportunity also to demand . . . the assurance that White Civilization will be assured?" (Harrison 1981, 112).

Whiteness was also encoded into many facets of the centenary trek. Not only were the festivities designed by and for white Afrikaners, but the color white was used symbolically to underscore racial purity, the "light of civilization," as well as Afrikaner femininity. The Voortrekker youth who carried the torches toward Pretoria were often photographed at night to emphasize the bright white flames of the new nation against the darkness of Africa. Women dressed in starched white bonnets and dresses featured prominently in every town the wagons visited.

On December 16, 1938, at Bloemfontein, nation-builder and theologian Father J. D. Kestell preached, "We have received a fire from God, that fire is our nationhood . . . a burning torch which is not extinguished. It has been kept burning all the way from the statue of van Riebeeck [in Cape Town] to here. It must be kept burning" (Moodie 1975, 183). A symbol of white civilization illuminating the darkness, the burning torch also ties in with the fascist symbolism of nation building.[33] At the same gathering, D. F. Malan charged the crowd of one hundred thousand spectators gathered before him to look backward, "back to your people; back to the pledge which has been entrusted to you for safekeeping; back to the sanctity and inviolability of family life; back to the Christian way of life; back to your church; back to your God" (Patterson 1957, 40). He constructed for them a ritornello, a call to return to a unified past that had not actually existed, a unity created for them by a select group of nation architects who sought to rescue their portion of the economic, political, and social pie. This ritornello required amnesia, the forgetting of the multiple struggles in a contested field of vying potentialities, and the replacement of multiplicities with a singular, white elitism. And it required performances—on grand as well as personal scales—to be effective. In these remarks, Malan sutured time and space together, tying Cape Town and Bloemfontein, 1652 and 1938, into a single narrative.

THE LAAGER ON VOORTREKKER HEIGHTS

The ultimate symbol of the Afrikaner nation, and shrine to whiteness, is the Voortrekker Monument. A spectacular, imposing structure, it sits on a hill outside Pretoria, the traditional seat of the apartheid government. This imposing granite edifice was erected to represent and enact Afrikaner volk identity, history, and power. The building is a carefully constructed testimony to the nationalist project, a paragon of control, precision, and sovereignty, an emblem of "the state's memory of itself" (Young 1994, 19). Architect Gerard Moerdijk claimed that his monument honored the Afrikaner's brave treks into the interior of South Africa and "had to remind people for a thousand years or more of the great deeds that had been done" (Vermeulen 1999, 129).[34]

The symbolic resonance of this chrono-monument was most evident in 1938 when, at the height of the nationalist propaganda campaign, the Centenary Trek was stage-managed to synchronize with the Afrikaner Sabbath, December 16. A decade later, on December 16, 1949, after the Nationalist Party's victory, the first cornerstone of the Voortrekker Monument was laid.

This building design shares the precision and sovereignty of Bentham and Foucault's panopticon (Foucault 1995), but reverses them. Whereas a panopticon allows the one to see the many, this monument focuses the gaze

Figure 6.
Voortrekker
Monument
in Pretoria.
© 2012
Megan Lewis.

of the many onto one singular narrative, controlling rather than empower-ing the observer. And the symbolic figure controlling the gaze is the Great Afrikaner Spirit, the sacred dimension of the national identity. The build-ing has a sanctified aura to it; its solemn marble interior is illuminated by stained glass windows, and it feels more like a church than a museum.

The monument is experienced spatially, both in physical and ideologi-cal terms, and the building controls the observer's gaze from within and without. Unlike a space like Daniel Libeskind's Jewish Museum in Berlin, which he planned as "'an invisible matrix or anamnesis of connections in re-lationship' between Germans and Jews" (Young 2000, 167), the Voortrekker Monument is far more direct and explicit in its aims and design. When first approaching the edifice, the visitor encounters its wall, a carved stone representation of a laager. The wall is made up of sixty-four wagons, just as the laager at the Battle of Blood River allegedly was. As I argued earlier, the iconic laager that haunts Afrikanerdom is a manifestation of anxiety turned outward. The laager delineates a border between Self- and Otherhood, maintaining a membrane between that which must remain without, and that which is desired within. Formed in times of crisis as a protective mechanism, the laager as symbolic signifier marks an identity built on fear and anxiety. And the center of the laager strives toward a pure, uncontaminated, bright whiteness.

Several central characters feature in the building's nationalistic narrative. Below the doorway to the Hall of Heroes stands Anton van Wouw's statue of the Volksmoeder (Mother of the Nation), looking steadfastly toward the future, facing due north toward the expanse of Africa. She embodies the Afrikaner's nostalgic patriarchal idealization of the woman as the engenderess of the volk; she preserves civilization and light amid the brutality and darkness of Africa and is the emblem of the Afrikaner's future. Each cornerstone of the building is presided over by a six-ton granite statue of a Voortrekker leader: Piet Retief, Andries Pretorius, Hendrik Potgieter, and an unnamed leader (representative of all leaders).

The monument houses the flame brought to it in 1938 during the centenary reenactment, as well a central cenotaph, the symbolic resting place of Voortrekker martyr Piet Retief. The cenotaph is low on the ground, says the official guidebook, so that visitors have to bow their heads in reverence. Above is an enormous domed roof. For spectators, the building elicits a sense of disequilibrium produced by the arch of the domed roof, which draws one in and produces an uneasy vertigo. The monument spirals in on itself with this single perspective, leading one's gaze through an imposing Afrikaner understanding of history and destiny.

I have always been most emotionally disconcerted by the specific events in Afrikaner history depicted along the museum's interior walls; these whitely versions of history read as scenarios of colonial justification. In the Hall of Heroes, twenty-seven marble friezes guide the viewer through the events of the Great Trek, each rich in Afrikaner patriotism. Frieze No. 7, entitled Battle against the Matabele at Kapain, 1837, depicts the slaughter of Matabele warriors on oxen by gun-wielding Voortrekkers on horseback. The central point of the composition is a Matabele warrior bent over backward as a Voortrekker's horse tramples him. *The Murder of Retief and His Men* (Frieze No. 13) pictures the stalwart Retief watching the murder of his comrades as he is being bound for his own execution. This composition focuses on Retief's rigidity as Zulu impis raise their assegais over his head. The fabric on Retief's trousers twists as an impi pushes his foot against Retief's leg to tighten his fetters, using his full weight to restrain the mighty hero. *The Battle of Blood River, 16 December 1838* is paired with the *Making the Vow* panel (Nos. 20 and 21), in a central position on the rear wall. In the latter, Sarel Cilliers stands on a cannon and raises his hands upward as seven men look on. The battle panel is divided into two halves: on the left the Zulus buckle and falter as the Voortrekkers, on horseback, fire their muskets. The Voortrekkers are full of motion—their horses' muscles are tensed as if in full gallop—while the Zulus are static. Interestingly, the laager is depicted in the background but the actual action occurs outside the circle of wagons. The artistic license taken in depicting this history underscores the nationalist mythmaking and the distortion of events to suit a homogenous notion of identity. The psychological—and psychosomatic—impact of the friezes is violent and unnerving.

The building's most precise mechanism of control is a small hole in the cupola. It connects the entire edifice to that central date in Afrikaner history: December 16. The guidebook proclaims, "Each year at 12 o'clock on 16 December (the Day of the Vow) . . . the ray of sunlight, the light of civilisation, falls directly onto the cenotaph. It falls onto the words you see there, from the national anthem: 'Ons vir Jou, Suid Afrika'—'We for thee, South Africa.' The ray of sunlight symbolises God's blessing on the work and aspirations of the Voortrekkers" (South Africa 1989, 6). The whole building is designed to *perform* a commemorative date, and linked to that date is a definition of a nation based upon white superiority and dominance. This architectural mechanism is designed to enact a reality, bringing history into the present, and justifying the white colonization of South Africa. The words "We for thee, South Africa" on Retief's cenotaph function in an Austionian sense to conjure up a cohesive white nation.

Museums require an audience to be activated. As Young explains, "By themselves memorials remain inert and amnesiac, mere stones in the landscape without life or meaning. Only when we animate the stone figures and fill the empty spaces of the memorial, only then can monuments be said to remember anything at all" (1994, 37). Thus, visitors to the monument, assumed to be sympathetic to the Afrikaner cause, are invited to enact their national nostalgia within this space. Disciplined by the stillness and pseudo-sacred ambiance of this large granite edifice, visitors are encouraged to take in the monument's narrative in silence, much like a Sunday sermon in the Dutch Reformed Church.

But the observer's experience is highly individualized (Young 1994). Although during the apartheid era, the monument was only open to white South Africans[35] and was frequented by school groups learning about South African history, since 1994, the monument has attempted to become more inclusive, shifting its language and framing of history to match the new political dispensation, as I will discuss further in chapter 2. Grundlingh (2001), Coombes (2003), and Hutchison (2013)[36] each make convincing arguments about the position of the monument in post-1994 South Africa, especially in relation to Freedom Park, the African-troped memorial on the neighboring hill, and on how the site has attempted to engage wider constituencies.[37]

The imposing building, which under apartheid occupied a Baudrillardian hyperreality, existing as an insulated white, Calvinist utopia, safeguarded by the laager of wagons outside, still stands on the hill outside Pretoria. Now it is a monument to an outmoded identity, and to a people whose identity must change if it is to be accepted in the dynamic and multiracial social field of South Africa. As Grundlingh suggests, the monument remains "cocooned in a 'tourist bubble,'" and its "political voltage hardly registers, nor is it meant to do so" (2001, 108). He also asserts that the monument reads in contemporary South Africa as "an episode of nationalist deception" (102). Today the monument stands as a monolithic testament to whiteness that reveals the fictions of its privilege.

Afrikaners, as a volk, leveraged performance—through public pageantry, monumentalized spaces, and political rhetoric—to stage themselves into power in the early twentieth century. The genesis of the Afrikaner nation demonstrates how nations are engendered through what Sommer (1991) calls foundational fictions. In the Afrikaner fiction, race and nation were intimate bedfellows; the volk was imagined as markedly white, or whitely marked. The laager, the central metaphor of Afrikaner *volkseie*, is not only a metaphor for this population of settlers in Africa, but can apply to the broader system of whiteness and supremacy. Like the laager, whiteness requires a belief in its infallibility, despite its fictive nature. Like the laager, whiteness is designed to delimit boundaries and separate those who benefit from its privilege and those who are excluded from it. And because white supremacy is a fundamentally imbalanced system, like the laager, it is precariously vulnerable to anxiety when faced with perceived threats. Hence, the Afrikaner ascendency and its nation-building theatrics can offer an instructive model for how whiteness and nation function and perform in mutual concord.

Rehearsing a White Nation

AFRIKANER PERFORMANCES OF

VOLK IDENTITY (1904–2009)

Having traced the Afrikaner ascendency and creation of the volk, I now explore the tenuousness and rehearsability of the laager as Afrikaners repeatedly perform their national cohesion at different points in their history. I tease out the anxieties at the core of such enactments in two particular moments: Deon Opperman's 2008–2009 Boer War musical *Ons vir Jou* (*We for Thee*) and the 1904–1905 Boer War Circus (or Transvaal Spectacle) in St. Louis, Missouri, and Coney Island, New York. Throughout the chapter, I time-hop between 2009 and 1904, tracing the rehearsability of the laager. I also weave several related arguments into the chapter: about the relationship of shame to the Afrikaner psyche, the longing for a worthy Afrikaner hero and the popular resurrection of the figure of General Koos de la Rey, and Afrikaners' reclamation of their minority status in South African culture.

THE FALLACY OF THE LAAGER

Across their history, Afrikaners have created real and symbolic laagers to protect themselves from Africa, and to justify their acts of colonization. Afrikaners justify this enclosure through a particular reading of Calvinist doctrine that posits God as the Great Divider, thereby rationalizing the separation of races and supporting a nation based on the logic of predestined whiteness (see Goodwin and Schiff 1995, 187–198). Yet in establishing such a structure, the inevitable happens: the laager walls have a permeability that is, or seems to be, anathema to the laager itself.

This porousness engenders a deep sense of psychological insecurity that requires iterative suppression to maintain the intactness of the laager. Such is the psychological formula of Afrikaner nationhood and whiteness in general. As I mentioned in the introduction, the psychological equation required to maintain the laager—and the larger system of whiteness—is a confident belief in its absolute integrity, or at minimum the denial of its permeability, and a willing blindness to its fallibility. Both Afrikaner nationalism and systems of whiteness (like in the United States) require such confidence in the integrity, infallibility and predestined nature of the system itself, and thrive when it is present. Whiteness is the norm, unexamined and ubiquitous; white privilege is taken for granted. When challenged, whiteness becomes reactionary, defensive and dismissive. For instance, when confronted with the realities of racism in the contemporary United States, white Americans put huge efforts into sustaining the myth that, in a country with a black president, racism no longer exists; claim color-blindness and ignore their own race; refuse to acknowledge that the system is rigged to benefit some and not others; believe that reverse racism is the real problem; and attempt to tell black Americans how to feel, think, or behave.[1]

Similarly, the Afrikaner psyche is informed by a fear of slippage. Afrikaners are, as Owen suggests, the "children of an open frontier" (1996b), born of the anxiety of being outsiders in Africa. If their identity is predicated on the absolute insularity of the laager that keeps them contained within their safe white space—what Jansen calls "togetherness on the inside"—then the fear of penetration, slippage, seepage, or permeability dismantles the thorny branches of the laager—or what Jansen suggests is "security from the outside."[2] Out of the fear of slippage is born a desire to secure the space against external invasion and to ward off extinction. This desire is evidenced by the singular assuredness of Afrikaner historical narratives, what eighth-generation Afrikaner Marq de Villiers calls the "post-colonial tribal power struggle" that characterizes settler culture in southern Africa: "There are no people with a greater dislocation between their political and private actions than the Afrikaners.... Politically, they're intolerant, arrogant, determined to get their own way. Privately they are hospitable and want badly to be loved. It's their tribal history: they have had to withdraw so often, have been dispersed so often, have been attacked so often, that group cohesion is their highest goal" (1990, xxv).

Jansen explores the lasting impacts of apartheid on white Afrikaner students, asserting that when contemporary Afrikaner selfhood is questioned or shattered, there is a "defensive falling back on group knowledge" (2009,

79), a circling of the wagons. Even though they are of the born-free generation, born since the end of apartheid in 1994 (Mabry 2013), these students
are still socialized to look to the past for their sense of themselves. "Unlike
German perpetrators [in World War II]," writes Jansen, "Afrikaners did not
seek to break all affective ties to the past. Rather, the past was reasserted and
embellished in an attempt to reclaim what is perceived as threat and loss"
(Jansen 2009, 69). For many Afrikaners the past is always being replayed to
stave off the fear of obliteration. "This latter-day assertion of cultural presence (we are still here)," says Jansen, "is a response to being declared invisible in the social and political domain" (2009, 77). The fear of invisibility
or obliteration explains why Deon Opperman's large-scale musical *Ons vir Jou*
touched an emotional nerve with Afrikaners in 2008.

Playing Boers: 2009, State Theatre, Pretoria

Draped across the monumental stage of the State Theatre in Pretoria, a ban-
ner festooned with rifles and the old Vierkleur flag of the Transvaal Republic
reads "Ons vir Jou" (We for Thee), which refers to the final line of the first
stanza of "Die Stem" ("The Call"), the old South African national anthem.[3]
It is July 2009 and I am attending a packed-house Sunday matinee staging of
the Boer War as a musical, by renowned Afrikaner playwright and producer
Deon Opperman. During the finale of the first act, the hero General Koos de
la Rey prepares to go to war against the British. A general during the Second
Anglo-Boer War (1899–1902), he was highly respected on both sides for his
even-handedness, humanity, and military acumen. In Opperman's musical,
the general, played by Rouel Beukes (figure 7), rallies his troops with a battle
hymn, "My Afrikanerhart," a heart-wrenching, militaristic anthem that begins "Kom, boere krygers wees nou helde" (Come, Boer soldiers, become
heroes):[4]

> The khakis aim to conquer our people
> Promising pain and hurt,
> But if you shoot, shoot me through
> But if you shoot, shoot me through
> My Afrikaner heart.
> (Opperman and Else 2008, my translation)

Smoke billows over the stage as de la Rey's soldiers march in unison toward
the audience. In blinding white light, reflecting off the smoke, they take

Figure 7. Rouel Beukes as General Koos de la Rey in Deon Opperman's *Ons vir Jou.* © 2013. Courtesy of Deon Opperman.

aim and shoot their guns, sending chills up the audience's collective spines and bringing the act to a close. As this (melo)dramatic scene ends, I turn around in my seat in the first row to look back at the thirteen-hundred-seat full house. To my surprise, the whole audience is weeping. Men and women, young and old; there does not seem to be a dry eye in the room.[5] What had touched this community so deeply to bring about a moment of collective emotional outpouring, a moment of *communitas*, like this? What is it about this particular narrative that moves grown Afrikaner men, like the man in the row behind me, to sob uncontrollably into his wife's floral hanky? Or to moisten the eyes of my family members sitting beside me? The melodramatic scene could be read simply as a retrograde recircling of Afrikaner wagons. But I cannot simply dismiss the emotional impact it has on such a large audience and am puzzled by the fact that this scene is playing out now, in 2009, in democratic South Africa.

To unpack the emotional and communal impact of this Afrikaans-language musical in 2009, and the scripts it draws from, I trace the genealogy of Afrikaner self-performance across the history of this unique national group. In the discussion that follows, I time-hop between 1904, when the

Boer War Circus performed in St. Louis, Missouri, and the teary reception of *Ons vir Jou* in 2009; the former's palimpsestic traces bleed into the latter as Opperman's musical cites past scenarios of Afrikaner self-representation.

Playing Boers: 1904, St. Louis, Missouri

It is 1904 in St. Louis, and twenty-five thousand people are gathered at the Boer War Concession, a multiacre arena in which two major battles from the Anglo-Boer War are being reenacted twice a day as part of the Louisiana Purchase Exposition. After entering through a massive fortified wall and turret, based on the original Fort de Goede Hoop in Cape Town, and under the Boer, British, and American flags, spectators enjoy almost three hours of spectacle, divided into three scenarios. In the first scenario, *The Battle at Colenso*, British redcoats in polished uniforms are surrounded by Boer commandos and their ox-drawn wagons. Showered with "a perfect hailstorm of bullets" (Anglo-Boer War Historical Libretto), the British lose their powerful fifteen-pounder field cannons to the plucky Boers in their threadbare clothing. At its finale, General Piet Cronjé (the actual general, not an actor) stands atop a wagon and waves his hat as one of his soldiers brandishes the Vierkleur flag (figure 8). In the second scenario, *The Battle of Paardeberg*, a burly Cronjé replays his historic surrender to the diminutive Englishman, Lord Roberts (played by an actor), as he walks stalwartly across the battlefield and extends his hand to his rival, his hat securely on his head, an image that evokes the historic photograph taken at the actual event only a few years prior.[6] While technically the reenactment of a historic defeat—Cronjé's surrender came only months before the Boers' capitulation on May 31, 1902—the general's performance in St. Louis is one of Boer dignity and pride. In the third and final scenario, *De Wet's Daring Escape*, an actor impersonating General Christian de Wet (George Prescott) makes a daring escape on horseback through a cordon of British troops and leaps from a height of thirty-five feet (eleven meters) into a pool of water, making a "daring dash for liberty" (Anglo-Boer War Historical Libretto).

Only two years after the Boers surrendered to the British in 1902, General Piet Cronjé and charismatic war hero Ben Viljoen went to America, not as war heroes or military personnel, but as *performers*.[7] Their entourage of South Africans[8] went to the Louisiana Purchase Exposition in St. Louis as part of a performance installation known popularly as the Transvaal Spectacle or Boer Circus.[9] As Jennie Sutton describes it, they re-created battles

Figure 8. Battle of Colenso, Boer War exhibit, Louisiana Purchase Exposition.
© 1904 Carleton H. Graves. Courtesy of Library of Congress.

from the South African War of 1899–1902 "for the amusement of American and international audiences [featuring] hundreds of veterans in the 17-acre amphitheater fir[ing] blanks at each other with rifles and artillery, along with dozens of horses, mules, wagons, and ox-carts crisscrossing the field" (2007, 272). This dramatic, large-scale event filled with "noisy explosions and dramatic scenes promised fairgoers a tantalizing and perhaps terrifying glimpse of the South African War" (Sutton 2007, 272). What was at play in St. Louis in 1904, when these former soldiers left South Africa to replay their own defeat twice a day for two straight months in front of paying audiences?

The South Africans were invited to America by enterprising promoters seeking to capitalize on Americans' common antipathy to the British and to assure Americans of an "atmosphere of reconciliation, stability, and sustained white racial control in postwar South Africa" (Sutton 2007, 272). The star of the show, General Piet Cronjé, a leader known as the "Lion of South Africa," gained fame during the First and Second Boer Wars (1880–1881; 1899–1902) but ended the war in shame when he had to surrender the 4,150 Boers under his leadership to Lord Roberts at Paardeberg[10] after an eleven-day siege. His participation in St. Louis earned him respect from Americans, who saw in him a robust hero and graceful loser, but also deep criticism from his fellow South Africans, who called him a sellout and a traitor. On September 21, 1904, the editor of the *Mafeking Mail* wrote of the "peerless buffoonery" of the Boer Circus, claiming that Cronjé and his cohort were "not heroes, but clowns," who were making "a harlequinade of their country's agony." The author's suggestion that Cronjé and his entourage were performing a falsity and making a spectacle of themselves also taps into deeply held Afrikaner notions of decorum, shame, and disgrace.

SHAME AND DISGRACE

The phrase "Skaam jou!" (Shame on you) is a common refrain in Afrikaner culture.[11] Given the manner in which Afrikanerdom has self-presented as an enclosed, exclusive national unit, the role of the concepts of shame (internal, private ignominy, or self-loathing), and its twin, disgrace (external, public dishonor, or humiliation), in the construction of white Afrikaner identity is important.

Scholars have explored the notion of shame from a variety of perspectives. On its most basic level, shame occurs when the self encounters an unpleasant, distasteful, or alienating version of itself. Giorgio Agamben, in *Remnants of Auschwitz* (1999), defines shame as a product of the inability to get away from oneself, of always having to face the self, and that "what is shameful is our intimacy, that is our presence to ourselves" (105). For Helen Lynd, shame is a "sense of degradation excited by the consciousness of having done something unworthy of one's previous idea of one's own excellence" (1958, 23–24). Stephen Pattison suggests shame is both an individual and a communal phenomenon: shame is experienced as "an acute sense of unwanted exposure," and "all shame is socially shaped [and] socially engendered" (2000, 40–43, 182). And according to Gershen Kaufman, "Because of the fundamental equation of difference [and inferiority] with shame," minority identity is psychologically informed by "scenes of shame" (2004, 273–274). Faced with the "totality of [their] existence" (Agamben 1999)—apartheid, moral responsibility, blame, complicity—contemporary Afrikaners are in an ongoing process of confronting the shame of that totality.

Afrikaners, as a minority of white Europeans in Africa, fear unwanted exposure; or considered another way, they fear the rupture of the laagers of their culture. When faced with alienating versions of themselves as racist colonialists, sexually repressed miscegenists, or complicit supporters of apartheid, they experience shame as the previous ideas of their own excellence become degraded. Shame also functions socially; when confronted with the costs of their privilege as an advantaged group, many Afrikaners, like many whites in contemporary America, have a hard time letting go of their narratives of belonging or taking responsibility for their history. Whether they participated actively as individuals in colonial or apartheid acts, or complicitly profited from them, Afrikaners in the post-1994 era are being called on to face the totality of an identity created as a supposedly impregnable whole, which ultimately has been disgraced and has produced shame. This, at a time when whiteness is being called to answer for its sins globally.[12]

Playing Boers: 1904

I return now to Cronjé's reply to the accusations that he and his entourage were making a shameful spectacle of themselves. Shame, here, is of the social corrective kind; Cronjé's breach of Victorian-era Afrikaner decorum challenged the cohesive narrative and social image of the volk. Such shameful displays were perceived to be particularly harmful at a time when the fledgling national group was attempting to prove itself after its massive defeat at the hands of empire. Cronjé replied: "I have a conscience to be at peace with, and so long as I am convinced that the means I adopt to retrieve what a long and perilous war has destroyed, so long will I not worry or be unbalanced by criticisms. . . . My mind is peaceful in the knowledge that every day I spend in America I am able to enlighten the Americans about my persecuted people" (1904 Programme). Cronjé's motivations were partially financial, partially pragmatic, and partially aimed at restoring his personal credibility as well as that of his fellow Afrikaners. For the general, the part he was playing in the Transvaal Spectacle was not just as a war hero or an actor in a historical pantomime, but as a temporarily defeated Afrikaner who came to America to win American support for the Boer cause. In his mind, he was upholding the Afrikaner volk as a proud patriot, even while critics at home read him as a traitor and a charlatan. When he presented his letter of surrender[13] to Lord Roberts in the Paardeberg scenario, he was not performing defeat; rather, he was playing the part of the sentimental hero for his sympathetic American audiences.

The historical context in which he performed is important. In 1877, the British government annexed the independent Transvaal Republic. The First Anglo-Boer War began on December 16, 1880, when Transvaal Boers attacked the British garrison at Potchefstroom. After four months of fighting and overwhelming British losses, including the famous Battle of Majuba Hill

in February 1881, the two sides called a truce. An uneasy peace lasted until 1899, when tensions between the two colonial powers flared again. Unlike its predecessor, the Second Anglo-Boer War was a protracted battle between the independent Boer republics of the Orange Free State and the Transvaal and the larger British Commonwealth.[14] At the end of the war, the Boer Republics became British colonies. This brutal war saw the first extensive use of barbed wire, trench warfare, and guerrilla tactics, and the establishment of concentration camps. It was also extensively documented, thanks to the recent advent of portable photographic technology. Under the leadership of Lord Kitchener (1850–1916), the British used a controversial scorched-earth policy to subdue the Boers, burning their farms, killing livestock, starving them out, and imprisoning 116,000 Boers, about 26,000 of whom, mainly women and children, perished in British concentration camps. On May 31, 1902, the Treaty of Vereeniging was signed and then in 1910, Briton and Boer were incorporated into the Union of South Africa, a dominion of the British Empire. The war left an indelible psychic scar on the Boer population, and this wound became a rallying point for the Afrikaner nation-builders. And this wound reopened in 2009, at a time when Afrikaners were wrestling with their positions as a white minority in a majority black democracy.

In 1904, at the Boer War Circus, fiction and reality were happy bedfellows. A spirit of play was central to the reenactments as was a cultivated verisimilitude and an aura of authenticity. Renowned circus impresario Frank Fillis,[15] along with his English business partner Arthur Waldo Lewis, produced the Anglo-Boer War Concession, which he touted as "the greatest and most realistic military spectacle known in the history of the world" (Anglo-Boer War Historical Libretto, 2). Featuring a British Army encampment, a native kraal (comprised of Zulu, San, Swazi, and Ndebele), as well as the large performance arena, Fillis's spectacle promised to deliver truth through staged imitations of real events. The souvenir program outlines this realism vividly in its many photo captions. For instance, one caption reads: "The actors are the survivors of the scenes they reenact." Another claims: "Topography of the ground selected for the reproduction of the battles is very like that on which the originals were fought" (Fillis 1904).

Thus, Fillis shellacked his reenactment performances with the veneer of authenticity. The dramaturgy of the reenactments also positioned audiences to receive the Boers with sympathy. In order to appear impartial and fair, especially so shortly after the Boer War, both British and Boer victories were portrayed. The first battle (act 1: Colenso), depicted a British defeat, which no doubt went over well with Americans, who had a long history of their own with the British Empire. The second scenario (act 2: Paardeberg) was the Boers' major defeat but by spotlighting Cronjé's surrender, along with a dramatic parade of the prisoners of war (women, children, and livestock),[16] this scenario instilled sympathy for the Boer cause. According to Sutton, Americans followed the Boer War closely and exhibited "mass demonstrations of pro-Boer sympathy" (2007, 275). The Transvaal Spectacle helped secure that pro-Boer support.

Perhaps most interesting is how Fillis played out the climactic third act of the spectacle. By ending with Christiaan de Wet's escape on horseback in the climactic scene (figure 10), the show left audiences with the image of a triumphant Boer getting away. By closing the show with De Wet the Boer Pimpernel, a man known for his ability to outwit and evade British forces during the war, Fillis dramaturgically framed the Boers—the actual losers in the war—as the heroes of the Transvaal Spectacle.

Playing Boers: 2009

More than a century later, in July 2009, I am watching Deon Opperman's Ons vir Jou at the State Theatre in Pretoria. In the opening scene of this historical musical, "the Lion of South Africa," General Cronjé (played by Jacques

Figure 10. General de Wet's escape, Boer War spectacle, World's Fair,
St. Louis, MO. © 1904 Charles L. Wasson. Courtesy of Library of Congress.

Combault), whips the Boer leadership into a fighting froth, calling on President Kruger to declare war on England so that they will feel the righteous might of the Afrikaner volk. Cronjé's battle cries are tempered by another Boer General: Koos de la Rey (played by Rouel Beukes) advises Kruger to be cautious. "Britain lies on our borders like a wounded lion ('n gekweste leeu). It's an arrogant hunter that underestimates a wounded lion." While it refers to the British here, the image of a wounded lion is also an apt metaphor for Afrikaner self-representation, as it encapsulates ferocity and courage intertwined with a profound sense of psychic wounding and political disenfranchisement. The character of the wounded lion marries the scarring impact of the Second Anglo-Boer War on the Afrikaner psyche with their self-depiction as fierce survivors in the harsh African landscape, competing against the mighty British Empire for political control.[17]

In 1904, reaction to the Transvaal Spectacle was sympathetic. "Courage is courage no matter the colors on the standard," one reviewer wrote (Boer and Britons 1905), and a heroic Afrikaner story permeated the event. In 2009, the reaction to Opperman's Boer War musical was far more conflicted, as one would expect. While Afrikaans-speaking audiences flocked to see the show, resulting in an extended run in Pretoria and the teary reception I witnessed, many critics chastised the piece and its creators for performing a nostalgic and exclusive "circling of the wagons." The late playwright and columnist, John Matshikiza, cautioned that *Ons vir Jou* "is an exclusive history at a time when [South Africa] needs inclusive history" (Watts 2008).

Ons vir Jou, which had several successful runs at the State Theatre between 2008 and 2010, and another in Cape Town in 2013, was a collaboration between Afrikaans playwright and director Deon Opperman—who is known for his epic Afrikaner history plays—and Mozi Records executive Sean Else. Deeply steeped in Afrikaner nationalist lore, the musical features in its central scene—and has capitalized, financially and culturally, on—the massively popular song "De La Rey," by pop sensation Bok van Blerk (a.k.a. Louis Pepler), Else's star client. The 2006 song, about the Boer War hero General Koos de la Rey, rocked up the pop charts and into the hearts of many Afrikaners. The refrain calls for de la Rey to come again and lead the Boers; many interpret it as a clarion call for white supremacy at a time when the black government is failing to provide for the basic needs of its citizens and to protect them from escalating crime. The media made much of the song, its accompanying video, and the "De la Rey" parties inspired by the music, complete with their apartheid-era South African flag-waving, and nostalgic performances of white solidarity and Afrikaner pride.[18] Opperman and Else based their musical on van Blerk's megahit, fleshing out the story of General de la Rey's attempts to stave off war as long as he could and then fight valiantly as a *bittereinder*.

The official music video for "De La Rey" is unabashedly nostalgic and melodramatic.[19] Bok van Blerk appears as a soldier, back pressed against the wall of a muddy trench, calling for a hero to lead the Boers: "De la Rey, De la Rey, will you come and lead the Boers?" Van Blerk sings of how the British burned his house and his farm to ashes, and how those flames and fire are now burning deep inside him. "My wife and child lie in a camp and rot," he sings, as we see women, dressed in Voortrekker kappies, staring out achingly at the camera through barbed wire as the old flag waves in the background.[20] In both the pop song and the musical, it seemed as if Afrikaners were performing their volk identity and racial exclusivity—circling their wagons—as they had done in the past.

Critiqued by some as an opportunistic commercial venture, *Ons vir Jou* played on the fears and alienation of many Afrikaners in post-1994 South Africa, after they no longer held political and symbolic power and their claims to truth came into question. Johrné van Huyssteen, a member of the band Ddisselblom, publicly criticized *Ons vir Jou*, saying that Opperman and his business partner, Sean Else, were exploiting the emotion, fear, and anger of Afrikaners who feel lost in contemporary South Africa (Watts 2008). This perception of wagon-circling has been fueled by Opperman's own public declarations of Afrikaner pride, which echo Cronjé's vision of himself as the ultimate patriot. "I will not apologise for being an Afrikaner," Opperman asserts, "And I understand that the word Afrikaner has basically been banned from the general lexicon of South Africa, you're not allowed to say the word anymore, you can say things like 'Afrikaanse,' 'Afrikaanssprekend.' Well you know my reaction to that is it's rubbish. I'm an Afrikaner, that is where my heritage comes from, that's my roots" (Watts 2008).[21]

Also, in May 2008, a huge black-and-white billboard went up next to the N1 highway outside Pretoria with Afrikaner slogans and later a giant Vierkleur flag on it. "For a week it caused an outcry," says Derek Watts of the television program *Carte Blanche*, "until it was revealed as *Ons vir Jou*'s advertising campaign" (2008). This marketing strategy pushed sensitive buttons. The Vierkleur flag is read as a marker of a conservative Afrikaner position in contemporary South Africa, much like the Confederate flag in the United States. Both flags are also distinct markers of whiteness. A billboard of a giant Vierkleur, posted just outside the gated community of Centurion,[22] at the gateway to the city of Pretoria/Tshwane, would read to many South Africans as a white Afrikaner provocation. While it was effective in recruiting white Afrikaner audiences, who might already have been sympathetic to such nostalgic symbolism, the marketing for *Ons vir Jou* simultaneously alienated the rest (the majority) of South Africans, who read the billboard as an exclusionary symbol.

The billboard marked a sense of belonging for Afrikaners who desire to see their history performed on stage, Afrikaners who believe, as Opperman has said several times, "any nation, like any person, who does not remember who he was, will not know who he is, and cannot dream about what he can be" (Opperman and Else 2008, my translation). But it also marked a clear boundary between those who "belong" in this equation and those who do not, rehearsing laager logic yet again. The billboard became like the boundary drawn by a laager, between what belongs within the safe enclosure and what is wild and threatening outside. When paired ANC Youth League leader Julius Malema's racialized incitements—in 2011 he whipped university students into a frenzy chanting "Dubula iBunu" (Kill the Boer!), and continued to do so despite a court ruling that this constituted hate speech ("Julius Malema's Political Timeline" 2012)—the *Ons vir Jou* billboard illustrates how conflicted negotiations for self-definition and power in the new democracy currently are.

At the end of *Ons vir Jou*, the chorus sings a modified version of the old, pre-1994 national anthem "Die Stem" ("The Call"). While the old anthem promised that citizens would live and die for South Africa ("Ons sal lewe, ons sal sterwe"), Opperman and Else's revision emphasizes how "Like a rock, a nation stands together." Now that singing the old anthem is no longer socially sanctioned (it would be akin to waving the Confederate flag in the United States), this play offers a space in which Afrikaners can express their volk pride through this not-so-veiled homage to the old regime and a nostalgic return to the fictionalized past.

WHITENESS IN UNCERTAIN TIMES

Almost two decades into the new democracy, Afrikaners—who ended up far better off than many feared after the 1994 transition—are returning to narratives of loss as they stage themselves. While the Boers of 1904 performed heroism in the face of real loss, today it seems as if many Afrikaners are performing loss in the face of a relatively stable reality. They perpetuate narratives of loss and obliteration despite Max du Preez's astute observation that the vast majority of whites, Afrikaners included, are still prospering under black rule. "The kids standing in the pubs in Pretoria with their hand on their heart ... go outside and they get into their BMW convertibles," says du Preez. "They're not suffering. It's an imagined suffering" (McGreal 2007).

Opperman's musical plays on this imagined suffering as it attempts to re-unify Afrikaners feeling lost in the new political order. In *Ons vir Jou*, the song "My Afrikanerhart" is filled with familiar tropes of dark clouds (*donker wolke*) forming over a nation under pressure; an enemy casts his shadow across the land, as the Boers stand armed to the teeth. The word *donker* ("dark" or "darkness") takes on particular resonance in contemporary South Africa, a country now under black majority rule. The opening scene of *Ons vir Jou* is reminiscent of D. F. Malan's speech at Bloemfontein in 1938, where he sutured time and space into a singular, white narrative of the Afrikaner nation; here, a man we later come to know as Siener van Rensburg, the Boer prophet-soothsayer and adviser to General de la Rey and President Steyn, sits downstage by a fire and talks to the audience. I translate from the Afrikaans: "You have already seen what I have seen, what I did not want to believe when I saw it: A *volk* pushed to the edge of an abyss . . . As the old people tell it, if you want to forge the strongest metal, you heat it in fire until it's white-hot (*witwarm*) . . . and then you dip it in blood, over and over. It's the same with a *volk*. I see. You see. *They* still have to" (Opperman and Else 2008, 5). In this speech, Opperman bookends "the Afrikaner story" between two moments of strife: the turn of the twentieth century—when over twenty-six thousand Boers died in concentration camps and they suffered deep losses against the British—and the contemporary moment—when stories continually circulate about Afrikaner farmers being murdered, where the battle of languages repeatedly rears up, and where ANC government corruption, skyrocketing crime, and unpoliced violence feed resentment toward the black government.[23]

From 2008 to 2010, while *Ons vir Jou* was playing, several events added fuel to the fire: the increasing popularity of Julius Malema's antiwhite political party, the Economic Freedom Fighters (EFF), and the brutal murder on April 3, 2010, of Eugène Terre'Blanche, the former leader of the white political militia movement, by Chris Mahlangu and Patrick Ndlovu, two disgruntled workers on his farm (BBC News 2010). Audiences at *Ons vir Jou*, almost all of whom were white, could easily connect the dots to these events. Siener's opening speech sutures a "nation on the edge" in 1899 and a nation in need of "white-hot forging" in 2010. And it binds the audience into a community of solidarity. But what gets erased in this "valley of fire and blood" is the entire apartheid era. It is also vital to unpack the tacit yet ubiquitous use of the word *white*. The volk galvanized by strife and battle is a white one, forged white-hot in blood. And who are the "they" that Siener tells us still have to see the Afrikaner volk in 2009 and 2010? In the context of the Boer War, it is the British, but *Ons vir Jou*, performed in contemporary South Africa, hints at a closer "other" as it draws on narratives and scripts from the past.

Ons vir Jou is written from a decidedly pro-Boer point of view. The British in the play glibly sing about their scorched-earth policy and imperial desires. Lord Milner sings, in English, about burning out the Boers, "Let them starve in a country that is scorched" (Opperman and Else 2008, 62). *Mail and Guardian* theatre critic Adriaan Basson questioned why the British were "depicted as silly, pale-skinned little men" (2008). Black Africans, of whom there is only one, fare less well. Samson Khumalo, as Samuel, carries burdens for his white masters, makes food, and saddles horses. His character is developed to its greatest extent when he tells his young master Kleinboet, in an awkward Afrikaans accent, that the war is like a mountain and it is growing bigger. He has only twelve speaking lines in the play, most which work to affirm his white masters or mirror their deeds.

Opperman selects those moments that serve Afrikaner identity and boost Afrikaner *volkstrots* (nation-pride) at a time when this group feels politically and socially lost. Yet Opperman also actively focuses on the noble figure of General Koos de la Rey, who was revered by Boer and Briton alike for his pragmatism, integrity, and courage both in challenging his superiors not to go to war and then in fighting valiantly once the decision was made. In an interview in June 2011, he explained to me what drew him to write about de la Rey. For him, de la Rey taps into the best part of being an Afrikaner: he has a clear moral compass. Opperman explains further that unlike Milner and Kitchener, Methuen and de la Rey were humane. "They followed a code of honor. It was the way of gentlemen" (M. Lewis 2011). Hence, Opperman chooses to perform a version of Afrikaners in *Ons vir Jou* that is grounded in honor, to counter their shameful relationship to apartheid.

Unabashedly disinterested in what critics say, Opperman cares about what his audiences think. He told me, "People cry [at *Ons vir Jou*] because they are remembering a time when they felt worthy. Who can be proud really of fucking [former prime ministers] P. W. Botha and or John Vorster? There's a yearning for a time when people were good and true. And honest. And clear. And fair. And they shook hands when they vanquished each other" (M. Lewis 2011). And Opperman makes a noteworthy point when he adds, "They were also weeping for the loss of something finer in their culture. It's not just a longing for the 'good old days.' It's more like 'we're not as good as we were'" (M. Lewis 2011). Such a self-reflexive comment is worth considering, especially when *Ons vir Jou*, both in its content (a pro-Boer history) as well as its genre (a large-scale musical reminiscent of *Les Misérables*), is read by many as exclusively patriotic. I understood Opperman to use *good* (in "we're not as good as we were") in a profoundly moral sense of the word, not a hierarchal one. For a population who after 1994 have been "declared invisible in the social and political domain" (Jansen 2009, 77), and who have been made to confront the shame of their past, what can they find in that past that is worth celebrating? As the architects and benefactors of apartheid, Afrikaners are easy—often legitimate—targets for derision. But there can be no denying that the 3.3 million white settlers are also an integral part of the complex social fabric of the vibrant post-1994 democracy, and they need to find new ways to express themselves and their culture. This is, for me, one of the quintessential questions whiteness faces in the postcolony: how are white subjects to perform, or dismantle whiteness, after the demise of their political privilege?

Contemporary Afrikaners are in tension between shame about the past and a desire to move forward as members of a multicultural democratic South Africa with pride in their culture and their contributions. The de la Rey song seems to have hit a nerve because of that tension. Journalist Max du Preez has written that contemporary Afrikaners are "search[ing] for identity ... search[ing] for pride" and find in General de la Rey something about their history of which they can be proud (A² Productions 2007). Perhaps the song's plea to de la Rey could also be read as a yearning for Koos de la Rey's principles and integrity to be the guiding spirit of young Afrikaners, rather than the outdated, racist logic of apartheid and white superiority. "[White] people feel uncertain," asserts sociologist Andries Bezuidenhout. "They're afraid, they feel disempowered. And I think that's what explains the deep emotions that [this song triggers]" (A² Productions 2007). *Financial Times* correspondent Alec Russell paints a portrait of conflicting claims and desires around van Blerk's song: "Commentators agonised over what it meant. Was it a sign of renewed Afrikaner confidence? A paean to white rule? Or a reminder of a happier and simpler time when Afrikaners did not have to feel guilty about their past? ... Whatever his intentions, young Bok had clearly roused a grassroots Afrikaner populism" (A. Russell 2007). "Whatever Pepler might have intended," writes Jansen, the song "absorbs and reflects" the fears, anxieties, anger, and confusion of many Afrikaners (2009, 48). He suggests that beneath the "loud bravado" are deep emotions about loss and change: "It is about a people unprepared for the suddenness of transition. It is about the disruption of a once-simple narrative about the past. It is about the travail of giving up privilege and power to those who only yesterday were tarnished as terrorists and enemies of the state. ... It is, in the end, about the gradual recognition of defeat" (Jansen 2009, 48). Acknowledging "the unpleasant truth" that "our people were responsible for apartheid and destroying the dreams of the majority of the population" (M. Lewis 2011), Opperman is nonetheless unwilling to recognize the type of defeat Jansen suggests. Yet in his desire to celebrate his own people's history, he also risks alienating the many South Africans (WESSAs and black South Africans) who echo John Matshikiza's rebuke of the musical as culturally and racially exclusive at a time when South Africa needs social inclusivity. Adriaan Basson asks, "Why, in 2008, does one of our best think it proper to put on stage a production that uncritically glorifies the role of the Boers in the Anglo-Boer War?" (2008). I would answer because of the ontological insecurity of whiteness at times of instability. At anxious times like these, the volk are soothed by the nostalgic and melodramatic comfort of the laager.

It is fitting, then, that a form such as melodrama—with its clear moral distinctions, emotionality, and escapism from political realities—would be deployed by Afrikaners. It appeals to their moral coding of the world and is an apt vehicle through which to circulate their historical narrative of a chosen few besieged on all sides. In a recent interview, Rouel Beukes, the actor who played de la Rey, said, "I said to Deon you should have called it 'Ons vir Jou and Bring Your Box of Tissues with You,' you know, because . . . it's the *soapie* (soap opera) element that's also been brought into this" (Watts 2008). In my interview with Opperman, he confirmed that melodrama was an effective genre for his storytelling because "I want [the audience] to have catharsis. I believe that if you make them feel, they think for days afterwards. Because they can't get it out of their hearts" (M. Lewis 2011).

Melodrama, as an exteriorization of internal conflict (Brooks 1995), relies on binary constructions of good versus evil, both of which are imagined to be pure and essential truths. Personalized characters stand in for larger social issues as melodrama depicts the "triumph of moral value over villainy, and the consequent idealizing of the moral views assumed to be held by the audience" (Frye 1957, 47). Melodrama also distorts reality, offering escapism and a conservative worldview, and functions to deliver ideology as false consciousness (Postlewait 1996). The form of historical musical that Opperman has perfected relies heavily on melodramatic conventions— musical underscoring of the story, heightened emotionality, a clear moral universe, tried-and-true historical narratives that exalt Afrikaner values, and powerfully drawn characters with strong personalities that stand in for larger social issues.

In *Ons vir Jou*, amid the story of war, Opperman frames a love story between de la Rey's son, Adaan (played by Adrian Poulsen), and his beloved Mariaan (played by Marisa Bosman) (figure 14). Their relationship follows classic lines of melodrama: the two fall in love but are then separated when Adaan must go to war to fight and Mariaan is left at home. Their duets are also imbued with nationalist rhetoric. They sing in Afrikaans: "And in our dream our land was still our land, Lead by God's hand, He's on our side" (Opperman and Else 2008, 21). As in *Bou van 'n nasie*, the heterosexual couple—the embodiment of the volk's future—are the personal emblems of the political issues at stake. By including this subplot, Opperman ensures that the stakes of loss and longing have an acute and personal hook that draws the audience into the political story. Opperman's framing of *Ons vir Jou* along melodramatic binaries seems to keep Afrikaners in a constantly performed state of defensive battle-readiness. From the trauma of the concentration camps and scorched-earth tactics of the Boer War rose the flames of Afrikaner nationalism that eventually became apartheid. Today, it is the murder of white farmers and Malema's call "Kill the Boer" that have Afrikaners re-traumatized—and reperforming their laagers.

In 2008, the same year *Ons vir Jou* premiered, Afrikaners joined the Unrepresented Nations and Peoples Organization (UNPO), an international organization dedicated to protecting the human and cultural rights of indigenous peoples, minorities, and unrecognized or occupied territories.[24] This membership, along with the formation in 1996 of the Commission for the Promotion and Protection of the Rights of Cultural, Religious, and Linguistic Communities, ensures Afrikaners ethnic minority status in the new democracy.[25] While protecting minority rights is a vital benchmark of "stability in multi-ethnic states" (van der Merwe and Johnson 1997), Afrikaners' symbolic use of this minority status is somewhat problematic. In post-1994 South Africa it rings false when fallen victors claim victimization. The sentiments of loss and persecution that fueled the recent Red October protest[26] have been echoed by Opperman before. "We were always the least, and we still are," he has said when challenged about the message *Ons vir Jou* sends to contemporary South Africans. In the play, General de la Rey gives a rousing speech about Afrikaners' being too few and yet strong enough to fight the British: "How few is too few to abandon our freedom? How few is too few to be a slave in our own land?" (Opperman and Else 2008, 66, my translation).

Ons vir Jou ends with Siener van Rensburg again on stage. The Boers have surrendered, de la Rey has lost his son in battle, the scene is bleak. But Siener reminds the audience in Afrikaans: "No matter how dead or dark (*donker*) the future looks—a small coal that glows in the white ash of the past (*wit as van sy verlede*) . . . all that is needed is a small piece of hard wood . . . and a little wind of change. Look and you will see how high those flames will burn!"

(Opperman and Else 2008, 104, my translation). Again, the words *dark* and *white* resonate in multiple registers, and the wind of change has indeed come to South Africa. While one can read a desire for progress and adjustments in identity in that "little wind of change," what do the flames represent in 2010 to a white minority within a black majority? What *hardehout* (hard wood) is it that seeks to ignite flames of *volkstrots* again out of the "white ash" of the past? This metaphor is an Opperman signature. He ended his epic 1996 play *Donkerland* with a small "hyphen of humanity, lost in the grass of Donkerland" (Opperman 1996, 157), apparently gripped by the notion of a small white speck adrift in a darkening, dark land. But whereas his 1996 version seemed to fear oblivion, his most recent metaphor calls for reignition.

The laager of Afrikaner whiteness is frequently rehearsed; it is a ritornello, the tune this population returns to at times of political or social instability. In 1904, General Cronjé performed the sympathetic Boer hero to thousands of Americans, inspiring his audience with feelings of courage and patriotism. Across South Africa in 1938, Afrikaner history was enacted through the Centenary Trek, offering onlookers and spectators the chance to participate in the performance by uttering Voortrekker vows, capturing wagon grease or *fakkel* flames with their handkerchiefs, and baptizing their children with the name of ox-wagons. And in 2009, Opperman's successful and popular musical brought tears to the eyes of thousands of Afrikaners who saw their now-shamed history proudly reenacted on the State Theatre's expansive stage. At each of these moments in their history, Afrikaners have leveraged the power of performance—both under the proscenium arch and in the public sphere—to galvanize a volk identity around a predestined white authority and to stage themselves, for themselves, as children of an open frontier. And that whiteness, ontologically precarious at its core, is inherently anxious, finding constant need to reassert and restage itself when it perceives threats or is questioned. In the next chapter, I explore one way Afrikaner whiteness often elects to perform itself out of anxiety, as Opperman does very effectively: through the binary comforts of melodramatic forms and by using the salve of nostalgia.

Hyphens of Humanity

WHITENESS AND NOSTALGIA IN

THE WORK OF DEON OPPERMAN

In this chapter I offer a deeper discussion of Afrikaans theatre impresario and playwright Deon Opperman, whose work often inspires passionate responses, but who remains the most prolific and successful playwright writing in Afrikaans today.[1] His work is enormously popular; he often sells out to audiences of forty-five thousand people. An avowed populist who cares more about his audiences than what any critic has to say, Opperman is committed to creating work for and about Afrikaners and the Afrikaner condition. "Categorically, I am an Afrikaner," he says. "It's the Afrikaans word for Africa. I'm from Africa" (M. Lewis 2011). Below, I analyze his powerful and important history play *Donkerland* (*Dark Land*, 1996) along with another recent musical, *Tree aan* (*Roll Call*, 2010), and the heroes commemorated at Freedom Park, on a hill opposite the Voortrekker Monument in Pretoria. I use these performance artifacts and sites to tease out the tensions in the transition around 1994 and in the following two decades of the new democracy. I explore Opperman's theatrical and larger social labors, his use of nostalgia, memory, and minority status as he wrestles with Afrikaner self-definition, masculinity, and the perceived demise of whiteness as well as the threats of land loss, miscegenation, and the interstitial space between two political camps: *verligte* (enlightened, liberal) and *verkrampte* (cramped, conservative) Afrikaners.

Opperman's work indexes white anxiety at moments when the Afrikaners' ethnic identity and political status are in question, and is simultaneously nostalgic, reactionary, insightful, and culturally relevant. His work registers the cultural complexities of performing whiteness in the new democracy, begging questions like (how) can whiteness perform in the postcolony? What are its limits? Is it possible to disentangle whiteness from the shameful associations of the past? And what happens when white bodies perform in the contemporary postcolony?

A WHITE MAN IN AFRICA

A Fulbright scholar, Opperman was educated at Rhodes (BA), Northwestern (MA), and Wits (MBA) Universities. He has written or directed over fifty theatre productions in both Afrikaans and English in every major theatre and festival in South Africa, as well as abroad, and he is as prolific as he is controversial. His plays explore many genres and topics, having exposed South African audiences to the taboo subjects of HIV and AIDS; right-wingers and racism; the trauma of the Border Wars and teenage conscription; homosexuality; and, of course, the ongoing challenges of white Afrikaner identity. Opperman is also a founding director of AFDA, the South African School of Motion Picture Medium and Live Performance, and of Packed House Productions, through which he produces much of his own work, as well as the work of other artists. Recently, Opperman has branched out into the world of television, with several highly successful series: *Getroud met rugby* (*Married to Rugby*) and his Afrikaner trilogy of *Donkerland* (*Dark Land*), *Kruispad* (*Crossroads*), and *Hartland* (*Heartland*).[2] He is an entrepreneurial theatrical businessman, a kind of trekboer for a new generation.

Opperman posted the following poem on his blog in April 2013, titled "I'm a White Man in Africa":

> I'm a white man in Africa a survivor in the south
> We got one man one vote but we live from hand to mouth
> Apartheid was a fuck up now we free, free at last
> But some of us are paying for the sins of the past
> I'm a white man in Africa from sixteen fifty-two
> I'm stuck here can't get out nothing I can do
> I've got my dobermans electric fence machete and a gun
> They'll get me in the end but 'till then I'm having fun.
>
> (Opperman 2013)

These lines index several key claims of Afrikaner (white) existence in the postcolony: an anchoring genealogy and aura of survivor pride (been here since 1652); the conflicting disgrace of—and obligation to pay for—the past; a continued laager mentality (defensive Dobermans, fences, and weapons);

and Afrikaners as Africans (rather than Europeans) with nowhere else to go. It also suggests the potentials and failures of the current ANC government: "We got one man one vote but we live from hand to mouth," and suggests a sense of inevitable impossibility about being white in Africa: "They'll get me in the end but 'till then I'm having fun."

Opperman's career has unfolded during a volatile time in South African history. If whiteness must be hidden to maintain its power, then 1994 marked a moment when whiteness became visible and therefore destabilized. In post-1994 South Africa Afrikaners were deposed—and exposed—at the same time. After decades of privileged machinations, in 1994 a once-secret society suddenly had to spill its collective guts at the Truth and Reconciliation Commission (TRC) and air its dirty laundry for the country, and the whole world, to see. With the implementation of Black Business Empowerment efforts under Mandela's presidency, many Afrikaners—who dominated the ranks of the civil service under apartheid—were replaced with black workers. The Land Commission was formed in 1996 to review claims from individuals seeking the return of property taken from them during the colonial period or under apartheid. To many Afrikaners, the threat of land loss was paired with a general fear of erasure as a minority group. Under the new constitution, Afrikaans, the sacred language of the apartheid state, lost its position as one of two official languages, instead becoming one of eleven. Anxiety about the future of the language—spoken by a relatively small number of people and by a mixture of white and Cape coloureds without a unified agenda—flared wildly in the years immediately after 1994.[3] By staging the loss of language rights, Afrikaners were also (re)articulating their presence. It was a savvy tactic, one Afrikaners had perfected for most of the past century. Convincing themselves, and others, that they are on the verge of extinction justifies their search for national self-determination.

In April 1996, Opperman debuted his drama *Donkerland* (*Dark Land*) at the Afrikaans-language Klein Karoo Nasionale Kunstefees (KKNK) in Oudtshoorn. It played at the same festival where rowdy racist conservatives hurled obscenities and beer cans at Miriam Makeba and her dancers while they performed on stage, and booed Afrikaner songstress Amanda Strydom when she sang "Amandla!"—which translates as "Freedom!" and is a rallying cry of the antiapartheid struggle.[4] This festival also sparked a debate about inclusiveness in the "New" South Africa and whether the event was preserving the Afrikaans language, as its organizers claimed, or actually only (white) Afrikaners. Two months later, *Donkerland* opened at the predominantly Anglophone National Arts Festival in Grahamstown,[5] where I saw it performed, followed by a three-week engagement at the State Theatre in Pretoria. The play's popularity has not dwindled since 1996: in August 2013, a twelve-episode television series of *Donkerland* premiered on the Afrikaans pay-TV channel KykNet.[6] Below I explore the fragmentation of the social fabric for white Afrikaners in the mid- to late 1990s and investigate what a play in Afrikaans, about Afrikaner history, staged at a principally Anglophone festival, can tell us about that new social landscape. In addition, I explore what *Donkerland* can reveal about how whiteness is performed at times of anxiety and nostalgia. I am interested in how Afrikaners, who for so long played the role of power architects, had to restage themselves differently in 1996, only two short years after the historic political transition.

AGAINST THE CANVAS OF HISTORY

Set against the context of the new ANC government, Opperman's play chronicles the life of one family: the de Witts (Whites), owners of a farm named Donkerland. Featuring a star-studded cast of South Africa's most accomplished actors (both English- and Afrikaans-speaking), *Donkerland* was presented in two parts, each of two and a half hours in duration, with an interval, and a dinner break in between parts I and II. In this epic history, Opperman selects the most common "signposts" of the four hundred years of Afrikaner history. Part I included six scenes in two acts. Act 1, "Plant die stok" ("Staking the Claim") had three scenes: "Die pad na Kanaán" ("The Road to Canaan"), set in 1838 at the beginning of the Great Trek; "'n stukkie grond" ("A Little Parcel of Land") in 1840 at the end of the Great Trek; and "Lank genoeg geterg" ("Teased Long Enough"), set in 1881, at the end of the First Anglo-Boer War around the time of the formation of Die Genootskap van Regte Afrikaners (The Fellowship of True Afrikaners). Act 2, "Graf in die gras" ("Grave in the Grass"), also had three scenes: "Vuur en bloed" ("Fire and Blood"), set in 1899, at the beginning of the Second Anglo-Boer War and years after the discovery of diamonds (1867) and gold (1886) on the Witwatersrand; "'n Balling gekom" ("An Exile Comes") in 1901, toward the end of the war; and "'n Merk vir die eeue" ("A Mark for the Ages"), set in 1902 after the signing of the Peace of Vereeniging.

Part II included four scenes in two acts. Act 3, "Boompie by die pad" ("Sapling along the Road"), included "Ver van die stadsgeluide" ("Far from the City

Noise"), set in 1929, portraying the economic hardships that accompanied the growth of Johannesburg,[7] and "Die salf van eie gom" ("The Salve of Self-Glue") in 1948, when the Nationalist Party came into power. Act 4, "Die wiele van Afrika" ("The Wheels of Africa"), included "Swart klip" ("Black Rock"), set in 1976, the year of the Soweto Uprising at the height of apartheid, and "'n Klein strepie mensdom" ("A Little Hyphen of Humanity") in 1996, the present moment, after the release of Nelson Mandela in 1990, the elections of 1994, and the 1994 Restitution of Land Rights Act went into effect.[8]

In his dramaturgical structuring of the play, Opperman decenters a purely linear historical trajectory by capturing the reverberations of macrocosmic sociopolitics through the microcosm of the de Witt family's actions and reactions to these events. For instance, he sets the scene titled "Swart klip" ("Black Rock") in 1976, the year students in Soweto protested against being taught in Afrikaans and were met with police violence, but the scene doesn't deal with those events directly. Instead of addressing the inauguration of D. F. Malan and the institutionalization of the National Party, for example, he sets a scene in 1948 and has the de Witts deal tangentially with those public events. In this way, he refracts the political through the personal, for as he told me, "As a playwright, I specialize in writing about ordinary people against the canvas of history" (M. Lewis 2011).

Donkerland received an audience at a time when the euphoria of the post-election period had subsided, reports of daily violence were common, and the struggles of daily life in the new democracy became tangibly strained. F. W. de Klerk resigned as deputy president in June 1996, just before the play opened in Grahamstown in July. The resignation signaled an indisputable shift in political power, particularly among staunch Afrikaners. In addition, the "New South Africa" was comprised of an open field of constituent citizens who now (at least legally) enjoyed the same rights and privileges. However, it was still a place of enormous tension, of struggles waged on a daily basis between competing individuals and groups fighting for their economic and social livelihoods and for how the narrative of the new nation would be told. The feeling on the streets in 1996 was palpably tense.

The play's title is deliberately multitoned. Donkerland is the name of the farm inhabited by generations of de Witts as well as the colonial term for Africa in general, the Dark Land or Darkest Africa; the de Witt family name is also symbolically coded. This title highlights dark (indigenous, black- and brown-skinned, African) versus light (settlers, white-skinned, European).

This binary also echoes the nationalistic doctrine embodied in the Voortrekker Monument, which as I observed in chapter 1, justified the Afrikaner nationalist political agenda of white superiority and cultural dominance. Opperman decenters the dark/light dualism at the end of his play as both the physical (land) and theoretical (hegemonic) landscape are ultimately inverted: the de Witts' farm, Donkerland, returns to the Zulus as Nelson Mandela becomes the country's first black president. Donkerland becomes a metaphor for the de Witts' legacy; dark (black) Africa is the symbol through which white settlers define themselves, yet ultimately it becomes the force that destabilizes them.

Donkerland, the play, examines and enacts the breadth of Afrikaner history since the arrival of Dutch colonials at the Cape of Good Hope in 1652. It serves as a metaphor for understanding Afrikaner history (a representation) and simultaneously a performative act (a political intervention) that marks a shift in Afrikaner theatre and self-representation. It also chronologically bookends the Voortrekker Movement of the 1930s (see chapter 1) and the ostensible "end" of apartheid after the historic 1994 elections. Such a move is similar to D. F. Malan's suturing of time and space, tying 1652 and 1938 into a single narrative in his 1938 speech. Thus, Donkerland offers a contemporary position from which to view and critique past acts of national imagining.

Donkerland was heralded as a watershed in South African drama, an incisive investigation of Afrikanerdom.[9] That this play emerged at a time of great social upheaval indicates a desire to assert a national discourse in a time of fragmented national narratives. Hermann Giliomee argues that a process of self-definition and self-justification is part and parcel of Afrikanerdom (1999). In his essay on turn-of-the-century identity, survival, and existential crises among Afrikaners over the past three hundred years, Giliomee marks the various transitional moments that have faced Afrikaners at the turns of the past three centuries. Whether over economic rights to farm and trade in the Cape Colony at the turn of the seventeenth century; over political status as "burghers (citizens) rather than koloniale onderhoriges (colonial subjects or subordinates)" (Giliomee 1999) under British rule in the eighteenth century; or over linguistic definition and exclusive nation-formation following the Anglo-Boer Wars (1899–1902) a hundred years later—at each century's turn, Afrikaners have been in an existential crisis. As a European settler culture inhabiting African space, competing for resources in that space with indigenes and other colonial forces, and beset by material and existential crises, Afrikaners are undergoing yet another moment of self-definition and justification in a long line of such crises.

Donkerland is a memory play that begins with a reflection on memory. A female narrator opens the play with an invocation, claiming that there is no place where one can see history clearly and know it as absolute truth (I translate): "A story is always burdened by all the pieces that are lied and dreamed onto it, and is disfigured by all that is forgotten. But like a child after nine months in the pregnant belly, disfigured or not, if he wants out, then he must out. And where was there ever a birthing without a groaning? And without blood? Yes, blood, because the soul can also bleed ... in its own way" (Opperman 1996, 3). Acknowledging the constructed nature of the past, Opperman weaves several key concepts together there: history, birth, and pain. History is narrative, he suggests, and one's historical positioning will necessarily impact which story one is able to hear. And birthing a new (or revised) nation is a troubled and difficult process, with much blood and pain involved in making social transitions such as the one from apartheid to democracy. Opperman also gestures toward the sadness and loss that many Afrikaners felt in the new political dispensation, with his claim that "the soul can also bleed ... in its own way."

In *Donkerland*, memory is established as a space in which past and future can meet, a site of flux between lies and truths, between dreams and desires. The temporal reality of this play, the present, is a space of memory where the past resurfaces and faces the future. This space is uncertain, for the past is neither entirely over, nor is the future a reality yet. Opperman recognizes that the search for Truth with a capital T, echoing the goals of the TRC, is not possible. The Afrikaner nation is, in Benedict Anderson's terms, a community distinguished, not by their falsity or genuineness, but by "the style in which they are imagined" (1991, 6). The style in which Opperman imagines history is a particularly Afrikaner one. Afrikaner identity is trapped within its limits, the boundaries of its own formation, but as Anderson would suggest—and as Opperman asserts—it also dreams of sovereignty, of being free of the fetters of the past.

After 1994, Afrikaners underwent a seismic—psychological if not material—shift in their reality. They went from being a dominant minority within the larger white minority (which includes WESSAs) who controlled the state and who enjoyed privileges based on their ethnic and racial identity, to one of many subcultures in a multicultural, polyglossic, and ethnically diverse democracy. This shift brought about a profound cultural anxiety among Afrikaners, a sense of rootlessness. On uncertain present footing, Afrikaners feared for their future, and thus returned to the past in search of a sense of security. For Dennis Walder, "nostalgia in a curious way connects people across historical as well as national and personal boundaries ... [in an] uncanny mix of individual and social desires" (2011, 1). Opperman plays on such a nostalgia in much of his work, seeking to "connect" contemporary Afrikaners to the best parts of their communal past.

Susan Bennett theorizes nostalgia as the representation of the past's "'imagined and mythic qualities' so as to effect some corrective in the present" (1996, 5). Nostalgia, which etymologically stems from the Greek *nostos* (home) and *algia* (pain), is a kind of homesickness. It is, for Bennett, a "marker of both what we lack and what we desire," or citing Susan Stewart, it is "the desire for desire" (1996, 5–6). Nostalgia relies on an imagined—and imaginary—past in its longing for a time and a quality that is "lost" now and which a population seeks to reclaim in the present. Thus, Opperman's play, which trades in images of an imagined past that is under threat of loss, aims to show the past—in all its bloodiness and longing—in order to "effect some corrective" (Bennett) in the new dispensation and to perform back into communal consciousness the history of the Afrikaner.

GENDERED LANDS OF WHITENESS

Early in Opperman's play, land—complete with all its associations of ownership and superiority—is established as a central myth of Afrikaner culture. A fundamental tenet of Afrikaner ethnomythology is the narrative of being the Chosen People, favored by God to inhabit and dominate the Promised Land at the southern tip of Africa, to bring civilization to a dark and unruly world. This civilization is patriarchal, heavily Calvinist, and racially marked. Opperman acknowledges this: "There's an innate cultural fascism in the Afrikaner. There's no room for disagreement or argument, it's all absolute. Everything in Calvinism is absolute. Calvinism breeds fascism because there's an unquestioned loyalty to an idea you don't even understand but you just go, yes" (M. Lewis 2011). By focusing on this central element of Afrikaner mythology, Opperman calls attention to the colonial legacy of his people. The play resounds with land references: in its title; in the site of the play (the farm itself); and in its constant battles by each of the characters to claim or detach themselves from it.

The play begins as the patriarch, Pieter de Witt (played by the exceptional André Odendaal), plants his land claim marker in the mid-nineteenth century in the scene titled "Die Pad Na Kanaän 1838" ("The Road to Canaan 1838"), setting into motion the long struggle that characterizes the narrative of Afrikaner history.[10] While women feature in the play, *Donkerland* is the story of men, of patrilineal inheritance and passing down the definition of what it means to be an Afrikaner man from generation to generation. "This land stays de Witt land until there is not one more of us left on earth to work it," asserts sixth-generation Ouboet. "From father to son," he says. "So it has been through the years, and so it will continue to be" (Opperman 1996, 121).

At the same time that Pieter de Witt claims the land, he also claims a young Mpondo woman, whom he calls Meidjie, as his sexual conquest. It is his right, as a white settler, to claim and to name. Described in the stage directions as "treffend mooi" (stunningly beautiful), (Opperman 1996, 14), Meidjie comes to him for protection from a Zulu man who wants to force her to be his bride. After Pieter shoots and kills the man, she gives herself to him, saying in Zulu, "You saved my life. Now I am yours" (Opperman 1996, 17). Pieter then takes her into the bushes, where she "ken sy drif eerste" (knows his passion first; Opperman 1996, 20); he plants his *stok* (stake) into African soil and into the body of the African woman, who is romanticized as giving herself willingly to her white master.

Given the entanglement of gender, sexuality, and imperial power, it is not surprising that Afrikaners marked their national space in gendered terms. The Afrikaner nation-state was created by white men, many of whom belong to the Broederbond. The nation-state was solidified in a masculinized military conflict (the Anglo-Boer Wars), that became anchoring moments for their nation-building even though the Boers lost. Tying the 1838 Battle of Blood River to the events of the early twentieth century, the nation's architects created a "divinely organized" military conflict that baptized the nation in a "male birthing ritual, which grant[ed] to white men the patrimony of land and history" (McClintock 1995, 369).

As an example of the manner in which women are linked with land in nation-formation and the Afrikaner imaginary, I turn to a scene in act 1 of *Donkerland*. Called away to fight the Zulus, the patriarch Pieter de Witt leaves his pregnant wife at the homestead under the care of his Zulu maid and secret sexual consort Meidjie (whose name means "Little Maid"). The wife's childbirth turns out to be difficult. Despite Meidjie's repeated attempts to tell the white neighbor woman — in Zulu, in broken Afrikaans, with gestures — that she knows how to turn the breach baby, the neighbor barks back at her, "I won't let you try your barbarian practices (*barbarse gewoontes*) on her. . . . You aren't in your kraal; this is a white man's house!" (Opperman 1996, 31, my translation). Pieter arrives as his wife is dying, and in the play's most melodramatic stage moment, uses his hunting knife to perform a cesarean on his dead wife's body. He pulls the male child from her belly and lifts him into a bright red wash of light as a chorus of Zulu singers chant faster and faster to a climax.

Amid the mise-en-scène of springbok skins and Voortrekker Bibles, this scene resonates with many elements of Afrikaner ethnomythology. The neighbor woman's reaction indexes a racially divided social schema, Pieter's authority in the scene is marked by an established and revered patriarchy, and a chivalrous erasure of white female subjectivity simultaneously confiscates black female agency. White women are relegated to roles as male supporters — bakers of *koeksisters* (crullers) and bearers of children — while black women become sexual objects to all men (black and white), and surrogate mothers, nannies, and maids to whites. Opperman depicts the gendered world of the early settlers to underscore the connection between land and women's bodies. And this scene is distinctly one of a masculinized birthing ritual: Jacob is plucked from the inanimate "swamp" that was his mother by the phallic knife of his father, like Zeus ripping Dionysus from Semele before inserting him into his own thigh, in an appropriated birthing ritual that erases female agency and replaces it with male authority.

DARK LANDS OF AFRIKANER MASCULINITY

Thus, throughout the play, a rigid and erect masculinity is contrasted with feminized spaces and characters, like Africa, women, weaker men such as Englishmen, black men (kaffirs), and later generations of sons who do not want to continue farming Donkerland. Pieter and his sons blatantly ignore the voices or interests of women. The de Witt men's definition of masculinity is based on stoicism and divine right rule, on naturalized hierarchies, and on shooting first and asking questions later. Pieter proclaims, "A man who doesn't stand firm will disappear like a grave in the grass, swallowed up into the bosom of Africa" (Opperman 1996, 9).[11] Opperman marks his character's Afrikaner masculinity as existing in so much as it is distinct from its feminine foil, the bosom of Africa. Pieter's masculinity is also threatened by

Africa—and by extension Africans—who throughout the play are feminized, ignored, ordered about, or possessed sexually and ultimately, dehumanized, oppressed, and shot at will. For Opperman's men, violence is not only a part of life but is also their first instinct whenever they are challenged. "Oorhees of wees oorhees" (Override or be overridden; Opperman 1996) emanates from the mouths of many a de Witt man throughout the play. They revel in stories about killing *khakis* (British soldiers) in the Boer War trenches, *kaffirs* (blacks) almost anywhere they encounter them, or *terrs* (terrorists or communists) in the Border Wars. Fathers constantly threaten to beat sons who disobey or counter them.[12] Violent acts are constant through the play. The de Witts tie up, blindfold, and almost kill an Englishman, John, caught courting their sister, Anna. They use a *sjambok* (bullwhip) on a black man caught instigating the workers and later hit his head so hard with a rock that he dies. And they throw punches at each other, brother against brother, when ideological differences divide them.

For much of the play, women feature as bearers of children and cups of tea, and as iconic Volksmoeders (Mothers of the Nation) that the men turn to when all else fails. In "Ver van die stadsgeluide," Henk returns from working in the mines with an amputated leg. He tries to hold his composure, but breaks down and falls into his mother's arms. The Afrikaans stage directions read: "He drops his crutches. And thus Henk becomes once again a small boy in his mother's arms" (Opperman 1996, 98). In "'n Balling Gekom" (1901), the mother Hester rallies the men back into war, much like the women after the Bloukrans Massacre in the 1938 film *Bou van 'n nasie*. "Don't return home until you have mended the wrong of your brother's death," she directs them with conviction (Opperman 1996, 73). Opperman hints at women's liberation in act 4 of the play, when the outspoken seventh-generation daughter Mariaan participates in the political discussion alongside the men. She tells her father, "You menfolk are going to have to learn to think differently; the blacks are not the only ones rebelling ... we women are short on their heels" (Opperman 1996, 134).

VERLIGTES AND VERKRAMPTES

In part I of *Donkerland*, Opperman explores the narratives that created the volk, leading up to the nation-building era; in part II, he explores what the transition into—and out of—apartheid means for white settlers. In a vignette titled "Die Salf Van Eie Gom 1948," set during the rise of the Nationalist Party, Opperman explores the tensions among Afrikaners when their political power is expanding.[13] These frictions are manifested through two brothers: Ouboet, a Nationalist Party supporter, who has maintained the farm and is the only male left on Donkerland, and his younger brother, Dirk, who holds very different political views and who has left to seek his fortune in the city. Dirk returns to claim his half of his inheritance after a twenty-year absence during which he has been a teacher in a black school. The intense battle over inheritance between these two brothers, who literally stand on opposite sides of a fence as they speak their lines, indicates the ideological rift between two camps of Afrikaners: the *verkramptes* (conservative, reactive, literally "cramped") and the *verligtes* (liberal, more progressive, literally "enlightened"). The National Party split into these two factions in the 1970s, and they also appeared among artists, writers, and journalists. Writers like André Brink, J. M. Coetzee, and Breyten Breytenbach, and later, members of the musical movement Voëlvry (Freebird or Outlaw)[14] like Koos Kombuis, Johannes Kerkorrel and the Reformed Blues Band, and Bernoldus Niemand and Die Swart Gevaar (the Black Peril) positioned themselves as Afrikaner antiestablishment countervoices to the official apartheid state.

This ideological battle continued into the new democracy. In May 2000, Willem de Klerk, brother of former president F. W. de Klerk, published a treatise titled *Afrikaners: Kroes, kras, kordaat* (*Afrikaners: Surly, Strident, Surviving*), to which independent journalist Chris Louw responded with venom in an open letter that has become known as the *Boetman Brief* (*Boetman Letter*). Reminiscent of the *verligte-verkrampte* debates and existential crises of the previous decades, here, for the first time since the apartheid era, a member of the younger generation publicly challenged his elders, and it raised many people's hackles. Louw blamed de Klerk and his cohort for selling the younger generation down the river. "Our whole future," he writes, "was predestined by You and Your God, there was nothing we could do about it" (Louw 2000, 7, my translation). The subsequent discourse around the de Klerk–Louw exchange was diverse. Conservatives attacked Louw for everything from insolence to petulance, from bad taste to treason. Progressives praised him for his boldness and for daring to articulate what many have felt but never uttered: that the apartheid architects essentially sacrificed their children (Louw's generation) to military conscription in Border Wars, replete with ensuing identity crises, posttraumatic stress disorders, depression, and lifetimes of guilt in the name of their grand racial delusions. In one of his most scathing comments, Louw writes: "Who or what gave you the right to surrender my whole generation to a dehumanizing system and to send us to a doomed war in the name of your fucking racist dreams (*fokken rassedrome*)?" (Louw 2000, 13).

Thus, the de Witt family's battle over who has the right to the land can be read as an analog for the long-running ideological battle over who has the right to be an Afrikaner. The border that divides brothers Dirk and Ouboet in the play is clearly seen in this exchange about Dirk's teaching at a black school and their different notions of race:

> OUBOET: 'n Onderwyser?! (A Teacher?! So, you're a master now.)
> DIRK: Mnumzana. [isiZulu for "teacher"]
> OUBOET: Mnumzana?
> DIRK: Ek het vir swart kinders skool gegee. (I taught black children.)
> OUBOET: 'n Kaffer skool? (A kaffir school?)
> DIRK: 'n Skool, Outboet. Vir kinders. (A school, Big Brother. For children.)
> OUBOET: Kafferkinders. (Kaffir children.)
> DIRK: Kinders. (Children.)
> OUBOET: *Kafferkinders.* (*Kaffir* children.) (Opperman 1996, 116)

In *Donkerland*, Opperman asked audiences to witness the tensions between members of the de Witt clan and to trace the cyclical nature of Afrikaner history, its repeated strivings and failures. He assigned actors multiple roles that created what David Graver termed "ironic resonances" across the timespan of the play (1997). The original patriarch, Pieter de Witt, is played by André Odendaal, and in the opening scene his horse is stolen by an English minister (played by David Clatworthy) while he is in the bushes with Meidjie (Seipati Montsho). One hundred thirty-eight years later, Arnold, Pieter's descendant (Odendaal again), is served with a paternity suit (by Clatworthy) on behalf of a descendant of Meidjie (again played by Montsho). These double castings, paired with the battle between the enlightened and conservative brothers, illustrate the fraught, complex negotiations that continue to surround Afrikaner identity.

HYPHENS OF HUMANITY

Recognizing the need for change after 1994, at the play's end Opperman quotes a verse from renowned Afrikaans poet and playwright, N. P. van Wyk

Louw, reminding us that "this land was not purchased / merely on loan" (1996, 129). The notion of borrowed land, and borrowed time, was especially poignant in 1996 in South Africa. Nelson Mandela lived on borrowed time for twenty-seven years while imprisoned by the state. The time had now come for the Afrikaner to pay up, and payment was taking effect at the very site of the volk's identity: land. Under the 1996 Land Commission, properties that originally belonged to indigenous peoples (and had been confiscated from black Africans under the 1913 Land Act) were being redistributed to the original owners or their descendants. Afrikaner farmers, many of whom had worked the land for six generations, were being required to sell their farms to the government for redistribution.[15]

Opperman leaves the Afrikaner at this moment of *landlessness* and uncertainty. Arnold, the last de Witt male, stares forlornly at a pile of stones on the edge of Donkerland where Pieter de Witt the patriarch planted his marker over three hundred years before. The female narrator's final speech bookends nicely with her opening invocation (I translate):

> While [Arnold] sat there, a snail slithered across a stone and left a little trail . . . a short hyphen of silver in the mighty wilderness (*'n kort strepie silwer in die magtige wildernis*); and then it hit him: we are only here momentarily. The wheels of Africa turn slowly . . . slowly, but as surely as death, and one day . . . someday only a disintegrated little pile of stones will survive, as witness to the little hyphen of humanity (*'n klein strepie mensdom*), lost in the grass of Donkerland. (Opperman 1996, 157)

By retelling the familiar stories and reflecting the Afrikaner Self vividly on stage, Opperman poses the troubling and risky question: Now what? and places the responsibility for answering it in the hands of the audience: the Afrikaners of 1996 and today. Framing Afrikaners as a hyphen of humanity echoes Giliomee's thesis about Afrikaners existing in a constant state of redefinition, a minority against the mainstream. It also problematically suggests that the only humanity in Africa is a white (Afrikaner) one. And such a framing repeats the white-haired pastor after the massacre at Bloukrans in *Bou van 'n nasie* (1938), who tells the surviving trekkers, "We are a mere remnant, overwhelmed by tragedy" and de la Rey's claim in *Ons vir Jou* of being "so few" against so many. It also echoes pop singer Bok van Blerk's lyrics to his hit song "De La Rey," in which he sings "a handful of us against their powerful forces." These claims of minority status have been mobilized by Afrikaners post-1994 into political action. Opperman acknowledges the possibility that the tiny trace of vanishing, *white* humanity has seen its day. Snails hide in their shells, and many Afrikaners in 1996 refused to envision any future other than the secure past they had known.[16] Opperman warns his fellow Afrikaners not to hide in their shells or all that will remain is an insignificant trace of white in a dark (*donker*) land. But how Afrikaners ought to perform now is still in question.

While it explores the notion that the Afrikaner's time has run out, that this hyphen of whiteness has come to an end, what does this play—staged at this particular moment in history and at the Anglophone National Arts Festival—enact in the larger social field? In reenacting this history in an epic play, *Donkerland* also reanchors that history; in other words, the play conceals its own history-production as it foregrounds history. To use Pierre Bourdieu's terms, Opperman is (re)circulating symbolic capital that for so long has formed the sense of Afrikaner history, truth, and nationalism. The stage is filled with the trappings of Voortrekker life, symbolic objects that resonate nostalgically for the audience. Additionally, a familiar historical narrative—complete with Meidjie's willing submission and black figures who are noble, albeit uncivilized—frames Opperman's examination of the de Witt family. *Donkerland* effectively (re)places Afrikaners on (center) stage in 1996, at a time when they felt their minority status most immediately and tangibly.

Just as the performance makes Afrikaans visible in the Anglophone Arts Festival, so too does the printed text for the play. In the text, Opperman punctuates each of its ten sections with excerpts of poems that then become the section's title. For instance, he quotes from Afrikaans poet S. J. du Toit for the section "Lank genoeg geterg" ("Teased Long Enough"). I translate:

But when the Brits still taunted us,
Then we took up our guns;
We had been teased long enough,
And could no longer [stand it].
(Opperman 1996, 37)

Each quotation also anchors the play within the larger context of Afrikaner literature. He cites the canon of Afrikaans literary figures, including du Toit, Jan F. E. Celliers, C. Louis Leipoldt, J. R. L. Van Bruggen, Totius, N. P. van

Wyk Louw, and, of course, D. J. Opperman.[17] These writers are then positioned among canonic elders of Western civilization like former president Jan Smuts and Horace as well as the Afrikaner canonical source, the Bible. Opperman cites Exodus 6:7 for the first segment, "Die pad na Kanaán," Horace's "Hoc erat in votis" for "'n Stukkie grond," and Jan Smut's political speech for "Vuur en bloed." This strategic move places *Donkerland*—and Opperman—within the genealogy of Afrikaans literature, connecting politics and poetics at a time when the future of Afrikaans was uncertain.

THE DEMISE OF WHITENESS

Opperman's play ends with an acknowledgment of the demise of whiteness. The play ends as it begins, with the land stake (*stok*) and miscegenation. An English lawyer and activist serves seventh-generation Arnold with a summons, charging him with the paternity of one of the farm workers, Nomthandazo's, baby. Arnold refuses to submit to the paternity test, making boastful claims to avoid giving the required blood sample until his father, Piet-Jan, brings out the family Bible and asks him to swear on it. When he cannot, his father exclaims "Skaam jou!" (Shame on you!), and his mother, Truida, flees in horror as his secret cross-racial sexual relations are revealed. Read against the apartheid-era Immorality Act and Mixed Marriages Act (1927), this revelation triggers Arnold's shame. Yet Arnold calls his father on his hypocrisy, "You say I should be ashamed of myself, Pa; put your hand on [that Bible] and swear yourself" (Opperman 1996, 149). The two men now share a secret shame as *meidenaaiers* (maid fuckers; Opperman 1996, 145), and this scene reminds audiences that despite the rhetoric of purity and whiteness, South Africa's history has been filled with interracial sex, mixing, and colouredness (van den Berghe 1960). The scene also references Afrikaner fears of airing one's dirty laundry in public, or Pattison's framing of shame as "socially shaped" (2000, 182). In my interview with Opperman, he explained how "*Skaam jou!* means dishonoring your parents, not being true to the calling of your culture, disobeying God, being seen *in public* to behave badly. It doesn't matter what environment, but *in public*. This has an enormous power in Afrikaner culture" (M. Lewis 2011, emphasis in original). Then he added, "And *trots* (pride) is shame's opposite. You know, we would rather have died on the border [referring to dutiful army conscription] than not go to it" (M. Lewis 2011). So Arnold's shame when faced with the exposure of his sexual affair with Nomthandazo is about his parents knowing his "sins" publicly and him having to attest to his paternity in public but also about his own acknowledgment of his flawed self.

Donkerland trades in a kind of necropolitics, as every single generation of de Witts end up burying their dead in the graveyard on Donkerland that grows larger with each passing generation; whiteness literally dies out across the course of the play. For Afrikaners, Opperman seems to say, suffering is a state of being, just as Giliomee suggests, a process of self-definition and self-justification is part and parcel of Afrikanerdom. In the penultimate scene of the play, Frederick, the brother obsessed with Arnold's army kit, gruesomely murders Nomthandazo's *basterkind* (bastard child) by "beat[ing] the child to death with the butt of his rifle" (Opperman 1996, 150) and is later shot by the police. This scene offers one of Opperman's self-reflective admonitions; it weaves the violence of the de Witt men, their views on racial purity, the seductive heroism of the army, soldiers, and fighting to the death, and the shame of miscegenation into a bleak yet powerful constellation.

In the final moments of the play, the lawyer Van Tonder brings Arnold—the last surviving member of the de Witt family on Donkerland—a contract to sign, the offer of purchase by the Land Commission. Van Tonder suggests that Arnold should "go and make a life for yourself in another place ('*n ander plek*)" (Opperman 1996, 155). The refrain of "'n ander plek" is a death sentence to Arnold, who bears the responsibility of carrying on the family name and ensuring the farm's survival. Like many Afrikaners, Arnold has nowhere else to go and, as a working-class farmer, has no means to get there. At a loss, Arnold asks his sister Mariaan in Afrikaans: "What chance do a few drops of white paint stand in a whole bucket of black?" (Opperman 1996, 156).[18] This is Opperman's deepest and most challenging question, as it queries the Afrikaner's right to exist in Africa at all. She replies, "Somewhere it has to stop. Someone has to be the first to stop. It's not just the end, it's also a beginning" (Opperman 1996, 156). Then Arnold tells his sister about a strange vision of a black man from the past that came to him in a dream: the Zulu man Pieter de Witt shot on the banks of the Umzimkulu in 1838. He is surprised by the fact that he does not go for his gun, then tells her he realized that had he shot this black man in his dream, another one would replace him, and another, and another. The image of the black hordes outnumbering the whites from *De Voortrekkers* and *Bou van 'n nasie* come easily to mind here. And then Arnold tells his sister that instead "we peered at each other ... Kaffir and Boer looking at each other over three hundred years of misunderstanding and betrayal and regret" (Opperman 1996, 156–157). Here Opperman offers his assessment of the tense state of racial and social politics for white Afrikaners and black Africans in 1996, when the democracy was still very young.

Then the female narrator explains the small snail trail in the grass. As 'n klein strepie mensdom, a trace or hyphen of humanity, Opperman's Afrikaners are portrayed (or self-identify) as a dying breed, an invisible pale trace in dark (black) Africa. This sentiment lingers among many white Afrikaners today, who see the new democratic dispensation as a death knell for their language, their culture, and their right to exist in Africa at all. The turmoil experienced by Afrikaners after the historic 1994 power shift is based on real and perceived threats from the black majority, loss of political and economic power, linguistic marginalization, and cultural minority status.

A poignant example of contemporary Afrikaner minority discourse occurred in October 2013, when singers Sunette Bridges and Steve Hofmeyr organized a day of action they called "Red October," and released red balloons into the sky to draw attention to the plight of Afrikaners, who claim an ethnic minority status. The project was aimed at global awareness about disenfranchised whites, which Nicky Falkof suggests means "the bits of the UK, US and Australia where embittered former South Africans live" (2013). The rhetoric of Red October was filled with racially coded language, dramatic capitalizations, and incendiary claims: "We are tired of Corrupt Governance, Racist Black Economic Empowerment and Affirmative Action policies. We can no longer tolerate the destruction of our infrastructure, our filthy government hospitals, our pathetic educational system, dirty dams and rivers, uninhabitable parks and public areas, dangerous neighbourhoods and filthy streets! The list is endless and we say it's ENOUGH!" (S. Hofmeyr 2013). Drawing on enduring Afrikaner rhetoric, the claims of "dirtiness" and "corruption" read in opposition to white purity and civilization. As Falkof notes, the visual registers used on the group's website, borrowed from adoption pamphlets, mainstream gay literature, and local government advertising, "emphasizes diversity: Old (white) people! Young (white) people! Blonde (white) people! Brunette (white) people! All the different types of (white) people one could possibly imagine!" (2013). Puzzlingly, the organizers seemed to miss the earlier associations of Red October with the Bolshevik Revolution and socialist worker movements. Ironically, they co-opted a

Bolshevik title for their unquestionably antisocialist claims. Or perhaps for white South Africans who feared communism under apartheid and continue to abhor integration, using the name Red October was a Freudian slip? Ultimately, the event was not as popular as the organizers had hoped. Approximately four hundred people showed up, waved old apartheid-era flags, made claims about genocide (supported by spurious statistics), and compared the fate of the Afrikaner to that of the rhino: both bordering on the edge of extinction. Christi van der Westhuizen characterized the event as "white supremacists trying to appropriate the discourses of struggles for equality and freedom to legitimise the privileging of some people on the basis of skin colour. Not just that: they are claiming that they are being victimised by the policies designed to overturn the very damage of the white supremacist systems of the past" (2013).[19] That the event did not garner sizable support suggests the limited priority, significance, and attention most South Africans (white, black, and brown) gave this minority complaint.

While it is easy to dismiss Red October as a lame attempt to claim minority status for deposed whites, Opperman's play is far more nuanced. A first reading of *Donkerland* might suggest Opperman's uncritical reenactment of ancient tropes, yet his characters are able to grow and reflect. The selfsame Pieter who shot Meidjie's pursuer without hesitation reflects on that murder later in his life. "He was somebody's son," Pieter tells his own son, Schalk. And fifth-generation Dirk asks his father Klein Piet and brother Ouboet, who has just killed a black activist on the farm by hitting his head onto a rock, "Jesus, Pa, you talk of the graves the English dug for us Afrikaners, but what about the hole we've dug for the kaffirs?" (Opperman 1996, 103). While Pieter is unable or unwilling to listen to women, he will take the advice of another man, even a black man. In "Lank genoeg geterg" (1881), Pieter defends Mehlokazulu, Meidjie's partner and Pieter's foreman, telling his son Jacob (I translate): "He's a warrior and he's entitled to respect. It's bad enough he no longer has his land; don't also strip him of his honor. The day that happens, we are lost. Listen to what I'm telling you" (Opperman 1996, 45). Thus, Pieter is depicted as a complex character with many conflicting qualities, much like many Afrikaners post-1994. He is a domineering, proud patriarch. He is racist, sexist, and intolerant. He is also hardworking and driven by a code of honor, even if that code is tainted by his biased worldview.

Opperman has been accused of being just as complicated a man, from many sides of the political spectrum. After the twelve-episode TV series of *Donkerland*, Opperman was called everything from a "sellout joiner-traitor of the Afrikaner volk" to "a racist because [he] tried to talk away the Afrikaner's sins" (Opperman 2013, my translation). In response, Opperman posted the following on the KykNet website (I translate):

> Every week was like this: "You should be ashamed (*jy hoort jou te skaam*), you racist—the Afrikaner's history should disappear along with his people" as well as "Deon, you should be ashamed that you depict our beautiful people in such a negative light." My position is this: in the past 30 years that I have been writing dramas for Afrikaans audiences I have always strived to show both sides of an issue. It's my deepest conviction that no people, or nation, have just good, or just evil, in them. Humanity is a mixed-up mess of both good and evil. (Opperman 2013)

Opperman is candid about the complexities of his own Afrikaner culture. He began his 2011 interview with me claiming, "I'm going to say things I shouldn't say, but nothing I am ashamed of." He describes Afrikaners as "a vigorous nation, adaptable and able to survive and change. But also fascists. Calvinists to the extreme. And hypocrites beyond your wildest imagining" (M. Lewis 2011). He also acknowledges the Janus-faced nature of the contemporary Afrikaner's position, a complicated negotiation of prideworthy and repellant elements. "Outwardly there is *'n skaamte* (a shame)," he says, "we are obliged to say that. But inwardly, at *braais*, people talk of what a fucking great time [the apartheid era] was. We didn't have to have Armed Response. We didn't get hijacked. So it's an outward performance of what's politically correct" (M. Lewis 2011).[20] Opperman calls South Africa the Southern Paradox: "Two poles that make a truth somehow. And they keep negotiating. Like a binary code. . . . I love the paradox of South Africa. It's very creative. . . . I could leave anytime. But I stay" (M. Lewis 2011).

That Opperman was moved to write a play in Afrikaans, about so Afrikaans a subject, at a time when the Afrikaner no longer held political power, suggested a need among "New South Africa" Afrikaners to find their niche in this Bhabha-esque nation of many narratives. Within the text itself, the colonial past was problematized—it explored the schisms that exist within Afrikaner families and political bodies; it questioned the assumptions held by the majority of Afrikaners about their legitimacy and what makes them a people; and it posited a dubious future for the Afrikaner. Yet in its mode of delivery as a melodrama—one that pulled at the heartstrings with its epic scope and was so naturalistic that it seemed as if the audience were watching their own families on stage—the play encouraged audience identification with the all-too-familiar images of themselves, essentially reiterating the volk's identity. Staged within the tenuous field of the "New" South Africa in 1996, *Donkerland* asserted a strong sense of Afrikaner pride even if the textual battle within it interrogated Afrikanerdom and highlighted its complex and shameful past. Opperman embraced his past and created characters that were as much Afrikaners as those in the audience: he literally "remembered" them, gave them substance. He tried to fathom how they have had to adapt to the ever-changing environment around them. But he did not forget them, for to do so would be to do the impossible: to accept the fate of that little hyphen of whiteness in the darkness of Africa. As the Afrikaans theatre world's favorite and most prolific playwright in contemporary South Africa, Opperman could not, and would not, do that.

Toward the end of *Donkerland*, the narrator ruminates on the Afrikaner's position: "To lose touch with the wisdoms of the past is one thing; to meet the future with wisdom is quite another" (Opperman 1996, 128). In his dramaturgical use of history, Opperman locates his Afrikaner heroes, Afrikaner patriarchs like Pieter de Witt (*Donkerland*) and honorable and principled Koos de la Rey (*Ons vir Jou*), in a time before apartheid. They function in a time when Afrikaner men could still be heroes, when, as rough as they were, they were guided by a code of ethics; a time before being an Afrikaner was as complex and fraught as it has been since 1994.

WHEN WHITE BODIES PERFORM:
FROM *BOERE* TO *BOSBOETIES*: 2010

Twenty years into the South African democracy, Opperman remains committed to making Afrikaans plays about the Afrikaner volk. In 2008, Opperman staged his hugely successful Boer War musical, *Ons vir Jou* (*We for Thee*), which I discussed in chapter 2. In 2010, he wrote, directed, and produced another large-scale historical musical, this one about the Border Wars.[21] *Tree aan* replayed a now-taboo history of the white victims of apartheid: those soldiers conscripted to fight communism and *die swart gevaar* during the so-called Border Wars of 1966–1989. *Tree aan*'s subject—the Border Wars—is a personal obsession of Opperman's. They feature in an earlier play, *Môre is 'n lang dag* (*Tomorrow Is a Long Day*, 1984), and *Donkerland* (1996) also includes references to the Border Wars. Opperman himself served in the SADF during the Border Wars and claims that he wrote *Tree aan* "because I fought that war. Because I was on the border. Because it was denied that we were there, like the Vietnam soldiers" (M. Lewis 2012). He told me that his aim with *Tree aan* was to "tell the story of the people's heart they cannot articulate in public. Because it is the public confessional of the narrative that is acknowledged, that gives them catharsis" (M. Lewis 2012). He is passionate about the need to provide a space of public witnessing for such a secretive part of South African history because, he says, "You can't know who you are today if you don't know . . . what the sins of the father were. And what the good things were. . . . If you wipe out a history, you take away a nation's sense of itself" (M. Lewis 2012).

Tree aan tells the story of a platoon of new recruits terrorized and bullied by their drill sergeant (figure 12), and it mirrors Anthony Akerman's 1983 play, *Somewhere on the Border*, which was originally banned in South Africa. When Akerman's play made its South African debut, under the censor's radar, Opperman was one of the performers. Under the direction of Gerard Schoonhoven, the cast secretly rehearsed the prohibited play in the Performing Arts Council of the Orange Free State (PACOFS), right in the belly of the beast. "It was a big fuck-you" to the apartheid censors, Opperman told me with relish (M. Lewis 2011). Whereas Akerman's play is a brutal critique of the harrowing indoctrination of young recruits in the name of an ideology, with the English-speaking pacifist Doug Campbell as the play's moral compass, Opperman's play emphasizes the duty these men felt in serving their country. It pivots around a love story between Christo and his beloved Christine. Several stanzas of the old South African anthem, "Die Stem," feature centrally in the musical's score, as they did in *Ons vir Jou*.

While the majority of the play skirts any direct political message, the finale lands *Tree aan*'s political punch. At the end of the play, the troops singing an adapted version of "Die Stem," claiming that they answered the country's call and sacrificed what they were asked to do: we lived, we died, for you. As they sing the old anthem, a list of all the (white) men who served South Africa during the Border Wars — and paid the ultimate price — scrolls across the enormous State Theatre's scrim. The company sings from behind the scrim, their bodies ghosting in the background. This act — of naming the

Figure 11. Calling up the roll in Deon Opperman's *Tree aan.*
© 2012 E. Meyberg. Courtesy of Deon Opperman.

Figure 12. Corporal Kotze intimidates young recruits in Deon Opperman's
Tree aan. © 2012 E. Meyberg. Courtesy of Deon Opperman.

names of those who served secretly and anonymously to protect the state—played off another contemporaneous event that audiences at *Tree aan* would have been familiar with: the memorial at Freedom Park.

Freedom Park is a new monument on a hill outside Pretoria created in 2004 to commemorate the lives lost during the colonial and apartheid eras in South Africa. Positioned dialogically on a hill facing the Voortrekker Monument, the monologic shrine to Afrikanerdom, Freedom Park features a reflecting pool, an eternal flame, a gallery, and a "symbolic resting place for those who have died" (freedompark.co.za). It serves as "a symbol of national identity" (freedompark.co.za) in the new democracy. Several enormous granite blocks—"A vast wall commemorating those who have paid the ultimate price for freedom" (freedompark.co.za)—commemorates those who died during eight conflicts within South Africa's history: the precolonial wars, genocide, slavery, wars of resistance, South African wars (first and second Anglo-Boer Wars), World War I and II, and the liberation struggle. There are thousands of names of freedom fighters and victims of the apartheid era: its political prisoners as well as civilians, including the names of those killed in the 1960 Sharpeville massacre and during the 1976 Soweto uprising. There is even a wall space honoring the Cuban fighters who died in Angola and Mozambique. What is omitted from these lists, however, are the deceased of the approximately six hundred thousand white boys and men who served during the Border Wars. The names were not omitted by accident, but after deliberations by the Freedom Park Board. In 2006, veteran's organizations submitted the names of fallen comrades in the South African Defense Forces to the Trust as part of their official solicitation process but were rejected. Their omission underscores the complexities of remembrance and memorialization in contemporary South Africa. The decision of the Freedom Park Trust, presided over by CEO Wally Serote, made it clear whose version of history will triumph—that of the black majority—and whose version is not considered worthy of record anymore in the "new" South Africa—that of the white minority.

Clearly, there are political, racial, and theatrical implications of remembering and representing The Border Wars after the end of apartheid. In his analysis of the Freedom Park fracas, Gary Baines suggests "If one person's 'terrorist' is another's 'freedom fighter,' then South Africa's white minority's 'Border War' was the black majority's 'Liberation Struggle'" (2009, 330). Given that it has been common practice throughout history that the victors control the narration of the nation, Afrikaners, who once wrote their white volk into power in the early twentieth century, at the expense of all other constituents of South African culture, must now confront being erased from the new national narrative by black Africans and the ANC government. Opperman understands the way history pivots, claiming "the ANC government is . . . doing exactly what the apartheid government did from '48 onwards, just with different color skin. [The ANC] is changing name places, they are giving jobs to their friends, the Civil Service [once an Afrikaner domain] is now all Zulu and Xhosa. We wiped out black history after 1948; the ANC is doing the same now" (M. Lewis 2011). To address such erasures, in the song "Wie sal ons onthou?" ("Who Will Remember Us?") from *Tree aan*, two soldiers, Andre and Kosie, sing in unison, "Twenty years from now, Will someone remember us?" They refer to "all the names — evaporated like morning dew" that would disappear into history (Opperman 2010, 90). Opperman justifies his dramaturgical choices, asserting, "I have particular issue with the denial of a people's history" (Watts 2008).

While Opperman's statement carries a certain irony, coming from a white Afrikaner after apartheid, it is important not to dismiss his performance intervention at the end of *Tree aan*. The title of the play, which means "roll call," can also mean "to act on." The act of listing thousands of names of white men and boys who served during the Border Wars is a political one, a provocation that reminds audiences that *everyone*, on all sides of the apartheid equation, was wounded by the racist apartheid system. The white boys conscripted and indoctrinated into the SADF are ultimately also victims of apartheid. Drawn into a hypermasculinized and discriminatory system, and indoctrinated into defending a flawed and racist regime, generations of white South African boys were formed — and deformed — during the Border Wars. Many individual men suffer from posttraumatic stress disorder (PTSD) to this day, but the negative effects of the Border Wars are also deleterious to the collective white psyche.[22] The brutality of the hazing process, the racist ideology programmed into young men's minds, and the horrific acts they committed against alleged *terrs* scarred generations of white men in South Africa. White masculinity has been stunted by apartheid. For many, imagining the perpetrators of apartheid as victims risks ignoring the black victims of South Africa's racism, nor are whites deemed a population worthy of attention anymore. But it remains vital to consider the effects of apartheid and the Border Wars on everyone involved if South Africa is to work through its past and become a fully democratic society in the future, and if we are to move whiteness out of its negative hegemonic history and strive toward more viable, productive ways of being in the future.

The Freedom Park naming question offers an exemplar through which to consider the stakes of performing whiteness in the postcolony. Because the Border War stories involve racially charged historical subjects (white men and boys, many of whom were Afrikaans-speaking), significant controversy arises when these bodies take to the stage or are proffered as names for the walls of Freedom Park. Within the shame-filled, contested, and secretive history of white Afrikaners in South Africa, Deon Opperman's theatrical works reveal the tensions at play when white bodies perform. Guided by John Fletcher's caveat not "to treat communities and groups that you politically oppose, however fiercely, as if their motivations and habitus aren't as complex and historically intricate as any other community or group" (2012, 8), I ask if we can consider Opperman's interventions for the savvy way in which they bring attention to a politically unpopular position, but one to which a significant portion of the South African population are drawn and in which they see themselves represented. Theatre—as a "liminal, negotiating arena of social efficaciousness" (Joseph and Fink 1999, 7)—can offer a space in which the voices of the white men conscripted into the Border Wars can be heard and where the now-taboo history of white victims of apartheid can be publicly performed and "written" on a large screen even if they cannot—or should not—be memorialized at Freedom Park.[23]

Perhaps Opperman—the spearhead of contemporary Afrikaner theatre who sees it as his role to keep the flame of their history alive for his Afrikaner audiences—is the wrong person to send the message, to attempt to right or write history in this moment in time, or to effectively correct an omission. His work—and his outspoken personality and unapologetic ethnic pride—risks reinscribing Afrikaner hegemony and can read as unyielding and conservative, even though I do not believe that is his intent. And perhaps the genre—a large-scale melodramatic musical—is the wrong key in which to sing the tune. Yet *Tree aan* challenges us to consider the stakes of representing history's *victors* as also history's *victims*. And it begs the question: can whiteness claim a nonhegemonic position in performance? And if so, how? The Freedom Park rejection suggests that former hegemons cannot claim the same space as new regimes, despite their own claims of victimhood or trauma. Whiteness needs to lay low, not seek attention or, as Vice suggests, perform "(a certain kind of) silence" that is "intended to diminish the impact of whiteliness in the public sphere" (R. Barnard 2012, 152). To do so requires a kind of humility and letting go that many white settlers in South Africa, and their American cousins, still struggle with today.

Opperman's oeuvre illustrates the nuances of performing whiteness around the political shift into democracy. In the next three chapters, I work through several performance artists' attempts at wrestling with whiteness, including Pieter-Dirk Uys, Peter Van Heerden, Jack Parow, and Die Antwoord, asking what possible performance repertoires each offers for white subjects in the postcolony.

Queering Afrikanerdom

THE PERFORMATIVE MANEUVERS

OF PIETER-DIRK UYS

While multitudes of Afrikaans-speaking playwrights and performers were active during the apartheid era,[1] here I focus on the
work of Afrikaner cross-dressing satirist and performance artist
Pieter-Dirk Uys, whose work deserves greater scholarly attention
because of its usefulness in understanding the gendered nature
of Afrikaner *volkseie* (national identity) and its racial intersections.
Returning to the Afrikaner nationalist project I discussed in chapter 1, here I explore a binary gender construction that emphasizes
Woman as the Mother of the Nation and propagates a hypermasculine identity for the nation as a whole. I return to such performance
artifacts as the 1938 film, *Bou van 'n nasie (Building of a Nation)* and the
Voortrekker Monument in Pretoria, which was completed in 1949
just as the National Party came to power. As a counterpoint, I turn
my analysis to Uys, his deployment of humor, particularly satire
and punning, and his use of drag or cross-dressing.[2] Interrogating conventional gender constructions through his various theatrical personae, Uys explodes the mythology of Afrikanerdom, radically critiquing—or queering—conservative, narrow definitions of
(white, heteronormative, patriarchal) power, and contesting gender norms by performing his alternative masculinity, in drag, as
Mother of the Nation, Evita Bezuidenhout. I work through Uys's
oeuvre, beginning with his first one-man revue, *Adapt or Dye* (1981–
1982), to his film work during the 1980s, including *Skating on Thin
Uys* (1985). I explore his work as South Africa transitioned out of
apartheid (*Funigalore*, 1994) as well as his activism since 1994 and
his continuing critique of the new ANC government. Uys offers a
performance repertoire for white subjects that differs sharply from

both Deon Opperman and Peter Van Heerden (whom I discuss in the chapters that bookend this one).

VOLKSMOEDER: THE MOTHER OF THE NATION

The Afrikaner's relationship with the figure of the Volksmoeder (Mother of the Nation) is one that finds its origins in the nationalist project of the early twentieth century, particularly at the shrine of Afrikaner mythology: the Voortrekker Monument in Pretoria. Visitors encounter a statue of the Volksmoeder, flanked by her two children, at the doorway (figure 13).

In 1949 she was erected as the steadfast symbol of the nation's future, its biological reproducer; the Latin word for birth, *natio*, is the root of "nation." She guards the entryway into the sacred nation-space, a space delineated by boundaries between racial groups. Not only is the Volksmoeder the guardian of the doorway, she is also metonymic of a national birth canal through which the volk emerge. She is positioned at the center of the edifice, just below the entry balcony, in the metaphoric "groin" of the building. "The woman suffers but she does not look down," states the Museum Guidebook. "She looks straight ahead. The children do not look back. They look up" (South Africa 1989, 2).

No discussion of Afrikaner culture can ignore its gendered dynamics. The institutions on which Afrikaner nationalism are based, such as the all-male secret society Die Broederbond, are decidedly male, and Afrikaner politics are dominated by men.[3] Yet the laager, the organizing principle of containment around which Afrikaners have defined themselves, is troped as a feminized space: a womblike enclosure from which Afrikanerdom was symbolically born and into which it retreats when threatened. The gendering of colonial space is not unique to Afrikaners, as Anne McClintock's work confirms, nor is the connection between "romance and republic" unique to South Africa, as Doris Sommer's work illustrates (1991, 7). McClintock argues that as "contested systems of cultural representation," nations are products of "masculinized memory, masculinized humiliation and masculinized hope" (McClintock 1995, 353) that are built on the marriage of what Sommer calls "private passions with public purpose" (1991, 7). I am interested in the Afrikaner state's marriage of a poetics and a politics of national identity and gender. In a double dilemma, the patriarchal nation denies women a political role while utilizing the idea of Woman to physically and symbolically engender the volk. The Volksmoeder icon—Woman with a

Figure 13.
Anton van
Wouw's
Volksmoeder
statue at
Voortrekker
Monument in
Pretoria. © 2012
Megan Lewis.

capital W— is "the symbolic bearer of the nation" (McClintock 1995, 354) as well as the boundary marker employed to resist and embody the masculine fear of penetration, contamination, or seepage. Woman thereby delimits the contained space of the nation through her presence. Yet she is absent in the political life of the laager that she symbolically represents.

The silent, enduring woman appears as a stock character in multiple places in the Afrikaner symbolic landscape. She is the Volksmoeder at the Voortrekker Monument who suffers but does not look down, or the seated woman at the Vrouemonument (Women's Monument) in Bloemfontein, looking eastward toward a new era while holding a dying child in her lap. Or she is Mevrou Retief, one of the Voortrekkers featured in the Bloukrans Massacre in the film *Bou van 'n nasie*.

Like Harold Shaw's *De Voortrekkers* before it, Joseph Albrecht's *Bou van 'n nasie* (1938)[4] feeds a discourse on racial difference and black threats to whiteness. But as a demonstration of how masculinized national power depends on the prior construction of *gender* difference (McClintock 1995), Albrecht's film establishes the racialized and gendered space of the laager in greater detail than Shaw's did in 1916. In addition to depicting the Zulu chief Dingane's ambush and murder of Retief and his men and the Battle of Blood River, Albrecht includes a vivid scenario of the Bloukrans Massacre of 1938. After murdering Retief's party, Dingane ordered the extermination of Voortrekker camps all along the Bushman River, including at Bloukrans. There, on February 17, 1838, the Zulus killed 41 men, 56 women, 185 children, and 250 Khoikhoi and Basuto who accompanied the Voortrekkers (Theal 1886). Albrecht provides a graphic depiction of the massacre. Below I describe this scene in some detail before analyzing the racialized tropes of masculine black savagery assaulting white civilization and femininity contained within it.

The scene begins at night, with an unnamed mother and her newborn son asleep inside a wagon. A little girl with blond curls sleeps near them, clutching a small puppy. Both she and her mother wear white nightgowns, visually and thematically linking the two bodies. Their slumber is interrupted by the barking of dogs. The mother awakens and we see her face take on a look of increasing terror. She urgently rouses her husband, sleeping beside her. Believing it to be a lion in the cattle pen, he says he will go and investigate, as is his gendered duty as the male provider and defender of his volk. But his wife stops him and tells him to listen closer. We cut from the couple sitting upright in their bed to the feet of Zulu *impis*, creeping through the darkness. Realizing they are under attack, the husband (Daniel Bezuidenhout) cries out, "Die kaffirs! Myn God!" As we transition between the Zulu's feet out in the darkness and the interior of the wagon, Daniel tries to rouse his postpartum wife, but she claims she is too weak. She implores him: "Promise me you will save our little child, our son!"

Just then, the Zulus begin to run and ululate, attacking the encampment at full speed. Assegais fly overhead and penetrate the white canvas of the wagon; as they do, the woman inside is hit and dies in Daniel's arms. Now the scene expands its scope: as the Zulus reach the laager itself, women flee from their wagons, their white nightgowns outlining their terrified, frantic bodies against the darkness of the night in a scenario of vulnerable and sexualized white femininity. A woman about to climb out of a wagon sees the approaching Zulus, who flow like a river from offscreen toward her. She retreats into the wagon, and her naked leg is the last thing we see before she is followed by eight or nine Zulu attackers. Then a woman runs across the screen as the Zulu horde follows close behind. A small boy watches as the woman (possibly his mother) is attacked. The little blond girl is enveloped by Zulu men from both sides, her tiny white-nightgowned body erased by their massive presence onscreen. In a scenario of rape and ravishment, Zulus pull the bedding out of a wagon, and one warrior brandishes a white nightgown in his hands. The camera pulls back to show the whole laager as the Zulus set fire to each wagon individually. Daniel is seen fleeing from the scene, his infant son in his hands. The Zulus sing in unison as the wagons burn, the huge flames reaching high into the night sky. As he turns to run, Daniel realizes his baby has been shot; he holds up his blood-soaked hand in horrified recognition. As the fire rages, the bodies of two women in their white nightgowns are silhouetted through the flames, and we see them lying dead in the burning wagon.

This scene is heavily coded with racial and gender markers. The battle between Boer and Zulu is framed through light/dark, good/evil, male/female binaries. Women are nameless fetishes, marked as bearers of children, to be protected within the selfhood of the laager, a space that the Zulu men, as black others, attempt to penetrate. The implication of sexual assault — McClintock's erotics of ravishment (1995, 22) — ghosts through the scene as the woman's naked leg and the brandishing of the nightgown suggest. And patriarchal ideology informs the action. Women are to be protected through a poetics of containment, but are also expendable; the nameless mother is killed, as is her curly-haired daughter. The father, Daniel Bezuidenhout, attempts to save his infant son but never thinks to protect his daughter from the enveloping Zulus. The choice to depict the attack at night was for dramatic effect, particularly when using fire. In reality the Bloukrans attack happened at daybreak, according to Andries Pretorius's journal (Preller 1938). The color white functions symbolically here; the white wagon canvas and the women's nightgowns (markers of not only whiteness but also of femininity and intimacy) stand out starkly against the dark night, affirming again the racial logic of white versus black, good versus evil, civilized female victims versus savage male perpetrators.

In the film, Bezuidenhout makes it to the camp at Moordspruit the next day to warn the other trekkers there. Hearing the news of the massacre,

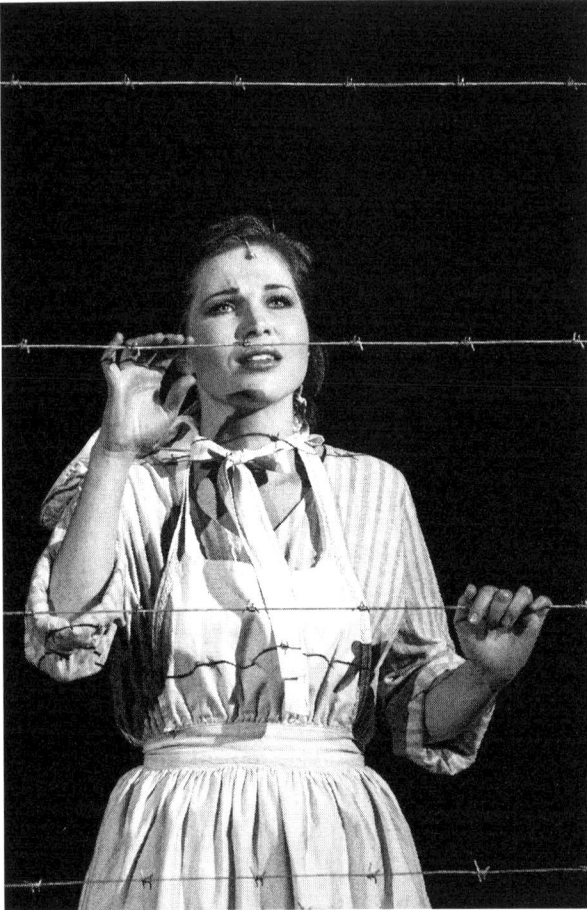

Figure 14.
Marisa Bosman as
Mariaan in Deon
Opperman's *Ons
vir Jou.* © 2008.
Courtesy of Deon
Opperman.

Retief's widow, Magdalena "Lenie" Johanna Greyling (played by Madge Fabian), sighs in disbelief, "Liewe God" (Dear God), and the camera lingers on Fabian's face for a full twelve seconds as she takes in the dreadful news. In this cinematic framing, she is the stalwart Volksmoeder of the Voortrekker Monument, who "suffers but does not look down" (South Africa 1989, 2). While the men suggest retreating to the Cape Colony, the women take up the rally cry and give moving speeches about moving forward rather than withdrawing: "We women will never agree to leave this land until our beloveds and the innocent blood of two hundred children are avenged." As Elke Boehmer puts it, "The idea of nationhood bears a masculine identity though national ideals may wear a feminine face" (1991, 6).

In the midst of South Africa's male-dominated Afrikaner nation stands the contradictory figure of the Volksmoeder. She becomes the upholder of the moral and spiritual life of the nation. As a literal and figurative gate-keeper, she also serves as a boundary marker embodying the racial purity of the Afrikaner nation. In her perfectly starched kappie, she is surrounded by an aura of Victorian physical and moral cleanliness, purity, and fragility. Standing with clusters of her husband's children around her, the Voor-trekker woman also evokes a sense of maternal fecundity that stands in for the propagation of the volk.[5]

Afrikaner women are venerated symbolically but are disenfranchised in practice. Treated as minors under the law, South African women were historically denied the right to "enter into contracts, to own and dispose of property, and to exercise guardianship over their children" (ANC 1954). Prior to the 1996 Constitution, a woman could not open a bank account in South Africa without her husband's consent. While black women suf-fered most under these laws, the gender discrimination applied to white women of privilege as well. In their astute analysis of South African patri-archy, several scholars enumerate the ways in which patriarchy functions within South African culture. For Daniella Coetzee patriarchy assumes an "almost 'religious' status" that "does not tolerate criticism, and adversely affects every aspect and structure of the culture" (2001, 301). In Afrikaner culture fathers were "the highest authority," and mothers were "the loving and understanding party who cared and served in silence" (Boonzaier and Sharpe 1988, 155). "Women were kept in their position of subservience," Coetzee argues, "through measures such as fewer educational opportuni-ties than men, economic dependence, physical harassment, exclusion from leading roles in education, politics, the church and society at large" (2001, 301). South African patriarchy leads to a "reductionist view of reality": not only do men view women as inferior, but "women have eventually accepted their subordinate and inferior position in society ... as natural and a fact of life that cannot be altered" (Coetzee 2001, 301).

THE BOERE DIVA

If Afrikaner national identity relies on gendered and racial schemas to jus-tify its policies and practices, then what happens when a queer Afrikaans-speaking man in drag breaks through the silence of the Afrikaner woman that Boonzaier and Sharpe describe? Tapping into, embodying, and satiriz-

Figure 15. Pieter-Dirk Uys as Evita Bezuidenhout, the most famous
white woman in South Africa, at the Boere Museum/Nauseum in Darling.
© 1997. Courtesy of Pieter-Dirk Uys.

ing the Volksmoeder motif of Afrikaner nationalist rhetoric, actor/writer/
drag artist Pieter-Dirk Uys has built his career on speaking truth to the
power structures of apartheid as well as to the new ANC dispensation after
1994.[6] While his repertoire includes many characters, it is as his most famous alter ego, the Afrikaner Volksmoeder Evita Bezuidenhout (figures 15
and 16)—whom he refers to as "the most famous white woman in South
Africa"—that Uys has been able to directly critique apartheid's leaders, its
policies and ideologies, and the racist Afrikaner underpinnings that supported it.[7] During apartheid's active years, Evita served in what Uys called the
"South African diplomatic corpse" as ambassador to a fictional homeland
called Bapetikosweti: an amalgam of Soweto, the enormous township outside Johannesburg where black workers had to live, and Bophuthatswana, a
fractured grouping of land parcels set aside for black use as a "homeland"
under apartheid.[8]

Often refereed to as Tannie Evita (Aunty Evita), this character combines
numerous Afrikaner tropes and conventions. She always wears an imposing,
almost architectural black wig with gray and white highlights whose curls

are reminiscent of a Cape Buffalo's horns. Her outfits drip with Nationalist Party insignia; she often sports an orange, white, and blue sash that resembles the old South African flag or, these days, the signature ANC colors of black, green, and yellow. In her formal portraits, she often poses with symbolic capital of the Afrikaner state: AK-47s (the state's military might), proteas (the state flower), a rugby ball (the national sport), roosters, cacti, or *boerewors* (farmer's sausage, for their inherent phallic puns), and she is always dripping with diamond rings, earrings, and necklaces (referencing the mining system that drove the apartheid economy).

Pieter-Dirk Uys describes himself as "born, bred and invented in Cape Town . . . a writer and an entertainer, more reactor than actor; more famous as a *boere diva* than a dramatist" (Uys 2001). He modeled Evita partially on his idol Sophia Loren and partially on Andrew Lloyd Weber and Tim Rice's 1978 musical about Eva Peron. He explains the emergence of Evita as follows:

> I was writing a weekly column for the *Sunday Express* in Johannesburg . . . during the time of the Information Scandal.[9] The land was abuzz with rumours of embezzlements, thefts, even murder, but because of the ever-increasing paranoia about press control and censorship, it was not possible to write about these things. So I created a character in my column . . . the wife of a Nationalist MP [Member of Parliament], someone on the fringes of power but elbow-deep in the catering, [who kept] informing the nation of the stench under the cloak of respectability. . . . Someone even gave her a name: the Evita of Pretoria. (Uys pdu.co.za)

The Evita character represents a satiric lens through which Uys examines, and critiques, white South Africa. "She could damn with faint praise," he says; "she could condemn with flattery" (Uys 1995, 15). "Tannie Evita stepped out of the chorus line, and took off into folklore," he explains (Uys pdu.co.za). The public wanted more of her all the time, so Uys created a family and a history for Evita: daughter Billie-Jeanne, who marries Leroy Makoeloeli, the family's black gardener-turned-politician; son Izan, whose name spelled backward is Nazi, and who is a member of the right-wing AWB movement; libidinal son De Kock, a member of the Gay Liberation Movement; estranged, sexually liberated sister Bambi Kellermann; outspokenly racist grandmother Ossewania Poggenpoel; and Nationalist Party member and henpecked husband Hasie (whose name in Afrikaans means "bunny"). As the wife of a Parliamentarian, Evita knows—and exposes—the intrigues in the Department of Information. Uys used Evita as socialite insider who could comment on real political scandals. In the guise of gossip, Evita exposed information that was banned, or restricted by media regulations, testing the limits of Afrikaner propriety.

Like the politician P. W. Botha (whom Uys often impersonates as a lip-licking, finger-wagging old crocodile), the fictional Evita assumes a like-minded audience for her casual racism and thus speaks to both those who support apartheid and those who see through its ruse. For example, Uys quips, "There were no questions asked about apartheid, our school considered it normal: we, the Afrikaners, were right and everybody else was black" (Uys 1999). "It is no secret," writes Uys in *Funigalore: Evita's Real-Life Adventures in Wonderland*, a book based on a television series Uys did in 1994, "that inside the studied façade of middle-aged glamour is an unglamourous, middle-aged man" (1995, 5). Yet even though Evita is obviously a man in a dress, Uys says that "not one of the guests on *Funigalore* ever referred to me as 'Pieter' while I was presenting Evita Bezuidenhout. . . . They all suspended belief and gave themselves over to the surrealism" (1995, 5). Such a suspension of disbelief marks the continued willingness of many South Africans to swallow national constructions—satiric, fictionalized, or officially partisan ones—"hook, line, and earring" (Uys 1995, 5).

APARTHEID CENSORSHIP

Uys comes from a prominent Afrikaner family. Born in 1945, he is the son of Calvinist Afrikaner father, Hannes Uys, who hails from fourth-generation Dutch-Belgian Huguenot stock, and Berlin-born Jewish mother, Helga Bassel Uys. Uys often quips that his mixed Jewish and Afrikaner heritage makes him a member of both Chosen People. Uys is also a cousin of the film director Jamie Uys, who is best known for *The Gods Must Be Crazy* (1980), and Uys's father was a cousin of Daniel Malan, the first prime minister of apartheid South Africa, from 1948 to 1954. His father worked for the apartheid state's Censor Board,[10] a later version of the 1954 Commission of Inquiry into "Undesirable Publications" that was charged with upholding morality and state interest by none other than Malan himself. Headed by Geoffrey Cronjé, a rabid apartheid ideologue guided by "racialized disgust," the Publications Commission sought out "moral repugnance" and was charged with combating "the evil of indecent, offensive or harmful literature" (McDonald 2010, 23). In 1963, with the passing of Publications and Entertainment Act No.

26, the commission's scope was broadened to include "entertainments." By 1974, the impact of theatre as a subversive force had been felt significantly enough to warrant the passing of the Publications Act, which required that all plays had to be approved by the Censor Board. Uys's early material, especially his scripted plays, continually challenged the Censor Board. For example, in 1975 the Control Board banned his play *Selle ou storie (Same Old Story)* on grounds that it was blasphemous, obscene, and it made Afrikaners look ridiculous (Ferguson 1977). In 1978, one of Uys's plays, a mock radio serial about an Afrikaner family entitled *Die van Aardes van Grootoor*,[11] was banned in its first three weeks at The Market Theatre. Uys writes in *Between the Devil and the Deep: A Memoir of Acting and Reacting*, that *Die van Aardes* "broke the stale mold of Afrikaans comedy. It was irreverent, vulgar, suggestive, camp, shocking and politically explosive" (2010, 68). In the final scene, the family farm is being sold to a black woman, who happens to be the granddaughter of the *Aia* (nanny) who raised the van Aardes family for generations. Radical for the time, this prescient ending offered a harbinger of how South Africa would eventually transform itself.

Apartheid South Africa was rife with what Bill Keller calls "the censor's paternalism," a world of "whited-out newspapers, happy-talk TV, sex-free cinema and laundered literature" (1993). Though haphazardly enforced, censors often shuttered plays. Banned playwright Anthony Akerman described the paradoxical position theatre held in those days: "People outside the country are often surprised to discover that the theatre is able to criticize the system at all. [South Africa] does not conform to their conception of what a police state should be.... The theatre has appropriated certain 'freedoms' for itself; these are limited, conditional and constantly under threat" (Akerman n.d.). Uys describes how the National Party took up *Kultuur* as a weapon, "inspired no doubt by the experiences in Nazi Germany of the architect of apartheid, Dr Hendrik Verwoerd" (Uys 2004). "I grew up in a constipated Afrikaner society," writes Uys in his signature ironic tone,

> where theatre was for whites only, opera was in German, Shakespeare was in Afrikaans and art was too important to share with just anyone. Like artists in the Germany of Hitler and Goebbels, our writers, painters and performers were rewarded with success and appreciation for looking only in the *right* direction. National awards were lavished on them and with great ease; these foot soldiers of the Boer "Kultuur" took up their

weapons of words and deeds and conquered the people. (Uys 2004, emphasis in original)

On his website, he jeers that "having survived the mediocrity of apartheid kultuur," it is his "therapy" and his "joy to expose the bones of that dinosaur for the entertainment of democratic audiences worldwide" (Uys pdu. co.za). Uys played with the censors, openly inviting them to see his work. He even wrote letters of complaint about his own work to entice them to see it. In his first one-man revue in 1981–1982, *Adapt or Dye*, Uys comments on the scrutiny of the censors. After one of the shows he was approached in the car park by three big Afrikaner policemen. "Now we have you, Pieter-Dirk Uys, you little bastard!" they shout at him. "You go too far. You mess with the Afrikaans language; you mock Afrikaans culture; you make us Afrikaners look laughable or like Nazis . . . but hell, you've got nice legs!" (Uys 1982).

While most of Uys's plays were censored, his one-man revues were not. Tannie Evita says that the Nationalists put up with Pieter-Dirk Uys "to show how democratic we were. Besides, the jails were full" (Trillin 2004). His *konserts* avoided the censors because they defied categorization, took place late at night, and were not considered serious enough to warrant censor scrutiny. And as Calvin Trillin suggests, "Uys glided under the radar in Evita Bezuidenhout's frocks [and] believes that a lot of Nationalists thought, Oh, it's just a *moffie* in a dress, *moffie* being the Afrikaans pejorative for a homosexual" (2004).

In *Adapt or Dye* (1982),[12] Uys takes a direct stab at the censors. Calling the Censor Board his "very own public relations department," he dons some trousers and a nice tie, because, as he claims, "to be a censor, you don't need to be able to spell but you must have a nice tie." As the scene begins, the song "Anything Goes" plays as he dons a bowler hat and opens up a pornographic magazine. Uys used a real pornographic magazine as a prop, which was banned at the time. "I hereby exercise [pronounced *ex-or-cize*] the powers invested in my singular person by the Publications Act," he claims and then begins to read an imagined legal document. "Whereas . . . " he says, articulating the "r" in the word heavily to indicate his censor character's Afrikaans-ness. He continues, "Because of the obscene nature of their shapes, the following objects are deemed undesirable as far as we are concerned: candles, cucumbers, *boerewors*, and orbs formerly known as nigger-balls."[13] As the scene progresses, the list of banned items becomes more absurd, marking the extent of apartheid censorship. "Tomorrow has been declared undesirable because of the obscene phrase *the crack of dawn*," Uys quips, and "all Afrikaans universities will hereby be closed due to the repeated and frequent usage of FAK (Federation of Afrikaans Culture) and *Fakulteit* (Faculty)."

Uys performed *Adapt or Dye* in 1981 in The Market Theatre's newly converted cafe space, aptly named The Laager. The title referenced Prime Minister Botha's 1979 claim that "we must adapt or we shall die" as well as the "total strategy" that he believed was necessary to counter the "total onslaught" against apartheid that the National Party perceived to be eroding their power (Giliomee and Mbenga 2007). Starting his show at 11 P.M. because, he said, "the Broederbond and the Kappiekommando[14] went to bed at nine," Uys played with linguistic and gender codes, claiming that the piece was "written, directed and performed by Pieter-Dirk Uys in both official languages and sexes" (Uys 1982). The show premiered, fittingly, on April Fool's Day 1981, and ran for over a hundred performances.[15]

As *Adapt or Dye* begins, Evita Bezuidenhout enters the theatre and vamps through the crowd before taking her place center stage, behind a makeshift podium draped in orange, white, and blue and encircled in barbed wire. Emblazoned on it are the words "Ons Land, Ons Volk, Onslaught." The barbed wire forms a symbolic laager and the slogan refers to the commonly used National Party phrase, "Our Land, Our People," with the word *Onslaught* printed aslant, as if sliding off the podium, thereby obscuring the complete word and evading censorship. Dressed in leopard print, a mink stole, and platform heels, Evita places a *Slegs Vir Blankes* (For Whites Only) sign on the podium and, as the national anthem plays, she corrects the technician, quipping in a lilting, tongue-in-cheek tone, "That is 'God Save the Queen.' We are a Republic and there are no queens in South Africa" (Uys 1982). Under apartheid, homosexuality was equated with the crime of sodomy; offenders could receive up to seven years in prison or be subjected to shock aversion therapy.[16] Thus, for Uys to play with gender like this—let alone to come out publicly as a homosexual—was a risky affair.

Evita's welcoming remarks are laden with jabs at the government. Reading off note cards, in a blend of English and Afrikaans, she welcomes "the various chairmen of the 143 National Commissions of Inquiry, our beloved guests from Paraguay, Adolf en Greta Goebbels, [and] members of the Security Police and your faithful dogs." She regales her audience with double-edged jokes, like recounting how Mrs. Kaunda [wife of Kenneth Kaunda, the first president of Zambia, who ruled from 1964 to 1991] told her that "swart mag sal Suid Afrika breek" (black power will break South Africa). And Evita replies, "Yes, but darling, the blacks break everything."

Uys makes puns or double entendres throughout his revue, like saying that the situation in South Africa is "*vrot* with tension," *vrot* (pronounced "frot") being the Afrikaans word for "rotten." Or that being a true Nationalist means never having to say "I'm sorry . . . *Baas.*" *Baas,* Afrikaans for "boss," is how black South Africans were required to refer to whites. And as Evita, Uys punctuates all his comments with a knowing look to the heavens and the phrase "Né, Doctor?" (Right, Doctor?). The "Doctor" here is Dr. Hendrik Verwoerd, apartheid's architect and South Africa's prime minister from 1958 until his assassination in 1966.

The sweet-talking Volksmoeder Evita delivers daggers of critiques. "Just look what our National Party has done *to* [rather than *for*] South Africa," Bezuidenhout beams as she lists all the ways in which democracy is being eroded. "Nou-ja,"[17] she croons, "our glorious Boere Republic has survived in spite of *the odds*: The Donald Woodses, the Breyten Breytenbachs, the Joe Slovos, the Peter Heyns, the Neil Agats, the Bikos, the Mandelas, the Sobukwes, the Buthelezis, the Tutus. *Ag, hemel* (Oh, heavens), the black list is endless" (Uys 1982). To even utter the names of any of these banned individuals was illegal at the time. And for Evita, as emblem of Afrikanerdom, to be doing the uttering was satirical on multiple levels: the Afrikaner exposing the illogic of Afrikanerdom and doing so through the usually silent Volksmoeder figure.

Uys has been described as a cuckoo in the nest of Afrikanerdom, a traitor to his own people (Ferguson 1977). His response is that he exposes those parts of his culture that are flawed and harmful to other people. "When I send up the *verkramptes* (conservatives), I am always sending up the *verkrampte* ghosts in me," he says. "But I never poke fun at people—it's their ATTITUDES that I find funny. Some of them seem to have their scripts all mixed up" (Allan 1983, 75). Through Evita, whom Melvyn McMurtry calls "the epitome of bigoted nurturing," audiences wonder "who Uys, through her, will dare to criticize, and how far he can draw them into a collision in which laughter can be a release and an indictment. She both frees them from the gravity of propriety and tests the limits of accessibility in a repressive society" (1994, 83).

SATIRE AND THE POWER OF THE PUN

Uys's use of humor, especially satire and the punning power of the Afrikaans language,[18] is a fluid, ambiguous entity open to interpretation and the perfect medium for his slippery politics. Griffin explains that satirists are "roused by a sense of urgency about moral ugliness or its idiocy, by the sense that something must be done or at least said" (1994, 48). For linguists and sociologists, humor functions by combining three elements: incongruity, ambiguity, and language. An incongruity stands out as an element distinct from a congruous, or intact, system and the degree to which we find something funny depends on "how firmly we are attached to the expectation system it attacks" (Davis 1993, 15). Thus, South African audiences (especially whites) see themselves in Evita—their privilege, their mannerisms, even their racism—and laugh at a system they know intimately.

In addition to incongruity, humor depends on ambiguity, or an element congruous with two opposing systems (Davis 1993, 17). When these elements intersect, they create what Arthur Koestler calls "associative contexts," the result of which is humor (Davis 1993, 18). Davis explains the tension between these two concepts: incongruity is "the real difference between things that seem alike," and ambiguity is "the real resemblance between things that seem to differ" (Davis 1993, 24). At the root of this understanding of humor is the notion of a disruption to a supposedly stable system.

As a "structured, rule-governed" system (Davis 1993, 33), language lends itself to such disruptions, the most common of which is the pun. Here, the focus of meaning is shifted from the word's meaning to the word's sound (Davis 1993, 37). Unlike ordinary speech, puns "pivot" focus from the primary to the secondary meaning of language (Davis 1993, 45, emphasis in original). Puns disrupt linguistic conventions and "transform language from transparent to opaque" (Davis 1993, 60). In the act of violating or disrupting linguistic codes, listeners are often made aware of the "imperfections of the higher cultural and social systems, of which we often need to be reminded" (Davis 1993, 65).

Afrikaans is a deliciously punning language, and Uys is one of its most artful manipulators. Consider the titles of his many plays and reviews, from *Strike Up the Banned* (1975), *Skating on Thin Uys* (1985), and *A Part Love a Part Hate* (1990) to *Truth Omissions* (1996), *Foreign Aids* (2001), and *Macbeki* (2009).[19] In the act of punning "an additional semantic layer is added to the otherwise stable relationship between signifier and signified" (Pedersen 2010, 8). A pun requires a context in which "multiple and disparate meanings for the pun word are acceptable" (Delabastita 1993, 70). Uys's work depends on the familiarity of South African audiences with the contexts of his puns. Thus, *Adapt or Dye* and *Total Onslaught* only work in reference to P. W. Botha's reformist policies in the dying days of apartheid in the 1980s. *A Part Love a Part Hate* and *Truth Omissions* require knowledge of apartheid and the Truth and Reconciliation Commission. The bilingual puns are predicated on a familiarity with Afrikaans words. For instance, the *kaktus* in *Tannie Evita Praat Kaktus* refers simultaneously to a desert succulent and the Afrikaans word for shit (*kak*); thus, *Aunty Evita Talks Shit*. Similarly, the *naai* (English: "nigh") in *The End Is Naai*, is Afrikaans for "fuck"; the "skating" in *Skating on Thin Uys* puns on the Afrikaans word *skyt*, meaning "to take a shit"; and the FAK (pronounced in English as "fuck") in *Bambi Sings the FAK Songs* refers to the Federation of Afrikaans Culture (Federasie van Afrikaanse Kultuur, or FAK). Many of these puns are sexual in nature and also play with Afrikaner social mores, which tend to be conservative in keeping with Christian (Calvinist) values and shun any outward expression of sexuality.[20] Like homosexuality, under apartheid prostitution was illegal, pornography was banned, and sexually explicit scenes were expurgated from printed and visual materials. Anyone who spoke out against the state risked banning, censorship, or even incarceration.

Satire can also be understood to serve a political purpose of exposing social flaws, and Uys is an enormously skillful satirist. For George Test, satire "exploits the ability of irony to expose, undercut, ridicule or otherwise attack indirectly, playfully, wittily, profoundly, artfully" (Gournelos and Greene 2011, 63). For example, in performing as Dr. Eschel Rhoodie (1933–1993), apartheid-era spin doctor and minister of information during the infamous Information Scandal, Uys spoofs Rhoodie's evasiveness and doublespeak. Wearing a pair of enormous ears (Rhoodie's signature feature), Uys-as-Rhoodie meets the press. "I'm very glad you asked that question," he claims loudly to the imaginary reporters and journalists, but constantly avoids answering by telling them, "I'll get to you now." His language is peppered with emphatic phrases like "most categorically" and "I say this with conviction." When it is suggested that, like Marie Antoinette, the government should let the people eat cake, Rhoodie offers a copy of *Kyk* (pronounced "cake"), a popular romance photo story magazine, whose title in Afrikaans means "Look." Uys's incongruous jab here asks audiences to look beyond the spin with which Rhoodie and his cronies tried to hide their sinister attempts to influence global public opinion about apartheid. By deploying humor, Uys is able to directly attack a government official, an impossible act if performed in a different genre.

If social systems have been constructed, they can also be deconstructed, as in the sense of *cracking* in the phrase *cracking someone up*. The comic "shows the social world to be disordered—or at least ordered in another way than most people ... believe" (Davis 1993, 155). Such a disordering often involves, as it does in Pieter-Dirk Uys's case, unmasking; splitting the subject matter into "an apparent phenomenon (what most people believe is going on) and an actual noumenon (what is 'really' going on)" (Davis 1993, 157). Unmasking is effective because of its ability to reveal "'dirt' behind reputable institutions, roles, groups and individuals: the government, the bureaucracy, the professions, the rich, the powerful, the celebrated" (Davis 1993, 157). In South Africa, the "dirt" was more sinister than mere corruption or deception; it was a systemic privileging of a select few at the expense of dehumanizing the majority of the population.

Satire is also useful in repressive regimes because it can protect itself from its object's aggression by retreating back into the literal (Gournelos and Greene 2011, 63). For Jamie Warner, "satirical pieces can circulate as simply ridiculous literal suggestions—although, hopefully, some will know better" (Gournelos and Greene 2011, 63). Gournelos and Greene claim that irony, as a form of humor designed to cause incongruity subtly rather than overtly, is "a potentially useful tool by which one can open up new ways of speaking about an issue" (2011, xxiv). According to Warner, in more "repressive rhetorical regime[s], the ambiguity inherent in irony can become a potent weapon" (Gournelos and Greene 2011, 63).

One of Uys's great skills as a performer is his ability to frame whiteness and its privilege ironically. In addition to Evita, *Adapt or Dye* included several other characters, including Noel Fine, the Jewish *kugel* (a type of pudding and a term for a stereotypical Jewish woman) who speaks in a nasal drone as she complains, "There are only two things we can't stand about this country: apartheid . . . and the blacks." If Evita is the epitome of Afrikaner conservatism and Uys's way of addressing that aspect of South African culture, then Noel Fine is Uys's vehicle for mocking white liberalism. She claims to support the antiapartheid movement yet constantly retreats into her white, upper-middle-class privilege. She and her garden boy, Nimrod, play kinky games (The Queen and Black Intruder, for instance) that index the apartheid-era Immorality Act, which forbade sexual relations across the color bar.[21] All is fun and games until she threatens him: "Nimrod, if you don't do exactly what Madam says, Madam will report you directly to the police!" (Uys 1982). Irony here is a potent weapon, exposing the real violence of the state and the white privilege of its citizens. Through Noel Fine, Uys exposes how white South Africans play with themselves, play liberal, and play with the fates of black South Africans.

Donning a brown wig and glasses with exaggerated eyes in his *Adapt or Dye* revue, Uys next becomes SAUK newscaster Riaan Cruywagen,[22] informing the audience in his serious, news-reading tone: "Pieter-Dirk Uys . . . is apparently protected by his left-leaning ability to laugh at himself. But truthfully, here at the SABC, it is impossible to laugh at ourselves. And besides, what's so funny?" (Uys 1982, my translation). Here Uys plays off of the humorlessness of the SABC/SAUK (South African Broadcasting Corporation / Suid-Afrikaanse Uitsaaikorporasie), in a culture of censorship where the broadcasting agency was considered a moral arbiter as well as a news source. He also underscores his use of satire when he tells his audience that there has been tremendous competition during the show's eighteen-month run. "There has been a better satire on in South Africa," he claims, "a satire more pertinent, more shocking, and in many ways, funnier than this one. Of course I refer to the production that ran at the Old Assembly Theater, Parliament Street, Cape Town" (Uys 1982). Here he is referring to the farce of the South African Parliament, which was housed in government buildings in Cape Town's Central Business District. Uys scoffs at "that, uh, star-studded production of Much Ado About Nothing," and "that very successful lunchtime production of Julius Caesar, with F. W. de Klerk as Mark Anthony and Hartzenburg and Treurnicht alternating as Brutus" (Uys 1982). Ferdinand Hartzenberg, Conservative Party leader, and Andries Treurnicht, former minister of education, both outspoken against what they saw as the "liberalism" of the National Party, left the NP in 1982 to found the right-wing Conservative Party. "Everything in this show has been done before," says Uys to his audience, "in real life. The nice thing is, at least here, we still can adapt." Riffing off of the title of the revue, he allows the audience to fill in what he suggests should happen to this illogical system of government: adapt or die off.

J. Douglas Canfield states that the traditional understanding of satire is "an attack, containing at least an implicit standard for judgment, by a moralist on deviant behavior" (1996). The satirist is the corrector and the object of the critique is a passive victim of the attack. In Uys's case, he is the "deviant" (the white homosexual cuckoo in the nest of Afrikanerdom) correcting the "moralists" (the *verkrampte* Afrikaner regime). Canfield also reminds his reader that in this poststructuralist moment in history, "the satiric form seems more open-ended; satiric motivation more complex; audience response more complicit with selfish or self-indulgent play" (1996). The complexity of audience reactions to Uys's work deserves a study unto itself, but Gournelos and Greene suggest that "as a system of social exchange," satire requires a savvy audience, one that "understands the second nonliteral ironic layer of meaning" (2011, 63). Uys's audiences, most of whom were white under apartheid (because laws prohibited mixed-race gatherings), occupied a dual position as the objects of his attacks on the one hand and complicit subjects who delighted in his lampooning of themselves on the other. They understood the "nonliteral ironic layer of meaning" in Uys's work as a critique of a system that benefited them. And the pleasure they gained from watching Uys throw javelins at the culture ranged from self-debasing delight to an examination of their privilege.

Canfield's suggestion that satiric motivation is more complex and audience response more complicit addresses a critique leveled against Uys's work by another South African satirist, the late Robert Kirby (1936–2007). Calvin Trillin describes how

> Kirby maintains that what was thought of as a devastating imitation of P. W. Botha actually made Botha into somebody "avuncular and a bit lovable instead of the horrible, lethal fascist that he was." . . . Some people on the left in those years did see the Nationalist Party's tolerance of Uys as an indication that he was serving as a court jester—someone who took the mickey out of the government, as English-speaking South Africans would put it, but pulled back when the opportunity came to go for the jugular. (2004)

Ambivalence theory of humor is "when an audience finds a text to be both attractive and repulsive," and the pairing of these two opposing desires "builds tension, which is released through laughter" (Gournelos and Greene 2011, xix–xxi). When Evita quips to Mrs. Kaunda that "blacks break everything," privileged white housewives laugh both with—and at—her, seeing their own racist thinking simultaneously expressed and ridiculed. As Griffin observes, "The excitement of satire (its bite) is based on our knowledge (or just our suspicion) that the victims are 'real,' even if we can't always identify them" (1994, 124). But it's not just Uys's victims that need to be real; it's also his characters that require realism to be most effective. "In a country which is absurd," says Uys, "the clown needs to be real to have impact" (McMurtry 1994, 95).

Once the mythological bedfellow of every important apartheid official, the "Free State Scarlet O'Hoera" (Uys 1995, 8),[23] Evita hopped into the ANC's bed in 1994, and now continues to serve and critique the state as the pendulum has swung to the other side of the political spectrum. All sectors of South African culture flock to Evita, be they black or white, liberal or conservative, victims of her satire or those who take pleasure in it. Minister Pik Botha faxed her. Archbishop Desmond Tutu kissed her on the cheek and danced the *toyi-toyi* with her in his garden. Former minister of African affairs Piet Koornhof visited with her in Darling, the town outside Cape Town that Uys painted pink, where he performs in regular cabaret shows at Evita se Perron (Evita's Platform).[24] "Designers designed for her . . . I dieted because of her," says Uys (Uys pdu.co.za). Politicians want to appear with Evita because she is an iconic celebrity, whose realism is so convincing, they forget she is a man in drag. Uys plays her so convincingly—with her *gasvreiheid* (hospitality), racist pleasantries, and *koeksisters* (crullers)—that she is read not only as a woman, but as the ultimate embodiment of Afrikaner femininity: the Volksmoeder.

Evita's convincing performance is supported by several public ploys, like writing to Margaret Thatcher as a fellow head of state, holding official press conferences, and starring with real political figures in her films.[25] It has also been bolstered by her autobiography, *A Part Love a Part Hate—The Biography of Evita Bezuidenhout* (1990). After many years of Evita's success, Uys wrote this "satirical look at the apartheid empire" that he maintains is "not just the story of a woman, or the story of a nation. It was in many cases the story of our lives" (Uys pdu.co.za). In 1995, he followed up with *Funigalore: Evita's Real-Life Adventures in Wonderland*, based on a television series he did for M-NET. *Funigalore* chronicles Evita's televised encounters with actual political figures from President Mandela to former foreign minister Pik Botha; from the Orange Free State's new premier, Patrick Lekota, to Conservative Party leader Tony Leon and radical Pan African Congresswoman Patricia de

Lille. During the interviews, both on and off camera, the guests referred not to Pieter, but only to Evita. Once Evita was accepted as a woman, suggests McMurtry, "once disbelief is not only willingly suspended but ignored, once the sense of man-as-woman is lost, Evita can makes comments Uys cannot and be a further satirical mask (and an object of satire) in her own right" (1994, 96).

"I'll never know what exact impact Evita has on people, but I'm told it can be pretty intimidating," says Uys. "She doesn't look like a man in a dress. In fact that's the point: the man in the dress has to make himself known before the guest seems to relax" (Uys 1995, 55). As he was busy transforming into Evita prior to his meeting with Mandela — making the change from "forty-something *boereseun* to middle-aged *supertannie*" (Uys 1995, 8) — a group of six black and coloured housekeepers at the Parliament buildings asked if they could watch him get dressed and become "Mevrou" (Madam). The women encouraged him as he struggled to get into his step-in corset, commented on what nice legs he had, and even passed around his false breasts and joked about the holes in them. The jovial banter ceased the minute Uys put on the wig. "Instantly Evita Bezuidenhout was there" and

> the ladies changed their attitude in a flash. Suddenly there was no chummy interest, no reference to *Meneer*, no familiar interest. They stuttered and tried to look busy. I gave them an Evita stare in the mirror.
>
> "*Haai, waarlik* (Wow, truly)," whispered the first lady, "there's Mrs Bezuidenhout. "*Môre, Mevrou* (Morning, Madam) . . ."
>
> "*Môre, Mevrou*," the others echoed, dry-mouthed, as if their nightmares had come true. The past was back! (Uys 1995, 243).

Evita is so readily accepted because the character embodies the familiar Afrikaner *tannie* or Volksmoeder, both loving and stern. Because the Volksmoeder is an idealized fiction, it is also easy to buy the fiction of Evita. The Volksmoeder icon sells the fiction of the imagined community of the volk; playing the Volksmoeder, Evita debunks and demythologizes it.

FOKKING WITH *DIE VOLKSMOEDER*:
QUEERING AFRIKANERDOM

For E. Patrick Johnson, to queer is "to resist or elide categorization, to disavow boundaries . . . and to proffer potentially productive modes of resistance against hegemonic structures of power" (2008, 166). Pieter-Dirk Uys,

Figure 16.
Pieter-Dirk
Uys's repertoire
of characters.
© 2012.
Courtesy of
Pieter-Dirk Uys.

as a homosexual and as a performing artist, queers Afrikanerdom. His drag acts are "productive modes of resistance" against one of the most repressive regimes of the twentieth century. Writing on one of his promotional postcards, "hypocrisy is the Vaseline of political intercourse," Uys offers an ever-present reminder of the constructedness, fallibility, and potential corruption of all political regimes, as well as the sexual and gender politics that undergirded them.[26]

As Uys mocks apartheid politics, he also articulates a countermasculinity to Afrikaner hypermasculinity.[27] In a scene in the 1985 film *Skating on Thin Uys*, staged in a caravan trailer with Springbok rugby captain Divan Serfontein, Evita proudly claims in English that she has always been involved in sport and was head of the "campaign to keep South African sport white." Then she whispers under her breath in Afrikaans, "I have naturally changed like so many other people in this country." Then lanky Evita moves closer to the short and compact Serfontein and refers to him using the Afrikaans diminutive *Divantjie*. In a patronizing, motherly tone, she asks Serfontein if he remembers when Tannie Evita came to his school and encouraged him to become a rugby player. Serfontein answers every question with an obedient and respectful, "Ja, Tannie" (Yes, Aunty). Uys outsizes Serfontein, who, pressed against the caravan's window, appears diminutive next to his host. Evita's broad arm wraps around his shoulder, and as Evita crosses her knee, her exposed leg touches the exposed knee of the rugby player. Then Evita chuckles, "Divantjie wil jy 'n roomys hê?" (Little Divan, do you want an ice cream?). "No, I will have a beer, thanks," he replies.

Rugby epitomizes Afrikaner masculinity, featuring beefy men who tackle one another without pads and helmets. Rugby in South Africa is, as the 2009 film *Invictus* illustrates, and as Maingard confirms, "exclusively male, mostly white, and often Afrikaner" (1997, 24). By infantilizing one of the icons of Afrikaner heterosexual manhood (Serfontein), Uys positions his own queer body as dominating the dominant version of masculinity. He is able to do this in a dress, coded as the Volksmoeder, because her sexualized advances, which conform to heterosexual paradigms, are acceptable, whereas Pieter the gay man would not have been able to play with sex so openly in 1985, especially to a famous rugby icon like Serfontein.

Uys's own history informs his performance work. In his memoir, *Elections and Erections: A Memoir of Fear and Fun* (2002), he shares his early sexual experiences under apartheid. Caught between the "essence of British reserve" and "Afrikaner Nationalism, Dutch Reformed Church morality and that all-powerful word, *sies!*" (Uys 2002, 12–13), he was left totally unprepared for his own sexual awakening and shrouded in feelings of shame and sinfulness. He describes the word *sies*—which translates as "shame on you" or "hush" and carries polyvalent meanings of disgust, disappointment, or annoyance—as "ten times worse than hush!" Between the word "'sies' and 'hush' we didn't ask questions for forty years," writes Uys, "not about politics; definitely not about sex" (2002, 13). In a chapter titled "Like Tasting Chocolate?" Uys describes how his sexual encounters, at a gay cruising spot, were fraught with danger and racial transgressions. As a good Afrikaner, Uys has been socialized to be ashamed of sexuality of any kind, let alone such a perceived deviance as homosexuality or such an illegal act as interracial sex. For Uys, sexuality, race, and danger were inextricably linked under apartheid. After a beautiful erotic encounter with a coloured boy at the beach, Uys describes running home thinking to himself

I had broken God's law! I had broken the Immorality Act! Not to mention the Acts Against Sex With Boys and the Act of Putting Your Penis Between the Thighs of a Naked Person on a Public Beach! Not to mention the Law of Loving Across the Railway Line and the Barbed Wire Fence.

God would punish me! (Uys 2002, 19)

But Uys continued his illicit dalliances at the beach, which made him feel "less white and more real" (Uys 2002, 20), and eventually he began to question the logic of the Immorality Act, the dogma of the Calvinist Church, and the rhetoric of the apartheid state. After studying in London (where he first saw images of the atrocities of apartheid on television, which was banned in South Africa until 1976), and his mother's suicide in 1969, he decided to become an actor and invent the Mother of the Nation, Evita Bezuidenhout, his mouthpiece for speaking truth to power.

Uys's most direct parody of the Volksmoeder comes in a sketch in *Adapt or Dye* that I call "Kakpraat met die Kappikommando" ("Bullshitting with the Bonnet Brigade"). Tapping into the proliferation of the Volksmoeder icon during the 1938 Eeufees, Uys emerges on stage in a black kappie as the Boer War–era Afrikaans song "Sarie Marais" plays overhead.[28] The scene is performed entirely in Afrikaans, plays on melodramatic tropes and gestures throughout, and directly tackles the sacred cows of the volk. Recalling the sacrificial tone of the inscription on the Women's Monument in Bloemfontein[29] — they will forgive but never forget — Uys performs the iconic protectress of the volk here. "I'm wearing black because whiteness is committing suicide," the lamenting woman informs us. Uys's parody draws on the kappiekommando's militant opposition to cultural liberalization and their fervent attempts to stem what they perceived as the erosion of traditional Afrikaner morality in the 1970s. "My country has become a whore. And she is lying and panting underneath dirty liberalism and his lies," she laments. With flailing, melodramatic gestures, she wails that her country has become a bad woman, or even worse, an unwed mother! Then she preaches to the crowd, claiming, "Dit *staan geskrywe* (So it is written), that he who doesn't stay with his own kind and with his own, reproduces and fucks forward, he shall perish!" Uys cleverly structures his language to sound like scripture, but then puns on words like *voortplant* (reproduces) and *voortneuk* (fuck forward) to undermine the kappiekommando's logic of racial purity and sexual morality. He adds a delightfully improper coda to the joke: "So it is written on the walls of the Women's Toilet at the Union Buildings!" She rants on: "The English are our arch enemies. The Catholics are the Antichrist. And the Jews are all thieves. The liberals stink. The enlightened Afrikaners stink even more. But the current National Party stinks like an abandoned nightsoil [sewage] wagon in the sun!" Here Uys makes a pointed jab at the government, but through the ironic mouthpiece of the Volksmoeder. Her racism, xenophobia, and moral outrage are turned, in the final line, toward the very system she proclaims to support; she is the cuckoo in the nest of the National Party. And he reminds his audience of the imperative of Afrikaners to see the failings of the apartheid system: "So it is written in Aunty de Villiers's Croxley fine-line notebook: Afrikaners are the chosen people and alone through us will the truth be carried forth." The "us" in this sentence draws the audience into the equation, asking them to consider what the "truth" is. She ends her scene by lamenting the diligent sons of Afrikanerdom who have betrayed their people through the Information Scandal: "The one after the other are standing up against the laws of apartheid. Well, you will also end up in the shit!" And then she dances across the stage, thrusting her hips from side to side as Queen's "Another One Bites the Dust" plays as a musical foreshadowing over the loudspeakers.

This scene relies on incongruity and ambiguity. The Volksmoeder is, on the surface, decrying the failure of politicians to uphold traditional Afrikaner values just as Uys (the man in drag) is using her language against her. "Let's face it," Uys says after he takes off the black kappie and dress and is once again a male performer on the stage, "I have had the best scriptwriters in the world. They keep giving me so much new material every day that I can keep on just adapting . . . and never die." Drag, or "gender transference humor" (Davis 1993), depends on stable notions of gender roles that are, in turn, disrupted by cross-dressing or gender-bending: a man in a dress, for instance. For Laurence Senelick, "the donning and doffing of the signs of gender [transvestism] offer an illusion of an essence. Its effects may be unsettling, even traumatizing, but since the effects derive from a semblance, they require an audience" (2000, 6). Thus, when audiences see a man in a dress, their stable notions of gender are disrupted. However, in Uys's case, Senelick suggests that "it was the character rather than the transvestism that was the real source of irritation. . . . White Afrikaner women of a certain class were venerated as the legendary belle had been in the Old South: by adopting the guise of one, Uys had simultaneously besmirched the image and become invulnerable behind it. . . . To prosecute Evita would not only look absurd, it would seem to be an assault on Boer womanhood" (2000, 475).

Dramaturgically, *Adapt or Dye* is self-reflexive; Uys makes several meta-commentaries about the revue or about himself as a performer to point to the constructed nature of the gendered and racial logics he satirizes. For example, as he removes his blond Noel Fine wig, and reveals his own balding head, Uys says, "Politics might be a pleasure, but most of the time it's a hell of a drag" (1982). Or in *Farce about Uys* (1983), Sophie the maid comments on De Kock's (Uys) unconvincing portrayal of his mother, Evita. "Jisis, De Kock," she admonishes him, pointing to the actor's cross-dressing, "stop walking like a man in drag, man. Your mother is a woman of experience. You walk like you're holding something between your knees" (Uys 1983).

Evita's celebrity affords Uys a uniquely influential position in South African culture. Daniel Lieberfeld claims that "Many Afrikaans women have been supportive purely because Evita represents something that Afrikaans women have not been allowed—a political voice" (1997, 63). As a strong female clown, grounded in a convincingly authentic performance of Afrikaner culture, Evita critiques the patriarchal center from within it. If the government keeps writing his material, then Afrikanerdom is writing his character, the double-edged diva. Evita embodies the sacred gendered space of the Afrikaner Mother who seems harmless because she is central to nationalist ethnomythology but who is precisely the site from which he can attack the system. Uys is a white, queer, Jewish-Calvinist, Afrikaans-speaking man, who *as a woman* takes South African politics by the horns. Under the guise of the Afrikaner Mother or Aunty, he emasculates apartheid by exposing it in all its stupidity, racism, sexism, and bigotry. Appropriating the patriarchal Volksmoeder, he parodies the category of Woman-as-subservient-being and inverts her power position. Evita is on the fringe of power, not included in it, yet she is the one wearing the pants and the one with the bullhorn to her lips. She speaks the subtext of a nation resisting its form of government.

Not being a woman, but being read and accepted as one, Uys's gender also points to the patriarchal loop in which South Africa operates: he can attack the government as a woman *because he is a man*. By playing on the fantasy of Woman as moral leader of the volk—like the rousing speeches the women give to spur on their men after the Bloukrans Massacre in *Bou van 'n nasie*—Uys offers his scathing critique. A self-admitted other on three counts—his Afrikanerdom, queerness, and Jewish heritage—Uys appropriated the central figure of Afrikaner nationalism—the Volksmoeder—in order to attack it during the 1980s. However, the gender politics here have worrisome implications for women in South African politics and culture. Uys can confront any issue head-on in his role as Evita, whereas Afrikaner women who attempt to speak out often get into trouble. Take Afrikaans author Marita van der Vyver, for example, whose 1992 best seller, *Griet skryf 'n sprokie* (*Griet Writes a Fairy Tale*), was adapted by Pierre von Pletzen for the stage in 1997. The story begins as Griet (whose name means something akin to Gretel), has just been asked to leave her husband's house (because she spends too much time writing and too little time on him and his home) and is struggling—with the help of friends, rebound lovers, psychologists, and her own imagination—to survive divorce, a suicide attempt, two miscarriages, and a stillbirth (all events written upon her body), to make a life on her own. Her childlessness forming a metaphor for the plight of women raised to be bearers of the volk but powerless to act, write, or articulate their own agendas, Griet is isolated, left out, not fully woman. Her survival mechanism is to process her life experience through fairy tales, writing and rewriting them to make meaning of her life, and to reject the system (and the men) that stifles her female identity.

Van der Vyver's work is sexually explicit, flouting Calvinist taboos such as masturbation, oral sex, lesbianism, and female orgasm in a reaction against the purity of the Volksmoeder archetype. Van der Vyver expertly blends the personal and the political into her fairy tales; the events of Griet's story begin in 1989 and end in February 1990, the time of Mandela's release from prison. Throughout the novel, Griet resists being included in politics even though she has friends committed to the antiapartheid struggle. Gradually, as she finds "a room of her own," she is forced to confront her country's politics in her stories.[30] The novel caused uproar among Afrikaners when it was published in 1992. Van der Vyver was hailed by many liberals as the Afrikaans Erica Jong. Conservatives, on the other hand, attacked the book as pornographic, and a heated debate over obscenity—in which woman was marked as either Virgin or Whore—ensued. One prominent Afrikaans magazine posed the question to its readers, "Are you a Griet?" (Hansen 1992). The Johannesburg City Council refused to allow the 1997 show's poster to be exhibited in public because it depicted a naked woman riding a horse with her breasts showing. Despite critique that such censorship violated the New Constitution (which includes the most tolerant and expansive Bill of Rights in the world), the council deemed the poster offensive and ruled that it could be put up only after the offending "bits" were covered with stickers. Thus, a woman like van der Vyver is publicly labeled immoral when she discusses sexuality candidly in Afrikaans. Moreover, all of the novel's political elements were eliminated in the stage production in favor of the coming-

of-age story. Uys—because he is a man—can speak freely even as he carica-
tures the sacred Volksmoeder figure. The performed Woman (Evita) is more
politically powerful than the flesh-and-blood woman (van der Vyver) who is
labeled a troublemaker. In the gendered schema of the Afrikaner, the icon
wields more power than a real woman, fiction overshadows reality.

FARCE ABOUT UYS (1983) AND
SKATING ON THIN UYS (1985)

Through Evita's extended family, Uys further interrogates Afrikaner culture
and mocks its sacred cows. In *Farce about Uys* (1983),[31] directed by Dawie
Malan at The Market and then at The Baxter, Uys first introduced Evita's extended family. The show plays out in the whitewashed Bapetikosweti am-
bassadorial residence, Blanche Noir, described by Sophie the black maid as
"a political asylum" (4). Uys plays De Kock, who in turn plays his "kaffir-
bashing" brother Izan, as well as his mother, Evita Bezuidenhout. By playing multiple roles throughout the play—and ending with Sophie (played by
Thoko Ntshinga) playing the Madam, Madame Quazilezi—this piece points
to the "arse about face" politics of real-life political role-playing and the
racial role reversals that are to come with apartheid's end. "Play a game,"
Sophie tells Sersant Uys (played by Chris Galloway, but named Uys, a common Afrikaans surname), "like politics—pretend" (38). The performativity
of these social types becomes evident when almost everyone is playing a
role, or playing someone else's role. Uys is both the mincing De Kock in
his pink leg warmers and the racist, leather-clad Izan. And he is neither,
for he is really Pieter-Dirk Uys, a real-life homosexual satirizing the system.
These characters were reprised in a Ster-Kinekor film titled *Skating on Thin
Uys* (1985), directed by Bromley Cawood, and starring Uys as Evita, Hasie,
Billie-Jeanne, De Kock, Izan, Bambi, and Ouma Ossewania. The title puns
on the Afrikaans word for shitting (*skyt*), as well as on the risk of censorship
and Uys's surname.

The opening sequence is framed as a news broadcast about Evita's life
produced by BAP TV. A black male narrator tells the story of Evangelie Poggenpol, who would later become the famous Evita Bezuidenhout.[32] She was
born in Bethlehem, a town in the Afrikaner bastion of the Orange Free State,
in 1935 in a time of upheaval, referencing the Afrikaner nationalist project
of the 1930s. "An outbreak of foot and mouth disease broke out in the Free
State," the narrator tells us, "and soon moved to Pretoria, where it became

policy." Evita's father was "unknown," suggesting her mother's loose sexuality and that scandal undergirds upstanding Evita's history. Her mother, Ossewania (Oxwagonia), was the organist (a sexual pun) in the local church, and Evita was good in biology, hybridity, and interbreeding of species. "But even then," Evita says directly to the camera as she references the apartheid discourse on racial purity, "I knew you can't cross a protea with a hydrangea."

In a humorous scene about her early acting career, Uys plays with the notion of repetition that was at the core of nationalist ideology. The narrator tells us how Evita made her "big break into *fillums* (films)" with *Boggel en die akkedis* (*Hump and the Lizard*, sexual puns) in 1956. We see a young Evita as a pregnant housewife, mixing a bowl of cake batter, saying to her husband: "Johan, wat bedoel jy?" (Johan, what do you mean? / you must be joking). Then, in *Meisie van my drome* (*Girl of My Dreams*) in 1957, Evita is a wife in a car, eating candy floss, asking her husband: "Tertius, my man, wat bedoel jy?" In *Duivelsvallei* (*Devil's Valley*) in 1958, Evita is now a dying nun, her body pierced with Zulu arrows, crying out to God: "Wat bedoel jyyyyy?" The joke is completed with the fourth iteration; in her screen test, Evita looks genuinely confused and asks Pierre de Wet, the director, "Mister de Wet, what do you mean? / you must be joking!" On the surface, the joke of this repeated refrain is about Evita as a ditsy woman, but her question carries a deeper satirical weight as Uys's broader social query about the meaning of the apartheid state. Uys points to the illogic of the regime with his "you must be joking" refrain.

Evita's biography includes many satirical jabs at apartheid. For instance, Uys plays with the double standard about miscegenation that obsessed the apartheid state. In a news report, titled "Trouble in Laagerfontein," Evita's husband Hasie Bezuidenhout is found in the back seat of his car with a black waitress and faces charges under the Immorality Act. Hasie is an upstanding leader of the community who, Evita tells us, "introduced the curfew, which kept the town black-free after sunset. And of course had that book, *Black Beauty*, removed from the library shelves." As the paparazzi hound them for answers, Hasie and Evita (both played by Uys) shoo the cameras off, frantically trying to deny the accusations against them. Evita then claims it was a ridiculous smear campaign from the so-called "English liberal press," just as government officials had during the Information Scandal in 1978. Then the real-life antiapartheid activist and politician Helen Suzman (1917–2009) tells us Evita was "absolutely and completely unbeatable. She knew all the tricks of the trade, especially the dirty tricks. The number of dead voters that she managed to persuade to come to the polls to vote for Mr. Bezuidenhout was remarkable!"

One of Evita's sons, De Kock (Uys again), is openly gay, dressed in rainbow leg warmers and a pink T-shirt reading "So Many Men, So Little Time." His sister, Billie-Jeanne (a pun on tennis player Billie-Jean King, the first professional female athlete to come out as lesbian), also played by Uys, is a country-and-western singer at the Glitter Pit (a reference to Sun City, the luxury resort casino in the apartheid-era Bantustan of Bophuthatswana; see Sannar 2011). As Billie-Jeanne (pronounced like the Afrikaans and French "Jean") and her band, BJ & Haar Koeksisters,[33] sings their hit song, "No Way," De Kock makes eyes at the handsome young Russian sailor wearing a "Navy" shirt. His friend Sergei (played by Scot Scott) is, in turn, making eyes at Billie-Jeanne. As BJ sings and twirls her white tassels, the camera pans across the diverse audience, which includes whites, blacks, Russians, Arabs, and Jews and signals the permissiveness and sexual fluidity possible in Sun City when the rest of South Africa was still under strict moral policing by the Nationalist Party. Billie-Jeanne sings, "I crave your kiss, I just can't rest" and engages the handsome Sergei eye to eye. The camera cuts from Sergei's doe eyes to Billie-Jeanne's (Uys's blue eye-shadowed peepers). And as she sings "No way, no way, no way, hey," Sergei mouths the words, his smoky eyes and parted lips signaling a coded homoeroticism between the two male actors (Uys and Scott). Sergei falls in love with Billie-Jeanne, and all the Russians end up in various beds at Blanche Noir the next morning.[34]

Skating on Thin Uys is also where Uys tackles whiteness head on. In a scene I call "Whitewashing the Nation," Ambassador Bezuidenhout partners with President Makoeloeli (played by Stephen Moloi), the titular head of Bapetikosweti, at a ceremony in which Evita is to bequeath a deserted mine dump to the homeland. As she signs over "this magnificent piece of land" to the black leader, Sersant Uys, the bumbling Secret Service Policeman (Chris Galloway) and BAP TV producer (Fats Dibeco) accidentally dig into an oil pipeline while trying to stabilize the flag pole that is blowing wildly in the wind and disrupting the ceremony. Thick black oil begins to coat the white Evita, Sersant Uys, and her ditsy assistant, Bokkie (Liz Meiring), who are all dressed entirely in white. The panicking Bokkie asks Evita, "Mevrou, what's happening? I'm becoming black!" (figure 17). As the white coffee cups become as black as the coffee in them, Bokkie fumbles around, unable to see,

Figure 17. Evita's assistant Bokkie (Lizz Meiring) blackwashed in homeland oil in *Skating on Thin Uys.* © 1985. PD Uys Productions CC. Courtesy of Pieter-Dirk Uys.

as her sunglasses and face are covered in black oil. "Mevrou, what's happening?" screams Bokkie, "I'm going blind!" Here Uys indexes the color-obsessed blindness of apartheid's logic. Faced with their greatest fear—of mixing with, or God forbid, becoming black—the white characters are sent into a panic.

One of the central black characters in the film is Sophie (Thoko Ntshinga), the all-knowing domestic worker. At Blanche Noir, Sophie is dusting the furniture around the aged Hasie, who is writing his memoir but keeps muddling his facts. Hasie speaks his notes into a voice recorder, talking of the "separate development policy." Sophie then corrects him, reminding him that it was called "apartheid, Doctor. The fancy name only comes later. After Verwoerd." It is Sophie and Leroi Makoeloeli (Winston Gama), the president's prodigal son, who concoct a scheme to get land in exchange for rights to the oil of Bapetikosweti. "They will do anything to get oil," says Sophie. So Leroi suggests, "Let's make them an offer they can't accept." Sophie manipulates Evita, the white madam, into seeing a local witch doctor for advice on how to handle the oil saga. "Sophia," asks Evita, "what would you do if you were me?" And Sophie replies, throwing one of the piece's most direct political punches, "If madam will forgive me, this a black homeland. Madam must stop thinking like a white. Madam must start thinking like a black.

Madam might think that is a contradiction in terms. But Madam, believe me, here, logic, white logic, and apartheid are not the answers." In 1985, Uys has a black maid speaking truth directly to power. Sophie plays ironically with the loaded term *homeland*, with its dual associations with Bantustans and white claims to the land.

Evita ventures into Johannesburg to consult the witch doctor, an accomplished psychiatrist who quickly converts his office by hanging animal skins, burning herbs, and throwing the bones while cauldrons bubble and drums play in the background so the "big white Madam" can experience her faked witch-doctor reading. Groaning over the bones, the *sangoma* (traditional healer) tells her that a Bezuidenhout must marry a Makoeloeli in exchange for the oil; that Evita's white daughter Billie-Jeanne must marry President Makeloeli's black son Leroi. Here the joke set up early in the film gets its hilarious payoff as Evita asks, incredulously, "Wat bedoel jy?" (What do you mean? / Are you joking?) Traumatized by the thought of breaking the Mixed Marriage Act, let alone the Immorality Act, Evita laments to Sarsant Uys, "Dit is de einde!" (This is the end!). And Sophie, who has been hiding in the wings whispers, "No, Madam. This is the beginning of the end." Sophie's suggestion in 1985 that apartheid was coming to an end would, of course, become reality less than a decade later.

UYS POST-1994

In 1994, the year Mandela was elected and the country shifted from apartheid into the unknown territory of a new democracy, Pieter-Dirk Uys partnered with M-NET, the subscription-funded television channel, on a two-part series in which South Africa's grand dame would interview real-life figures. Called Evita's *Funigalore*,[35] a pun on *fanagalo* (the Zulu, Xhosa, Sotho, English, and Afrikaans pidgin spoken in the mining industry), it featured Evita meeting famous figures in their homes, talking about the transition, dispelling myths, and making a few jokes in the process. Uys describes it as his "honeymoon with hope" after a lifetime of fighting for democracy. "*Funigalore* was not satire. It wasn't even meant to be investigative journalism," claims Uys. "It didn't have brooding anger. It had a gentle stroke, a light tickle" (1995, 262). Now that the democratically elected government was in place, Uys says he "wasn't going to lift up my blood-stained toothpick and stab them in the cocktail of life." Instead he wanted to celebrate the heroes, to "applaud a culture of life" after the exhausting "culture of death" of the

Figure 18.
Pieter-Dirk Uys
as Evita and Piet
Koornhof as
himself in their
own dangerous
liaison. © 1995.
Courtesy of
Pieter-Dirk Uys.

apartheid years (1995, 262). His multiracial guests included apartheid activ-ists Joe Slovo, Mac Maharaj, Jay Naidoo, and Tokyo Sexwale; "newly hatched and hatching super-comrades of the new democracy" (Uys 1995, 16) like Cyril Ramaphosa (ANC deputy minister), Terror Lekota (premier of the Free State), Frene Ginwala (Speaker of Parliament), Patricia de Lille (Pan African-ist Congress leader), and Tony Leon (leader of the Democratic Party); whites from both the old and the new guards, Pik Botha (former minister of foreign affairs) and Roelf Meyer (leader for the Nationalist Party); and, of course, the "world's greatest hero" (Uys 1995, 255), Nelson Mandela himself.[36]

The show positioned Evita, the ambassador and MP's wife (the ultimate insider), as "rising from the ashes of her former fascism like a phoenix with lip gloss" (Uys 1995, 5) and taking on the new government as she did the apartheid regime in the past. As a political comic, "all parties must 'belong' to me as the essence of my material," writes Uys (1995, 7). It was time, Uys writes, "to take Mevrou across her Rubicon. . . . She had to be seen to make the giant leap for Afrikanerdom, from racist to clenched fist!" (Uys 1995, 15).[37] How apt that a cross-dresser—a hybrid figure who embodied pluralities—midwifed the cultural crossing from apartheid to democracy. Claiming herself as the Africanized "iVita b'Zuidenhout," this "reborn democrat" (Uys 1995, 5, 18) became the embodiment of the old guard adapting to the new dispensation, who is able to prod-while-praising as a man-in-a-dress playing the Mother-of-the-Nation.

In the episode with Terror Lekota, the new black premier of the conservative Orange Free State [now just the "Free State," losing the colonial "Orange" from its title], Uys plays with the cultural and color divides that were the obsession of the apartheid regime and that the new "Rainbow Nation" aimed to dispel. Evita says to Lekota, "For so many years, your people said 'Amandla' and our people said 'Vrystaat,' and both words meant the same thing."[38] Then Lekota replies, completely unprompted, "Now today we say 'Amandla-Vrystaat!'" (Uys 1995, 59). Evita, the ever-hospitable Afrikaner woman, offers to pour tea for the premier, asking him, "Do you take it black or white?" Lekota replies, "I take it with milk." "Oh? White!" says Evita, and then, murmuring under her breath, "That's nice to hear." Then she coos, "Do you take any sugar?" One teaspoon, he indicates to the bowl of unprocessed sweetener. "So it's black tea, white tea, and brown sugar!" exclaims Evita with delight.

For all "its camp and fantasy, this was *détente* in the making," writes Uys of the impact of the *Funigalore* series. "Many [white, conservative Free State] officials would only allow the black politician into their domain because he was brought there by Evita Bezuidenhout! The two sides were actually meeting for the first time. This was true Reconstruction and Development" (Uys 1995, 69).[39] This scenario also is an example of Evita Bezuidenhout's effect. As Davis suggests, the impact of humor depends on incongruity. What is more incongruous than this scenario of a queer Afrikaner in drag bringing a black politician into the heart of whiteness and the conservative community of the Free State? Or the image of two "extraordinary women" in the episode with Speaker of Parliament and Women's National Coalition leader, Frene Ginwala? The two women are embodied incongruities — "one not white; the other not a woman!" (Uys 1995, 78).

Uys plays with gender expectations in his work, creating ambiguous and incongruous moments that place marked and encoded bodies in situations to reveal new meanings and new possible readings. For example, during a break between takes in the Houses of Parliament with Ginwala, Uys visits the men's toilet to shave his five o'clock shadow. In the spotless, museum-like men's room, where Verwoerd, Vorster, Botha, and their ilk used to urinate, Uys is in complete Evita costume and wig, shaving cream all over his/her chin. Suddenly, Uys writes,

> A man in a grey suit walks in confidently, already with one hand going towards his zip. He glances to his left and sees a familiar woman in a sari. Shaving! His need dries up. He turns and flees!
>
> I giggle and shave on. . . . Another man in a grey suit enters. He gives me a casual glance as he walks to the porcelain.
>
> "Môre, Mevrou! (Morning, Madam!)" he says cheerfully.
>
> "Môre, Meneer! (Morning, Sir!)" comes from behind the razor. (Uys 1995, 83)

Another episode focuses on former foreign minister Pik Botha, who Uys says "treated Evita like he would any attractive woman. Disconcerting, but rather sweet" (Uys 1995, 128), and of whom Evita constantly says, "Pik faks my elke middag teen die tyd" (Pik faxes [pronounced "fucks"] me this time every day; Uys 1995, 61). After hunting with Pik Botha, the minister shows Evita his collection of prehistoric artifacts. "And as you know, man, *Homo sapiens*, only appeared on earth for the first time about fifty thousand years ago," Botha schools Evita. "Before him was his predecessor, *Homo habilis*, *Homo erectus*, and *Homo neanderthalensis*." For Uys "this cluster of homos couldn't go by unzipped," so Evita coos ironically, "But I am so pleased to hear that the Homos have been here from the beginning!" much to the surprise of Botha, who "looks somewhat startled to have his prehistorics painted pink" (1995, 207).

Running through the *Funigalore* series is a metacommentary on performance. Uys's written account frames much of the series through the language of performance, marking how South Africans all play parts in the larger theatre of the country's sociopolitics and culture. Uys recounts the many unscripted scenes that required his interviewees to improvise and "play their parts." All her interviewees played along with the silliness and spirit of mockery, making coy or sexual innuendos with Evita and fabricating mutual histories together on the fly. When Evita goes to Robben Island with former prisoner Mac Maharaj, the two don Groucho Marx disguises before boarding the ferry in Cape Town Harbor that goes to the island out in the bay. This act of disguising simultaneously references Evita's early theatrical career, Uys's drag practice, and Maharaj's history of donning disguises to evade the secret police as an antiapartheid activist in the 1970s and '80s. "I don't think anybody recognized us," sighs Evita with relief. "We got away with it," whispers Mac, playing along. Then he improvises, "I was worried that your dress is so obvious. That they might think that you were disguised and that you were really a man!" (Uys 1995, 115). Revealing that Uys is in drag, Maharaj marks the performed nature of all sociopolitical roles. Then Uys describes suddenly having a change of heart and "feeling like a real *poephol* (arsehole)" once on the island in the "amphitheatre of protest" that had been the site of real suffering for Mac and his compatriots; his "courage seeping," Uys feels the conceit of Evita in the ghosted space of Robben Island to be "so feeble, so trite" (Uys 1995, 116–117). But it is Mac who reminds Evita that "in all conditions of adversity, human beings have a capacity to partly grapple with that adversity by resorting to humor. And sometimes it's a wry sort of humor" (Uys 1995, 123).

The opening sequence of the second season of *Funigalore* featured Evita and Piet Koornhof, former National Party cabinet minister and ambassador to the United States from 1987 to 1991, in an absurd pas de deux modeled around Pierre Choderlos de Laclos's 1782 novel *Les liaisons dangereuses* (figure 18). Koornhof was an avid fan of Evita Bezuidenhout and was one of the few government officials who actually came to see himself lampooned in Uys's revues. Uys describes the scene: "The minuet starts. . . . Piet and Evita touch hands, twirl around each other, never break eye contact. She simmers and boils, he giggles and counts. His pink tongue peeps out from between his smiling lips. She opens her fan. . . . It is bizarre and strangely beautiful" (Uys 1995, 132). The absurdity of this scenario lies in the fact that a real-life politician would willingly parody himself and stage a blatantly queer scene with a man in a dress. Yet Koornhof endorsed the performance and put himself, and all the baggage he represented as an apartheid official, within such a performative frame to be laughed at and simultaneously admired. Later in the day, Evita in her Marie Antoinette gown, approaches Koornhof during some downtime in the shoot. "Gosh, Dr. Piet, look at us now!" says Evita in Afrikaans. And Koornhof, who is wearing a yellow brocaded outfit with a snow-white coiffed wig, replies playfully, "Yeah, this is now genuinely a bloody tomfoolery (*geneukery*)." The word *geneukery* has a double meaning as fooling around, both in the clowning and sexual senses. That a former cabinet minister (who married a coloured woman after his first wife's death) would be seen in a scene of *geneukery* with a man in drag was both revolutionary and reassuring. *Funigalore* showed that Afrikaners, even those from the highest echelons of the regime, possessed a sense of humor.

In his reflection on Evita's *Funigalore*, Uys speaks candidly about how the guise of Evita allowed him to "re-educate himself" of the many apartheid prejudices he carried with him. "I was born racist," he confesses. "How could it be otherwise, with the structures of apartheid so superbly woven around me? Not like rusty bars of a prison, but as silken cords of something even more effectively constraining. Education. Religion. Attitude. Opinion. Fear. . . . I am a racist; therefore I will never allow myself to be racist" (Uys 1995, 263). *Funigalore* was more than "a comedy turn with a man in drag," claims Uys. "In its own carnival way, [it was] a contribution to the Reconstruction and Development Process," for, as Madiba himself said, "Evita says things that people listen to" (Uys 1995, 239, 264, 245). Uys writes that the series made him realize that despite the flawed political system that had been scarred by apartheid, the new democracy was in good hands. He was confident that "the healing energy of democracy will prevail—if we out here in the real world can stop being comfortable, frightened by the non-existent bogeymen created on an A4 page by the political pornographers of the past" (Uys 1995, 264). With *Funigalore*, Evita made her transition—mirroring the macrocosmic changes around her—from "relic-in-opposition" to a direct involvement with the Government of National Unity, "this gnu that she helped create." In this 1994–1995 TV series, Uys committed to continue Evita's damning with faint praise or, if needed, damning them to "the hell of humor through flattery," a promise he has not failed to keep.

Since the transition of power in 1994, Uys has arguably had an even greater impact on South African culture than he did under apartheid. Despite claims and fears that he would be out of work once apartheid had fallen, he has continued to perform in the new democracy. Satiric endings, suggests Griffin, "generally eschew closure, partly because the satirist's anger has not been resolved, partly because closure seems too contrived" (1994). Uys is one of contemporary South Africa's most outspoken activists, putting his efforts into voter education, campaigning, and AIDS education. In 2007, Australian Julian Shaw made his directing debut with a documentary film about Uys's activism called *Darling! The Pieter-Dirk Uys Story*. In advance of the 2014 election, Uys penned a piece in the *Cape Times* encouraging young South Africans, who have never lived under legalized racism, to vote. "The born-frees could change the future of our democracy. If they register to vote. If they cast their ballot. If they understand that the vote is sacred and secret," Uys writes ("You Have a Voice" 2013). He is currently rallying the people to exercise their democratic rights, just as he did for the historic election in 1994. However, some of the hope Uys held during the filming of *Funigalore* has been challenged as the South African democracy has started to show its flaws; he is particularly concerned about rampant government corruption and the erosion of free speech. In his sold-out show at the 2012 National Arts Festival, *An Audience with Pieter-Dirk EISH!*, he reminded audience members, especially younger ones, that apartheid could very easily return under another name. He defended the freedom of expression guaranteed by the Constitution, particularly of artistic creativity, without which, he warned, festivals like the one in Grahamstown may cease to exist.[40] In a piece he wrote for the *South African* in September 2013, Uys said, "Unfortunately the Rainbow Nation is showing shades of grey." Freedom of expression and speech are being threatened "by draconian laws giving government rights of control that echo our desperate and dark past," he warned (2013a). "Democracy demands freedom of choice. Freedom of expression. Freedom of speech. Freedom to mock and freedom to embrace," Uys wrote earlier, in June 2013. "Citizens of a democracy always deserve what they get. If we all are involved with the protection of that democracy, the news will be encouraging. If we sit back, whinge and whine, sigh and snooze, the country will be lost" (2013b).

Despite his misgivings about the future of his country, Uys remains optimistic, as his poetic piece in *Die Burger* in September 2013 affirms. He writes, and I translate:

My South Africa is exciting, frightening, hot, cold, dry, wet, hilly, flat, crowded, empty, arrogant, friendly, dangerous, gentle, non-racial, racist, wealthy, poor, healthy, sick, hopeful, corrupt, unbearable and addictive.

My South Africa has not forgotten the past while looking forward to the future.

My South Africa is where no democrat has been before. It is the blueprint for hope where everything once looked hopeless. It is building a future in the faded footprint of despair.

My South Africa is a nineteen-year-old teenager on the edge of adulthood with all the confusions, expectations, demands, fears and fantasies that entails. (Uys 2013d)

Celebrating the complexities of South African culture, Uys frames the democracy as a teenager coming of age; South Africa is still in a state of becoming. Whiteness, too, is always in states of becoming, constantly morphing and being checked as it articulates itself. It is precisely because of his whiteness—and his privileged status as a white, male, Afrikaner—that Pieter-Dirk Uys has been able to stand in opposition to white supremacy, to begin to untie those "silken cords" of racism that kept whiteness in power, through humor and satire. Because he is a white man in drag, cloaking his whiteness within the skirts of the whitest woman in the land, he was able to say things during apartheid that no black person could say without violent repercussions. Because he is a white man in drag in the new democracy, he is able to say things about the black ANC government's failures that no other whites feel comfortable saying. His whiteness and masculinity in drag destabilize and make his position fluid, allowing him to critique both regimes.

So what model might Uys offer for whiteness in the postcolony? Querying, and queering, the sacred cows of his culture through satiric humor allows him to puncture the invisible facade of whiteness and make its racism visible. Once shown to be absurd, or shamed into consciousness, his audiences, including members of the government he critiques, are asked to think critically about power and their positions of privilege within it. The extent to which they then effect change, or not, marks the limits of satire's effects on political regimes. I argue Uys is effective because he is not merely a clown who "takes the mickey" but never really goes for the jugular, as Robert Kirby suggested (Trillin 2004). Instead, the combination of his satiric critique *as*

Evita Bezuidenhout with his political and health-related activism *as Pieter-Dirk Uys* makes him a vital moral compass for South Africans. His work teaches that while satire and humor are important performance strategies toward critiquing whiteness, they are not enough; to dismantle whiteness requires material and political actions as well as cultural or symbolic interventions.

Abject Afrikaner, Iconoclast Trekker

PETER VAN HEERDEN'S PERFORMANCE

INTERVENTIONS WITHIN THE LAAGERS

OF WHITE MASCULINITY

If Deon Opperman works within the world of nostalgia and memory, and Uys sends up whiteness satirically, then performance artist Peter Van Heerden offers another possible answer for white subjects in the postcolony: to interrogate and question Afrikaner history and the logic that supports it through iconoclastic interventions that critique Afrikanerdom in contemporary South Africa. Focusing on the Afrikaner male, Van Heerden creates provocative performance installations around taboo subjects that involve visceral abjections of his own body and ask his audiences to reflect on outdated narratives of the past and to imagine new ways of being in a multicultural democracy. In this chapter, I weave Julia Kristeva's work on abjection (1982) with my own formulation of betrayal, and examine how Van Heerden's iconoclastic interventions offer critiques of Afrikanerdom in contemporary South Africa.[1] I unpack several of his major pieces, including *So is 'n os gemaak* (*Thus Is an Ox Made*, 2004), *Bok* (*Ram/Goat*, 2006), *Totanderkuntuit* (*Throughtheothercuntout*, 2008), and a one-man piece about masculinity called *Ubuntu* (2010) that he performed (and I helped produce) in the United States.

Aiming to activate change in the world, Van Heerden works through his own body, which is marked by, and carries the baggage of, his upbringing under apartheid. Born in Johannesburg in 1973 to an Afrikaner father and a Brazilian mother, Van Heerden, like many white South Africans, was a child of privilege, schooled at the all-boys St. Peter's Prep and St. Stithians College before attending Rhodes University for a BA in Drama and Classical Civilization. At university he came to political and artistic consciousness, and committed himself to working through the performing arts to address challenging, often unspoken, social and cultural issues impacting South Africans in the new democracy, especially white identity and masculinity.

Van Heerden focuses on the Afrikaner male, a figure containing a mixture of registers and multiple truths that collide within and upon his body. Historically, the Afrikaner male presents a figure laden with negative associations—as a racist patriarch, he blindly and bullheadedly dominates everything in his path, be it women, children, black Africans, or animals. Yet he is also heroic, a risktaker, trekking forward through challenge, stalwart protector of his volk, levelheaded, thoughtful and a creative problem-solver. Van Heerden wrestles with this sense of discordance through performance. He works in close collaboration with social activist and farmer André Laubscher, and the two present work as the erf (81) cultural collective. Van Heerden is a *beeldestormer* (iconoclast), literally an image breaker, someone who attacks cherished ideas or traditional institutions to expose outdated beliefs; he not only reveals, but also explodes, familiar images of Afrikanerdom to reconfigure the ways in which white South Africans can participate as citizens in this young democracy.

Concerned with South African masculinity and race in a moment when white men have undergone a seismic (symbolic if not material) shift in power, Van Heerden's work circulates around the question of how the privileged perform themselves once their privilege is deflated. His work demands a reimagining of old identity formations, a deep rethinking of possibilities, to forge a future for all South Africans in this multicultural, multiracial society.

"I have always been fascinated by the past, by old things, and by the residue the past leaves on our bodies," Van Heerden told me as he was preparing for his one-man show, Ubuntu,[2] at the University of Minnesota in January 2010. In order to work through the past, create change for the future, and rid ourselves of outdated habits of the past, Van Heerden believes we require a process of catharsis, the kind of visceral encounter with embodied ideas that performance art offers. Van Heerden makes whiteness strange to itself in order to see it for what it is. His performance art creates spaces for catharsis by offering both the performer and audiences a space to journey through ideas, identities, symbols, visual and visceral images, and to reflect on our own reactions to what we encounter through his work. "As new places and spaces are created and discovered," suggests Van Heerden, "so [my] body [and those in the audience] has to negotiate its behavior to the rules of these new spaces; and in so doing develops new behavioral vocabularies that will manifest, inscribe and imprint on the inner landscape of the[se] bod[ies]" (2004). Van Heerden uses performance, that "pedagogically inflected field of play in which culture is liminal or liminoid and available for intervention" (Dolan 1993, 431–432), as the space in which to catalyze South Africans into examining their (white) culture and to work toward change.

SO IS 'N OS GEMAAK (2004)

In his first major solo piece, *So is 'n os gemaak* (*Thus Is an Ox Made*), which premiered at the 2004 National Arts Festival in Grahamstown, Van Heerden dangled by his feet from an ox yoke, the words *bok* (ram), *skyt* (shit), *Piet* (Pete), *volk* (people/nation), *harnass* (yoke), and *bitch* scrawled across his naked body (figure 19). Thrashing his head through a large pile of earth below him, he struggled to breathe, drowning in the soil of his birth, swallowing mouthfuls of dirt, regurgitating, choking, breathing. Then, with his testicles tied to the yoke, he pulled it forward, literally *voortrekking*, straining with and against his manhood, caught between the past and the future in a gesture of castration, tension, risk, and masculine vulnerability. Through images of struggle and determination, Van Heerden offers up his white masculinity in a ritual sacrifice. "It is only through abjection of white masculinity," he claims (2004, quoting Van Der Watt 2003), "that a new practice can be celebrated. The process of holding up whiteness for exploration is not in praise of its hegemony, but rather as a condition for sacrifice.... This ritual sacrifice of whiteness must become a feast and celebration, to enable the formulation of a new non-racialised practice." Holding his own body, particularly his own genitalia, in such tension, Van Heerden demonstrates that he *has the balls* to model the sacrifice required for a transformation of whiteness. Often called a *soutpiel*[3] as a child by Afrikaners who read him as "one of them" through his Afrikaans surname, even though he was raised in an English-speaking household (as I was), Van Heerden also offers his hybrid identity up for scrutiny.

Below, I trace Van Heerden's performance strategy of attracting audiences and then refracting what they encounter, as well as his use of iconoclasm, wordplay, strategic blasphemy, and physical abjection in his 2008 performance installation, *Totanderkuntuit*. Situating his performances in the larger genealogy of Afrikaner self-presentation, Van Heerden operates within the

Figure 19.
Peter Van
Heerden in
*So is 'n os
gemaak.* © 2004
T. J. Lemon.
Courtesy of
Peter Van
Heerden.

notion of the laager and works through the shame and betrayal that permeate much of Afrikaner culture. Through my position as an insider/outsider,
I examine his challenges to audiences to rethink their own positions in relation to South African history and Afrikaner identity and his interrogation
of Afrikaner male whiteness.

TOTANDERKUNTUIT (2008)
It is Good Friday, 2008, the first day of South Africa's annual Afrikaans-
language Klein Karoo Nasionale Kunstefees (KKNK)[4] in the dusty ostrich

town of Oudtshoorn, in the Western Cape. The words *Wit Kaffir* (White Nigger) are scribbled in black ink across a middle-aged white man's chest. Van
Heerden is blindfolded and strapped to a cruciform scaffold in the blaz-
ing sun. The crucifixion scene is part of his nine-day installation, a dissi-
dent passion play, called *Totanderkuntuit* (literally, "Through-the-other-
cunt-out").[5] By crucifying privilege and abjecting whiteness, Van Heerden
is engaged in what I call acts of *volksveraad* (race betrayal), that reveal the
symbolic and material privilege through which white men have dominated
Southern Africa since the seventeenth century.

Van Heerden begins by literally and figuratively stringing up the Afrikaner male, putting him under performative scrutiny. When asked by observers what he is doing, he speaks in antiquated High Dutch, telling them,
"Ye Olde Voortrekkers, who for a long time hath been wankers, hath now
trekked together to set up a laager here." Below Peter on the cross, a *dominee*
or preacher (played by André Laubscher) in top hat and tails gives a mock
sermon on the history of white settlement at the Cape of Good Hope. Reactions to the crucifixion scene were mixed, ranging between appalled outrage, confusion, and smirks of acknowledgment.[6] Some irate bystanders
shouted Calvinist warnings of eternal damnation and divine punishment
at the two performers: "God will punish you! You devils will burn in Hell!"
Their anger was fueled by two elements: religious blasphemy and racial betrayal. To call a white man a kaffir is the ultimate insult, equating the Self
with the degraded Other. And to enact a mock crucifixion is to profane the
sacred, to make this private Christian ritual a public spectacle. Such acts of
betrayal were exactly what Van Heerden intended. He slaughters sacred cows
and offers up their innards for our inspection, reflection, and encounter.
In these viscera white South Africans may see another way of being, see
themselves from the inside out. Playing on Christian associations of Christ
dying for the world's sins, his use of a crucifixion might also evoke a sense
of redemption for white masculinity. He calls upon all South Africans—
regardless of race, class, or creed—to engage in "acts of transformative behaviour" (Van Heerden 2004), and he specifically models this for white men
by embodying this transformation with his own body.

Any group that predicates its existence on a totalizing understanding of
belonging and the active exclusion of nonconforming ideologies sets itself
up for betrayal. In fact, whiteness itself, which is predicated on a totalizing
understanding of identity and the active exclusion of nonconforming iden-

tities, might also be said to set itself up for betrayal.[7] By betrayal, I refer to the *violation of a presumptive social contract* and to a *revelation*, the giving away too much, letting slip a secret, or the laying bare of something. At its core, betrayal produces moral and psychological conflict, exposing a system's flaws. The apartheid state, built on the idea of racial purity, could not tolerate race betrayal and legislated against dissent, intermarriage, and assembly across color lines. The state's draconian police system ensured that those who betrayed the state were summarily punished, silenced, or disappeared.

As counterhegemonic interventions, Van Heerden's performances invite audiences to engage in acts of *volksveraad*, to question and examine the difficult truths of white privilege and colonial, patriarchal power. For those Afrikaners who remain committed to the idea of the laager—even in post-1994 South Africa—betrayal of the volk, or breaching of the laager, causes fear, anxiety, and a recircling of the wagons. Van Heerden's performances incite such anxiety for conservative viewers. Yet simultaneously, his work allows sympathetic viewers, or those willing to entertain uncertainty and to question their positions, to vicariously unburden themselves of past baggage through performance and to discuss new possibilities for their future as ethical participants in a democratic, multicultural South Africa.

The man playing the dominee is social activist André Laubscher,[8] Van Heerden's coconspirator in the erf (81) cultural collective, whose mission is to "expose the past in the present" and to "chip away at" racism through "a new South African cultural dialogue" engaged in *saamtrekking*, "journeying together," and *saampraat*, "together-talk" (erf [81] cultural collective 2008). "Three hundred and fifty years of Bibles and bullets and the *dop* system[9] and look at it now," Laubscher preaches. "When our Jan[10] landed in Table Bay with his three little ships full of brutal outsiders and illiterate rapists, there were golden people living here . . . for thousands of years in relative peace. Only a psychopath can believe that this 'civilization' is progress" (Van Heerden and Laubscher 2008c, 1). Embodying the persona of the Calvinist dominee, whose fire and brimstone are deemed the direct words of God by many Afrikaner traditionalists, Laubscher invites the audience to consider the impact of the "brutal outsiders" on indigenous people at the moment of encounter and through the apartheid era. He asks his audience to consider the psychopathology of the European colonial project, with its religious (Bibles), military (bullets), and social (*dop* system) forms of domination. And he includes the audience in a community of cultural familiarity—"our

Jan," he says—implicating contemporary South Africans in his project of historical scrutiny.

Approaching the *Totanderkuntuit* encampment, I notice a huge ox-wagon and the Vierkleur flag. As I described in chapter 1, the ox-wagon is a potent icon of national identity. The orange, white, blue, and green Vierkleur marks the independence of the Boer Republics from British rule and is a coded marker of whiteness. As I near the performance space—an open plot of land by the edge of a cement drainage creek, fenced in on four sides with wire and corrugation, with a farm gate onto St. John's Street—flag and wagon read to me as a right-wing encampment of the Afrikaner Weerstandsbeweging (AWB), a paramilitary neofascist organization committed to preserving the Afrikaner Nation, and led, until his murder in April 2010, by Eugène Terre'Blanche.[11]

Knowing the KKNK festival to attract a certain ilk of Afrikaners [bottle-throwing racists had pelted Miriam Makeba, South Africa's first lady of jazz, as she performed here in 1997],[12] I assumed that what was playing out before me was a right-wing attempt to reclaim the "glory" of the past. My heart pounding, I approach a bearded and khaki-clad Van Heerden by his ox-wagon to hear what this lunatic was on about. Putting on my best American accent—to shield myself from being affiliated in any way with these apparent AWB supporters—I *assk* [American inflection] don't *ahsk* [British / South African inflection] Peter what is happening. "We are trying to suggest that there is something wrong with our social system," he told me, "through a living performance art installation that tackles issues about our cultural identity, both now and in the past. We've brought a wagonload of questions to the festival."

Each of *Totanderkuntuit*'s nine days was bookended by a flag raising and lowering. These militarized acts framed the installation dramaturgically, structuring a more formalized playing space out of a found space. The flag protocol associated the space with Afrikaner nationalism and the apartheid state while simultaneously creating a sense of ceremony and marking this as a site for, and of, performance.[13] The scene I encountered was laden with highly charged objects, the symbolic capital of Afrikaner culture. Imagine a Voortrekker encampment, complete with military-style canvas tents, a two-ton vintage ox-wagon, campfire kitchen with three-legged *potjie* cooking pot, and three potbellied piglets. Adorning the space were several iterations of the South African flag (the new ANC flag; the *oranje-blanje-blou* of the apartheid era; and the Vierkleur flag of the old Boer Republic)[14] and standard issue bushveld memorabilia—a rack of kudu horns, a cow's pelvic bones, and a springbok skin. The scene could have been the set for Deon Opperman's *Donkerland*.

Van Heerden's installation involved a series of iconoclastic (*beeldestorming*) performances, many framed by religious references. Like stations of the cross, each day was dedicated to a particular topic drawn from Afrikaner history, mythology, and lore while simultaneously addressing pressing, often taboo, contemporary issues. Day 1 was called *Dag van die kruis* (*Day of the Cross*) and consisted of the crucifixion scene described above. Then there followed eight additional days, in order: *Die laaste maragmaal* (*The Last Lunch*), *Boeremagdag* (*Boer Power Day*),[15] *Familiedag* (*Family Day*), *F.A.K.- plaas dag* (*F.U.K. Farm Day*),[16] *Bloedrivierdag* (*Blood River Day*),[17] *Kunstedag* (*Art Day*), *Heldedag* (*Heroes Day*), and *Geloftedag* (*Day of the Covenant*). By using a Christian structure and scripture, Van Heerden was citing the logic of organized religion (in this case, Dutch Reformed Calvinism) that has historically been used by white Europeans to justify their exploits in Africa. Through such citations, he then exploded these religious icons, revealing the ugly truths about the cost of white privilege. For example, an inflatable sheep circulated throughout the installation, particularly on the days dedicated to family murder and the sexual abuse of children.[18] Scrawled across its flanks in black ink were the words *Die lam van God* (*The lamb of God*). Fusing an inflatable sex toy with a lofty religious image asked audiences to consider how Calvinism and sexuality function under Afrikaner ideology to create dysfunctional relationships within families. As the sex toy sheep was made of white plastic, it also made an iconoclastic suggestion of "fucking whiteness."

Totanderkuntuit was not the first time Van Heerden had engaged in provocative acts and performative race betrayals. In 2005–2006, he created *Bok* (*Ram/Goat*), a piece commissioned by the KZNSA Gallery for their Young Artist Project in Durban, and he also performed it for the FNB Dance Umbrella in Johannesburg that year. In *Bok*, Van Heerden staged several mock executions of the Boer by having his blindfolded and shackled body pelted with sacks of white lime and flour. A video, by filmmaker Brad Schaffer, captured the piece in extreme close-ups. The white powder explodes against Van Heerden's naked chest; a chair falls as his body collapses, we watch as he struggles for breath. Inspired by a photograph of the execution of a Boer War General by the British, this performance literally *scapegoated*[19] his white body; a body marked and laden with baggage; a body contested, vulnerable, visceral, capable of remorse and pain. Multiple echoes of whiteness permeate the piece: the white blindfold covering his eyes, the white lime that exploded over his body, clinging to the hairs of his beard and marking his white skin with yet another layer of whiteness. *Bok* is anchored in the shame of the Afrikaner past—the Boer War defeats at the end of the nineteenth century, a pivotal rallying point for Afrikaner nationalists. Simultaneously, *Bok* excavates the white man's position now, asking if we ought to "execute" the Afrikaner for the horrors of the past, and if so, what part of that identity must die and what can remain a part of a South African future? White Afrikaners in the audience vicariously vomit and gag as saliva and breath ooze from Peter's mouth; audience members take the blows of the repeated sacks of venom, hatred, shame, and anger into the body politic as his individual body absorbs the shock of them.

In *Totanderkuntuit*, as in much of their other work, Van Heerden and Laubscher used several tactics that I will call the attract/refract dyad to draw in their audiences.[20] They performed outwardly alluring acts or they set up installations of familiar signs and tropes to pique audience curiosity and bring them into the performance space.[21] Then, once inside, they worked on refracting ideas, illuminating issues, or interrogating the familiar symbols, asking visitors to think about, reflect on, and articulate what they experienced, saw, and believed. For example, the giant ox-wagon and the flags were potent symbols that incited spectator curiosity. Inflatable sex dolls hanging from a tree on *Familiedag* were also strategic lures. And André often played the part of the *laerpredikant* (the camp preacher), while Peter performed the role of *laerkommandant* (the camp's commanding officer).[22] These two figures are familiar to Afrikaners and carry with them a certain degree of authority. Visitors would approach these two performers with a desire to either identify with (attraction) or resist that authority (repulsion). A young man saluted Peter as he entered the space; a woman deflected her eyes in deference as she spoke to André the *predikant*; at first, I feared Peter's bearded character. Once inside the world of *Totanderkuntuit*, audiences experienced mixed metaphors—the "lam van God," André the patriarchal Boer in khaki uniform cooking food for hungry children of color, a white man on a cross with the words *Wit Kaffir* across his chest—that asked them to consider history, racism, the power of symbols, and their own beliefs about race, religion, whiteness, and Others. This type of work is what Flockemann calls

Figure 20.
Peter Van Heerden
as the trekboer
or frontiersman in
flux. © 2008 Megan
Lewis.

thick complicity, "textured work using physical images, generating multiple meanings through innovative stage metaphors which challenge common assumptions." Such productions "question hegemonic knowledge, its production and dissemination. In the process these works often draw on history in order to play with contemporary realities" (2011, 139).

Guiding audiences through history, and each station of the installation, was Van Heerden, sporting a bushy beard, suspenders, rope belt, and *velds-koene* on his feet. He embodied the frontiersman: daring, driven, and not afraid of getting dirty. As the trekboer pioneer, he positioned himself in a fluid role, able to travel—like the migrating trekboere did—across time and space (figure 20). He anchored his journey in the familiar Afrikaner ethnomythological tropes: God's chosen, entrepreneurial pioneers stoically forging their way into uncharted territories, and bearers of the "light" of civilization into the "darkness" of Africa. It is the assumed authority and blind nostalgia behind the trekboer figure that Van Heerden wanted his audiences to reconsider and deconstruct. Drawing on his own reading of Judith Butler, Van Heerden deployed the trekboer figure to mark the reiterative, performative nature of identity as well as to make visible how such figures have been repeatedly deployed by the Afrikaner nationalist project to galvanize an ideology of whiteness. And as an iconoclast, he strategically employed and then destroyed, or attracted and refracted, the icons of Afrikaner nationalism, interrogating the white privilege on which apartheid and its logic have been based.

By fully inhabiting the iconic persona of the trekking frontiersman in flux so convincingly that both conservatives and radicals in the audience accepted him as legitimate, Van Heerden could then implode the icon from the inside out and take on white Afrikaner identity and mythology from within. Peter walked, talked, acted, looked, smelled like a trekboer. As this character, he facilitated dialogue about the impact of patriarchy, Calvinism, racism, and the cult of masculinity that permeate Afrikaners' sense of self. Within his trekboer persona, he spoke his mind as a socially engaged, gender-aware white man committed to social justice and a radical transformation of culture. And he addressed the charged ideologies of South African racism and patriarchy, which have historically been expressed through the metaphor of the Voortrekker—the forward-moving, fiercely independent pioneer—and of the laager, or circle of wagons.

In the journey through the performance space of *Totanderkuntuit*'s laager, participant-onlookers encountered language operating catachrestically and symbolism deployed strategically. While radically different in tone from Pieter-Dirk Uys's wordplay,[23] Van Heerden also playfully violated the norms of Afrikaans, asking his audience to see the irony, instructiveness, and puns of familiar words. For example, he and Laubscher introduced themselves as *Voortrekkers* ("pioneers," those who pull forward), *Draadtrekkers* ("wankers," those who pull their own chains), and *Saamtrekkers* ("journeyers," those who pull together). This clever verbal triad served as a guide for a new way of thinking about—and imagining—white identity in Africa. As a white man and product of the privilege of both whiteness and masculinity, Van Heerden engaged in critical self-reflection, as a *voortrekker* or pioneer moving forward rather than remaining fixed in the past. As a *draadtrekker*, he was also able to parody himself and satirize his own privilege. And, through his performance art and practice of *saamtrekking*, he made a reflective space of dialogue available and pulled people together in a new way of being in this new democracy. Van Heerden's performance engaged his Afrikaner audience in a playfully sincere mode, asking them to consider the trajectory of their volk in Africa, the narcissism and errors of their ways, and the potential for new modes of participating in the South African democracy.

As well, *Die laaste maragmaal* (*The Last Lunch*) on day 2, deliberately inflected the coloured or brown Afrikaner pronunciation of *marag* instead of the white Afrikaans *middag* to remind listeners of the *kombuistaal* (kitchen language) roots of the Afrikaans language and of the presence of brown Afrikaners, particularly in Oudtshoorn and the Western Cape, where they are the cultural majority.[24] Mixing a formal religious metaphor of the Dutch Reformed Church with the informality of *kombuistaal*—and thereby evoking the mixed-race (brown) Afrikaners from whom the Afrikaans language stems—was perceived as an act of blasphemy for many in conservative white Afrikaner circles who often frequent this festival. For Van Heerden it was strategic blasphemy; his aim, he told me, was to "shake things up, make people think twice about what they take for granted." Through this linguistic intervention, he made visible the tensions and effects of Calvinism as a colonizing force.[25] He also reminded viewers in Oudtshoorn of their brown-skinned cousins who share Afrikaans as their mother tongue but who are often invisible, artistically and on the streets of the KKNK.[26]

And by identifying as Voortrekkers/Draadtrekkers/Saamtrekkers, Van Heerden and Laubscher exposed the illogic of the past (and present), by asking their audiences to delve into their own (un)consciously held beliefs. They asked viewers to consider that the venerated Voortrekkers and their descendants are actually wankers, flawed and self-absorbed. Consider, for example, the way in which Laubscher called for a reevaluation of the myth of the Dutch encounter with Africa in his opening-day mock sermon at Peter's crucifixion. First he referenced the familiar mythical icon of Jan van Riebeeck, then he parodied and critiqued the colonial project.

In addition to language-play, symbols in *Totanderkuntuit* were deployed strategically to create mixed metaphors that required people to consider plural rather than monolithic cultural meanings. For example, on *Heldedag*, Van Heerden impersonated Gideon Nieuwoudt, one of the apartheid government's top operatives, who was denied amnesty at the Truth and Reconciliation Commission for his commanding role in the death of Black Consciousness activist Steve Biko in 1977 and in the burning of the bodies of three freedom workers from Port Elizabeth in 1985. Dressed in knee-high rugby socks, shorts, and a sleeveless T-shirt, his arms covered with the scribbled names of South African Security Police officers and their victims, Van Heerden labored all morning in the summer heat to dig three graves in honor of the Pebco Three.[27] On the one hand, he played the part of the agent of an oppressive state, calling attention to his—and by extension all white South Africans'—complicity in the atrocities perpetrated on black African bodies in the name of their whiteness. As he performed Nieuwoudt, though, he was also parodying the Afrikaner male braaivleis[28] attire of shorts that are too short and socks that are pulled up too high, creating an image of an infantile male figure.[29] And by physically digging the graves, Van-Heerden-as-Nieuwoudt not only offered a symbolic burial for apartheid's victims, but also engaged in an act of contrition (to return to a religious metaphor), opening up a space where guilt, shame, and culpability can be openly faced, named, and processed with his audience. He engaged visitors throughout the entire morning in conversation, asking them what they thought, saw, and believed about Nieuwoudt, Biko, policing by the Secret Service, his own actions/performance, and so on. His *Heldedag* performance was one of many instances in which he deployed this Voortrekker/Draadtrekker/Saamtrekker strategy.

Resisting a singular, fixed notion of the trekboer, in favor of complex, multiple shades of Afrikaner masculinity, Van Heerden and his creative collaborator, André Laubscher—who embodied various iterations of Pa (Father), Dominee (Preacher), and Boer (Farmer/Afrikaner)—performed complex, nuanced characters that offered audiences alternative identities to wrestle with and encounter. Through their bodies—which are made visible, vulnerable, porous, transformative—Peter and André enacted a *different way* of being Afrikaner, or white, men. André's repertoire of characters also performed strategic blasphemies and attractions/refractions. Laubscher enacted a simultaneous and opposing set of identities as various incarnations of the Afrikaner male psyche: as preacher, patriarch, father, farmer, caretaker. André-as-dominee served up daily benedictions and plates of food, which he willingly shared with any hungry passerby. On the surface, he performed the patriarchal "Boer" whose masculine authority presided over the space; yet, simultaneously, he performed a more tender role of farmer (boer), opening up new possibilities within the space. A caring gardener, he also tended the *erf* everyday with broom and rake, clearing pathways in the dusty soil and sweeping piles of grass and leaves to create walkways and borders, physically enlarging and shaping the playing space to accommodate each day's sequential topic. As a *saamprater*, one who encourages dialogue, he embodied—and modeled for the conservative members of the audience— a self-reflexivity almost unheard of in traditional Afrikaner circles. For example, André brought with him his six-year-old adopted Xhosa son, Theo, and engaged visitors in open and honest conversation about their relationship, Theo's parents' death due to AIDS, and our (all South Africans') responsibility to orphans like Theo. Then, shifting his persona yet again, each night in *Sweepslag*[30] he took the Afrikaner hegemon-patriarch figurehead on as he played the abusive, domineering Pa to Peter's Adam-esque character in a thirty-minute playscape of stage pictures, short scenes between father and son, and heavy use of symbolic objects.

ABJECTION

Sweepslag (*Whiplash*) started as Peter birthed himself from a bag suspended in a tree like a giant womb—invoking the *kunt* in the title of the installation. Suggesting a parthenogenic rebirthing of the white Afrikaner male, this act severed the symbolic tie between Afrikanerdom and the Volksmoeder. Having grappled his way out of the plastic placenta in which he was suspended, he dropped to the ground, naked and bloody, his body viscerally abjected and without preassigned meaning. The image of a naked human form, both nude and vulnerable, emerging from primordial ooze before the social markers of rank, race, and identity have defined him, was striking. A primal man crawling blindly through the dirt, snorting and grunting like a wild animal, he searched for language, meaning, and identity. Then he gradually acquired a sense of time (several alarm clocks), clothing (underpants and khaki shorts), and two suitcases (the "baggage" of whiteness, masculinity, Calvinism, and Afrikanerdom that burden his body).

Van Heerden, who counts feminist cultural theorist Julia Kristeva as one of his influences, believes that "in order to . . . re-map itself, re-locate itself, [the physical body requires] a shedding . . . a type of catharsis" (2004). For Kristeva (1982), the abject marks the human reaction (horror, vomit) to a threatened breakdown in meaning between self and other. The abject dis-

Figure 21. Peter Van Heerden and André Laubscher's patriarchal power plays in *Sweepslag*. © 2008 Majak Bredell.

turbs order and identity and does not respect boundaries, rules, or social station; hence, Van Heerden is drawn to the abject as a site from which to interrogate the hierarchal logic and identity politics of white Afrikaner masculinity. If we imagine Van Heerden to be examining the social body through his own body, then instead of ignoring unpleasant or distasteful elements, he offers them up to audiences to confront them head-on. Rather than avoid the ugliness and shame of the past, he engages it directly and asks his audiences to do the same. Engaging his own body in cathartic abjection, Van Heerden pares himself down to a prelinguistic state of Kristevan *chora*, that space in which the self and other are indistinguishable. He becomes a mudman, crawling in the muck and slime, his body barely distinguishable from the dirt and matter around him.[31] In doing so, he strips whiteness and masculinity of their symbolic power. Working in the nude, Van Heerden claims, means he has nowhere, and nothing, to hide; he is completely exposed and open to the performance (Schaffer n.d.). Witnessing his naked human form, the audience is given an opportunity to reimagine what this white man — and by extension, all white South Africans — can be as they encounter his live body stripped of its usual integrity, the fragility of his whiteness and masculinity exposed for examination, critique, and reflection.

As well, *Sweepslag* excavated the iron fist of Afrikaner patriarchy's impact on fathers and sons.[32] "We need to talk about abuse, we need to talk about what the fuck's going on in our culture," says Van Heerden (Schaffer n.d.). As red welts lashed out on his naked skin, Peter was baptized by Laubscher's Pa figure with a wet oxtail switch. "I baptize thee Peter the Ox," declared

André as he whipped him, "in the name of God die Vader (God the Father), Sot die Seun (the Idiot Son), en Die Heilige Bees (the Holy Ox)" (figure 21). The ox is a powerful symbol for Van Heerden. As the beast that literally carried Voortrekkers across the Drakensberg Mountains in their ox-wagons during the Great Trek, it midwifed a nation into existence. "[Oxen] dragged our country into being," he claims. As a beast of burden, laden with baggage, oxen also are often used sacrificially. Peter describes his use of the ox as follows: "In this trek of transformation I am the ox. As a white South African man I am harnessed to my lived experiences, which I must pull through the present in to the future" (Van Heerden 2004). And Peter the Ox sacrifices his white masculinity to the performance to make such a transition visible.

In another moment, André probed Peter's mouth with a stick, deliberately gagging him until he regurgitated bile onto the floor. Then André blindfolded Peter with the old orange-white-and-blue flag and made him run to exhaustion. At the end of the play, André's character died and Peter had to wrestle with the weight of his father's dead body, as if struggling with the baggage and burden of Afrikaner male culture, the proverbial sins of the father. The play ended with Peter, dressed in a suit, standing over the body of the deceased Father, which was draped in the new ANC flag. With a heavy suitcase in each hand, he let out a primal howl and stood there for several minutes in a white-hot spotlight as scratchy military gramophone music played itself out and the play ended.

Choric spaces incite fear and horror for many, because in them the structures by which we order our social world no longer function. Many observers who watched Sweepslag found it disturbing, threatening, even blasphemous. "He's making fun of being a man, mocking our God," one perturbed man told me in Afrikaans after the performance. Peter's messy, nonlinear performance not only challenged the standard aesthetic taste of middle-class theatregoers, but also invited a reexamination of how white Afrikaner masculinity is usually performed: as intact, powerful, and painted in clear, broad strokes. It is in the audience's encounter with this fear and horror, in seeing the Afrikaner male transformed into a choric other-self, that Van Heerden's work is most powerful. He enacts abjection to actively deconstruct and examine what (white) South Africans thrust aside in order to live. Or, as Christina Landman might suggest, Van Heerden's performance asks audiences to "face rather than ignore" the past and Afrikaners' "culpability in and for it" (Daley 1998, 11). Van Heerden deliberately holds up whiteness for exploration, exposing what lies inside to the outside, or reversing the logic of the laager. It's in this choric space of undefinedness, where the inside is exposed outwardly, and where the self confronts its otherness, that the potential for a reimagining of whiteness lies. In this *reorientation* of the self—to borrow from Boucher, Carey, and Ellinghaus (2009)—and in asking the white Afrikaner self to confront its own complicity in the past and examine its darkest psyche, Van Heerden's work opens up new possibilities for white Africans to rethink themselves not as unconsciously central and all-powerful, but as conscious and ethical participants in a democracy.

I theorize Van Heerden's performance as a form of betrayal, because his work *breaks or violates the presumed social contract* of what it means to be an Afrikaner—stoic, reserved, and distinctly never airing dirty laundry in public. In his performances, Van Heerden also betrays, or *reveals*, the uncomfortable truths of white privilege (the assumed power of the Boer male) and racial superiority (the economic, social, political, and symbolic power of whiteness) that have afforded whites their position in Africa for centuries. Such laying bare can make spectators, especially those with more conservative leanings, feel betrayed—as if *delivered to an enemy by treachery*.[33] American author Henry Miller, in his 1945 travelogue, suggested that "the new always carries with it the sense of violation, of sacrilege. What is dead is sacred; what is new, that is *different*, is evil, dangerous, or subversive" (1970, 172). Hence, the irate insults and damnations that bystanders directed at Peter on the cross betray, or reveal, the shame and anxiety his performance triggers within their Afrikaner psyches, both personally and in the communal sense of shame as socially shaped (Pattison). On Crucifixion Day, an angry viewer called Peter "the worst Afrikaner that I have ever seen!" To people like this man, Peter became a Judas, a *volksveraaier* or "race traitor," blaspheming the linguistic, cultural, and religious structures that hold their identities as whites and Afrikaners intact. He is perceived as different and dangerous and they read his work as what Miller might call sacrilege. A number of visitors to the installation used the Afrikaans phrase, "Skaam jou!" (Shame on you!) in reaction to Peter and André's work, to publicly correct them for breaking the Afrikaner social order.

As I discussed in chapter 2, scholars and theorists have explored the notion of shame from a variety of perspectives. On its most basic level, shame occurs when the self encounters an unpleasant, distasteful or alienating version of itself and experiences "an acute sense of unwanted exposure" (Pattison 2000, 40–43), both individually and on a social level. Afrikaners, as a minority of white Europeans in Africa, fear unwanted exposure; or considered another way, they fear the rupture of their comforting cultural laagers. When faced with alienating versions of themselves as exploitative and racist colonialists, sexual deviants, or supporters of apartheid, they experience shame as previous ideas of their own excellence become degraded (Lynd 1958). Anger and violence are often reactions to shame, as "a persecuted or disenfranchised minority can insulate itself against humiliation [read: exposure] by responding with contempt" (Kaufman 2004, 276). One night, bottle-wielding and stone-throwing drunkards attacked Peter and André's encampment. I quote (and translate) from André's account of the event:

> "Hey, Piet Retief, hey you with your beard, hey Paul Kruger,[34] hey faggot, hey kaffirfucker, wake up, tomorrow is the blood of slaughter river!" The next moment stones and rocks rained down on us; it's 2 A.M. and the Day of Blood River [the day was dedicated to AIDS]. This brave *impi* of drunken sots are the *brandewyn* (brandy) bastards, a youth lost in the machismo of protestant patriarchal dogma, they rub themselves off between the ice cubes in their Klipdrift & Cokes. . . . The dumb Afrikaner *is* scared, his god-given right to the land, his power and his nation is gone. He knows this but refuses to acknowledge that what was lost was a myth based on the abuse of other people. (Van Heerden and Laubscher 2008a, 1)

The artists offer an astute analysis of the machismo of the *brandewyn bastards* in this reflection. They identify the sexually charged, masculinist impulse in these men who operate through fear rather than understanding, and whose sense of history is blinded by their own white-sight. Of note is the way in which each of the insults volleyed by the *brandewyn bastards* marks the various forms of betrayal Afrikaner masculinity is unable to tolerate: calling the artists "Retiefs" and "Krugers," the race traitors who historically negotiated with enemies of Afrikaners (black Africans and the British); "faggots" or perceived traitors to a heteronormative sexual code; and "kaffirfuckers" or miscegenist traitors whose desire flows across laagered color lines. Van Heerden and Laubscher's performances expose many Afrikaners to difficult, shame-filled issues and trigger shameful feelings when the self confronts itself and does not like what it sees.

Betraying Afrikaner logic is central to Van Heerden and Laubscher's work. Through their interventions as the itinerant trekboer and dominee, infiltrating the laager of the KKNK,[35] and asking disquieting questions, they reveal the flawed, nostalgic, and melodramatic narratives and icons that have reinforced Afrikaner identity over the past century. They explore stories of our stoic pioneers, our role as paternalistic (white) caretakers in (black) Africa, the iron-fisted rule of our patriarchs, our shame-filled enactments of sexuality, our secrets, and our secret police force.[36]

HYBRIDITIES

During the KKNK festival, the complexity of my identity formation encountered the complexity of Van Heerden's. As Joseph and Fink define it, hybridity is a "nexus of affiliations that self-consciously perform continued acts of citizenship" (1999, 2). At first, I read Peter as an Afrikaner, and even as a right-wing member of the AWB. But then I detected in his Afrikaans accent a British inflection, not unlike my own. Van Heerden, whose Afrikaans surname comes from his Afrikaner father, is a hybrid, like me.[37] He too was raised in an English-speaking household. He tells me that he was drawn to the Afrikaner male persona as an interstitial identity in democratic South Africa, an identity on the edge of realignment between privilege and minority status and thus a space for dialogue and transformation. And perhaps, because of his own insider-outsider hybridity, as an Anglo-Afrikaner soutpiel[38] like myself, he is able to comment critically on the ways in which whiteness and Afrikanerness are intertwined. Following Jansen, our "outsider status . . . yields valuable analytical advantage" (2009). For Van Heerden, who is as much a critic of South Africa's past as he is hopeful for South Africa's future, "Afrikaner identity is still in motion, his 'uitspan' [the place in the trek when oxen and men were given a chance to rest, eat, and recuperate] is yet to be decided" (2004).

When I asked Peter to self-identify, he answered: "[Former president] Mbeki says that if you are white you are not an African. I don't feel fuckin' English. My blood feels like soil. But I'm not an Afrikaner" (Van Heerden 2008). His response indicates the constellation of affiliations that make up only one small portion of the multilingual, ethnic, and cultural South African population—in this case, whites. Refusing the fixity of identity, he sees himself as an African, not as a European of either Dutch or English descent.

His response betrays (reveals) the journeying of identities in this social space, as multiple acts of affiliation and disaffiliation. His blood "feels like soil," the marker of his hybrid birth and his position in a postcolonial world.

Echoing Pieter-Dirk Uys's "Mý Suid-Afrika" and Opperman's "I'm a White Man in Africa," but in a different register, Van Heerden's 2004 poem, which features in So is 'n os gemaak, reads (I translate):

ek is wit (I am white)
maar wat beteken dit (but what does that mean)
where the fuck is my script
ag, it's alright I live in a republic

I am a white man
my color like cum
people call me a dutchman
doesn't matter
I am a white boss

whitey, nigger, coolie, coon
we all stand together in one room
knock on the door say hello come in
we live in a fuckin' rainbow
                    (Van Heerden 2004, my translation)

Van Heerden muses on the positionality of whiteness in the postcolony and its relation to the other subjectivities of the democracy. Asking where the new script is for white men, he references the associations of power (baas), sexual prowess (cum), and European roots (dutchman) with white identity. And ultimately he suggests that multiple ethnicities, and their pejorative identities, share the same space in contemporary South Africa. Yet it is important to unpack his use of the rainbow here. The color white does not have a place in a rainbow; rather, it is composed of all frequencies of light in the visible spectrum—it claims on behalf of all. South Africa is a "fuckin' rainbow" nation, where whiteness remains the dominant social position (I'm a white boss) among many diverse constituencies.

Van Heerden does not create work with a particular audience in mind; rather, he makes work that is "necessary . . . that feels vital to [him] as a person" (2010). His audiences are comprised of a mélange of South African identities: local community members; visiting festinos; enlightened, left-leaning intellectuals; art lovers who also question and examine the past and present; confused bystanders; right-wing, bottle-throwing thugs; and Bible-quoting conservatives to whom his work is a threat and a challenge. By creating *free* installations at festivals around the country, he is also able to attract nontraditional audiences—street kids, working-class black and coloured South Africans—for whom most mainstream theatre is often financially and socially inaccessible. Van Heerden's goal in *Totanderkuntuit* was not simply to trick audiences or to mock sacred symbols; rather, the process of trust building within this space was central to the project and the commitment to *saampraat* extended to every single person who entered their encampment. Within the "negotiating arena" (Joseph and Fink 1999, 7) that performance offers, he made space for conversations that might not otherwise have occurred. There were many deep and meaningful conversations that happened around the campfire each night, around the daily installations, and after the nightly performances of *Sweepslag*.

Audiences at *Totanderkuntuit* represented a diverse swathe of the festival crowd.[39] They reacted with everything from reactionary slurs and physical assaults, to religious proscriptions of Calvinist doctrine, to transformative discussions across race, gender, and class boundaries about issues impacting South Africans in the past and today. For the first few days, until press attention over the crucifixion drew festinos into the installation, most people simply stood outside the fences and just looked *at* the installation and the ox-wagon that loomed over the encampment. Perhaps South African theatregoers' lack of familiarity with performance art as a genre caused this hesitation? Perhaps reading the site as challenging, threatening, or confusing stopped people from entering the space? Perhaps onlookers did not recognize it *as* a performance space in the first place? Perhaps, like me, festinos read the camp as an AWB event to avoid? Or perhaps the way in which festivalgoers' bodies are disciplined to consume rather than engage with what they encounter was the cause of their reluctance to engage?[40] Those who came into the encampment usually walked silently through the installations, contemplating what they encountered. Many people wrote in the visitor's book, housed in a wooden voting booth that created a private space where people poured out emotions, reactions, insights, and attacks.[41] Others asked questions and engaged in dialogue with Peter or André, their assistant, Chelwyn,[42] or fellow visitors. I recall one conversation with two Afrikaner men who visited the site three days in a row.

I approached them in Afrikaans, inquiring what they thought was happening in this performance, what these lunatics were on about. "It makes a person think," said Cassie, the most outspoken of the two: "When you walk outside [the installation], and a dark person bumps against you, you think, 'Dumb Hottentot!' But in here, this guy [indicating André] offers a black man his own plate of food, with his clean fork. My forefathers taught me you don't sleep with them, eat with them, drink with them. But this man [André] shows us the opposite. He is a real human being."[43] André modeled a way of behaving toward black South Africans that caused him to question his own assumptions and to imagine new possibilities. Cassie said he thought the purpose of this installation was "to ask questions. Like, are we [suggesting whites, Afrikaners] maybe the lunatics, the mad men?" Rubbing his hands together to illustrate his meaning, he told me, "Outside in the festival, it's all mulling and scraping against each other." Tapping his hand over his heart, he said, "In here, it makes your heart beat. Out there, it beats here," he said, tapping his jugular vein. Cassie's thoughtful reflections were illustrative of the saampraat at the core of Van Heerden's project. He found a physical metaphor—his own pulse—with which to articulate the realizations he had experienced in the Totanderkuntuit camp. He was clearly moved by the performances he had seen, performances that made him question his beliefs and assumptions, and was curious enough to return several times to revisit the space Peter and André had made possible.

Yet for many visitors, Totanderkuntuit was a troubling, frightening, even sickening experience. Some, like the brandewyn bastards who attacked in the night, reacted violently to what they saw. After Sweepslag one night, two visibly outraged Afrikaner women told me: "It's filthy/nasty (vieslik)! Aren't they ashamed of how they are mocking God?" Some chose to write their responses—"I will pray for you" or "Jesus lives"—as inscriptions in the visitor's book. Perhaps they were trying to deny or erase what the work had brought up for them? Perhaps they read the religious framing of the installation literally and were responding in kind? Or might they have wanted to out-symbolize Peter's strategic blasphemy by inundating his symbols with their own Biblical scriptures? Some saw this as an opportunity to recircle the wagons around a blind belief in racial and religious entitlement. I translate, again, from André's journal on Heroes Day, around the graves, which I described previously:

We invited people to write messages on little pieces of paper and to throw them into a grave ... dug in honor of the Pebco Three. One woman asked if we had found Jesus. In answer, she was invited to throw a message into the grave. She peeked into the grave and said, "What I want to write is already there." As she walked away, a paper lay in the grave with the words "Fuck the Kaffirs" scribbled on it. It was one of six pieces of paper with the same message on it. (Van Heerden and Laubscher 2008a, 1)

For every racist slur thrown at the artists, *Totanderkuntuit* also inspired transformative *saampraat* across racial and class boundaries. On *Bloedriveierdag*, visitors were asked to contemplate, not the blood spilled in the Ncome River in 1838, nor the nationalist rhetoric enshrined in the Voortrekker Monument in Pretoria, but the more relevant manifestation of blood in contemporary South Africa: AIDS. Visitors could sculpt and adopt an AIDS orphan out of a pile of rubbish—plastic bags, empty cans and bottles, the throwaway stuff of the new democracy. Participants took to this activity with energy, love, and hope. As I was sculpting my baby out of a garbage bag and a fragment of bubble-wrap, three coloured women and a young girl joined me. They were wearing shock-yellow reflective jackets with the slogan "Bambanani against Crime" [*bambanani* is a Xhosa word meaning "stand together" or "unite"] and explained that they were a community watch organization committed to reducing crime and making safer working, playing, and living spaces for coloureds in the Oudtshoorn area. We discussed how AIDS was impacting their communities and then, spontaneously, we began making an AIDS baby together. My white hands held the black plastic torso as their brown fingers wove a straw ribbon around the baby to create its body and head. Then one of the women discovered an unopened tampon amid the rubbish and we all decided to strap the little piece of cotton onto the baby, who had now morphed into a mother carrying its little child on its back. As we created together, we talked of being mothers; one woman proudly introduced the girl as her daughter, and I showed her a photograph of my son. We talked about AIDS orphans and the impact of this disease locally and across the nation. In the shared symbols of babies and feminine hygiene products, we engaged in *saampraat* (together-talk) that revealed to us the spaces of commonality between us.

Yet, lest I depict too utopian a scene here, there also remained lacunae in our engagement with each other, even in this post-1994 world. I never did get to know their names, nor they mine. We would not share a meal at a restaurant in town, nor visit one another's homes. Cultural and economic barriers, as well as my own distance from the intimacies of their lives in Oudtshoorn as an American, kept us apart. But for that brief moment, we crossed the barriers that otherwise kept us separated in South African society, and we shared a moment of communitas, a spirit of social equality, solidarity, and togetherness brought about through performance (Turner 1969, 94–130). In the liminal space of the *Totanderkunuit* encampment, we were given license to engage one another, albeit temporarily, on the most basic human level: as mothers of children concerned about the toll AIDS is taking on families. As the women were leaving, I asked them what they thought of Peter's installation. "Hy's heeltemal mal" (He's totally crazy), chuckled one of the women. "But he's wise," interjected her companion. To her, Peter was a white man willing to sit down and talk, to create art that allowed people to talk together. He also did not charge a fee for *Totanderkuntuit*, so he made his art accessible to her. And because of this she told me she thought he was "the smartest whitey she had ever met."[44]

In contrast to other contemporary performances of Afrikaner identity that trade in the nostalgic, or look backward to the past for solace, Van Heerden's *Totanderkuntuit* embodies a future-oriented approach, emphasizing the *voor* (forwardness) in the word *voortrekker*. He pulls the past forward in what he calls "his journey of discovery, a mobile trek," rather than looking backward to the past, as Afrikaners have so often done. Van Heerden treks through what he terms the "landscapes of mobility" that define South African culture and heritage. By disrupting the comforting, reiterative understandings of his white male body through abjection, by catachrestically wrenching familiar language and symbols away from their usual associations, and by laying bare the ethno- and gender-mythologies of many white Africans, within the laager of the KKNK, Van Heerden's acts of betrayal are the "transformative acts of behaviour" he sees as vital to the development of new ways of being in a democratic South Africa. Van Heerden is what Walter Benjamin might term a revolutionary intellectual: making his own (white; male) body public in order to confront his audiences and activate critical dialogue. Playing traitor to his *race*—and *gender*—he challenges audiences to work through and move beyond the structures that have afforded white men privilege in Africa.

As an iconoclast, he is engaged in the "rough work" that Oliver Wendell Holmes suggests is the "only way to get at truth" (1891, 54). Through his performance art, Van Heerden avoids stasis; he stays in motion, never allowing thinking to freeze, constantly requiring the intellectual and emotional reworking of ideas. Provoking viewers, and activating *saamtrekking* in his audiences, Van Heerden hopes that "through representations enacted in performance, spectators' cultural perceptions [are] challenged, [and] this becomes the first step in the dialogue towards a new practice": a fluid new practice, I suggest, that is historically conscious, is willing to embrace contradiction, and that lives up to the Voortrekker spirit by pulling Afrikaner whiteness and masculinity out of its shame-filled past, productively forward into the future.

UBUNTU (2010)

Through the process of physically performing, Van Heerden undergoes a cathartic change, which he describes as follows: "The character I am enacting or using becomes othered and changes for the better or worse" (2010). In *Ubuntu*, a one-man piece that Van Heerden performed in Baltimore and Minneapolis in 2010, Van Heerden took audiences on an imaginative journey through masculinity. Van Heerden began the piece as an animal-esque figure perched atop a makeshift set he constructed himself from wood and scrap metal he found in dumpsters. Sitting spread-eagled on the top of the set, Van Heerden was naked and covered in clay. Attached to his penis was a snaking tube of mottled fabric stuffed with old newspapers; it stretched from his body all the way to the floor, where it coiled center stage. This exaggerated phallus suggested the mythic Zulu *tokoloshe*, an evil water spirit who frightens children, ravages women, and bites off the toes of sleeping victims. Small and hairy, once caught by a witch as her familiar, the tokoloshe becomes sexually rapacious.[45] For the opening minutes of the piece, he watched from his perch, taking in the audience as a primate might when encountering something new, occasionally barking out guttural, baboon-like articulations at the audience.

Exploring the Self/Other dichotomy, Van Heerden's piece is titled *Ubuntu* in citation of the African philosophy of human interconnectedness. For Rita Barnard, "Ubuntu entails not only the idea that a person is a person because of other people, but also that one is bound by complicated relations of reciprocity, of duties and obligations to others; these relations are not easily lived out in a situation where some obviously prosper, while others remain mired in poverty and illness" (2012, 167). Praeg and Magadla explore the "emancipatory potential" of ubuntu as both "a function and a critique of Western modernity" (2014, 5). They understand ubuntu as a way of justice that imagines "equity, justice and rights" as interconnected and codependent, and dignity as a central to all humanity. Drucilla Cornell argues for ubuntu as a "new ethical vision of what being human together can mean and look like" (Praeg and Magadla 2014, 7); in other words, ubuntu is human solidarity.

In this piece, Van Heerden examines what ubuntu might mean across the racial divide. And what kind of hybridity do such crossings engender? How do audiences encounter a white body performing in unexpected, provocative ways? What might this encounter suggest about the potentials, as well as the pitfalls, of the I-am-because-you-are philosophy? Can a white body be included in the ubuntu formulation? Like in *Sweepslag*, Van Heerden's character gradually morphed from a choric, animal state toward a more human one. He covered his body with a Xhosa initiation blanket and dragged his enormous phallus-snake through the playing space. After a while, he stripped off the blanket and washed the red clay off his body, revealing his naked white skin. Wherever or however he moved, the phallus had to follow; he was always tied to, and at times burdened by, this masculinity. Eventually, he donned a schoolboy's uniform (a crested blazer, khaki shorts, and leather boots), creating an awkward image of a grown man in an infantilized costume. He then covered his face in black paint and approached the audience, offering us his tokoloshe penis. Some members of the audience touched or stroked it, others recoiled, a few smiled or laughed. This complex set of symbols — the schoolboy innocence, the racially charged blackface, the enormous phallus, the reference to the tokoloshe — were layered onto his white male body and became a coded web the audience had to process. Presenting an amalgam of symbols, Peter's whiteness became simultaneously abjected, vulnerable, innocent, racially charged, and disturbing.

Through the visceral change Van Heerden experiences in public, he suggests, "the audience is forced to engage with the othering/abjection process [and] to question their assumptions . . . to react and act with an encounter in the present moment, a visceral moment that engenders some form of change" (2010). In the postshow discussion, Peter encouraged audience members and students in Minneapolis, many of whom were confused or

Figure 22.
Saampraat
(together-talking)
with Peter Van
Heerden. © 2008
Megan Lewis.

unnerved by the piece, to take from the performance their own meaning and to consider what happens when these complex symbols are placed in relation to one another. What does it do when a white South African man uses blackface? Or when a naked man stands before you on stage? Or when a performer offers you his giant penis or births an image of Africa from between his thighs? How do we experience these acts and what do they bring up in us as audience members situated in a culture different from the one being presented? Van Heerden is interested in the motion of social fabric and sites of conflict particularly in a new democracy-in-the-making. "What happens when we put it against this?" he asks, gesturing with his hands to indicate two opposing forces in dialogue (Schaffer n.d.).

In order to live up to the ideal, at least, of Mandela's Rainbow Nation, Van Heerden believes South Africans must practice new ways of being, "whether it's through art, or politics or picking up [trash] thrown on the floor, we must keep *practicing* to get rid of old habits and create new ways of living as a nation" (2010). His use of the abject body—the body placed in contorted relation to its usual functions—is his way of calling for transformation in thinking, being, and embodying identity in contemporary South Africa. Modeling the courage and daring required of such transformation with his own body, Van Heerden commits physically to this work—he lives and breathes his art for nine days straight; he contorts and tortures his own flesh and risks his body in performance; and he takes a brand on his right shoulder after each major installation to mark its impact on him.

Encountering Peter's physical body in the "role" of trekboer, animal, or

schoolboy, audiences are asked to question systems of belief. As an artist using performance to catalyze dialogue around cultural issues, we encounter him in his multiple layers—as actor, trekker, radical, madman,
hybrid, provocateur—and in varied shades of the "character" he inhabits
during the installation—tough, risky, bold, incendiary, vulnerable, controversial, naked, open to dialogue, thoughtful, mortal. Putting his own (literal
and metaphoric white, male, Anglo-Afrikaner) body at risk, he debases himself, turns himself inside out, exposes his naked, vulnerable masculinity.
Offering his body to the performance and to the audience, he *roots* himself in
the familiar metaphors and symbols of the colonial and apartheid past as he
(re)routes the discourse in the present. His routing stands as example of how
one white artist can stretch the boundaries between physical endurance and
mental elasticity, and expand our understandings of how whiteness is imagined and how is could possibly function in the postcolony. As he undergoes
his physical and creative journey through performance, he also invites his
audiences to *trek* intellectually, emotionally, and politically.

Vuilgeboosted Gangstas and Romanties Afrikaner Rappers

THE ZEF WHITENESS OF

DIE ANTWOORD AND JACK PAROW

In this final chapter,[1] I offer other possible performance repertoires for white subjects in the postcolony; resisting past logics of whiteness by sampling and remixing identity using ironic framing and kitsch aesthetics. Locating my analysis in white-trash-chic performances of rave-rap group Die Antwoord and Afrikaner rapper Jack Parow, I work through their (re)negotiations of Afrikaner whiteness in contemporary South African music and Internet culture. I unpack several of Die Antwoord's videos, including "Enter the Ninja," "I Fink U Freeky," "Baby's on Fire," and "Rich Bitch," as well as Jack Parow's "Afrikaans is dood" ("Afrikaans Is Dead") and "Ons behoort mos saam" ("We Belong Together"). I also explore the use of kitsch in Pieter-Dirk Uys's Boere Museum/Nauseum in Darling outside Cape Town, at the 2007 annual Klein Karoo National Arts Festival, and in a Pretoria restaurant called Boer'geoisie. I conclude my study with a return to the 2013 Whitewash Conference at the University of Johannesburg to consider where whiteness is currently positioned in South African culture and where it may be headed.

ZEF SIDE OF WHITE

As I have argued, post-1994 Afrikaners are (re)negotiating their position within the social fabric of a new political dispensation; they could be said to be experiencing what Claire Scott calls a "crisis of delegitimacy" (2012, 746). This crisis has sparked conservative wagon-circling as well as radical new ways of performing whiteness. If Pieter-Dirk Uys sees South Africa as a nineteen-year-old teenager trying to grow up, the entrepreneurial Deon Opperman reclaims his culture nostalgically, and Peter Van Heerden asks where the white man's script is in the new South African democracy, then what do Internet sensations and Afrikaans rap artists Jack Parow and Ninja of Die Antwoord contribute to the conversation about whiteness and Afrikaner identity in post-1994 South Africa?

Both Parow and Die Antwoord are part of what is known as *zef kultcha*, a contemporary counterculture movement of Afrikaner heterodoxy and self-deprecation. Deliberately positioning themselves as low class, ill bred, and boorish (Krueger 2012), these artists use the hip-hop practices of sampling and remixing, combined with rave hooks and hip-hop beats, as they question orthodox white (Afrikaner) values and the logic of the apartheid past. I argue that they offer another possible answer for white subjects in the post-colony: to resist the past logic of white supremacy in favor of a slippery, foul-mouthed sampling of identity that dares to offend rather than complies with political correctness, is opportunistic rather than outcast from power, and stirs up controversy in order to remain visible.

Die Antwoord are Watkin (Waddy) Tudor Jones, a.k.a. Ninja; Anri du Toit, a.k.a. Yo-Landi Vi$$er; and Justin De Nobrega, a.k.a. DJ Hi-Tek.[2] Formed in 2008, Die Antwoord (The Answer) describe themselves as "a fre$, futuristic, flame-throw-flow-freeking, zef rave-rap krew from da dark dangerous depths of Afrika" (dieantwoord.com). They are "self-consciously uncool" (Stephens 2013) and perform "kommin" (common/vulgar) poor white identities as zef (cool) or white-trash chic. They borrow conventions from global hip-hop: an adversarial tone supported by raps and rhymes boasting about destroying their enemies sung or spoken over a live DJ's beats; "representing" an antiestablishment position; celebrating street, gang, and prison culture; leveraging music videos to boost sales; replacing S's with dollar symbols; and the cultivation of a unique fashion style. Ninja is rail thin, sporting gold *grillz* on his teeth, and is covered in crude (in style and content) *rou tjappies* (homemade tattoos), reminiscent of those worn by inmates and coloured gangs in Cape Town. Written on his chest is "How can a angel break my heart?" [complete with incorrect grammar]; on his larynx, the words *Pretty Wise*; on his right arm, Evil Boy with an enormous erection; Richie Rich covers his heart, and a dagger stabs his left pectoral muscle.[3] Yo-Landi Vi$$er is a petite white-trash pixie; her hair is blunt cut across her forehead, and her eyelashes and hair are bleached snow white. She presents a type of sex appeal that is always tinged in creepiness or forbidden desire;

in their videos, she often has rats crawling across her body, wears dark contact lenses that give the otherworldly effect of her having only pupils and no irises, or plays a little girl in hypersexual scenarios. Ninja and Yo-Landi sing, rap, and perform over DJ Hi-Tec's beats in a "street venac mix of English and Afrikaans" (Marx and Milton 2011, 739).

Die Antwoord seeks to recast the dominant construction of white (Afrikaner) identity as oppressive, *verkrampt*, and unoriginal. Instead, Ninja and Yo-Landi aim to make Afrikanerdom (and South African whiteness in general) cool, irreverent, and unique. Using what Stephens describes as a combination of "griminess, Ninja's prolific primitivist art, Yo-Landi's creepy seductiveness, and shots that celebrate the physically unusual" (2013), Die Antwoord exploded onto the international music scene in 2010 via their online videos, most of which include what Stephens calls "stylised filth, disturbing tableaux, revelment in anything and anyone that looks strange, and a paradoxical sensuality that arouses as it repulses" (2013). Die Antwoord introduced themselves first with "Enter the Ninja," which has received over 20 million online views. At the start of the video, Ninja tells viewers in a voiceover, in his markedly Afrikaans-tinged South African English accent, "Chekkit. I represent South African kultcha. In this place, you get a lot of different tings [note the lost h]. Blacks, whites [pronounced "whaaats"], coloureds, English, Afrikaans, Xhosa, Zulu, *wat ook al* (whatever). I'm, laaik, all these different things, all these different people, fucked into one person" (Die Antwoord 2010a). Referencing the forbidden subject of miscegenation that was at the core of much apartheid-era anxiety for Afrikaners in power, Ninja—and by extension, Die Antwoord, or the answer for South Africa as a whole—is an amalgam of identities, all "fucked" into one. Their stage personae, music, and video performances offer versions of South African race and ethnicity that are multiple rather than singular or monolithic, constantly in flux, and fluid in borrowing from diverse cultures and weaving together of a new zef style that shifts away from old paradigms.

Jack Parow, the stage name of thirty-one-year-old Zander Taylor, is from Bellville, a coloured and working-class white suburb of Cape Town neighboring the town of Parow. He named himself after a drunken evening watching Jack Sparrow in *Pirates of the Caribbean*, claiming: "I'm Jack Parow, pirate of the caravan park" (Socialite 2010). His first album, *Cooler as ekke* (*Cooler as/than Me*), was released in 2009 and was followed by the eponymous *Jack Parow* in 2010 and *Eksie ou* (*I' the Man*) in 2011. He is known for collaborating with other

Figure 23. Die Antwoord's Yo-Landi (Anri du Toit) and Ninja (Waddy Jones) put a new spin on whiteness in "Ugly Boy." © 2012 Die Antwoord.

Figure 24. Ninja as the Chosen One in "Fatty Boom Boom." © 2012 Die Antwoord.

artists.[4] Parow's videos parody their genre as well as white working-class culture as they simultaneously celebrate it. His signature fashion statement is a baseball cap with an enormous, exaggerated brim and animal prints over shoddy tank tops and shiny athletic shorts. Self-identifying as a "Zef Gevaarlik Romanties Afrikaans Rapper" (Zef Dangerous Romantic Afrikaans

Figure 25.
Jack Parow's boerekitsch. © 2012 Sascha Waldman. Courtesy of Jack Parow.

Rapper), Parow is far less in-yer-face than Die Antwoord, though just as popular.

Describing the impact of Parow and Die Antwoord, *Thought Leader* blogger David Smith explains:

> [We] had little time for Afrikaans.... it was dumb, intellectually inferior. A blunt language with no creative value.... The tongue of the unfashionable and the conservative. The language of the oppressor. The language of apartheid. But *fok* did we get it wrong! The Afrikaans kids are here to take the power back. To show us who is *baas* (boss). But this time, the politics and the weirdo white power stuff is gone. They are here to kick it hard and party like its 2099. They are here to show us no-one throws down like an Afrikaner rushing on klippies[5] — the cocaine of the working-class man. (2010)

Smith's assessment marks how Afrikaans was historically deemed "uncool" because of its cultural and political imbrication with the apartheid state. Afrikaans was long considered the language of the oppressors; but now, with the advent of zef acts like Parow and Die Antwoord, Afrikaans has suddenly regained its "cool" status. And by taking up hip-hop, which equates "black" with "cool" according to Bakari Kitwana in *Why White Kids Love Hip Hop* (2005, 15), these white South Africans can shift their affiliations away from the shame of Afrikaner nationalism and bring whiteness toward an affiliation with cool blackness. Against the highly proscribed world of Afrikaner and Calvinist morality, claiming an affiliation with a form of expression responsible for "sullying the pure and white moral values of . . . culture" (Kitwana 2005, 20) is a way of defying antiquated ways of performing whiteness. Thus, perceiving whiteness as "corrupt, bad, and oppressive" these artists in turn refuse to identify as white in what Fraley calls a "denunciation of Whiteness" (Fraley 2009, 46).

Zef, zefness, or *zef kultcha* refer to white Afrikaner working-class culture of the 1960s and '70s, complete with Ford Zephyrs [hence the term *zef*], men with greased coifs and combs in their socks, cars up on bricks on the front lawn, and a certain vernacular slang. Die Antwoord and Parow have reclaimed the term, and made its Afrikaner working-class connotations equate with a no-holds-barred, in-yer-face commoner's white pride.[6] The term refers to racial or ethnic rather than racist elements in contemporary South African culture but also encompasses a strong class ethic. Although distinct in their styles of zefness, both Die Antwoord and Parow stand out drastically against mainstream Afrikaans music, which Chris du Plessis describes as "saccharin crooning with a disgusting *schlager-lager* [German drinking anthem] syndrome" (2009, my translation). Melissa Steyn claims that in the contemporary democratic landscape South Africans are now "selecting, editing, and borrowing from the cultural resources available to them to reinterpret old selves in the light of new knowledge and possibilities" (2001, xx). Die Antwoord and Jack Parow's pastiche draws from Afrikaner zef, coloured gang culture, and hip-hop and rave trance musical repertoires in their kitsch aesthetics to disrupt mainstream apartheid-era social configurations.

Afrikaans journalist Max du Preez suggests that definitions of Afrikanerness have changed with the shift in the political status of the country. He proffers:

> Being Afrikaans is more than church bazaars, "the day of the vow" celebrations . . . Broederbond . . . Bles Bridges, the minister and the headmaster. You can be bohemian in Afrikaans, you can be a citizen of the world or a communist or a socialist or a Catholic or a Hare Krishna—you can be whatever you want to be and still be Afrikaans. And you can most definitely be a democrat and Afrikaans. (2005, my translation)[7]

Du Preez's pronouncement broadens the possible definitions of volk identity in the new democracy and allows for diverse rather than monolithic performances of whiteness, one of which is zefness.

In "Raging Zef Boner," Ninja proclaims that his motto is "If it doesn't fit, force it." There has been much debate over cultural appropriation; whether or not Die Antwoord has the right, as white artists, to use rap and hip-hop as their means of expression. That Die Antwoord and Parow deploy hip-hop and rap, genres that originate with African Americans and are globally marked as black, might challenge for Marx and Milton "the type of social expectations which demand that people act out their supposed racial identities" (2011, 737). Much of the music criticism around these acts echoes the critique waged at Detroit-based white rapper Eminem, considered by many to be the Elvis of hip-hop, who Stuart Hall claims "turn[ed] up in the wrong category" (1997, 236). When white bodies take on hip-hop, it brings old notions of race into sharp focus and "rattles our wildest assumptions about race even as it indulges and bears out every stereotype imaginable" (Kitwana 2005, 110). Kitwana argues that hip-hop's value lies in suggesting that "identity is fluid. One can make of oneself another self from other selves" (2005, 125). Thus, when Ninja claims to be "all these different people, fucked into one person," he is constructing a white South African self that is no longer following an imagined, singular, exclusive narrative (complete with its apartheid racial classifications, passbooks, and race tests) but is instead claiming multiple affiliations that cite the cultural, linguistic, and racial mixings of South Africa across its history.

Hip-hop as a genre and as a practice can both reaffirm and maintain essentialized notions of race (and gender, for that matter) but it can also, as Todd Fraley suggests, "mark Whiteness" and provide a space "to critically interrogate and question its normalcy" (2009). By using hip-hop to claim a poor-white-trash, or zef, position from which to articulate themselves, Ninja and Yo-Landi make whiteness visible. "White trash" is also an unusual position for whiteness to take, as it subverts the unmarked, ubiquitous power status that whiteness usually wields in culture and replaces it with a distinctly marked, local, and at times even abjected, articulation. Hence, Yo-Landi's bleached white eyelashes and the white rats that she cuddles in their music videos serve as explicit markers of whiteness, just as their choice of "kommin" vocabulary—zef (cool), poes (pussy/vagina, sissy, asshole), laanie or *laarney* (fancy, high society), and *kif* (awesome, from *kief*, potent marijuana) — mark them as whites belonging not to mainstream, upper-middle-class culture, but to lower-class, poor white Afrikanerdom.[8]

For whites, as well as blacks, hip-hop appeals to an antiestablishment logic. Quoting one of his interviewees, Kitwana claims "Like punk, hip-hop was counterculture. It gave youth a voice to tell to the truth and exposed the ills of society, especially racism and our hypocritical government" (2005, 27). Hip-hop's antiestablishment ethos is particularly meaningful in South Africa, where whiteness has historically been associated with the racist apartheid state. Post-1994, when the South African population is redefining the racial, class, and gender categories of the past, whites are engaging in various new performances of their ethnic identities and are seeking ways to be white that allow them to participate in the new democracy without always being linked to the shame of the past.[9] Die Antwoord present a meaningful "counter-narrative of nation" (Scott 2012, 745) within a South African context in which 'being "white" is replete with dissonance' (Steyn 2005: 122). For Homi Bhabha, such counternarratives of the nation "continually evoke and erase its totalising boundaries" and disrupt "those ideological manoeuvres through which 'imagined communities' are given essential identities" (1990, 300). For Zoë Wicomb, whiteness, "the condition once assumed by diverse European settler communities, is no longer one to be cherished. Indeed, it is no longer a nice word" (2001, 169). By choosing to disassociate from the whiteness of the past and attempt to forge new white futures, Die Antwoord might offer an option — an answer — for white subjects in the postcolony through their visually charged videos and provocative lyrics. And their key strategies include intertextuality, pastiche, and cultural borrowing from a variety of sources: nineteenth-century imaginings of Africa, 1970s zef references, American artists like Grant Wood and Roger Ballen, South African artist Jane Alexander, and twenty-first-century hip-hop conventions. One of their fans (Andy on mhambi.com) sums it up: "This is what happens in a melting pot. Shit coalesces."

REVISED CHOSEN ONES: "ENTER THE NINJA" (2010)

In their first music video, "Enter the Ninja,"[10] Ninja asserts, "You can't fuck with the Chosen One," referencing a double meaning of the Afrikaner covenant as well as a common refrain rappers use to boost themselves and degrade their enemies, or haters (figure 24).[11] Setting up the Chosen One

(Afrikaners as the Chosen People), he then counters such a potentially hege-monic reading with

> Ninja *skop befokte rof taal* (Ninja kicks befucked rough language)
> Fantastically poor
> Rough rhymes for tough times
> *Met fokol kos, skraal* (with fuckall food, emaciated).

He places the former power of whiteness (the Chosen One) in relation to poverty and hunger (*fokol kos*), displacing, or debasing, it from its usual posi-tion of power. In the music video for "Rich Bitch," Yo-Landi, draped in more gold than a De Beers mine, sings as she sits on the toilet

> Wasn't always a rich bitch
> Used to be a poor girl
> . . . .
> I was a victim of a *kak* (shit) situation
> Stuck in the system
> With no fuckin' assistance
> . . . .
> No butter on my *broodjie* (sandwich)
> *Geen koeldrank nie, net my strootjie* (No cool drink/soda, just my straw).
>   (Die Antwoord 2011)

Like Ninja, she also places symbols of whiteness, power, and the trappings of capitalist success (gold, fancy bathroom fixtures) in relation to poverty (not having enough money to buy butter or a Coke) as she sings while sitting on the toilet (from an intimate, vulnerable, and humorously abject position). Her whiteness, she claims, was "stuck in the system," a "kak situation" until she "got her game on" and now she is "Yo flame on (yo yo yo Yo-Landi)." Yo-Landi uses a distinct, Cape coloured–inflected accent that clips words into a kind of shorthand rather than *suiwer* (pure) Afrikaans. Thus, she claims a more expansive version of the language that extends its affiliations beyond whites only and includes bruin (brown) Afrikaners or coloureds.

DIRTY AFRIKANER FREAKS: "I FINK U FREEKY" (2012)
As Yo-Landi's toilet song suggests, one of the performance strategies Die Antwoord uses across their work is to offer up disturbing visual and verbal provocations that pit decorum and decency against the primitive, bestial,

and sordid. In collaboration with American photographer Roger Ballen, "I Fink U Freeky" is shot in black-and-white, and every single frame is skillfully art-directed.[12] Ballen is well-known internationally for his 1994 book *Platte-land: Images of Rural South Africa* [platteland, literally "flat land," means "heart-land"], which included portraits of Afrikaners from rural communities. "*Platteland* was born of the profound irony that despite the political privilege apartheid had bestowed on whites," Ballen claims, "in the physical heart of the land there is inescapable testimony to the failure of the regime even to secure the well-being of the privileged minority" (Ballen 2013). Probably the most famous image from *Platteland* is titled "Dresie and Cassie, Twins, Western Transvaal, 1993" and features two drooling men with distinct signs of inbreeding, including microcephaly, and distended ears.[13] By collaborating with Ballen on the video for "I Fink U Freeky," Die Antwoord perform an abjected version of whiteness and make associations with inbreeding and retardation — in the sense of both disability and backwardness. In a 2010 interview with Norwegian TV, Yo-Landi explains that "Afrikaans culture is *retarded* and boring, you know, so kids are just natural to break out of it" (Die Antwoord 2010c, emphasis mine). And the lyrics for "Fatty Boom Boom" claim, "All these rappers sound exactly the same / It's like one big *inbred* fuck-fest, Sies / No, I do not want to stop, collaborate or listen" (Die Antwoord 2012b, emphasis mine).[14] Calling Afrikanerdom "retarded" evokes both the idiocy of the apartheid state and references Afrikaner's propensity to always look backward to the past.[15]

As in *Platteland*, whiteness in "I Fink U Freeky" is also decidedly abjected, as images of Ninja and a cast of freaks fill the screen. Symbols of whiteness and poverty pervade every frame of the video. Skinny white men and boys grimace with sharpened teeth, dance in dirty underwear, or wear toy elephant noses as prosthetic penises. Covered in homemade tattoos, they are all thin and bony, suggesting not having enough to eat. Yo-Landi sports a hairstyle that's part bowl cut, part mullet, and she bites her underlip and snarls at the camera. Naked, she looks up at the camera from a bath of dark black water [possibly, blood] or from a bed strewn with skulls as hands caress her skinny body from under the mattress. An aura of kink pervades the scene. There is an abundance of white skin in the video, all of which is smeared with ash, as if the characters live in abject poverty. Whiteness is troped as dirty, in the sense of both sexual perversion and filthy poverty.[16] One online respondent described Die Antwoord as "The Filthiest People

Figure 26. Whitewashed: Yo-Landi Vi$$er in "I Fink U Freeky."
© 2012 Die Antwoord.

Alive for sure. A paean to the OxyContin Age" (Barshad 2011). Dirt is juxta-posed with stark whiteness in the video. As Yo-Landi sings, "Yo fuck the rat race, my style is rap rave," she is in close-up, with six rats crawling around her neck. She wears two stripes under her eyes, like a footballer's eye black, but her stripes are bright white (figure 26). Her hair and eyebrows are also all bleached snow white. And she tells us that "I'm the type of chick who rolls with *spif giftige* (stylin' toxic) misfits."

Playing on Afrikaners as the "white tribe" of Africa,[17] Ninja and Yo-Landi then pose as a tribal couple over a dead lion. Ninja wears a loincloth with an elephant trunk attached at the groin. Yo-Landi is wrapped in a gray-and-white-striped wool blanket used in South African institutions like mine hostels and prisons. Behind them, two children's heads peek out of two oil drums; the blond white girl is in blackface and the black boy's face is painted white. Ninja holds a spear over the scenario, which reads as a racially inverted nineteenth-century travel postcard. Whereas such postcards depicted black bodies in primitive settings, "I Fink U Freeky" features the white couple in the role of "savages." On their website, Ninja explains what Die Antwoord represents: "The common man, the man in the street, the bottom of the fuckin' level. That's what we relate to, you know, that funkiness [like when] you haven't changed your underpants, and it's smelling funky. South Africa's pretty fuckin' funky" (Die Antwoord, "Take No Prisoners," n.d.). Aligning

Figure 27. African Gothic: Yo-Landi Vi$$er and Ninja of Die Antwoord in "I Fink U Freeky." © 2012 Die Antwoord.

South African whiteness with dirt, filth, and fetid "funkiness," Ninja discredits its former desire toward racial purity, white supremacy, and Calvinist morality by suggesting that whiteness stinks.

In the video's middle interlude, Yo-Landi prepares eggs for Ninja in a dirty kitchen; a cockroach falls into the eggs; Yo-Landi sneers at it in disgust and flicks it out of the frying pan. In direct reference to *American Gothic*, Yo-Landi and Ninja each clutch forks and knives as a pig head sits on a plate between them. Ninja's plate is full of chicken feet and Yo-Landi has *pap en wors*, a traditional Afrikaner dish of farmer's sausage and cornmeal porridge. The scene is filled with poor man's food and "garbage cuts" of meat. By citing and sampling Grant Wood's Depression-era iconic Americana, whiteness moves beyond the local Afrikaner context to poor whites in Depression-era America; Afrikaners are framed in a lineage of global whiteness (figure 27).

As Ninja whips the song to its climax, he stares fixedly at the camera as a boa constructor curls around his face, mouthing the words "I Fink U Freeky and I like you a lot." Cut to his groin, where he strokes the boa's head as it stretches between his fingers, becoming an enormous snake erection. As we are asked to fixate on Ninja's phallic surrogate, he drops the following phallic rhymes: "Ek's a laarney, jy's a gam, Want jy lam innie mang, met jou slang in a man" (I'm from high society, you're low class [a gam, or Cape Flats coloured], because you're stuck in prison, with your snake [penis] in a man). As the video comes to an end, the snow-white Yo-Landi with the enormous dilated black pupils sinks into the black water of her bath, leaving only a ripple — a hyphen of humanity, perhaps? — as a reminder that she was there.

"I Fink U Freeky" traffics in a problematic symbolic mélange of images. Ninja dares to offend rather than comply with political correctness. Within the performance frame of the video, whiteness is abjected and made filthy, demoted on the rungs of the usual social hierarchy, and made savage and primitive. Simultaneously, Ninja wields his phallic masculinity and insults his enemies as imprisoned sodomites, positioning homoerotic sex from the penetrator's, not the penetrated's, point of view (your snake [penis] in a man). Yo-Landi's eerie blackened eyes without irises suggest the white-sight that has dominated South African culture, asking what the world might look like if not through white eyes. Simultaneously she wears the gray-and-white blanket of migrant labor hostels and prisons, spaces un-familiar to most South African whites and in which they received preferen-tial treatment under apartheid. She and Ninja pose as pseudo-regal African Gothics in a tableaux of poor white foods that alternately celebrate and de-base whiteness. The final image of Yo-Landi's disappearing ripple echoes Opperman's claims about the small hyphen of humanity and the minority status of whites in Africa in general. And the overall celebration of freaks and freakiness, punctuated by the pulsing refrain of "I Fink U Freeky and I like you a lot," reads as a forthright declaration of whiteness on new terms, terms that resist its former hegemony and instead celebrate its scaly under-belly. Whiteness gets its freak on.

What Die Antwoord are trying to do, is to adapt, chameleon-like, to a new social position and to move away from binary, essential constructions of race in favor of a messy web of borrowed and enacted affiliations. They play with racial categories, trying to undo racist ones. I agree with Claire Scott's assessment that "Die Antwoord do not present a utopian or unproblematic engagement with white identity, but rather focus the audience's gaze on all that is uncomfortable, distasteful and undesirable about 'white' as a racial category, as opposed to a purely racist category" (2012, 754). But it is vital to note that as whites, they occupy the privileged position of being able to bor-row culturally and racially shapeshift.

References to inbreeding and incest are picked up again in the video for "Baby's on Fire" (2012a).[18] This video echoes Afrikaans novelist Marlene van Niekerk's award-winning novel *Triomf* (1994, 2001), which chronicles the lives of a dysfunctional family of *armblankes* (poor whites) in the bulldozed and reclaimed suburb that was once the vibrant Sophiatown, outside Johannesburg, and Michael's Raeburn's 2008 film adaptation of her novel.[19] Set in a poor white neighborhood of cheap concrete row houses, "Baby's on Fire" opens with a domestic scene around the dining table. Whiteness is directly foregrounded in the design choices. Yo-Landi's tiny body is pale white, her hair, eyelashes and eyebrows bleached white, and she wears a pink T-shirt reading "Who needs tits . . . ." At the other side of the table, Ninja, also with bleached hair, thanks his mother for the delicious food she serves. The parents wear ultra-blond wigs, smoke while they eat, and the entire scene is somewhat overexposed, giving off an aura of extreme brightness (whiteness). The art on the walls of this small house include a kitten stuck in a tree with the caption, "I need a hug," hanging alongside a masturbating '50s pinup called "Inviting Cunt." The art evokes the double standards of Afrikaner culture that simultaneously prohibit sexuality and yet engage in perversions in secret. The mother passes labor down to her daughter, who is on the lowest rung of the family's hierarchy, and reluctantly, Yo-Landi goes to the fridge to get Ninja a Redbull. As she bends over, we see the back of her T-shirt, which reads " . . . when you have an ass like this," and we see her father leering at his daughter's petite body as he inhales deeply on his cigarette in a disturbing depiction of forbidden familial desire.

The song's chorus—"She got me going vokken crazy soos a mal naaier [like a crazy fucker]"—suggests the sexual taboos of incest and desire for underage girls, and also makes explicit male control over female desire. Marking the power of the alpha male (Ninja the brother) over the family (including his beta male, silent father), everyone must wait for Ninja to gulp down his Redbull before they can say grace and begin eating. As Yo-Landi says grace in a little-girl voice, thanking God for the food, their success overseas, and their pitbull named Satan, whiteness, pornography, and Calvinism are brought into revealing constellation as we pan across more art on the walls: a framed *Playboy* pinup alongside a little white Germanic girl holding flowers and Jesus with outstretched hands. When she asks if a boy can come visit after dinner, Ninja, the overbearing brother figure, shouts back at her, "No, I don't want any of these scaly motherfuckers from this hood getting fresh with my little sister!" (Die Antwoord 2012a).

The rest of the video entails Ninja, himself "getting fresh" with several women in his own leopard-themed bedroom or lounging by a kiddy pool filled with baby oil, constantly beating up all the boys who come to seduce Yo-Landi (and marking a sexual double standard). As his own sexual exploits move toward climax, he smells his sister's impending sexuality; he literally sniffs the air each time she is with a boy, running to her defense like a human pitbull. Sister Yo-Landi is depicted in pastel hot pants, gyrating her skinny pelvis, singing about how easy rapping comes to her, how many "bad boys want a piece of me." Performing against a constant backdrop of pinks, pastels, and stuffed animals, Yo-Landi combines a direct eroticism with the infantilized kink of pedophilia.[20]

This video—paired with "Cookie Thumper," the story of white Yo-Landi's love affair with ex-prisoner Bra Anies, a tattooed coloured gangster who, at the video's climax, penetrates her anally—plays with sexual taboos at the core of Afrikaner morality, including incest, miscegenation, and the spectrum of sexual practices beyond procreation. Die Antwoord's use of sexuality serves to draw in audiences (sex sells, after all) and to challenge conservative Afrikaner mores. But it also picks up on Ninja's proclamation of "all these different people, fucked into one person" and, in offering a spectrum of sexual practices, from the traditional and accepted to the forbidden and kinky, also advocates for a greater fluidity in South African social practice.[21] Die Antwoord miscegenates the assumed purity of Afrikaner whiteness, making explicitly visible the crossings and mixings inherent in South African culture and resisting the isolationism and logic of racial purity of the laager.

WHITE KAFFIRS

In "Never le nkemise 1" ("You Can't Stop Me"), off their second album, Ten$ion, Ninja proclaims himself "Ninja, die wit kaffir" (the white nigger), and in "Fok julle naaiers" ("Fuck You Fuckers"), he says, "All hail da great white ninja." As mentioned before, calling someone a kaffir is to deem them a degraded Other. In "Never le nkemise 1," Ninja claims the othered insult of kaffir for himself as a white body in the postcolony. The strategic move of equating whites with kaffirs performs several important moves. On the one hand, it indexes the apartheid-era term as a label for the lowliest members of society, those relegated to subhuman status. By using this label for whites in post-1994 South Africa, Ninja suggests that whites are now the underclass, the lowliest members of the new society. And it could also suggest that whites or whiteness itself is subhuman, a despicable position to occupy. This move uses the symbolic category of kaffir (lowest member of society, invisible, degraded, or denigrated one) to speak about poor whites both as the new kaffirs of the culture (lamenting the loss of power) as well as place whiteness into a denigrated category unto itself (something to discredit or abhor). By "kaffir-izing" whiteness, by claiming all its zefness, its dirtiness, and its distastefulness, Die Antwoord knocks it off its historic pedestal. Such an act, at least metaphorically, levels the racially charged historic playing field where whites in South Africa have always been in control.

Die Antwoord combines a "kaffir-izing" of whiteness with lyrics that are designed to shock and appall, particularly resisting mainstream Afrikaner culture and social mores. There are aggressive attacks like "Wat kyk jy? Fokof! Wat kyk jy? Poes! Wat kyk jy? Fok jou! Wat kyk jy? Jou naai!" (What you lookin' at? Fuck off! What you lookin' at? Cunt! What you lookin' at? Fuck you! What you lookin' at? You fucker!). There are articulations of the unmentionable, like "'Binne-poes-pienk' aan die moerefokken brand ("Inner-pussy-pink" on muthafuckin' fire), or the unpalatable, like "jy lyk so mooi met my piel in jou keel / ag siestog! Now try say my name / Man-botter binne in jou slym-konyn" (you look so pretty with my dick in your throat / oh poor you, Now try say my name / Man-butter inside your slimy-bunny).[22]

Actively engaged in spectacle, Die Antwoord makes glossy, seductive, shocking and provocative videos set to funky beats and filled with expletives. They trade in a currency of these images, which are knowingly provocative. Their lyrics even point to their own shock value. For instance, at the end of "Fatty Boom Boom," after a giant mucous-covered cricket, known as a Parktown prawn, is removed from the Lady Gaga character's vagina by a street abortionist, a male voice decries in Afrikaans, "Jeeziz, dude! Chill out a little bit, please!" This distasteful and vulgar tone even bleeds into reviews of the group's work; for example, Stephens says of the album Ten$ion, it "doesn't flirt with controversy, so much as buttfuck it without buying it dinner first" (2013, 6).

So what might the shock vulgarity of Die Antwoord and their slippery racial affiliations amount to? Simply dismissing them as puerile shock jocks out to get a rise out of stuffy old folks ignores their enormous international reach and popularity. Waddy Jones, himself a seasoned forty-year-old, is a sophisticated spinner of culture, having reinvented himself and his musical style multiple times before hitting gold with the zef formula. In "So What?" he sings, "I've been rapping for 20 fucking years / A whole lot of fucking blood sweat and tears."[23] Might Die Antwoord's version of whiteness be an attempt to make whiteness indigestible, in the sense of resisting assimilation? By performing the most distasteful, vulgar, and obscene versions of whiteness, and enacting and fetishizing the biggest taboos of white Afrikaner culture, especially in relation to—or in defiance against—Afrikaner ordentlikheid (propriety), Die Antwoord become indigestible, fluidly remaining outside mainstream standards of decorum and opposing white hegemony. Ninja claims the difference between Die Antwoord and conservative Afrikaans people: "Maybe, like Satanism was spawned from Christianity. Dat's the difference" (Die Antwoord 2010c). "Fuck da system, we got our own system," spits Yo-Landi Vi$$er in "Never le nkemise 2," adding, "We make our own rules. We don't answer to no one."

Beyond being an irreverent boast, her claim has some real-world grounding. After being signed by Jimmy Iovine at Interscope Records, the power-house producer of much of the hip-hop music scene, Die Antwoord broke off with the label in an unprecedented move for such a new group, "forgoing a million dollar guarantee on the new record and choosing complete creative independence" (Jardin 2011). Claiming that Interscope wanted to "make us sound like everyone else out there at the moment," they instead released Ten$ion through their own independent label, Zef Recordz.[24] For an international newcomer to reject the lucrative offer and prestige that Interscope represents is quite a boldly defiant act. In a move that could be read as the Global South speaking truth to the Global North, Die Antwoord essentially refused to be constrained—and consumed—by Interscope, which represents the larger capitalist music-making machine. Die Antwoord had to have been aware that when Insane Clown Posse (ICP)—a white "circus-themed swear-rap" group (Morton 2007) that was about as indigestible and out of the mainstream as you could imagine—was signed by Interscope, they became part of the corporate machine they started out defying.[25] Ninja and Yo-Landi instead refused the lure of American dollars, aware of the corporate hook and its concomitant artistic pigeonholing.

All the controversy surrounding their work—including having to pull the video trailer for their new album Ten$ion because they used South African sculptor Jane Alexander's iconic Butcher Boys without permission—keeps them in the spotlight. They cultivate controversy in order to remain visible. If I consider Die Antwoord as a metaphor for South African whiteness writ large, then their controversial position keeps them from becoming obsolete; they remain visible in order to avoid falling into oblivion, or what Opperman might call a small hyphen of whiteness in a vast black continent.

Yet even though they operate outside the American-based musical machine, Die Antwoord do utilize digital space and the technologies of the Internet to circulate glossy, consumable images (albeit shocking and provocative ones), and as white artists, they also have access to the mechanisms of success that many of their fellow coloured and black South Africans do not. Recently, a debate raged in the Cape Town press over how much credit Jones and du Toit were giving coloured street kids like Wanga Jack, who is featured in their "Evil Boy" video. The critique was launched by none other than André Laubscher, Peter Van Heerden's collaborator. Laubscher accused Die Antwoord of exploiting the boys and suggested that "Ninja and Yo-Landi stole their image and creative material from the boys living on his farm, including Wanga, through pursuing them with booze and drugs" ("Die Antwoord Reacts" 2013). Die Antwoord posted a lengthy response to Laubscher's accusations, as reported by Charl Blignaut of City Press. Delivered in a patronizing tone, it chronicles the story of Wanga's apprenticeship under Die Antwoord's tutelage and claims that Jack was paid for his work but that Jack's consistent unprofessionalism forced them to break off ties with him. The response ends by admonishing Wanga for "being naughty and telling lies" and explaining that Wanga was "getting 'guidance' from the wrong people" ("Die Antwoord Reacts" 2013). News coverage of the scandal died down immediately after Die Antwoord posted their response on their Facebook page and it was picked up verbatim and reprinted in multiple news outlets. Whether or not Laubscher's claims of exploitation were founded, Die Antwoord got the last word. The claims of black orphans potentially exploited for their artistry and talents would not be heard over the loud proclamations of now mega-successful white artists who remain opportunistic rather than outcast from power.

JACK PAROW'S KITSCH

If Die Antwoord cultivates and thrives on controversy, Jack Parow is far more subdued and scandal-averse. Parow's performance style is a combination of clever Afrikaans lyrics, catchy beats, and an "everyday Joe" personality that is exaggerated to make ironic and humorous commentary on itself. In his video for "Byellville," a zef pronunciation of his hometown of Bellville, Parow is depicted as a dejected loser in a buttoned-up collar sitting alone at the bowling alley on his birthday. A rich man with two girls on his arms throws napkins at him as he looks forlornly at the single sparkler in his Coke float. After he finds his bike wheel stolen, he transforms into cool Jack Parow the "zef, romanties Afrikaner rapper" wearing a foot-long brim on his signature baseball cap. His tacky costuming all point to his marked status as a working-class white South African. As a proponent of zef style, he defines himself through an ironic frame, one that is grounded in a kitsch aesthetic.

Defined as lowly, sentimental, tacky, garish, or in poor taste, kitsch artifacts are works that are calculated to have popular appeal and are appreciated ironically or for camp value. According to Walter Benjamin, kitsch is a utilitarian object lacking all critical distance between object and observer; it is "art with a 100 percent, absolute and instantaneous availability for consumption" (Menninghaus 2009, 39). According to Menninghaus, the monosyllabic word connotes "'lowly' objects or actions" conjoined "with a slight degree of funniness." Such objects are excluded from formal discourse, as they represent "a vulgar and/or childish form of expression" with a tendency toward "debasement" (2009, 39–40).[26] Kitsch is also tied to irony; to appreciate the kitsch value of an object, one must understand meaning beyond its literal signification. Kitsch is poor taste appreciated knowingly, or in an ironic way. Parow's exaggerated cap brim references baseball caps worn to be cool while also parodying the very trappings of such coolness. Parow often stages poor whites ironically. In one publicity shot (figure 28), Parow and his "family" are posed beside a camping caravan: a shirtless father figure holds a cocktail in an everyday drinking glass; a woman in stylish sunglasses holds a baby; a girl smirks at the camera in her socks; and a tattooed young woman lies on the ground with a tabby cat curled between her legs. Unlike the dirtiness of Die Antwoord's images, Parow's are stylized amalgams of old tropes with new glossy finish, a combination of nostalgia and ironic commentary.

Figure 28. Jack Parow's boerekitsch. © 2012 Sascha Waldman. Courtesy of Jack Parow.

"AFRIKAANS IS DOOD" ("AFRIKAANS IS DEAD") (2011)

The video for "Afrikaans is dood" plays on the culture of violence and home invasions that many (white) South Africans fear, as the Oscar Pistorius case affirmed.[27] Parow, our protagonist, is in his pajamas and fuzzy slippers, tied to a chair with duct tape over his mouth. "Everyone is screaming *Afrikaans is dood* (Afrikaans is dead)" echoes loudly under the scene, referencing the 1990s *taalstryd* battles over the future of Afrikaans and the 2015 flare-up over Stellenbosch University's decision to move toward English as the language of instruction. At first glance, the image of a white man tied up and gagged is a distillation of the Afrikaner's position in contemporary South Africa. Then the camera reveals his three captors: a coloured man in a welder's helmet wielding a grinding saw; a tall white man with a mean right hook; and a large white woman with a cricket bat. As they tear off his duct tape, the song's refrain changes slightly, now rhyming *dood* (dead) with *groot* (big). Afrikaans morphs from being dead, irrelevant, or out of style to being hot, in demand, and great. Parow then outsmarts his captors and beats them with their own weapons. Enacting a form of self-debasement by proclaiming himself "king of the shit, the new Afrikaans icon," Parow says he's "straight out the suburbs, *top van die middle klas* (top of the middle class)."

Here he shifts the usual social hierarchy and places himself in an elevated position (as king) of his domain (the world of shit). He also plays on Voortrekker mythology when he claims, "No one can save me / But I still push / forge on forward." By the end of the video, the title has been inverted and Afrikaans is no longer *dood*; rather, now it is *groot*. Parow refuses the narrative that Afrikaner culture is no longer valid by reclaiming cultural freshness (*groot*) from the pronouncements of its death (*dood*).

Parow combines incongruous elements in his rhymes, at once celebrating and denigrating his Afrikaner heritage. In his breakout hit "Cooler as ekke" ("Cooler as/than Me," 2009), he plays a browbeaten waiter at a drive-in restaurant abused by his rich customers in flashy cars. In revenge, he sings:

Ek's original jy's gecopy (I'm original you're copied)
Ek's 'n flash drive jy's 'n floppy (I'm a flash drive you're a floppy)

But even his revenge deprecates his own status. He compares his own success with that of the rich boy in the car:

Jack Parow, brother, I'm pussy-wild (*poes-woes*)
You eat caviar and couscous
I drink Klipdrif, you drink Peroni
You've friends in Sweden,
I have friends in Benoni

He positions his enemy—mainstream South African whites—as high class, eating caviar and couscous, and drinking imported Italian beer, while he is the working-class hero who drinks cheap brandy and has friends in the working-class suburb of Johannesburg. The song's chorus, "You think you're cooler than/as me" utilizes the Cape dialect of the first-person singular— *ekke* as opposed to *ek*—and marks Parow's language as working class rather than *suiwer* (pure) or upper-class Afrikaans. The video features Parow and his friends having a *braai* (barbeque) in a parking lot and hanging out beside a junkyard kiddy pool, both locations marking the class of the characters. The video ends with Parow in the middle of the road beside his car, which has run out of gas on the curb. If whiteness has run out of gas after the fall of apartheid, then Parow is giving it new life, on new terms, through zefness.

Parow also collaborated with EJ von Lyrik, a coloured female musician and human rights activist, on "Ons behoort mos saam" ("We Belong Together"), the title track for Tim Greene's 2011 film *Skeem*, about two wannabe gang-sters who discover a million bucks in the trunk of their car. The video is a love story between Parow and Lyrik. He sings that he loves everything about her, including her freckles, her belly, her pimples, and even her snot. She sings of loving him, and says in coloured-inflected Afrikaans, "kannie wag virre dag wanna ons twee vasmaak in holy matrimony" (can't wait for the day that we two connect in holy matrimony). In a scene of interracial coupling, they snuggle together in Parow's zef car at a drive-in movie, watching images of a black man and white woman flirting on screen in *Skeem*. In this love song to cultural unity, Parow sings of Lyrik as "his popcorn and movie, chocolates and champagne," all complementing elements that make a united whole. His format is melodramatic, but here the binaries bleed into each other, rather than remain locked in a historic stare down (as Opperman's Boer and Kaffir) and Parow's storyline allows for cross-racial love.

Parow's kitsch borders on nostalgia at times. In the song "I Miss" off his *Jack Parow* (2010) album, he sings of all the things he misses from "the old days": "Monday morning *skoolsaal* (school assembly)," "the days when I thought all the movies were real," "Voortrekker camps and CSV kampe / Mufasa, Aladdin, Bambi and Thumper." The song's chorus samples popular culture references that were imported from America: Tweety and Sylvester, Ninja Turtles, Smurfs, Greyskull from *Masters of the Universe*, and *Ghostbusters* (1984). He sings,

> There's so much I miss from the old days
> There's so much that I learnt from the old ways
> Another kid fokken raised by the 80's
> Kytie, Kytie, jy was nie net 'n mytie (Katy, Katy, you weren't just a maid)

Here Parow uses a coloured-inflected dialect and waxes nostalgic about the "good old days," complete with references to interracial sex and the practice of young white Afrikaner boys losing their virginity to black maids. But he ultimately recognizes the past as past, when he sings: "There's a lot of good things that happened back then / But I can't keep going on about way back when" (Parow 2010). "I Miss" suggests a longing for the innocence of child-hood and the heyday of white South Africa; structured as a list of all the things he misses, it becomes a chronicle of a white teenage boy's privilege under apartheid.

Parow's kitsch is simultaneously tacky, lowly, and sentimental. It is designed to have popular appeal; he often sings of *tannies* who say of his work, "Wow, that guy raps lekker (nice)." His songs are anthems to partying, populated with references to popular liquor brands Klipdrift and Ricky Louw, and to the celebration of the tacky, common characteristics of Afrikaner life. But because celebrating whiteness outright in the new democracy is considered in poor taste, the tactic he takes is to make his love songs to his culture into kitsch, so that they are appreciated ironically. That way, he can honor his cultural heritage without coming across as a white supremacist. Whereas the inhabitants of the all-white enclave of Orania, or members of the conservative Afrikaner Resistance Movement, are easily written off as right-wing fanatics and their expressions of racial pride are often regarded as outdated, Parow's kitsch irony makes his *volkstrots* palatable. Thus, if Die Antwoord make themselves indigestible to the capitalist machine and the machine of whiteness, then Jack Parow makes whiteness in the postcolony palatable—even lovable—through kitsch. The significance of such a strategy for global whiteness is important; as a subject position that has historically been responsible for terrible injustices against other groups, performing whiteness as nonthreatening is a way of acknowledging—and remedying—those past dynamics. Yet performing whiteness as lovable also suggests how ontologically insecure such as system is; whiteness always desires to be included in, even central to, the social sphere.

SERIAL KITSCHERS, BOER'GEOISIE, AND THE BOERE MUSEUM/NAUSEUM

Parow is not the only one using boerekitsch as a strategy. There is a popular restaurant in Pretoria called Boer'geoisie that serves traditional Afrikaner fare such as *pap en wors, poffadder, waterblommetjie bredie,* and *koeksisters*.[28] The décor is boerekitsch to the extreme; the entire restaurant is filled with memorabilia from the apartheid era. Statuettes of Verwoerd and Paul Kruger sit beside official portraits of P. W. Botha and commemorative china plates from the 1938 Centenary Trek festival. The walls are covered in etchings of the Battle of Blood River, Jan van Riebeeck, and the Voortrekker Monument. Ox-wagons of every imaginable size and material litter the place and there is even a sewing machine made to resemble the Voortrekker Monument. Diners, whose class status afford them the privilege of frequenting the establishment—hence the ironic name: *Boer'geoisie*—consume their favorite Afrikaner dishes surrounded by the outmoded symbolic capital that built their nation. History is consumable as ironic capital, a far stretch from its sincere deployment as the stuff of the nation-building project. Whereas Afrikaans-speakers genuinely and wholeheartedly internalized that symbolic capital in the early twentieth century, in democratic South Africa they can regard the artifacts with irony, feeling partially nostalgic and yet not shameful as they consume mouthfuls of *boerewors* and wash them down with shots of *bucchu* (South African herbal grappa) or cups of *rooibos* tea.

An entire exhibition of boerekitsch, titled *Serial Kitschers*, was on display at the 2007 Klein Karoo National Arts Festival in Oudtshoorn. The installation included sepia portraits of Afrikaners framed in wooden toilet seats; an image of Marilyn Monroe in a Voortrekker kappie, her panties revealed by her billowing skirt patterned with the old South African flag; and aerodynamic ox-wagons being pulled by the world's fastest land animal: the cheetah. There were also paintings of Paul Kruger in the style of South African kitsch art favorite, Vladimir Tretchikoff, and Elvis as a trekboer smoking a corncob pipe.

And at Evita se Perron in Darling, outside Cape Town, Pieter-Dirk Uys has installed his ironically named Boere Museum/Nauseum. Housed within an old zinc-roofed farmhouse adjacent to his cabaret performance space, the Nauseum houses Uys's collection of apartheid-era memorabilia and Afrikaner kitsch artifacts. He displays all the official letters Evita wrote to the government and the formal replies she received, as well as documents from the Censor Board. There are portraits of apartheid's architects—Verwoerd, Malan, Strijdom, Botha—alongside paintings of Evita in multiple incarnations—Evita as Frida Kahlo, Mona Lisa, Klimt's Judith, and Liberty in Eugène Delacroix's *Liberty Leading the People* (1830). There is a "golliwog" doll riding on a taxidermied antelope head, the official government portrait of the all-white Parliament dating from the mid-1980s, and, outside in the garden, an apartheid sign from the Cape Town City Council stating "This Area for Whites Only."[29] My favorite artifact is a wall-mounted lamp that shines through an image of Verwoerd's head: the "light" of civilization indeed.

Boer'geoisie and the Boere Museum/Nauseum serve as ironic archives of the Afrikaner past. They stand as testaments to the absurdity of the nation-building and apartheid eras, as parodies of the former authority of a powerful racist machine. They are archives of the symbolic capital the nation architects leveraged to build and uphold the white apartheid state. Framed as kitsch, the collections in these two popular sites have both an "element

Figure 29. Boerekitsch memorabilia at Pieter-Dirk Uys's
Boere Museum/Nauseum in Darling. © 2012 Megan Lewis.

of 'debasement' about them" (Menninghaus 2009, 40) and a nostalgia, in
Susan Bennett's terms, a representation of the past's "'imagined and mythic
qualities' so as to effect some corrective in the present" (Bennett 1996, 5).

While it is seductive to believe whiteness may escape its hegemonic past
through irony, I'm weary of too rosy a framing. Viveca Greene (2012) suggests that irony has limits. In her exploration of the ethics of humor, she
points to hipster racism — "the practice of someone in a dominant racial
group making a derogatory joke about people in a historically disadvantaged
racial group under the guise of being ironic" (2012, 154) — and suggests that
the veneer of irony often obscures systems of privilege and social inequali-
ties (2012, 155). Thus, Die Antwoord and Jack Parow's ironic frames may be
effective for white subjects seeking to disavow the power dynamics of the
past; but at what price does zefness co-opt coloured vernacular and street
culture to do so? I wonder: is the only way for whiteness to undo its privilege
to look, yet again, to blackness and brownness?

CONCLUSION

In conclusion, I return to the Whitewash Conference at the University of Johannesburg in March 2013. In my own metacommentary on whiteness and performance, I unpack some of the performances I witnessed at the conference, which are indicative of the complexities and stakes of whiteness in contemporary South Africa. There was only one person of color invited to speak at the conference: *City Press* editor Ferial Haffajee.[1] She was on the prestigious plenary panel at the center of the event, alongside noted academics Melissa Steyn and Sarah Nuttall. The plenary was an awkward affair and tensions were high. The first speaker was Steyn, the best-known scholar on whiteness in South Africa, who eloquently reported on the work she has been doing through interviews of whites in the new democracy. She catalogued the range of responses she got from her interview subjects, including lingering attitudes among white South Africans that perpetuate outdated narratives of belonging and continue to cultivate an ignorance or blindness about the past. While Steyn's work is vitally important to Whiteness Studies in South Africa, it was read by some in the room, including Haffajee, as a recentering of the privileged white academic voice. Perhaps the dramaturgical choice of having her speak first on the panel may have inadvertently fed this interpretation. The concern about recentering whiteness was immediately taken up by Professor Nuttall, who spoke next. Nuttall, who seemed visibly uncomfortable, commented on how studying a topic could inadvertently recenter its power. "Ours is not the most important story," she claimed, and warned the assembled group not to construct alibis, recenter white privilege, or make claims about white victimization (none of which had occurred, nor ever did, throughout the conference). She reminded the group that black radical voices were needed as part of the discourse. This was the perfect segue to introduce Haffajee, who then proceeded to enumerate the reasons she was "unbearably bored" with the conference and its topic. Haffajee left immediately after giving her remarks and followed up the next day with an op-ed piece in *City Press* called "The Problem with Whiteness" in which she wrote off the entire conference as an "obsessive navel-gazing" enterprise that "continues to place privileged people at the centre of the gaze of the academy" (2013). One of the conference participants, Christi van der Westhuizen from the University of the Free State, offered a response in the same issue of *City Press*. Van der Westhuizen claimed that while "it has been a feature of whiteness studies to continually interrogate its raison d'être, as whiteness scholars are alive to the danger of degenerating into reproducing whiteness," the "proviso for studies of whiteness should be to continue the dismantling of whiteness as part of a larger political project against race and racism" (2013a). Haffajee's critique is one that is often waged at scholars engaged in Whiteness or Critical Race Studies, and, frankly, one waged at academics by nonacademics. I can understand that Haffajee was put on the defensive as the only woman of color in a room of white academics. And her concerns about recentering privilege—especially since she was the only person of color involved—are compelling and valid. What was unfortunate, however, was that she ended up publicly dismissing the conference, including the important work of the many talented and committed scholars who gathered for this conference, without having a chance to listen to the scholarship itself. I was saddened that she wrote off the conference based on the fact that it was populated by white people, without considering how those people were engaged in the difficult work of attempting to dismantle privilege, interrogate its supremacy, and unpack how it functions (from every imaginable disciplinary perspective) in order to build a more equitable and democratic society. The organizers of the conference should have thought about the racial dynamics of such an event and made sure that people of color were not only included, but directly invited to participate. Just as antiracism efforts require white allies, so too does the effort to dismantle whiteness require the commitment and participation of white, black, and brown academics and activists.

Haffajee's reaction to the conference marks just how fraught race still is in the new South African democracy, especially the sensitivity around any discussions of whiteness. In her response to Haffajee, van der Westhuizen quoted sociologist Zimitri Erasmus, who argued that "white people should do the white work" (van der Westhuizen 2013a). In other words, the reason for the whiteness of the conference was that it is our responsibility *as white people* to begin the work of dismantling whiteness. What was most interesting to me about the performances of the plenary panel was the way in which race—and whiteness—were harnessed to old ways of thinking about race. The findings of a white academic voice were unable to be heard because her whiteness got in the way. Another white academic felt it was "impossible" to do the work of Whiteness Studies and became awkward and dismissive. And the lone black voice wrote off the whole affair, judging the book by the whiteness of its cover and not its content.

As only one racialized event in the complex South African democracy, the Whitewash Conference demonstrated how difficult it is to even begin to take on whiteness. Because of its position as the center of power—the hegemon, "The Man," or what Steve Garner calls the "Greenwich Mean Time of Identity" (2007, 47)—whiteness can never occupy a position as subaltern, marginal, antihegemonic, or the Sticker-to-the-Man. No matter how much it borrows from subaltern practices, or claims prison tattoos, or coloured Afrikaans turns of phrase, it seems always to be trapped in its own power construct. If "sticking it to the man" means "to take some action intended to defy a source of oppression such as globalization, commercialization, big business or government" (allwords.com), can whites ever stick it to themselves? And if such a maneuver is impossible, then what are the options for whiteness in the postcolony and our global world? Can whiteness ever escape its own hegemony?

One possible answer was offered by Whitewash Conference plenary panelist Samantha Vice, who suggested that white South Africans should downplay their public selves in the new democracy. Vice opts for a reformation of the "morally damaged white self, constituted by psychical and somatic habits of privilege" (2010, 338). She prescribes humility and silence—"(a certain kind of) silence" (Vice 2010) that is "intended to diminish the impact of whiteliness in the public sphere" (Vice 2012, 152). Her prescription was misread by many as a "blanket banishment" (R. Barnard 2012, 153) of white people from public life, but her intent was far more nuanced. It involved what Max du Preez described as giving "black South Africans enough space for self-expression and self-fulfillment without feeling that over-critical whites are constantly supervising them" (R. Barnard 2012, 154); in other words, whites have to stop imagining themselves as bosses over black servants. Rather, Vice posits such silence as a kind of restraint that *listens for the other's voice.*

South African theatre, and Afrikaner performance in particular, offer several additional answers, no single one of which is entirely satisfactory.

One way that South African satirist Pieter-Dirk Uys "sticks it to the man"—in good left-progressive fashion—is to parody the power structures and to queer Afrikanerdom, inverting the value system and making the powerful laugh at themselves. As a white man in a dress, he is able to speak back to the system of patriarchy and white supremacy. Peter Van Heerden offers yet another alternative for whiteness: to abject it, eviscerate it, and expose its ugliness in order to understand it, move forward, and imagine new ways of being. Or, when stripped of their privilege, the privileged might follow Deon Opperman's populist performances of nostalgia and look to the past for some semblance of honor or elements in white culture that are deemed prideworthy. Contemporary artists like Die Antwoord might suggest that "the answer" lies in becoming indigestible, by rejecting connections to white privilege in favor of a foul-mouthed irreverence that claims poor white trashiness as a place from which to articulate and affiliate itself (through cultural borrowing) with black and brown culture rather than mainstream whiteness. In other words, to embrace the claim that in a melting pot of racial affiliations, "shit coalesces" (Andy on mhambi.com). Following Jack Parow, the answer might lie in commenting ironically on privilege, from an underprivileged position, with lovable humor and kitsch.

At this moment in history, there are no clear or easy solutions to the issue of how whiteness is to perform itself ethically. It seems safe to say that whiteness is always haunted by its own historicity and part of performing as a white subject in the postcolony means coming to terms with the fact that whiteness may never be untangled from power, imperialism, and hegemony. In this study, I have attempted to put Afrikaners in the spotlight to better understand how whiteness and hegemony are created, enacted, and contested and in ways that neither deify nor demonize it but rather demonstrate the complexities and entanglement of whiteness with history. It is my hope that this specific Afrikaner context offers a parable for global whiteness. As a case study in our postcolonial moment, I have looked to Afrikaners to see how whiteness plays out (to use a theatrical term) within a specific culture; how it has been leveraged toward nation-building efforts; how the privileged perform themselves into power and, then again, once their privilege is deflated; and also how performing artists have attempted to resist, challenge, abject, queer, and refashion whiteness. The Afrikaner scenario offers a lens through which to see both the potentials and pitfalls of these performances, the nostalgic acts that regress toward the past as well as the bold new performance negotiations of their identity, that make whiteness strange. It is imperative that scholars, artists, and citizens continue to work through whiteness, no matter how "guilt-etched [an] endeavor" (Bethlehem 2013), so that we disassemble its power as the default category of existence and address the problematics of "whiteliness" (Vice 2010) that still permeates South African culture—and the global Anglosphere—its everyday spaces, its academy, and its theatre. Performance, which marks behavior "in inverted commas" (Bonnett 1999), offers us a perceptual frame through which to see the world's historic color-codedness and racial constructions and to conjure up alternate ways in which to see, and enact, the world less whitely . . .

NOTES

PREFACE

1. Diana Taylor defines scenarios "as culturally specific imaginaries — sets of possibilities, ways of conceiving conflict, crisis, or resolution — activated with more or less theatricality" (2003, 13).

2. Garner, a forty-three-year-old African American man, was stopped by a white officer, Daniel Pantaleo, for selling loose cigarettes on a street in Staten Island. Pantaleo put Garner in a choke hold, threw him down, and pushed his face into the ground while four other officers restrained him. Garner plead with the officers, saying "I can't breathe" eleven times before losing consciousness, and eventually dying, while face-down on the sidewalk (Baker, Goodman, and Mueller 2015).

3. Drawing on contemporary practice in the United States, throughout this book I use the terms *white*, *black*, and *brown* in the manner in which African Americans reclaimed blackness or Latinos claimed brownness as sources of pride rather than derision. I have opted to deploy these color terms in lowercase rather than capitalizing them in an attempt to divorce such terms from the totalizing way in which they were used in classificatory regimes of power such as apartheid. Wherever possible, I also use more specifically descriptive terms such as WESSAs (White, English-Speaking South Africans), Afrikaners, Cape coloureds or bruin Afrikaners, African Americans, etc.

4. In November 2015, the Supreme Court of Appeal overturned his culpable homicide conviction and found him guilty of murder in the death of Reeva Steenkamp (BBC News 2015).

5. The postcolony, for Mbembe, is a simultaneously temporal and subjective entity. Characterized by "chaotic plurality" and "political improvisation" driven by "corporate institutions and a political machinery" that constitute a "distinct regime of violence," the postcolony offers a "dramatic stage" on which the lasting effects of colonialism and contemporary neoliberalism play out. It is a space and place that defies "the binary categories used in standard definitions of domination" in favor of an understanding of the "entanglement" of postcolonial relations (Mbembe 2001, 102–103).

INTRODUCTION

1. According to 2011 census figures, white South Africans make up 8.9 percent of South Africa's population of 51,770,560, which also consists of black Africans (79.2 percent), coloureds (8.9 percent), and Indians and Asians (2.5 percent). The white population is further divided linguistically/culturally: 61 percent Afrikaans-speakers, 36 percent English-speakers, and 3 percent who speak another primary language (www.statssa.gov.za/census/census_2011/census_products/Census_2011_Census_in _brief.pdf, 27, accessed April 10, 2016). Not all Afrikaans-speakers are white. Col-

oureds, who often self-identify as bruin Afrikaners (brown Afrikaners), speak Afrikaans as their mother tongue. For the purposes of my study, when I use the term *Afrikaners*, I mean white settlers of European descent who identify as a volk (nation). For more on coloured South African identity, see the works of Hein Willemse, Grant Farred, Zoë Wicomb, Mike van Graan, Mohamed Adhikari, and Zimitri Erasmus.

2. In claiming American allegiance here I mark how difficult discussions of race and taking responsibility for history continue to be in the United States, especially for white Americans. As an educator, I have worked tirelessly to bring such discussions into my classrooms, but my students continue to struggle with how to speak about the unspeakable in what they are told is a postracial society. Derald Wing Sue (2015) identifies how "politeness" and "colorblind" protocols and internalized fears of appearing racist prevent many people from tackling the taboo subject of race in America.

3. Anton Botha (2011) discusses several other instances of Hollywood visions that depict Afrikaners as villains, often in contexts that have nothing to do with South Africa: *Hard Target* (1993), *Sum of All Fears* (2002), *The Manchurian Candidate* (2004), and *Red* (2010). I would also add *Blood Diamond* (2006) and *Avengers: Age of Ultron* (2015).

4. Note the explicitly racial tones of his name: Eugène (well-born or good-genes) Terre'Blanche (white earth).

5. Orania is a whites-only enclave along the Orange River in the northern Cape, and Kleinfontein is a suburb of Pretoria. F. Brinley Bruton describes how Kleinfontein residents have fenced themselves into their community in reaction to the country's high crime rates and institutionalized affirmative action policy, which has resulted "in white people being frozen out of jobs and university places" (2013).

6. In fact, the "poor white" issue was raised at the turn of the twentieth century. For more on the *Carnegie Commission on the Poor White Question in South Africa*, see Grosskopf et al. 1932.

7. Here my South African allegiance (first person) marks the complexities and nuances of my claim to a settler culture that is responsible for terrible things yet simultaneously seeks belonging in Africa. I refuse blanket dismissals of white Africans as a whole; rather, I seek to understand the inner workings of such identity formations.

8. Unlike *extractive colonialism*, in which "an imperial power moves into a society and, through a variety of violent, ideological, bureaucratic, manipulative, coercive, and discursive means, gains control of its economy, typically its natural resources and labor, redirecting those resources and that labor to the benefit of the metropole," *settler colonialism* is a system in which "the colonizing society is intent not simply on gaining control of the resources and labor of the local community, but on owning its land as well." Accomplished by marginalizing indigenous inhabitants, and "seeking through various institutional means to destroy their traditional cultures," settler cultures also create "enduring social and political institutions to normalize and perpetuate the settler project" (Lynch 2014, 376–377).

9. The plenary included white scholars Sarah Nuttall from the Wits Institute for Social and Economic Research, Melissa Steyn of the University of Cape Town, Louise Bethlehem of Hebrew University in Jerusalem, and journalist Ferial Haffajee, who edits

City Press and was the only one person of color on the panel. See Haffajee's (2013) op-ed critiquing the conference as well as Christi van der Westhuizen's (2013a) response.

10. See also Falkof 2013; Van Der Watt 2003, 2004; and van der Westhuizen 2013a.

11. From Heidegger's formulation of *sous rature*, crossing out text yet allowing the erasure to remain visible. See Sarup 1993.

12. See, for instance, Crais 1992 on white supremacy in the colonial Cape; Zaal 2005 on antimiscegenation legislation in the seventeenth-century Cape colony; and Comaroff 1989 on the "intricate web of relations" that made up colonial Cape society.

13. Professor Vice was recently involved in a public debate about whiteliness after a paper she wrote about white privilege became a news sensation. In her 2010 essay, "How Do I Live in This Strange Place?," published in the *Journal of Social Philosophy*, she called for "whites in South Africa . . . to see themselves as a problem" (326).

14. According to a 1996 Arts and Culture White Paper, "The current arts and culture dispensation still largely reflects the apartheid era in the distribution of skills, access to public resources, geographical location of arts infrastructure and the governance, management and staffing of publicly-funded arts institutions." The "Revised White Paper" (2013) still referred to persistent inequities in the arts sector: "The equitable delivery of ACH [Arts, Culture, Heritage] to all has yet to reflect the transformed society envisaged by government, despite the advances made by the sector since 1994" ("Revised White Paper" 2013).

15. One notable exception is The Market Theatre. Of the three artistic directors who have led the organization since the 1994 transition—John Kani (1995–2005), Malcolm Purkey (2005–2013), and James Ngcobo (2013–present)—two have been black Africans.

16. Arts activist Mike van Graan notes that while diversity is a priority for the theatre industry in South Africa, there is a lingering perception of the theatre world as a "dominant White Director theatre environment." He also points out that "mainstream structure attitudes" do not alleviate this perception, particularly in the festival circuit, "which do allow spaces for development of new work but don't encourage new participants" (van Graan 2014).

17. I take this term from Breyten Breytenbach, who said in *Return to Paradise*, "I am smitten with white-sight" (1993, 28).

18. There is general consensus among scholars that the imagined category of whiteness holds its symbolic and real power through its repetition. Much of the scholarship on whiteness, however, skirts around the performativity of this racial category. I follow Warren and Heuman, who work under the premise that "we are essentially performing beings, constituted in/through our everyday, minute acts" (2008, 215). Elsewhere, Warren and Fasset read whiteness as a performative construct; they suggest that "white identity is considered a discursive construct that is made and remade through our reiterative patterned communication choices" (2004, 413). Whiteness, then, is a politicized, situated, and relational cultural *performance*. For Shona Hunter, whiteness is "symbolically, materially, and affectively *enacted* through and across time and space" (2013, my emphasis).

19. In my analysis of the constructed nature of white Afrikaner identity, I draw on Butler's assertion that gendered identity is perpetuated through a *stylized repetition of acts*. Following Butler's calculus, it stands to reason that other types of identity formations, like one's racial identity, are similarly construed. And I would suggest that repeated iteration over time is the key here. Thus, each time whiteness is performed—explicitly or by implication, intentionally or subconsciously—we are offered another opportunity to "try a range of different significations for spectators willing to read them" (Dolan 1993, 432).

20. See a further discussion of Pieter-Dirk Uys's caricature of Botha in chapter 4 and his impersonation of the former head of state: "Pieter-Dirk Uys Does a PW Botha Impersonation—The Morning Show," YouTube video, posted January 12, 2012, www.youtube.com/watch?v=TpWgLchnurc.

21. Afrikaans, an amalgam of Dutch, French, and indigenous African languages, is spoken by approximately 3 million white Afrikaners or Boers (Afrikaans for farmers), as well as by the 4 million brown Afrikaners or coloureds, people whose mixed ancestry includes indigenous Khoisan and Xhosa people, European settlers, and slaves imported to South Africa from Malaya, Indonesia, and Madagascar.

22. The two most famous films about Afrikaner history are *De Voortrekkers* (1916) and *Bou van 'n nasie* (1938). A third, *'n Nasie hou koers*, about the 1938 Centenary Trek reenactments, was produced in 1940.

23. For more on the 1910 and 1952 events, see Merrington 1997, Kruger 1999b, and Rassool and Witz 1993.

24. The term *voortrekker* is the Afrikaans word for pioneer and literally means "to pull or journey (trek) forward (voort)."

25. *Bittereinder* is a term used to describe the faction of Boer guerrilla soldiers who decided to fight on rather than surrender at the end of the Boer War (1899–1902).

26. For studies on Afrikaners, the Afrikaner nationalist project, and the culture of Afrikanerdom, see, in chronological order, Sheila Patterson's *The Last Trek: A Study of the Boer People and the Afrikaner Nation* (1957); T. Dunbar Moodie's *The Rise of Afrikanerdom* (1975); André Du Toit and Hermann Giliomee's *Afrikaner Political Thought: Analysis and Documents 1780–1850* (1983); J. Alton Templin's *Ideology on a Frontier: The Theological Foundation of Afrikaner Nationalism, 1652–1910* (1984); Isabel Hofmeyr's "Building a Nation from Words: Afrikaner Language, Literature, and Ethnic Identity, 1902–1924," in *The Politics of Race, Class and Nationalism in Twentieth Century South Africa*, edited by Shula Marks and Stanley Trapido (1987); Charles Bloomberg's *Christian-Nationalism and the Rise of the Afrikaner Broederbond in South Africa, 1918–48* (1989); and Hermann Giliomee's *The Afrikaners: Biography of a People* (2003). I would add to these scholars, Vincent Crapanzano's *Waiting: The Whites of South Africa* (1985), Marq de Villiers's *White Tribe Dreaming: Apartheid's Bitter Roots as Witnessed by 8 Generations of an Afrikaner Family* (1990), June Goodwin and Ben Schiff's insightful oral history *Heart of Whiteness: Afrikaners Face Black Rule in the New South Africa* (1995), and Jonathan Jansen's *Knowledge in the Blood: Confronting Race and the Apartheid Past* (2009).

27. Afrikaner Dutch Reformed Calvinism is a religious and political system; the

apartheid state asserted not only legal controls on its citizens, but also social conservatism fueled by Calvinist morality. Roxanne Dunbar-Ortiz (2015) calls this a *covenant nation*, driven by an elite of purportedly divinely sanctioned *chosen people*.

28. A common notion about and by Afrikaners is that they are a "white tribe." See, for instance, Marq de Villiers's autobiographical history *White Tribe Dreaming* (1990), the work of anthropologist Laurence van der Post, or David Harrison's *The White Tribe of Africa* (1981). As a colonial construct, the term *tribe* was used by anthropologists to categorize peoples (Xhosas, Zulus, Swazis, Shangaans, etc.) and to justify unilinear cultural evolution. From a postcolonial perspective, deeming Afrikaners a tribe erases the long history of oppressive dominance over the indigenous tribes in southern Africa. Whites belong to a European *settler culture* that might have justifiable claims to South Africa as their birthland, but are not an indigenous tribe. Thus, I use the terms *settler* (to indicate the particular tension between European and African allegiances of those whites born in, and marked by, Africa) and *ethno-myth* (as a descriptor of the narrative of belonging constructed to justify settler status), which I borrow from Marianne de Jong (Goodwin and Schiff 1995, 297). Yet using this term for white South Africans marks the paradox of the Afrikaner: as European colonizers (outsiders) seeking internal belonging and wishing to identify with the continent (insiders). De Villiers describes the history of the Afrikaners as a "history of tribal maneuverings," suggesting that Afrikaners are concerned primarily with the survival of the tribe and that this "dominant reality" determines all other decisions and thought processes, from economics to politics, social behavior to internal thinking (1990, xxiv–xxv).

29. For scholarship on Afrikaans literature and drama, see J. C. Kannemeyer's *Die Afrikaanse Literatuur, 1652–1987* (Kannemeyer 1988); L. W. B. Binge's *Ontwikkeling van die Afrikaanse toneel: 1832 tot 1950* (J. L. Van Schaik, 1969); F. C. L. Bosman's *The Dutch and English Theatre in South Africa, 1800 till Today, and the Afrikaans Drama: Short Surveys* (de Bussy, 1951); Jill Fletcher's *The Story of Theatre in South Africa: A Guide to Its History from 1780–1930* (1994); and Loren Kruger's seminal history of South African theatre: *The Drama of South Africa: Plays, Pageants and Publics since 1910* (1999).

30. In determining the scope of this study, I chose to focus on male playwrights and theatre-makers because of my interest in the intersections of Afrikaner whiteness and masculinity. However, I also feel it is important to mention Afrikaans playwright Reza de Wet (1953–2012), who deserves an entire study to herself. For more on Reza de Wet, see Blumberg and Walder 1999; Hauptfleisch 1999; Keuris 2004; and Krueger 2010a, 2010b.

1. The Afrikaner nationalist project reinforced a singular narrative of domination and made visible a trajectory of whiteness while concurrently erasing, overlooking, or challenging the histories of black, coloured, or Anglo South Africans, who were in turn attempting to mobilize in their own rights. See Kruger's work (1999a, 1999b, 1997); also Gavin Lewis's *Between the Wire and the Wall* (1987).

2. I use the following appellations to refer to the historic periods in South African

history: the *colonial era* (the period of encounter in the mid-seventeenth century and the colonization of the Cape by the Dutch and then the British); the *Voortrekker era* (from the 1830s, when Dutch framers trekked north to establish independent states from the British); the *nation-building era* (from the 1870s, when Afrikaners first began mobilizing into a unified volk, up to 1949, when the National Party took over power); the *apartheid era* (from the NP victory in 1949 to the historic transition into democracy in 1994); and I use *democratic, post-1994*, or *contemporary* interchangeably to refer to present-day South Africa under ANC rule.

3. See, for reference, Crais 1992.

4. The South African socialscape is a performative space of representation: a constellation of real (material) and imagined (symbolic) spaces which exist at times in dialogic relation to one another, and which at times coexist independently in a larger field with varying degrees of temporal and spatial overlap. I build on Henri Lefebvre's claims that the *spatial practice* of a society "secretes that society's space; it propounds and presupposes it, in a dialectical interaction; it produces it slowly and surely as it masters and appropriates it" (1991, 38). Lefebvre defines *representations of space* as "conceptualized space, the space of scientists, planners, urbanists, technocratic subdividers and social engineers . . . tend[ing] towards a system of verbal (and therefore intellectually worked) out signs" (1991, 38–39). And *representational space* is that space "directly lived through its associated images and symbols, and hence the space of 'inhabitants' and 'users'" (1991, 39).

5. British colonization (1795) followed on the heels of the Dutch (1652) and these two European forces battled for political, economic, and social control of the country into the twentieth century. Tensions were most acute during the Anglo-Boer Wars (1881; 1899–1902). Britain's use of concentration camps and scorched-earth tactics against the Boers became a significant rallying point for Afrikaner nationalism in the 1930s. See Moodie 1975; Packenham 1979; Templin 1984; I. Hofmeyr 1987; Crais 1992; Giliomee 2003; Jansen 2009; and van Heyningen 2013.

6. For Bruce Cauthen, "the concept of chosenness, that is of a particular people . . . who collectively possess a divine warrant to subdue, and propagate the faith in, a heathen land, has been throughout history a uniquely potent catalyst for social mobilization and national coherence" (2004, 20). Afrikaners share with Jews across the diaspora the belief in being God's Chosen People (Beker 2008).

7. See Mary F. Brewer's discussion of Manifest Destiny (2005, 18–20).

8. Such encounters in South Africa began as early as 1488, when Vasco da Gama reached and named the Cape of Good Hope; were most intensive in 1652 with the arrival of the Dutch East India Company (represented by Jan van Riebeeck and his crew); and continued through the arrival of approximately four thousand British settlers in Port Elizabeth in 1820. Subsequent waves of immigrants altered the landscape as they arrived for the gold and diamond rushes in the late nineteenth century, and this influx continues as migrants from neighboring African countries such as Zimbabwe and Mozambique flock to South Africa today.

9. I draw my subtitle from Eric Hobsbawm and Terence Ranger's (1992) study on the creation of national cultures, *The Invention of Tradition*.

10. The HNP was an amalgam of Malan's Gesuiwerde Nasionale Party (Purified National Party) and J. B. M. Hertzog's Afrikaner faction of the United Party. The HNP unexpectedly won the elections of 1948, ushering in the apartheid regime. After 1948, the HNP became the Nasionale Party (National Party).

11. *Regte* means "right," both "correct or true" and "conservative (right-wing)."

12. See Sheila Patterson 1957 and Isabel Hofmeyr 1987 on this history.

13. According to Alan Barnard (1992), Khoisan (also spelled Khoesaan, Khoesan, or Khoe-San) is a unifying name for two ethnic groups of Southern Africa: the Khoikhoi (also spelled Khoekhoe) and the San. Formerly, the Khoikhoi were derogatorily referred to as "Hottentots" and the San were called "Bushmen." These were the first indigenous peoples the Dutch encountered in the Colonial Cape; later, they made contact with Bantu tribes like the Xhosa, Zulu, and Basotho.

14. *Trekboere* (plural of *trekboer*) were seminomadic subsistence farmers of Dutch and French descent who, between the 1790s and 1830s, trekked eastward and northward into the interior of southern Africa in search of better grazing lands and to evade the imperious Dutch East India Company, which administered the Cape Colony. The mythology of these pioneering Voortrekkers became a foundational metaphor of the Afrikaner nationalist project.

15. The so-called First and Second Language Movements lasted from 1880 till the 1920s and were committed to two major tasks: the publication and dissemination of vernacular Afrikaans as opposed to High Dutch, and the unification of Afrikaans-speakers as a nation.

16. The Afrikaans language is derived from Dutch, with imported vocabulary from Malay, Portuguese, Bantu, and Khoisan languages. For more on the development of the Afrikaans language, see Mesthrie 2002 and Ponelis 1993.

17. In the 1920s and '30s, Afrikaner Calvinist faith and myths of rightful inheritance of the land were inflected with Broederbonder rhetoric, which espoused Aryan supremacy. See Bunting 1986 and Bloomberg and Dubow 1989.

18. Here it is worth citing Leslie Witz's 2003 study, *Apartheid's Festival*, in which she suggests "South Africa was curated as a national entity following a singular, historical narrative" (12) but that localized commemorations revealed "deep fractures," often pluralizing and problematizing coherent narratives of the nation rather than affirming them.

19. See data from the South African Social Attitudes Survey (SASAS) conducted by the Human Sciences Research Council at www.hsrc.ac.za/uploads/pageContent/256/6004 _Gaibie_Qualityoflife.pdf, accessed April 10, 2016.

20. It is important to note that despite the legal and political shifts after 1994, racism, discrimination, and unequal access are still facts of life under the new ANC government, which is plagued by cronyism, corruption, and mismanagement.

21. See Maingard 2007, 24: "*De Voortrekkers* probably matched [Shaw's] ideological

inclinations, rooted in his Kentucky childhood, especially in the light of his comment that 'the colonial always appeals to me'" (*Stage and Cinema*, December 30, 1916, 2).

22. December 16 has a colorful and contentious genealogy. It has been honored as a day of remembrance by white Afrikaners since 1864. Not coincidentally, December 16 is also the anniversary of the founding of the military wing of the ANC, Umkhonto we Sizwe (Spear of the Nation), in 1961. The ANC organized a series of antiapartheid sabotages to coincide on this date in 1961, signaling the shift from passive resistance to armed struggle against the state. In 1994, the date was renamed Reconciliation Day (under Act No. 36 of 1994) to foster reconciliation and national unity in the new democracy.

23. I have been unable to find out who these two performers were beyond an unsupported reference to "Tom Zulu" (Dingane) and "Goba" (Sobuza) on IMDB.com. Not a single piece of scholarship mentions their anonymity.

24. As the legend goes, on December 16, 1838, three hundred Boer trekkers were cornered at the banks of the Ncome River by three thousand Zulus. The trekkers formed their wagons into a laager and waited the night. That night, trek leader Sarel Cilliers prayed, promising that if God helped the Boers win the battle the next day, the Boers would erect a church and commemorate the day every year thereafter as a sabbath. The next day the tiny band of Boers won the battle. So many Zulus were killed that the river ran red with their blood and was thereafter renamed Blood River. December 16 has become the key date in Afrikaner history because it is considered the moment that God defended the Afrikaners as his Chosen People. Historians have found several incongruences in this myth. In 1952, in the year in which many of the apartheid regime's most notorious laws were passed, the original Dingane's Day was renamed Geloftedag (Day of the Covenant or Day of the Vow).

25. The Broederbond's public front, the FAK or Federasie van Afrikaanse Kultuurvereenigings (Federation of Afrikaans Cultural Organizations), was founded in 1929. It clandestinely controlled almost every public or cultural organization, including the South African Broadcasting Corporation (SABC), the agency controlling radio and TV (until 1994), and M-NET (South Africa's only "cable TV" channel).

26. "Ritornello" is Gilles Deleuze's term for a recurring theme or refrain that staves off chaos and fear. It is always territorial, linked to region, province, or physical land (Boundas 1993, 210–213).

27. Meintjies would eventually write *The Voortrekkers: Story of the Great Trek and the Making of South Africa* (1973).

28. Founded in 1932, the Afrikaanse Taal-en Kultuurvereeniging (ATKV) was designed to raise the cultural level of thousands of South African Railways workers, who were predominantly Afrikaners. A similar organization was created for postal workers in 1953.

29. This wagon also served as a reminder of the women brutalized in British POW camps in the Anglo-Boer War. See McClintock's critique (1995, 352–389).

30. The naming and renaming debate is alive and active in post-1994 South Africa, where now the Afrikaans streets and towns are being renamed with Africanized names,

causing considerable divides between blacks and whites and between competing narratives of belonging. See Beresford 2006 and "Residents Stick to 'Old' City Names" 2011.

31. See www.info.gov.za/aboutgovt/symbols/anthem.htm.

32. Note the use of the royal we; any European, even if Portuguese and not Dutch, is deemed more civilized than indigenous Africans.

33. As Brian Bunting asserts in *The Rise of the South African Reich* (1986), fervent affinities existed between Nationalist Party leaders in South Africa and the Nazi movement in Germany during the 1930s.

34. It is worth noting how Moerdijk's claim resonates with the Nazi millennial belief in a *Reich* that would last a thousand years.

35. Until 1994, a sign stating *Slegs Vir Blankes* (For Whites Only) hung on the main gate, which ironically, is made up of rows of wrought-iron Zulu assegais.

36. See Hutchison for an astute comparative analysis of the Voortrekker Monument's solidification of history versus Freedom Park's "public rehearsal of reconciliation" (2013, 99).

37. Intriguingly, two South African women organized a yarn-bombing of the monument; though not explicitly political, their intervention placed women's labor against the backdrop of the giant granite phallus. See crochetinpaternoster.wordpress.com /2014/08/05/voortrekker-monument-yarn-bomb-1-august-2014/, accessed December 13, 2015.

CHAPTER TWO

1. See, among many others, E. Gray and Samakow 2015; Wines 2014; Kristof 2014; and Woods 2014.

2. Poet N. P. van Wyk Louw's 1941 epic poem "Raka" encapsulates this fear and distrust of the bestial outsider. The feared outsider (black Africa, bestial, uncivilized, childlike) remains forever at the gate, haunting the "civilized" (white, colonial) world. See van Wyk Louw 1968.

3. The Vierkleur (literally, "four-color") was the flag of the original Transvaal Republic, the second independent Boer state to resist British rule (in 1857). The words "Ons vir Jou" are also emblazoned on Voortrekker leader Piet Retief's cenotaph.

4. All references to the play are from the unpublished script provided to me by Deon Opperman (Opperman and Else 2008).

5. My experience was affirmed by the number of comments on Opperman's Facebook page; Petro Heydenrych Gouws wrote in Afrikaans: "Ons vir Jou was outstanding, I experienced so many emotions and couldn't stop the tears, they just came by themselves"; Lydia Kok added, "I think I cried the entire time. Such an incredible portrayal of our people's passion, desires and feelings. Proudly South African, forever!!xxxx" (www .facebook.com/deon.opperman.official, accessed December 13, 2015).

6. Cronjé's surrender to Lord Roberts was captured on film on February 27, 1900, and is included as part of L. S. Amery's *Diamond Mines of South Africa, Vol.* 2. See commons .wikimedia.org/wiki/File:Surrender_of_Cronje.jpg, posted July 2, 2009.

7. In 2011, novelist Sonia Loots wrote a historical fiction account of Cronjé and Viljoen's journey called *Sirkusboere*.

8. According to the *St. Louis Post-Dispatch*, April 9, 1904, the entourage included generals Cronjé and Viljoen, as well as "150 Briton and 200 Afrikaner veterans, 40 Kaffirs, Zulus, and South African blacks of other tribes, and 50 Afrikaner women and children" (Sutton 2007, 271).

9. The Boer Concession was the highest grossing military concession of the Fair; based on its success, it moved to Coney Island in 1905 (Sutton 2007; Boer and Britons 1905).

10. See Davitt 1902 for an account of the Battle of Paardeberg, available online via www.angloboerwar.com/books/37-davitt-boer-fight-for-freedom/860-davitt-chapter-xxx-paardeberg.

11. Blame, guilt, disgrace, and shame are concepts used frequently when discussing South Africa, especially in relation to white South Africans and the Truth and Reconciliation Commission (TRC) of the 1990s. See Cole 2009; Nyquist Potter 2006; W. Verwoerd 1999.

12. While whiteness studies is several decades old, mention of whiteness has come into common parlance acutely post-Ferguson, being widely used in the news and on social media, and addressed outside the academy. Trending search terms on Google in 2015 included *whiteness, white people,* and *white privilege*. See www.google.com/trends, accessed December 13, 2015.

13. A facsimile of the actual letter of surrender was on display at the Boer War Concession, adding to the event's aura of authenticity.

14. Australia, Canada, and New Zealand all sent troops to aid the United Kingdom's efforts against the Boers.

15. Floris van der Merwe has written extensively about the British-born Fillis, whom he describes as a circus master, horse trainer, world traveler, and showman in his own right.

16. This exodus of prisoners referenced the actual capture by the British of Boer prisoners and women and children who died in concentration camps during the Anglo-Boer War.

17. The Transvaal Spectacle presented American audiences with a story of an underdog, upstart nation (not unlike their own) fighting the imperial beast of Britain.

18. Van Blerk's song was played at informal parties and concerts across the country. See "De La Ray Song," YouTube video, posted June 23, 2008, www.youtube.com/watch?v=KHcFm3dXcQA.

19. See Bok van Blerk's official video for his song "De La Rey," with English subtitles, at www.youtube.com/watch?v=esnz_hhsZXo. For a bilingual translation of van Blerk's song, see lyrics.wikia.com/Bok_Van_Blerk:De_La_Rey, accessed December 13, 2015.

20. This image is rehearsed on stage in *Ons vir Jou*, as the two main female characters, Mariaan (Marisa Bosman) and Nonnie (Michelle Botha), are imprisoned by the British and stand behind barbed wire strung across the stage (figure 14).

21. The term *Afrikaner* denotes a political position as well as a linguistic and ethnic

one. The more politically correct terms *Afrikaanse* (Afrikaans) and *Afrikaanssprekend* (Afrikaans-speaking) are identity terms that attempt to separate the political from the linguistic and to undo the historical association of Afrikaners with apartheid.

22. Centurion, previously known as Verwoerdburg (after architect of apartheid Hendrik Verwoerd), is where Oscar Pistorius shot his girlfriend, Reeva Steenkamp, on February 14, 2013.

23. Much has been written about farm murders in contemporary South Africa; see, for example, Reuters 2012 and Conway-Smith 2012. For the anxiety around the current language debate, see De Vos 2011. Or see the fracas caused when Afrikaans author Anneli Botes admitted that she feared black people because of the rate of crime committed by blacks in contemporary South Africa (Groenewald and Harbour 2010.)

24. I discuss the UNPO and Afrikaner minority status again in chapter 4.

25. For deeper analysis of Afrikaner minority status, see van der Merwe and Johnson 1997 and Southern 2008.

26. In October 2013, Afrikaans singers Sunette Bridges and Steve Hofmeyr organized a day of protest they called "Red October," claiming, "We can no longer be silent about the brutal torture of the elderly and defenceless people of our Ethnic Minority!" (www.redoctober.co.za, accessed October 30, 2014). See analyses by Falkof (2013) and Christi van der Westhuizen (2013b).

CHAPTER THREE

1. An earlier version of this chapter first appeared in *Text and Presentation* under the title "De/Re-Constructing Borders: Afrikaner Language, Mythology and Nostalgia in the New South Africa's Drama" in 1998. All references to *Donkerland* are from the published playtext (Tafelberg, 1996) and the production I saw at the Grahamstown Festival in 1996.

2. *Kruispad*, the second in the trilogy but the first to be aired on KykNet in 2010, follows two Afrikaner families in the thirteen years after the 1994 election as they adapt to the new democracy. *Hartland*, the third in the trilogy and the second to be aired in 2011, is an Afrikaner family saga based on three of Opperman's plays, *Kaburu*, *Stille nag*, and *Boesman, my seun*. *Donkerland*, the first in the trilogy but the last to air, premiered in 2013. *Getroud met rugby* (2008) is a South African analog to *Footballer's Wives*.

3. See De Vos 2011 on the Stellenbosch University Afrikaans language summit (*taal-stryd*).

4. See Eyal 1997 for an account of these events.

5. It is important to note that *Donkerland* was performed in *Afrikaans* at the predominantly English-speaking Grahamstown Festival. The National Arts Festival (NAF) offers an annual showcase of amateur, professional, regional, national, and international theatre. During its forty-year lifespan, the NAF has mirrored the larger social field and reflected sociopolitical issues; it has also been critiqued as a bastion of whiteness, controlled by and performed for white middle-class South Africans. See Grundy 1994. Ironically, the festival was established in 1974 as a Shakespeare festival, in response to what was perceived as "the onslaught of Afrikaner nationalism" (McNeil 1996). The

festival created a space in which artists could address the nation, speak truth to power, and push against censorship. That a nationalistic Afrikaans play succeeded here is quite remarkable.

6. See the television trailer: "Donkerland: Een Plaas. Een Familie. Een Bloedlyn. Sewe Geslagte. 158 Jaar," YouTube video, posted August 8, 2013, www.youtube.com/watch?v=uRttMOTqoxs&feature=youtu.be.

7. See the Carnegie Commission's 1932 report on white poverty in turn-of-the-century South Africa, *The Poor White Problem in South Africa* (Grosskopf et al. 1932).

8. Act No. 22 of 1994, the Restitution of Land Rights Act, provided for the restitution of land to people dispossessed under apartheid (and the 1913 Land Act, which allotted the majority of South Africa to whites) and the establishment of a Commission on the Restitution of Land Rights and a Land Claims Court.

9. See, for example, reviews by Carklin and Alcock (1997), Graver (1997), and Keuris (2009).

10. De Witt plants his land marker as Bartolomeu Dias did in the film *Bou van 'n nasie*, both claiming Africa as their own. The *stok* he plants into the soil to mark out Donkerland features in every scene: first as Pieter plants it center stage in 1838; then as the leg of a table in the next scene in 1840; again as the mount for some taxidermied antelope heads in 1881; and finally at the top of the fireplace in the de Witt farmhouse, which is featured in the final three scenes of the play. The stake even survives the burning of the farm by the British during the Boer War scenes. Thus, this phallic marker of patriarchal authority ghosts through every scene as an ever-present reminder of the power of the male de Witts (white men).

11. In my 2011 interview with him, Opperman talked in depth about the gender politics of Afrikaner culture: how his own father was the "unquestioned head and authority in our house" but also that he "could make no decision without the approval of my mother" (M. Lewis 2011). While this type of gender balance is the reality for many Afrikaner families, in the space of the play—which is governed by dramatic forces that thrive off binaries—such nuances in gender dynamics do not appear.

12. See Diane Russell 1993 and Daniella Coetzee 2001 for more on South African patriarchy's abusiveness.

13. The discovery of diamonds and gold in the 1880s, and the subsequent explosive growth of cities like Johannesburg, caused a schism among Afrikaners between those who remained farmers and those who broke family tradition to seek their fortunes in the city. See Loren Kruger's oeuvre for more on Johannesburg's rich tapestry of competing forces in the early twentieth century.

14. The Voëlvry Movement was an alternative Afrikaans music movement of the 1980s, built on the literary circle of *verligte* writers, whose goal was "the emancipation of Afrikaner youth from the strictures of their authoritarian, patriarchal culture" and to "make it cool to be an Afrikaner" (Hopkins 2006).

15. In his use of the Land Commission in 1996, Opperman registered a threat to whites that, at that point in time, was not that pressing. At the time of the play's pre-

miere, the Land Commission was completely swamped with requests that it has taken decades to sift through, and the process is still ongoing.

16. See, for instance, Marlene van Niekerk's 1994 novel *Triomf*, which chronicles the lives of a dysfunctional family of *armblankes* (poor whites) — Mol Benade, her brothers Treppie and Pop, and her incestuous son Lambert — in the bulldozed and reclaimed suburb that was once the vibrant Sophiatown. Set on the eve of the democratic election in 1994, the twisted family implodes as they are unable to adapt to the new political dispensation.

17. S. J. du Toit (1847–1911) was one of the cofounders of the Genootskap van Regte Afrikaners in 1875 and wrote the first play to be published in Afrikaans, *Margrita Prinslo* (1896). He was also editor of *Die Patriot* from 1878 to 1904. (See Keuris 2012 for more details.) Jan F. E. Celliers (1865–1940), C. Louis Leipoldt (1880–1947), and J. D. du Toit, the son of S. J. du Toit, who published under the pseudonym Totius (1877–1953), were three of the most important poets and writers of the Second Language Movement in the early twentieth century. Opperman quotes Leipoldt's poem "In die konsentrasie-kamp (Aliwal Noord, 1901)" ("In the Concentration Camp [Aliwal North, 1901]") in this play. J. R. L. Van Bruggen (1895–1948) is a lesser-known poet; Opperman cites his poem "Heimwee" ("Homesickness" or "Longing"), which became a popular Afrikaans song sung by opera star Mimi Coertse. N. P. van Wyk Louw (1906–1970) is one of the most famous Afrikaans poets and playwrights, and author of the epic poem "Raka" (1941), about a community disturbed by a primitive force at the periphery of their consciousness. D. J. Opperman (1914–1985), a relative of Deon Opperman and one of the best-known poets in Afrikaans, also served as a journalist for *Die Huisgenoot* between 1946 and 1948. He was also a professor of Afrikaans literature from 1949 to 1979. In addition to poetry, Opperman wrote three verse plays: *Periandros van Korinthe* (*Periandros of Corinth*) in 1954, *Vergelegen* (*Faraway*) in 1956, and *Voëlvry* (*Outlaw*) in 1968.

18. In her essay entitled "Optic White: Blackness and the Production of Whiteness" (1994), Harryette Mullen suggests, building on Ralph Ellison's *Invisible Man*, that a drop of black paint in a bucket of white makes the white whiter. The diametric opposition of black to white on the color spectrum, and in this case on the racial spectrum of South Africa, makes the penetrated color (white) even stronger in its whiteness. The color bar is a kind of laager that, when threatened with penetration, tightens its defenses.

19. For the polarized reactions to van der Westhuizen's piece, see "The White Angst of Red October," October 14, 2013, www.thoughtleader.co.za/christivanderwesthuizen /2013/10/14/the-white-angst-of-red-october/. And for reactions to Nicky Falkof's piece, see "Provocation Triple Distilled," October 7, 2013, www.dailymaverick.co.za /opinionista/2013-10-07-red-october/#.UqyF3Y3Oxow.

20. Carjackings, especially in wealthy neighborhoods, are commonplace (Carroll 2006).

21. *Boere* is the Afrikaans plural of Boer; *bosboeties* (literally, "bush brothers") was a term white comrades used for one another during the Border Wars, the period of active military defense of South Africa's national borders to the north and inside the coun-

try. The conflict between South Africa and its allies, and communist-backed Angola and South West Africa, lasted from 1966 to 1989. Over six hundred thousand young white men were conscripted to do their national service (*diensplig*) in the South African Defense Force. Recruits, who were as young as seventeen, endured a system of brutal hazing and indoctrination and each served an average of two years in the army. The war was disavowed and conducted in secret, so these damaged men were not able to speak of their experiences upon returning home.

22. See Spanierman, Todd, and Anderson 2009 on the psychosocial costs of racism to whites (known as PCRW).

23. In 2007, the names found a more appropriate home on Salvokop, the hill on which the Voortrekker Monument is erected. See Baines 2008.

CHAPTER FOUR

1. To name only a few: Hennie Aucamp, Breyten Breytenbach, André Brink, W. A. de Klerk, Charles Fourie, Athol Fugard, Uys Krige, Bartho Smit, Anna Neethling-Pohl, and N. P. van Wyk Louw. And those working predominantly after 1994: Marthinus Basson, Saartjie Botha, Reza de Wet, Anton Krueger, Deon Opperman, Mike van Graan, and Christiaan Olwagen.

2. It is worth noting Steven Cohen's work, as he is often compared to Uys. Cohen is another white Jewish South African (though not an Afrikaner) who deploys queering practices to critique whiteness and masculinity. See Van Der Watt 2004.

3. The extent to which women participated in Die Broederbond, for example, was extremely limited. According to Marianne de Jong, "They licked the stamps and baked the *koeksisters* for the elections. That was how they took part in the political process, as a subordinate group" (Goodwin and Schiff 1995, 94).

4. All references are from the film (African Film Productions, 1938), and all translations are my own.

5. In the final scene of *Bou van 'n nasie* (1938), a Boer woman sows seeds in field, solidifying Woman as engenderess of the volk, as she grows the seeds of the next generation.

6. For analyses of Uys's work see Ferguson 1977, S. Gray 1979, McMurtry 1994, Lieberfeld 1997, Jenkins 1998, and Trillin 2004.

7. Bezuidenhout is a common Afrikaans surname; Evita could be a distant, imagined cousin of Daniel from *Bou van 'n nasie*.

8. Under apartheid, black South Africans were assigned to small parcels of land known as homelands or Bantustans, similar to Native American reservations in the United States.

9. Nicknamed Muldergate after Dr. Connie Mulder, the minister of information in John Vorster's government (1966–1979), the 1978 Information Scandal involved the illegal funneling of government money to boost South Africa's public image at home and aboard. This caused the downfall of Vorster and Mulder and the rise of P. W. Botha in the process ("The Information Scandal," January 27, 2005, www.sahistory.org.za /topic/information-scandal).

10. For more on the Censor Board and apartheid-era censorship, see McDonald 2010 and McDonald's resource-rich website: www.theliteraturepolice.com. See also Merrett 1995.

11. See S. Gray 1979 for a review of the piece, which translates as the Van Earths of Big Ear.

12. All references to *Adapt or Dye* are from the DVD of the 1982 performance (PD Uys Productions). All translations are my own.

13. Licorice-flavored candies eaten by children in apartheid South Africa. These large black sweets turned white when sucked.

14. The Kappiekommando (Bonnet Brigade or Petticoat Commando), an arch-conservative Afrikaner Women's organization established in the 1970s, demanded a return to traditional moral values inspired by Johanna Brandt's 1913 account of life for women during the Boer War.

15. While I have seen much of Uys's work in person, I am relying here on the video version of *Adapt or Dye*, which was filmed live on the last night's performance at The Market Theatre in 1982.

16. See Gerald Kraak's 2003 documentary, *Property of the State: Gay Men in the Apartheid Military*. The new Constitution made discrimination based on sexual orientation illegal.

17. Nou-ja (literally, "now-yes") is a common colloquialism in Afrikaans.

18. See also Peter Van Heerden's use of puns in chapter 5.

19. Uys's repertoire also includes: *Adapt or Dye* (1981–1982), *Farce about Uys* (1983), *Total Onslaught* (1984), *An Uys up My Sleeve* (1986), *Bite the Ballot* (1989), *One Man One Volt* (1994), *Bambi Sings the FAK Songs* (1994), *Tannie Evita Praat Kaktus* (1996), *Dekaffirnated* (1999), *For Fact's Sake* (2000), *The End Is Naai* (2004), *It's Just a Small Prick* (2004), *The Great Comedy Trek* (2004), *Icons and Aikonas* (2005), *Pieter-Dirk Eish!* (2006), and *Evita's Kossie Sikelela* (2010).

20. See Sonderling 1998, Klausen 2010, and Keegan 2011.

21. The Parliament of South Africa passed the Immorality Act No. 5 of 1927 to prohibit extramarital sex between white and black people. The Prohibition of Mixed Marriages Act No. 55 of 1949 followed. In 1950 the act was amended to apply to sex between "Europeans" and all "non-Europeans."

22. Cruywagen was appointed the first Afrikaans news anchor for the state-controlled South African Broadcasting Corporation (SABC, or SAUK in Afrikaans) in 1975, when South Africa first allowed television. He is considered an icon of Afrikaans culture.

23. *Hoer* is the Afrikaans word for "whore."

24. A pun on "train station," "political platform," and "stage platform" and also a reference to Argentina's former first lady, Eva Peron.

25. In *Skating on Thin Uys*, for instance, opera singer Mimi Coertse, Progressive Party politician Helen Suzman, and former minister of information Dr. Connie Mulder play themselves alongside Uys's fictional creations.

26. A note about the subhead for this section: In an homage to Uys's punning ability, I remind readers that *v* in Afrikaans is pronounced as an *f*, hence *fok* (fucking) and *volk* (nation) are homophonic.

27. For more on Afrikaner hypermasculinity, see Conway 2008, Mooney 1998, Maingard 1997, and Grundlingh 1994.

28. *Sarie Marais* was also the first talkie ever filmed in South Africa, directed by Joseph Albrecht (of *De Voortrekkers*) in 1931. The film plays out in a Boer War concentration camp, and the passionate, patriotic song is sung by one of the prisoners, who sings of his beloved far away. The contemporary popular Afrikaans women's magazine *Sarie* is also named after this song. *Sarie* was established in 1949 as an exemplar of the modern Afrikaans womanhood.

29. See Marschall 2004 and Cloete 1992 for further analysis of the gendered politics of the Vrouemonument.

30. Unfortunately, all the political moments of the novel were eliminated in the stage production, which I saw at the National Arts Festival in Grahamstown in 1997.

31. All references to *Farce about Uys* are from the 1983 playscript, available at pdu .co.za. All references to *Skating on Thin Uys* are from the DVD. All translations are my own.

32. There are class associations with these two surnames; Poggenpol is a "common" or working-class name, while Bezuidenhout is a distinguished surname.

33. "BJ" (short for Billie-Jeanne) is also slang for oral sex, and *koeksister* is a pun on the braided dough and syrup dessert and the term *koek*, which in Afrikaans refers to a vagina. Hence *koeksisters* becomes code for lesbians.

34. A common apartheid-era fear was that there were Russians (communists or terrorists) hiding under every bed. Here, the Russians are *in bed* with the whites.

35. References to *Funigalore* are drawn from the TV series as well as Uys's book of the same name (1995).

36. Uys attempted to interview F. W. de Klerk for *Funigalore*, but the former president's handlers refused the offer.

37. On August 15, 1985, P. W. Botha made his infamous "Crossing the Rubicon" speech, wagging his finger at the camera in his signature style. The speech is considered by many to be one of the pivotal moments in the gradual dismantling of apartheid. See Giliomee 2012.

38. *Amandla* means "power" in Zulu and Xhosa; "Vrystaat!" (Free State!) is a common cry at rugby games.

39. Terms used by the Government of National Unity (GNU) in the early stages of the new democracy. In the episode with Pik Botha, Evita puns the GNU with a wildebeest (a gnu) and remarks that people called her a gnu because of her hairstyle, "parted in the center with those two horns" (Uys 1995, 201).

40. Brett Murray's painting *The Spear*, which depicted President Jacob Zuma as a Lenin-esque revolutionary figure with his genitals hanging out, was defaced by two separate attackers as it hung in the Goodman Gallery in Johannesburg after the ANC government attempted to remove and censor it for depicting Zuma in a less-than-favorable light. See M. Lewis 2013.

CHAPTER FIVE

1. Material in this chapter has been previously published as "Abject Afrikaners and Iconoclast Trekkers: Peter Van Heerden and the Laagers of White Masculinity," *Journal of Dramatic Theory and Criticism* 26, no. 2 (Spring 2012): 7–30, and "Uprooting and Re-routing the Afrikaner Male: Peter Van Heerden's Abject Performance Art," *Positions South Africa*, vol. 3, edited by Matthew Krouse (Berlin: Goethe-Institut and Pretoria: Jacana Media, 2010), 90–104.

2. In *Ubuntu*, Peter explored his own South African masculinity through the mythic tokoloshe, a troublemaking creature with an enormous penis; rituals of initiation; and othering through the use of blackface.

3. *Soutpiel*, or "salt dick," is a derogatory term Afrikaner men use for an English-speaking man with one foot in Africa and one in Europe, his genitals dangling in the ocean.

4. The KKNK is an annual Afrikaans arts and culture festival established in 1995. It includes a nine-day program of music, theatre, entertainment, visual art, food, and drink in a sociable atmosphere in the middle of the South African summer. Demographically, the average festino is forty-four years old; 93 percent claim Afrikaans as their home language; the majority are from the Western Cape (52 percent), Eastern Cape (19 percent), and Gauteng (14 percent); and the majority are women (male 38 percent; female 62 percent) (M. Kruger, M. Saayman, and S. M. Ellis, 2010). The authors, quite notably, do not provide data for race; however, the KKNK attracts a majority of white attendees and has been criticized as a bastion of white Afrikanerdom. See Kitshoff 2004.

5. The title puns on *kant*, the Afrikaans word for "side." Van Heerden performed *Totanderkuntuit* at the KKNK from March 21–29, 2008. All quotations are from these performances and my interviews during the nine days of the installation.

6. The press coverage was muddled, with one report confusing Van Heerden and Laubscher with a white power group and not realizing it was a performance; see Gerber 2008. Other reviews combined praising the work and registering the audience's shock and horror; see van Bosch 2008 and Myburg 2008.

7. Noel Ignatiev has called for the abolition of the white race. In the journal he founded, *Race Traitor*, he suggests "treason to whiteness is loyalty to humanity" (racetraitor.org).

8. Laubscher, an Afrikaans farmer in Tamboerskloof, cofounded Hope for the Children, an NGO that helps orphans by bringing them to his farm on 81 ERF Military Road. See www.hopeforthechildren.co.za/.

9. A system whereby vineyard laborers were paid in alcohol.

10. Jan van Riebeeck (1619–1677) was an administrator for the Vereenigde Oost-Indische Compagnie (VOC) or Dutch East India Company. On April 6, 1652, he landed his three ships—the *Dromedaris*, *Reijger*, and *Goede Hoop*—at what would become Cape Town, a way station for the VOC trade route between the Netherlands and the East Indies.

11. Terre'Blanche founded the AWB during the apartheid era and was known for

threatening civil war to maintain white rule in South Africa. After 1994, he fought for the formation of a *boerevolkstaat*, or independent Boer (whites-only) state.

12. See chapter 4 and Eyal 1997.

13. The flag raising was reminiscent of other militarized elements of Afrikaner culture, including conscription to fight the Border Wars (1967–1989), flag ceremonies as part of the nationalist school system, and the convention of Veld Schools (Bush Schools), week-long sleep-away camps in which white schoolchildren (like me) were indoctrinated into Afrikaner nationalism under the guise of nature study.

14. The Vierkleur flag flew over the Boer Republic of the Transvaal intermittently 1857–1874, 1875–1877, and 1881–1902. The orange, white, and blue South African National flag, based on the van Riebeeck or Dutch flag, represented the Republic from 1928 to 1994. The new black, gold, green, white, chili red, and blue ANC flag was first flown on April 27, 1994, during the historic general election.

15. Boeremag, meaning Boer Power or Force, is a white separatist movement that has sought to overthrow the ANC government.

16. The FAK (Federasie van Afrikaanse Kultuurvereenigings) is the Federation of Afrikaans Culture, formed in 1929. Its aim was to promote Afrikaans-language arts, music, publication, and culture to support the larger nationalist political project, especially in the face of black and British competition in the early twentieth century.

17. See chapter 1.

18. *F.A.K. Plaasdag* involved an installation called Bang Kock—punning on the Thai city known for its sexual exploits and the Afrikaans word *bang* (afraid) with the word *cock*—in which the audience moved through a series of makeshift shanties, each containing a scenario of conflated images of masturbatory and sexual acts, Calvinism, and Afrikaner patriarchy. On *Familiedag*, which confronted the high incidence of family murder, shame, incest, and sexual abuse among poor white Afrikaners, visitors encountered the Family Murder Tree: inflated sex dolls lynched on a dead tree stump.

19. Bok is also short for *sondebok*, or "scapegoat."

20. Attraction involves drawing in an object (in this case, the audience) and refraction involves deflection or alteration of an object by viewing through a medium (in this case, performance.)

21. Van Heerden and Laubscher did not charge an entry fee for *Totanderkuntuit* and relied on random passersby as their audience.

22. Van Heerden gave himself the title of Laerkommandant P. A. H. W. R. V. O. Van Heerden, and André was Laerpredikant Ds [Dominee] André Laubscher. These characters echo roles played in South African Veld School and military culture.

23. While Uys draws his audiences into complicity with his characters, Van Heerden's work is more incendiary.

24. Demographic data are available at www.statssa.gov.za.

25. For more on Calvinism, colonialism, and apartheid, see Carr 2001.

26. See M. Lewis 2008.

27. Antiapartheid activists Sipho Hashe, Champion Galela, and Qaqawuli Godo-

lozi—the Pebco Three—were abducted and murdered in 1985 by the South African Security Police.

28. A *braaivleis* (or *braai*; literally, "grilling of meat") is a South African barbeque, and the cooking of meat on a fire is a decidedly male activity.

29. It is also useful to remember the many instances of what Hannah Arendt might call the "banality of evil" that surfaced during the Truth and Reconciliation Commission. Several times South African Security Police were reported to be having a *braai* while victims were being tortured or while their bodies were being burned to ashes.

30. *Sweepslag* was performed nightly at 7 P.M. at the Klein Karoo Nasionale Kunstefees in Oudtshoorn, South Africa, March 21–29, 2008.

31. In several of Van Heerden's other performance pieces, including *So is 'n os gemaak* (2004) and *Bok* (2006), he confined himself inside bags of sheep and cow blood and innards.

32. See Daniella Coetzee 2001 and Diane Russell 1993 for more on Afrikaner patriarchy as a culture of abuse.

33. Peter and André wrote an op-ed piece after the *Totanderkuntuit* installation, describing the violent reactions to their work. See Van Heerden and Laubscher 2008b.

34. Piet Retief, a trek leader, was trapped and executed by Zulu chief Dingaan. Despite his heroic status, Retief is considered by far-right conservatives to be a race traitor because he sought to negotiate with Dingaan. President Kruger negotiated with the British several times, and he too is critiqued for this "treachery." Kruger, like the bearded Van Heerden, was known for his bushy beard.

35. Media coverage of the annual KKNK festival often describes the insularity of a gathering that is ostensibly open to all Afrikaans speakers but in actuality remains entrenched in racially exclusive practices.

36. Here the first-person plural marks the importance and necessity for white citizens, myself included, to recognize our complicity in systems of oppression.

37. The battle between Boer and Briton has a long and troubled history, as the Anglo-Boer Wars affirm. Marrying across the cultural line was considered taboo; my parents broke such a taboo in 1967.

38. A Euro-African hybrid or "salt dick."

39. I witnessed middle-class Capetonians and Pretorians on holiday mixed with rural famers from the Orange Free State, art lovers and aficionados, journalists and scholars like myself, coloureds from the Oudtshoorn area, Indian families from Durban, a feminist artist from the Limpopo Province, and a tour group of white women in their seventies.

40. The food stalls were located just across the creek from the installation, and many visitors came to the space consuming what they had just purchased.

41. The Afrikaans word for "vote" is *stem*, which also means "voice," and the voting booth became a space where reactions to the installation were voiced.

42. Chelwyn Engelbrecht, a street kid whom André adopted as a teenager, assists him and Peter on their performance projects.

43. My translations based on notes from a personal conversation with Cassie at KKNK, March 2008.

44. My translations, based on notes from personal conversations with the Bambanani against Crime women at KKNK, March 2008.

45. See "What Is a Tokoloshe?," June 19, 2012, occultzulu.wordpress.com.

CHAPTER SIX

1. Translations: dirty or ill (*vuil*) turbo-boosted (*geboosted*) gangsters (*gangstas*) and romantic Afrikaner rappers.

2. In live tour shows, DJ Hi-Tek is replaced with DJ Vuilgeboost because Hi-Tek fears flying.

3. In their song "U Make a Ninja Wanna Fuck," Ninja claims he has *Wat kyk jy* (What you lookin' at) "tattooed on [his] dick."

4. Parow's collaborators include Gazelle and DJ INVIZABLE (on "Hosh Tokolosh," the first Afrikaans-language single to ever reach number one on 5FM radio); Dawid Kramer (on *Biscuits and Biltong*); Francois van Coke of Afrikaans alternative rock band Fokofpolisiekar (English: Fuckoffpolicecar; on *Dans Dans Dans*); Pierre Greeff of Die Heuwels Fantasties (on *Die Vraagstuk*); and Die Antwoord (on *Wat Pomp?* and *Doos Dronk*).

5. Short for Klipdrift, a cheap, potent brandy often drunk with Coke.

6. An American analog would be the recent proliferation of hillbilly or redneck-themed reality TV programming.

7. Bles Bridges (1947–2000) was a popular crooner who sang saccharin odes in both English and Afrikaans.

8. For a dictionary of zef slang, see www.watkykjy.co.za/zef-slang/, posted March 30, 2015, and en.wikipedia.org/wiki/List_of_South_African_slang_words, posted April 6, 2016.

9. See also Sarah Nuttall's (2004) analysis of Y or *loxion kulcha* by black youth in Johannesburg.

10. All references are from the official music video and its lyrics (Die Antwoord 2010a).

11. For an image of Ninja as the Chosen One, see http://i.imgur.com/wiEmA.jpg, posted October 25, 2012.

12. All references are from the official music video and its lyrics (Die Antwoord 2012d).

13. The twins were also developmentally disabled. For a more detailed account, see "Two Kindly, Jovial Fellows" 2011. View the image of Casie and Dresie by Roger Ballen at www.rogerballen.com/wp-content/uploads/2014/10/Dresie-and-Casie-twins-Western -Transvaal-1993.jpg, posted October 31, 2014.

14. Ninja's intertextual citation is the hook from the 1989 hit "Ice, Ice Baby," by another white rapper, Vanilla Ice, a.k.a. Robert Van Winkle.

15. See my discussion, in the preface, of Oscar Pistorius's disability.

16. Consider how Die Antwoord's dirt resonates against Steve Hofmeyr and Red

October's claims of "dirtiness" and "corruption" that read in opposition to white purity and civilization, which I discussed in chapter 2.

17. See my discussion, in the introduction (esp. note 28), of the use of the phrase *white tribe*.

18. All references are from the official music video and its lyrics (Die Antwoord 2012a).

19. In van Niekerk's *Triomf* (1994), Mol Benade, the matriarch of the band of poor Afrikaner misfits, serves the sexual needs of both her husband Pop and her grown son Lambert.

20. Pushing political incorrectness in the song "$copie" off of their Ten$ion album, Yo-Landi pants "No-no-no!" and then coos, "No means yes."

21. The song "Beat Boy" is a chronicle of sexual fantasies that include BDSM, anal sex, bloodsports, and necrophilia.

22. The English transaltion loses the rhyme and punning of the Afrikaans.

23. See Jimbo Stephens's 2013 documentary *AKA: The Lives of Waddy Tudor Jones* for a chronicle of his oeuvre.

24. See Katie Cunningham 2011 for the controversy surrounding the single "Fok jullie naaiers" that caused the breakup with Interscope.

25. See Rushkoff 2005 for more on ICP and the cycle of "cool hunting."

26. Interestingly, in the first book on kitsch in 1925, the term was paired with the word *degeneration*, which the Nazis took up as part of their racial politics.

27. "Afrikaans is dood," YouTube video, posted January 1, 2013, www.youtube.com /watch?v=fZQEq6avIq8.

28. *Pap en wors* is farmer's sausage with cornmeal porridge, *poffadder* is intestine stuffed with organ meats, *waterblommetjie bredie* is a water-lily-pod stew, and *koeksisters* are syrup-drenched fried knots of dough. A virtual tour of Bistrot Boer'geoisie is available at www.bistrotboergeoisie.co.za/virtual-tour/, accessed April 10, 2016.

29. Of note, recently another sign was attached to the apartheid sign stating, "This is an apartheid sign. Pre-1994." Presumably some visitors read the sign literally and did not see its irony.

CONCLUSION

1. Haffajee has since published a book titled *What If There Were No Whites in South Africa?* (2015).

REFERENCES

1904 Programme of the St. Louis World's Fair. Louisiana Purchase Exposition Company.

A² Productions. 2007. "De la Rey Lives Again." *Carte Blanche Television Programme.* beta.mnet.co.za/carteblanche/Article.aspx?Id=3251.

ABC Australia and Journeyman Pictures. 2006. "Poor Whites—South Africa." June. www.youtube.com/watch?v=pFjoHdW2iDs.

Agamben, Giorgio. 1999. *Remnants of Auschwitz: The Witness and the Archive.* New York: Zone Books.

Akerman, Anthony. N.d. "The Last Bastion of Freedom under Siege." *South African History Online,* www.sahistory.org.za/archive/last-bastion-freedom-under-siege-0. Accessed April 10, 2016.

Allan, Jani. 1983. *Face Value.* Cape Town: Longstreet.

ANC (African National Congress). 1954. *Women's Charter.* April 17. www.anc.org.za /show.php?id=4666.

Anderson, Benedict. 1991. *Imagined Communities.* London: Verso.

Anglo-Boer War Historical Libretto: Official Program of Boer War Concession. 1904. St. Louis, MO.

"Arts and Culture White Paper." 1996. Government of South Africa, June 16, www.dac .gov.za/content/white-paper-arts-culture-and-heritage-0.

Associated Press. 2014. "Answers to Questions about the Ferguson Grand Jury." November 24, bigstory.ap.org/article/996a212325cc46dc93b46925fdf6b34a /answers-questions-about-ferguson-grand-jury.

Baines, Gary. 2009. "Site of Struggle: The Freedom Park Fracas and the Divisive Legacy of South Africa's Border War / Liberation Struggle." *Social Dynamics* 35, no. 2: 330–344.

———. 2008. "Coming to Terms with the 'Border War' in Post-Apartheid South Africa." National Arts Festival, Winter School Lecture, July 1, www.researchgate .net/publication/29807044.

Baker, Al, J. David Goodman, and Benjamin Mueller. 2015. "Beyond the Chokehold: The Path to Eric Garner's Death." *New York Times,* June 13, http://www.nytimes.com /2015/06/14/nyregion/eric-garner-police-chokehold-staten-island.html?_r=0.

Baldwin, James. 1998. "The White Man's Guilt." *Ebony* (August 1965), reprinted in *James Baldwin: Collected Essays,* edited by Toni Morrison. New York: Library of America.

Ballantine, Christopher. 2004. "Re-thinking 'Whiteness'? Identity, Change and 'White' Popular Music in Post Apartheid South Africa." *Popular Music* 23, no. 2: 105–131.

Ballen, Roger. 2013. Official website. www.rogerballen.com. Accessed April 10, 2016.

———. 1994. *Platteland: Images of Rural South Africa*. Rivonia, South Africa: William Waterman.

Bank, Rosemarie K. 2002. "Representing History: Performing the Columbian Exposition." *Theatre Journal* 54, no. 4 (December): 589–606.

Barnard, Alan. 1992. *Hunters and Herders of Southern Africa: A Comparative Ethnography of the Khoisan Peoples*. Cambridge: Cambridge University Press.

Barnard, Rita. 2012. "Ugly Feelings, Negative Dialectics: Reflections on Postapartheid Shame." *Safundi: The Journal of South African and American Studies* 13, nos. 1–2 (January–April): 151–170.

Barshad, Amos. 2011. "Die Antwoord Made a Sad and Violent Short Film with Harmony Korine." *Vulture.com*, March 16, www.vulture.com/2011/03/die_antwoord_made_a_sad_and_vi.html.

Basson, Adriaan. 2008. "Unspectacular Spectacle." *Mail and Guardian*, September 25, mg.co.za/article/2008-09-25-unspectacular-spectacle.

BBC News. 2015. "Oscar Pistorius Guilty of Murdering Reeva Steenkamp." December 3, http://www.bbc.com/news/world-africa-34993002.

———. 2010. "Anger and Anxiety after Terreblanche Murder." April 4, news.bbc.co.uk/2/hi/africa/8602967.stm.

Beker, Avi. 2008. *The Chosen: The History of an Idea, and the Anatomy of an Obsession*. New York: Palgrave Macmillan.

Bennett, Susan. 1996. *Performing Nostalgia: Shifting Shakespeare and the Contemporary Past*. London: Routledge.

Beresford, David. 2006. "A City, by Any Other Name." *Guardian*, October 10, www.theguardian.com/world/2006/oct/10/worlddispatch.southafrica.

Bester, Martie. 2013. "Donkerland: For the Love of the Land." *Screen Africa Magazine*, March, www.screenafrica.com/.

Bethlehem, Louise. 2013. Plenary panel discussion. Whitewash Conference, University of Johannesburg, March 19–21.

Bhabha, Homi K. 1990. *Nation and Narration*. New York: Routledge.

Bickford-Smith, Vivian. 1995. *Ethnic Pride and Racial Prejudice in Victorian Cape Town: Group Identity and Social Practice, 1875–1902*. Cambridge: Cambridge University Press.

Biebouw, Hendrik. 1707. "Ek ben een Africaander." newhistory.co.za/Part-1-Chapter-2-The-rise-of-the-new-communities-Afrikaners-Hendrik-Biebouw-the-first-Afrikaner/. Accessed September 9, 2013.

Binge, L. W. B. 1969. *Ontwikkeling van die Afrikaanse toneel: 1832 tot 1950*. Pretoria: J. L. Van Schaik.

Blaser, Thomas. 2008. "Looking at *The Heart of Whiteness* in South Africa Today." *Safundi* 9, no. 1: 81–96.

Bloomberg, Charles, and Saul Dubow. 1989. *Christian-Nationalism and the Rise of the Afrikaner Broederbond in South Africa, 1918–48*. Bloomington: Indiana University Press.

Blumberg, Marcia, and Dennis Walder, eds. 1999. *South African Theatre as/and Intervention*. Amsterdam: Rodopi.

Boehmer, Elke. 1991. *Motherlands: Black Women's Writing from Africa, the Caribbean, and South Asia*. Edited by Susheila Nasta. London: Women's Press.

"Boer and Britons in Conflict Once Again: Waging Battle Twice a Day at Brighton Beach." 1905. *New York Times*, May 28.

Bonnett, Alastair. 1999. *White Identities: An Historical and International Introduction*. New York: Routledge.

Boonzaier, Emile, and John Sharpe. 1988. *South African Keywords: The Uses and Abuses of Political Concepts*. Cape Town: D. Philip.

Bosman, F. C. L. 1951. *The Dutch and English Theatre in South Africa, 1800 till Today, and the Afrikaans Drama: Short Surveys*. Pretoria: de Bussy.

Botha, Anton. 2011. "The Afrikaner as Villain." *Thoughtleader.co.za*, February 28, www .thoughtleader.co.za/mandelarhodesscholars/2011/02/28/the-afrikaner-as-villain/.

Botha, Martin. 2006a. "110 Years of South African Cinema." Part 1. *Kinema* (Spring).

———. 2006b. "110 Years of South African Cinema." Part 2. *Kinema* (Fall).

Bou van 'n nasie. 1938. VHS. Directed by Joseph Albrecht. South Africa: African Film Productions.

Boucher, Leigh, Jane Carey, and Katherine Ellinghaus. 2009. *Re-Orienting Whiteness*. New York: Palgrave Macmillan.

Boundas, Constantin V., ed. 1993. *The Deleuze Reader*. New York: Columbia University Press.

Brandt, Johanna. 1999. *Die Kappiekommando, of, Boerevroue in geheime diens*. Menlopark: Protea Boekhuis.

Brewer, John D. 1994. *Black and Blue: Policing in South Africa*. Oxford: Oxford University Press.

Brewer, Mary F. 2005. *Staging Whiteness*. Middletown, CT: Wesleyan University Press.

Breytenbach, Breyten. 1993. *Return to Paradise*. New York: Harcourt Brace & Co.

Brogden, Mike, and Preet Nijhar. 1998. "Corruption and the South African Police." *Crime, Law and Social Change* 30: 89–106.

Brooks, Peter. 1995. *The Melodramatic Imagination: Balzac, Henry James, Melodrama and the Mode of Excess*. New Haven, CT: Yale University Press.

Bruton, F. Brinley. 2013. "All-White Town Fights to Preserve Segregation in Mandela's 'Rainbow Nation.'" *NBC News*, June 20, worldnews.nbcnews.com/_news/2013 /06/20/19039961-all-white-town-fights-to-preserve-segregation-in-mandelas -rainbow-nation?lite.

Bunting, Brian. 1986. *The Rise of the South African Reich*. London: IDAF.

Butler, Judith. 1993. *Bodies That Matter: On the Discursive Limits of "Sex."* New York: Routledge.

———. 1990. *Gender Trouble: Feminism and the Subversion of Identity*. New York: Routledge.

Canfield, J. Douglas. 1996. "Satire: A Critical Reintroduction (Review)." *Eighteenth-Century Studies* 29, no. 3: 330–332.

Carklin, Michael, and Daid Alcock. 1997. "Standard Bank National Arts Festival. Grahamstown, South Africa. 4–14 July 1996." *Theatre Journal* 49, no. 1: 53–56.

Carr, T. K. 2001. "Apartheid and Hermeneutics: Biblical Interpretations, Neo-

Calvinism, and the Afrikaner Sense of Self (1926–1986)." *Contributions to the Study of Religion* 65: 49–59.

Carroll, Rory. 2006. "Carjacking: The Everyday Ordeal Testing South Africa." *Guardian*, March 2, www.theguardian.com/world/2006/mar/02/film.oscars2006.

Cauthen, Bruce. 2004. "Covenant and Continuity: Ethno-symbolism and the Myth of Divine Election." *Nations and Nationalism* 10, nos. 1–2: 19–33.

Chang, Jeff. 2005. *Can't Stop, Won't Stop: A History of the Hip-Hop Generation.* New York: Picador St. Martin's.

Chaudhuri, Una. 1995. *Staging Place: The Geography of Modern Drama.* Ann Arbor: University of Michigan Press.

Cibane, Brad. 2014. "Is It Because Oscar Pistorius Is Privileged White Male?" *Law Thinker*, September 14, thelawthinker.com/is-it-because-oscar-pistorius-is -privileged-white-male/.

Cloete, Elsie. 1992. "Collaborative Confinement: The Case of the Twentieth Century 'Afrikaner' Woman." *SAVAL Conference Papers* 11 (April): 60–71.

Coetzee, Amanda. 1997. "Meiring wil ook mans raak met 'Griet.'" *Beeld*, February 25.

Coetzee, Daniella. 2001. "South African Education and the Ideology of Patriarchy." *South African Journal of Education* 21, no. 4: 300–304.

Coetzee, J. M. 1988. *White Writing.* New Haven, CT: Yale University Press.

Cole, Catherine. 2009. *Performing South Africa's Truth Commission: Stages of Transition.* Bloomington: Indiana University Press.

Comaroff, John L. 1989. "Images of Empire, Contests of Conscience: Models of Colonial Domination in South Africa." *American Ethnologist* 16, no. 4 (November): 661–685.

Conway, Daniel. 2008. "The Masculine State in Crisis: State Response to War Resistance in Apartheid South Africa." *Men and Masculinities* 10: 422.

Conway-Smith, Erin. 2012. "South African Farmers Fearing for Their Lives." *Telegraph*, December 1, www.telegraph.co.uk/news/worldnews/africaandindianocean /southafrica/9716539/South-African-farmers-fearing-for-their-lives.html.

Coombes, Annie E. 2003. *History after Apartheid: Visual Culture and Public Memory in a Democratic South Africa.* Durham, NC: Duke University Press.

Crais, Clifton. 1992. *White Supremacy and Black Resistance in Pre-industrial South Africa: The Making of the Colonial Order in the Eastern Cape, 1770–1865.* Cambridge: Cambridge University Press.

Crapanzano, Vincent. 1985. *Waiting: The Whites of South Africa.* Ann Arbor: University of Michigan Press.

Cunningham, Katie. 2011. "Die Antwoord Split with Interscope over 'Faggot' Controversy." November 8, http://fasterlouder.junkee.com/die-antwoord-split -with-interscope-over-faggot-controversy/824107.

"Dagbreek: Kalklig—Ons vir Jou." 2013. YouTube video, October 15, www.youtube .com/watch?v=3G1sIOqGXO8.

Daley, Suzanne. 1998. "Africa's 'White Tribe' Fears Dark Past Is Prologue." *New York Times*, February 22.

Darling! The Pieter-Dirk Uys Story. 2007. DVD. Directed by Julian Shaw. Cape Town, South Africa: Green Light Productions.

Davey, Monica. 2015. "Ferguson One of 2 Missouri Suburbs Sued over Gantlet of Traffic Fines and Jail." *New York Times*, February 8. www.nytimes.com/2015/02/09/us/ferguson-one-of-2-missouri-suburbs-sued-over-gantlet-of-traffic-fines-and-jail.html.

Davidson, Patricia. 1998. "Museums and the Reshaping of Memory." In *Negotiating the Past: The Making of Memory in South Africa*, edited by Sarah Nuttall and Carli Coetzee, 143–160. Oxford: Oxford University Press.

Davis, Murray S. 1993. *What's So Funny? The Comic Conception of Culture and Society*. Chicago: University of Chicago Press.

Davitt, Michael. 1902. *The Boer Fight for Freedom*. New York: Funk and Wagnalls. Available online at http://www.angloboerwar.com/books/37-davitt-boer-fight-for-freedom/828-davitt-contents-and-dedication.

de Certeau, Michel. 1988. *The Writing of History*. Translated by Tom Conley. New York: Columbia University Press.

de Klerk, W. A. 1960. *Die Jaar van die Vuuros*. Pretoria: Nasionale Pers.

de Klerk, W. J. 1972. "The Concepts of 'Verkramp' and 'Verlig.'" In *South African Dialogue: Contrasts in South African Thinking on Basic Race Issues*, edited by Nic Rhoodie, 519–531. Johannesburg: McGraw-Hill.

Delabastita, Dirk. 1993. *There's a Double Tongue: An Investigation into the Translation of Shakespeare's Wordplay, with Special Reference to Hamlet*. Amsterdam: Rodopi.

de Villiers, Marq. 1990. *White Tribe Dreaming: Apartheid's Bitter Roots as Witnessed by 8 Generations of an Afrikaner Family*. Johannesburg: Penguin Books.

De Voortrekkers. 1916. DVD. Directed by Harold M. Shaw. Cape Town: African Film Productions.

de Vos, Pierre. 2011. "Why the Taalbulle Will Destroy Afrikaans." *Constitutionally Speaking Blog*, November 8, constitutionallyspeaking.co.za/why-the-taalbulle-will-destroy-afrikaans/.

de Wet, Phillip. 2014. "Oscar Pistorius: The Judgment Unpacked." *Mail and Guardian*, September 12, mg.co.za/article/2014-09-12-oscar-pistorius-the-judgment-unpacked.

Die Antwoord. 2014. Official Facebook page. www.facebook.com/DieAntwoord.

———. 2012a. "Baby's on Fire." Official music video. Zef Filmz in association with Egg Films, posted June 5, www.youtube.com/watch?v=HcXNPI-IPPM.

———. 2012b. "Fatty Boom Boom." Official music video. Zef Filmz, posted October 16, www.youtube.com/watch?v=AIXUgtNC4Kc.

———. 2012c. "Fok julle naaiers." Official music video. Zef Filmz, posted March 7, www.youtube.com/watch?v=L-wpS49KNoo.

———. 2012d. "I Fink U Freeky." Official music video. Zef Filmz with Roger Ballen, posted January 31, www.youtube.com/watch?v=8Uee_mcxvrw.

———. 2011. "Rich Bitch." Official music video. Interscope Records, posted March 7, www.youtube.com/watch?v=8bdeizHM9OU.

————. 2010a. "Enter the Ninja." Official music video. Interscope Records, posted August 3, www.youtube.com/watch?v=cegdRoGiJl4.

————. 2010b. "Evil Boy." Official music video. Interscope Records, posted October 11, www.youtube.com/watch?v=KbW9JqM7vho.

————. 2010c. "Interview Gone Wrong." Norwegian TV, posted October 14, www .youtube.com/watch?v=bG9ZtQ3phoE.

————. N.d. "Take No Prisoners Interview." YouTube video, posted February 8, https://www.youtube.com/watch?v=vx1cYUb-0f4.

"Die Antwoord Reacts to Exploitation Allegations." 2013. *Channel 24 News*, September 30. www.channel24.co.za/Music/News/Die-Antwoord-reacts-to-exploitation -allegations-20130930.

Dixon, Robyn. 2014. "Pistorius' Lawyer Urges Leniency; Prosecutor Calls for 10-Year Term." *LA Times*, October 17, www.latimes.com/world/africa/la-fg-pistorius-lawyer -urges-leniency-20141017-story.html.

Dlanga, Khaya. 2014. "Does Race Distort the Scales of Justice?" *Mail and Guardian*, October 23, mg.co.za/article/2014-10-23-khaya-dlanga-does-race-distort-the -scales-of-justice.

Dolan, Jill. 1993. "Geographies of Learning: Theatre Studies, Performance Studies, and the 'Performative.'" *Theatre Journal* 45, no. 4 (December): 417–441.

Du Bois, W. E. B. 1920. "The Souls of White Folk." In *Darkwater: Voices from within the Veil*. Project Gutenberg EBook #15210. 2005. http://www.gutenberg.org/files/15210 /15210-h/15210-h.htm#Chapter_II.

Dunbar-Ortiz, Roxanne. 2015. *An Indigenous Peoples' History of the United States*. Boston: Beacon.

Duncan, Patrick. 1964. *South Africa's Rule of Violence*. London: Methuen.

du Plessis, Chris. 2009. "Baie hype en swak musiek." *Rapport*, November 28.

du Preez, Max. 2005. *Oranje, Blanje, Blues: 'n Nostalgiese Trip*. Cape Town: Zebra Press.

Du Toit, André, and Hermann Giliomee. 1983. *Afrikaner Political Thought: Analysis and Documents 1780–1850*. Berkeley: University of California Press.

Dyer, Richard. 1997. *White*. New York: Routledge.

Edwards, Ezekiel. 2015. "The DOJ Ferguson Report Isn't Just an Indictment of Ferguson Police, but of American Policing Writ Large." *American Civil Liberties Union*, March 6. www.aclu.org/blog/criminal-law-reform/doj-ferguson-report-isnt-just -indictment-ferguson-police-american-policing-.

Engelbrecht, Leon. 2006. "The Life and Times of P W Botha." *IOL News*, November 1, www.iol.co.za/news/politics/the-life-and-times-of-pw-botha-1.301045#.VQsNn GbZc-8.

Enloe, Cynthia. 1989. *Bananas, Beaches, and Bases: Making Feminist Sense of International Politics*. Berkeley: University of California Press.

Enoch, Nick. 2013. "Welcome to Orania . . . as Long as You're White: Remote Town in South Africa Where Afrikaners Dream of Building Their Own State." *Daily Mail Online*, May 8, www.dailymail.co.uk/news/article-2321236/Orania-Whites-town -South-Africa-Afrikaners-dream-building-state.html.

erf (81) cultural collective. 2008. Official website. www.erf81.co.za/. Accessed August
20, 2008; site discontinued.

Eyal, Dror. 1997. "Beer Cans and Boer Wars." *Mail and Guardian*, April 4.

Falkof, Nicky. 2013. "Red October." *Daily Maverick*, October 7, www.dailymaverick.co
.za/opinionista/2013-10-07-red-october.

Fanon, Frantz. 1991. *Black Skin, White Masks*. New York: Grove/Atlantic.

Farber, Leora, and Nicky Falkof. 2013. Whitewash Conference. University of
Johannesburg. March 19–21. www.whitewash.co.za/.

Faul, Michelle. 2013. "South Africa Violence against Women Rated Highest in the
World." *Huffington Post*, March 8. www.huffingtonpost.com/2013/03/08/south
-africa-violence-against-women_n_2837804.html.

Ferguson, Ian. 1977. "Three Profiles from the South African Theatre: Pieter-Dirk Uys,
Ken Leech, Robert Mohr." *Theatre Quarterly* 28: 87–94.

Fillis, Frank E., and the South African Boer War Exhibition Company. 1904. *The South
African Boer War Exhibition: The Greatest and Most Realistic Military Spectacle Known in the
History of the World*. St. Louis: J. F. Hilton.

Fleishman, Mark. 2011. "Cargo: Staging Slavery at the Cape." *Contemporary Theatre
Review* 21, no. 1: 8–19.

Fletcher, Jill. 1994. *The Story of Theatre in South Africa: A Guide to Its History from 1780–1930*.
Cape Town: Vlaeberg Uitgewers.

Fletcher, John. 2012. "Theatrical Histories of/as Activism: Critical Generosity,
Paranoid Readings, and Assumptions of Good Faith." Paper presented at
American Society for Theatre Research (ASTR) Annual Conference, Nashville, TN,
November 1–4.

———. 2010. "Sympathy for the Devil: Nonprogressive Activism and the Limits of
Critical Generosity." In *Theatre Historiography: Critical Interventions*, edited by Henry
Bial and Scott Magelssen, 110–122. Ann Arbor: University of Michigan Press.

Flockemann, Miki. 2011. "Facing the Stranger in the Mirror: Staged Complicities in
Recent South African Performances." *South African Theatre Journal* 25, no. 2: 129–141.

Foster, Gwendolyn Audrey. 2003. *Performing Whiteness: Postmodern Re/Constructions in the
Cinema*. Albany: SUNY Press.

Foucault, Michel. 1995. *Discipline and Punish: The Birth of the Prison*. London: Vintage.

———. 1972. *The Archaeology of Knowledge*. New York: Routledge.

Fraley, Todd. 2009. "I Got a Natural Skill . . . : Hip-Hop, Authenticity, and Whiteness."
Howard Journal of Communications 20, no. 1: 37–54.

Frankenberg, Ruth. 1993. *White Women, Race Matters: The Social Construction of Whiteness*.
Minneapolis: University of Minnesota Press.

Freedom Park. Official website. freedompark.co.za. Accessed April 10, 2016.

Frye, Northrup. 1957. *The Anatomy of Criticism*. Princeton, NJ: Princeton University
Press.

Garner, Steve. 2007. *Whiteness: An Introduction*. New York: Routledge.

Gerber, Jan. 2008. "Agtertrekker-vonke spat." *Die Burger*, March 26.

Giliomee, Hermann. 2012. "The Day Apartheid Started Dying." *Mail and Guardian*, October 26.

———. 2008. "The Rubicon Revisited." *PoliticsWeb*, August 20, www.politicsweb.co.za /politicsweb/view/politicsweb/en/page71619?oid=100899&sn=Detail. Includes link to full text of Rubicon speech. www.politicsweb.co.za/politicsweb/action /media/downloadFile?media_fileid=1065.

———. 2003. *The Afrikaners: Biography of a People*. Charlottesville: University of Virginia Press.

———. 1999. "Eeuwendings en bestaankeuses vir wit Afrikaner-inboorlinge." *Aambeeld*, June, general.rau.ac.za/aambeeld/junie1999/eeuwendings.htm.

Giliomee, Hermann, and Bernard Mbenga. 2007. Companion website for *New History of South Africa*. Cape Town: Tafelberg. newhistory.co.za.

Giroux, Henry. 1997. "Racial Politics and the Pedagogy of Whiteness." In *Whiteness: A Critical Reader*, edited by Mike Hill, 294–315. New York: New York University Press.

Goodwin, June, and Ben Schiff. 1995. *Heart of Whiteness: Afrikaners Face Black Rule in the New South Africa*. New York: Scribner.

Gournelos, Ted, and Viveca Greene. 2011. *A Decade of Dark Humor: How Comedy, Irony, and Satire Shaped Post-9/11 America*. Jackson: University Press of Mississippi.

Graver, David. 1997. "1996 Standard Bank National Arts Festival." *Theatre Journal* 49, no. 1: 56–59.

Gray, Emma, and Jessica Samakow. 2015. "11 Things White People Need to Realize about Race." *Huffington Post*, July 23, www.huffingtonpost.com/entry/11-things -white-people-need-to-realize-about-race_55b0009be4b07af29d576702.

Gray, Stephen. 1979. "Review of *Die van Aardes van Grootoor* by Pieter-Dirk Uys." *English in Africa* 6, no. 2 (September): 78–84.

Greene, Viveca. 2012. "Irony and Ideology: Oppositional Politics and Cultural Engagement in Post-September 11th America." PhD diss., University of Massachusetts Amherst.

Griffin, Dustin. 1994. *Satire: A Critical Reintroduction*. Lexington: University of Kentucky Press.

Groenewald, Yoland, and Tarryn Harbour. 2010. "Author Anneli Botes Stands by Racist Comments." *Mail and Guardian*, November 26. www.mg.co.za/article/2010 -11-26-author-anneli-botes-stands-by-racist-comments.

Grosskopf, J. F. W., R. W. Wilcocks, E. G. Malherbe, W. A. Murray, and J. R. Albertyn. 1932. *The Poor White Problem in South Africa: Report of the Carnegie Commission*. Stellenbosch: Pro ecclesia-drukkery.

Grosz, Elizabeth. 1995. *Space, Time, and Perversion*. New York: Routledge.

Grundlingh, Arthur. 2001. "A Cultural Conundrum? Old Monuments and New Regimes: The Voortrekker Monument as Symbol of Afrikaner Power in a Postapartheid South Africa." *Radical History Review* 81 (Fall): 95–112.

———. 1994. "Playing for Power? Rugby, Afrikaner Nationalism and Masculinity in South Africa, c. 1900–70." *International Journal of the History of Sport* 11, no. 3: 408–430.

Grundy, Kenneth W. 1994. "The Politics of South Africa's National Arts Festival: Small Engagements in the Bigger Campaign." *African Affairs* 93, no. 372: 387–409.

Haffajee, Ferial. 2015. *What If There Were No Whites in South Africa?* Johannesburg: Picador Africa.

———. 2013. "The Problem with Whiteness." *City Press*, March 31, www.citypress .co.za/columnists/the-problem-with-whiteness-ferial-haffajee.

Hall, Stuart. 1997. "The Spectacle of the Other." In *Representation: Cultural Representation and Signifying Practice*. Thousand Oaks, CA: Sage.

Hansen, Corrie. 1992. "Is jy 'n Griet? Of is jy 'n Elizabeth? Sekskapades van die Afrikanervrou." *Huisgenoot*, May 2.

Harker, Richard, Cheleen Mahar, and Chris Wilkes, eds. 1990. *An Introduction to the Work of Pierre Bourdieu: The Practice of Theory*. New York: Palgrave Macmillan.

Harrison, David. 1981. *The White Tribe of Africa*. Berkeley: University of California Press.

Hauptfleisch, Temple. 1999. "Unwilling Champion—An Interview with Reza de Wet." *Contemporary Theatre Review* 9, no. 1: 53–63.

Hazlitt, William. 1930. "Lectures on the Comic Writers, etc. of Great Britain." In *The Complete Works of William Hazlitt*. 1819. London: J. M. Dent & Sons.

Hees, Edwin. 2003. "The Birth of a Nation: Contextualizing *De Voortrekkers* (1916)." In *To Change Reels: Film and Culture in South Africa*, edited by Isabel Balseiro and Ntongela Masilela, 49–69. Detroit: Wayne State University Press.

———. 1996. "The Voortrekkers on Film: From Preller to Pornography." *Critical Arts* 10, no. 1: 1–22.

Hill, Mike. 1997. *Whiteness: A Critical Reader*. New York: New York University Press.

Hobsbawm, Eric, and Terence Ranger. 1992. *The Invention of Tradition*. Cambridge: Cambridge University Press.

Hofmeyr, Isabel. 1987. "Building a Nation from Words: Afrikaner Language, Literature, and Ethnic Identity, 1902–1924." In *The Politics of Race, Class and Nationalism in Twentieth Century South Africa*, edited by Shula Marks and Stanley Trapido, 95–123. London: Longman.

Hofmeyr, Steve. 2013. Red October website. www.redoctober.co.za.

Holmes, Oliver Wendell. 1891. *The Professor at the Breakfast Table*. Project Gutenberg EBook #2665. 2006. www.gutenberg.org/files/2665/2665-h/2665-h.htm.

Hopkins, Pat. 2006. *Voëlvry: The Movement That Rocked South Africa*. Cape Town: Zebra Press.

Hunter, Shona. 2013. Presenter. Whitewash Conference. University of Johannesburg, March 19–20.

Hutchison, Yvette. 2013. *South African Performance and Archives of Memory*. Manchester: Manchester University Press.

Ignatiev, Noel. 1996. *Race Traitor*. New York: Routledge. www.racetraitor.org/.

Jansen, Jonathan. 2009. *Knowledge in the Blood: Confronting Race and the Apartheid Past*. Palo Alto, CA: Stanford University Press.

Jardin, Xeni. 2011. "Die Antwoord Leave Interscope, Will Release 'TEN$ION' on Their

Own New Indie Label." *boingboing.net*, November 7, http://boingboing.net/2011/11/07/dieantwoordleave.html.

Jenkins, Ron. 1998. "South African Political Clowning: Laughter and Resistance to Apartheid." In *Fools and Jesters in Literature, Art, and History*, edited by Vicki K. Janik, 419–427. Westport, CT: Greenwood.

Johnson, David. 2012. *Imagining the Cape Colony: History, Literature, and the South African Nation*. Edinburgh: Edinburgh University Press.

Johnson, E. Patrick. 2008. "Queer Theory." In *Cambridge Guide to Performance Studies*, edited by Tracy C. Davis, 166–182. Cambridge: Cambridge University Press.

Joseph, May, and Jennifer Natalya Fink. 1999. *Performing Hybridity*. Minneapolis: University of Minnesota Press.

"Julius Malema's Political Timeline." 2012. *IOLNews*, April 24, www.iol.co.za/news/special-features/julius-malema-s-political-timeline-1.1283102#.Um6nIySkBNg.

Kannemeyer, J. C. 1988. *Die Afrikaanse Literatuur, 1652–1987*. Cape Town: Human & Rousseau.

Kaufman, Gershen. 2004. *The Psychology of Shame*. New York: Springer.

Keegan, Timothy. 2011. "Gender, Degeneration and Sexual Danger: Imagining Race and Class in South Africa c. 1912." *Journal of South African Studies* 27, no. 3 (September): 459–477.

Keller, Bil. 1993. "The Urge to Suppress Persists in South Africa." *New York Times*, August 1, pdu.co.za/freedom%201993.html.

Kelto, Anders. 2014. "Did Oscar Pistorius Get Away with Murder?" NPR, Morning Edition, December 30, www.npr.org/2014/12/30/373934271/did-oscar-pistorius-get-away-with-murder.

Keuris, Marisa. 2012. "'Theatre as a Memory Machine': *Magrita Prinslo* (1896) and *Donkerland* (1996)." *Journal of Literary Studies / Tydskrif vir Literatuurwetenskap* 28, no. 3 (September): 77–92.

———. 2009. "Deon Opperman's *Donkerland*: The Rise and Fall of Afrikaner Nationalism." *Acta Academica* 41, no. 3: 1–15.

———. 2004. "Found in Translation: Chekhov Revisited by Reza de Wet and Janet Suzman." *Journal of Literary Studies* 20, nos. 1–2 (June): 148–164.

King, Shaun. 2015. "Ferguson an Apartheid Police State: 21,000 Residents Have a Staggering 16,000 Open Arrest Warrants." *Daily Kos*, March 16, www.dailykos.com/story/2015/03/16/1371220/-Ferguson-an-Apartheid-Police-State-21-000-residents-w-a-staggering-16-000-open-arrest-warrants#.

Kinghorn, Johan. 1994. "Social Cosmology, Religion and Afrikaner Identity." *Journal of South African Social Studies* 20, no. 3: 393–404.

Kirchick, James. 2008. "In Whitest Africa: The Afrikaner Homeland of Orania." *Virginia Quarterly Review* 84, no. 3: 74–87.

Kitshoff, Herman. 2004. "Claiming Cultural Festivals: Playing for Power at the Klein Karoo Nasionale Kunstefees (KKNK)." *South African Theatre Journal* 18: 65–81.

Kitwana, Bakari. 2005. *Why White Kids Love Hip Hop: Wanksfas, Wiggers, Wannabes, and the New Reality of Race in America*. New York: Basic Civitas Books.

Klausen, Susanne M. 2010. "Reclaiming the White Daughter's Purity: Afrikaner Nationalism, Racialized Sexuality, and the 1975 Abortion and Sterilization Act in Apartheid South Africa." *Journal of Women's History* 22, no. 3 (Fall): 39–63.

Koestler, Arthur. 1974. "Humor and Wit." *Encyclopedia Britannica*, 15th ed., 5–11.

Kristeva, Julia. 1982. *Powers of Horror: An Essay on Abjection.* New York: Columbia University Press.

Kristof, Nicholas. 2014–2016. "When Whites Just Don't Get It." Six-part online series. *New York Times*, August 30, 2014–April 2, 2016, nyti.ms/1B4Zfr6.

Krog, Antjie. 2009. "A New Ancestor for Our Alienated Afrikaner Youth." *Sunday Times*, November 7, www.timeslive.co.za/sundaytimes/article183988.ece.

Krueger, Anton. 2012. "Zef/Poor White Kitsch Chique: South African Comedies of Degradation." *Safundi: The Journal of South African and American Studies* 13, nos. 3–4: 399–408.

———. 2010a. "Keeping It in the Family: Incest, Repression and the Fear of the Hybrid in Reza de Wet's English Plays." *Literator: Journal of Literary Criticism, Comparative Linguistics and Literary Studies* 31, no. 2: 45–60.

———. 2010b. *Experiments in Freedom: Explorations of Identity in New South African Drama.* Newcastle upon Tyne: Cambridge Scholars.

Kruger, Loren. 1999a. *The Drama of South Africa: Plays, Pageants and Publics since 1910.* London: Routledge.

———. 1999b. "The Premodern Postcolonial? The Drama of the Autochthonous Settler." In *Post-Colonial Stages: Critical and Creative Views on Drama, Theatre and Performance*, edited by Helen Gilbert, 26–39. London: Dangaroo.

———. 1997. "The Drama of Country and City: Tribalization, Urbanization and Theatre under Apartheid." *Journal of Southern African Studies* 23, no. 4 (December): 565–584.

Kruger, M., M. Saayman, and S. M. Ellis. 2010. "Does Loyalty Pay? First-Time versus Repeat Visitors at a National Arts Festival." *Southern African Business Review* 14, no. 1: 79–104.

Lake, Marilyn, and Henry Reynolds. 2008. *Drawing the Global Colour Line: White Men's Countries and the International Challenge of Racial Equality.* Cambridge: Cambridge University Press.

Lefebvre, Henri. 1991. *The Production of Space.* Translated by Donald Nicholson-Smith. Oxford: Blackwell.

Lethal Weapon 2. 1989. DVD. Directed by Richard Donner. Burbank, CA: Warner Bros.

Lewis, Gavin. 1987. *Between the Wire and the Wall: A History of South African "Coloured" Politics.* New York: St. Martin's.

Lewis, Megan. 2013. "Power Plays in the Cradle of Humankind." *PAJ: A Journal of Performance and Art* 35, no. 3 (September): 55–60.

———. 2011. "Interview with Deon Opperman." Unpublished transcript, Johannesburg, June 29.

———. 2008. "(Un)Patriotic Acts of an Imagined Community: The Klein Karoo Nasionale Kunstefees." *Theatre Journal* 60, no. 4: 654–659.

Lieberfeld, Daniel. 1997. "Pieter-Dirk Uys: Crossing Apartheid Lines: An Interview." TDR 41, no. 1: 61–71.

Loots, Sonja. 2011. Sirkusboere. Cape Town: Tafelberg.

Lopez, Alfred J., ed. 2005. Postcolonial Whiteness: A Critical Reader on Race and Empire. Albany: SUNY Press.

Louw, Chris. 2000. Ope brief aan Willem de Klerk. Dainfern: Praag Uitgewers.

Lynch, Tom. 2014. "'Nothing but Land': Women's Narratives, Gardens, and the Settler-Colonial Imaginary in the US West and Australian Outback." Western American Literature 48, no. 4 (Winter): 374–399.

Lynd, Helen Merrell. 1958. On Shame and the Search for Identity. London: Routledge and Kegan Paul.

Mabry, Marcus. 2013. "Generation Born after Apartheid Sees Mandela's Fight as History." New York Times, December 6, www.nytimes.com/2013/12/07/world/africa/south-africas-born-frees-move-past-apartheid.html?pagewanted=all&_r=0.

Maingard, Jacqueline. 2007. South African National Cinema. London: Routledge.

———. 1997. "Imag(in)ing the South African Nation: Representations of Identity in the Rugby World Cup 1995." Theatre Journal 49, no. 1: 15–28.

Marks, Shula, and Stanley Trapido, eds. 1987. The Politics of Race, Class and Nationalism in Twentieth Century South Africa. London: Longman.

Marschall, Sabine. 2004. "Serving Male Agendas: Two National Women's Monuments in South Africa." Women's Studies 33, no. 8 (December): 1009–1033.

Martinot, Steve. 2010. The Machinery of Whiteness: Studies in the Structure of Racialization. Philadelphia: Temple University Press.

Marx, Hannelie, and Viola Candice Milton. 2011. "Bastardised Whiteness: 'Zef'-Culture, Die Antwoord and the Reconfiguration of Contemporary Afrikaans Identities." Social Identities 17, no. 6 (November): 723–745.

Mbembe, Achille. 2001. On the Postcolony. Berkeley: University of California Press.

McClintock, Anne. 1995. Imperial Leather: Race, Gender and Sexuality in the Colonial Contest. New York: Routledge.

McDonald, Peter D. 2010. The Literature Police: Apartheid Censorship and Its Cultural Consequences. Oxford: Oxford University Press. Accompanying website: www.theliteraturepolice.com.

McGreal, Chris. 2007. "Afrikaans Singer Stirs Up Controversy with War Song." Guardian, February 27, www.theguardian.com/world/2007/feb/26/music.southafrica.

McKaiser, Eusebius. 2012. A Bantu in My Bathroom: Debating Race, Sexuality and Other Uncomfortable South African Topics. Johannesburg: Bookstorm.

McMurtry, Mervyn. 1994. "'The Rise of the First Ambassador Bezuidenhout': Pieter-Dirk Uys's Creation of Evita Bezuidenhout, Her Fictional Actuality and His Approach to Female Impersonation." South African Theatre Journal 8, no. 2 (September): 79–107.

McNeil, Donald, Jr. 1996. "With Apartheid Done For, What's a Festival to Do?" New York Times International, July 16.

Meintjies, Johannes. 1973. *The Voortrekkers: Story of the Great Trek and the Making of South Africa.* Worthing, West Sussex: Littlehampton Book Services.

Menninghaus, Winfried. 2009. "On the 'Vital Significance of Kitsch': Walter Benjamin's Politics of 'Bad Taste.'" In *Walter Benjamin and the Architecture of Modernity,* edited by Andrew E. Benjamin and Charles Rice. Prahran, Australia: re:press.

Merrett, Christopher. 1995. *A Culture of Censorship: Secrecy and Intellectual Repression in South Africa.* Cape Town: David Philip; Pietermaritzburg: University of Natal Press; Macon, GA: Mercer University Press.

Merrington, Peter. 1997. "Masques, Monuments, and Masons: The 1910 Pageant of the Union of South Africa." *Theatre Journal* 49, no. 1: 1–14.

Mesthrie, Rajend, ed. 2002. *Language in South Africa.* Cambridge: Cambridge University Press.

Miller, Henry. 1970. *The Air-Conditioned Nightmare.* New York: New Directions.

Moodie, T. Dunbar. 1975. *The Rise of Afrikanerdom.* Berkeley: University of California Press.

Mooney, Katie. 1998. "'Ducktails, Flick-Knives and Pugnacity': Subcultural and Hegemonic Masculinities in South Africa, 1948–1960." In "Masculinities in Southern Africa," special issue, *Journal of Southern African Studies* 24, no. 4: 753–774.

Morrison, Toni. 1992. *Playing in the Dark: Whiteness and the Literary Imagination.* New York: Random House.

Morton, Thomas. 2007. "In the Land of the Juggalos a Juggalo Is King." *Vice.com,* September 30. https://www.vice.com/read/land-of-juggalos-v14n10.

Mostert, Dirk. 1940. *Gedenkboek van die ossewaens op die pad van Suid-Afrika: Eeufees 1838–1938.* Cape Town: Nasionale Pers.

Mulholland, Rosemary. 1997. *South Africa 1948–1994.* Cambridge: Cambridge University Press.

Mullen, Harryette. 1994. "Optic White: Blackness and the Production of Whiteness." *Diacritics: A Review of Contemporary Criticism* 24, nos. 2–3 (Summer–Fall): 71–89.

Myburg, Johan. 2008. "Heilige koeie geslag vir stof tot nadenke." *Beeld,* March 30.

Nuttall, Sarah. 2009. *Entanglement: Literary and Cultural Reflections on Post-apartheid.* Johannesburg: Wits University Press.

———. 2004. "Stylizing the Self: The Y Generation in Rosebank, Johannesburg." *Public Culture* 16, no. 3 (Fall): 430–452.

Nuttall, Sarah, and Carli Coetzee, eds. 1998. *Negotiating the Past: The Making of Memory in South Africa.* Oxford: Oxford University Press.

Nyquist Potter, Nancy. 2006. *Trauma, Truth and Reconciliation: Healing Damaged Relationships.* Oxford: Oxford University Press.

Opperman, Deon. 2013a. "Deon Opperman oor Donkerland." *KykNet.dstv.com,* November 6. kyknet.dstv.com/category/programme/donkerland/.

———. 2013b. "I'm a White Man in Africa." *deonopperman.blogspot.com,* April 14.

———. 2012. *Ons vir Jou* Facebook page. May 10, www.facebook.com/onsvirjou/posts/336533719748315.

———. 2010. *Tree aan.* Unpublished play script with lyrics.

———. 1996. *Donkerland*. Cape Town: Tafelberg.

Opperman, Deon, and Sean Else. 2008. *Ons vir Jou*. Unpublished play script with lyrics.

Orania. 2012. DVD. Directed by Tobias Lindner. Berlin: Dreamtrader Films.

"Orania: New Afrikaner Homeland?" 1991. *Chicago Tribune / Seattle Times*, May 1.

"Outcry in South Africa over Racist 'Fear Factor' Video." 2008. LiveLeak, February 27, www.liveleak.com/view?i=c68_1204141216#XjjIHA5dbsAsIGEF.99.

Owen, Ken. 1996a. "No Need for a Language Laager." *Weekly Mail and Guardian*, December 6.

———. 1996b. "The Taal I Was Once Ashamed Of." *Mail and Guardian*, December 8.

Packenham, Thomas. 1979. *The Boer War*. Johannesburg and Cape Town: Jonathan Ball.

Parow, Jack. 2013. "Afrikaans is dood." Official music video. Little Big Productions, posted January 1, www.youtube.com/watch?v=fZQEq6avIq8.

———. 2011a. "Byellville." Official music video. SFR, posted March 31, www.youtube.com/watch?v=2yQ1FNoFZoY.

———. 2011b. *Eksie Ou*. Jack Parow, featuring Dawid Kramer, Francois van Coke, Pierre Greeff, Haezer, P.H.Fat and SiboT. Produced by Justin de Nobrega. Parowphernalia. LP. Compact disc.

———. 2011c. "Ons behoort mos saam." Official music video. Jack Parow, posted October 12, https://www.youtube.com/watch?v=yeWP1ACrCTo.

———. 2010. *Jack Parow*. Jack Parow, featuring Francois van Coke and Die Heuwels Fantasties. LP. Compact disc.

———. 2010. Official website. jackparow.com.

———. 2009. *Cooler as ekke*. Jack Parow, featuring Francois van Coke, Reënboogperde, and Rufio Vegas. Debut EP album released as a USB flash drive.

Patterson, Sheila. 1957. *The Last Trek: A Study of the Boer People and the Afrikaner Nation*. London: Routledge & Kegan Paul.

Pattison, Stephen. 2000. *Shame: Theory, Therapy, Theology*. Cambridge: Cambridge University Press.

Pedersen, Camilla Østergaard. 2010. "The Translation of Puns: An Analysis of the Fate of Puns in Subtitling with *Sex and the City* as an Empirical Example." BA thesis, Aarhus University, Aarhus, Denmark. December 1, pure.au.dk/portal/files/14202/The_translation_of_puns.doc.

Ponelis, Fritz. 1993. *The Development of Afrikaans*. Frankfurt am Main: Lang.

Postlewait, Thomas. 1996. "From Melodrama to Realism: The Suspect History of American Drama." In *Melodrama: The Cultural Emergence of a Genre*, edited by Michael Hays and Anastasia Nikolopoulou. New York: St. Martin's.

Praeg, Leonhard, and Siphokazi Magadla. 2014. *Ubuntu: Curating the Archive*. Thinking Africa Series. Grahamstown: University of KwaZulu-Natal Press.

Preller, Gustav. 1938. *Voortrekkermense VI*. Cape Town: Nasionale Pers.

Pretorius, Fransjohan. 2001. *The Great Escape of the Boer Pimpernel Christiaan de Wet*. Pietermaritzburg: University of Natal Press.

Property of the State: Gay Men in the Apartheid Military. 2003. DVD. Directed by Gerald Kraak.

Rassool, Ciraj, and Leslie Witz. 1993. "The 1952 Jan van Riebeeck Tercentenary Festival: Constructing and Contesting Public National History in South Africa." *Journal of African History* 34, no. 3: 447–468.

"Residents Stick to 'Old' City Names." 2011. *News24*, August 15, www.news24.com /SouthAfrica/News/Residents-stick-to-old-city-names-20110809.

Reuters. 2012. "Killings of White Farmers Highlight Toxic Apartheid Legacy in South Africa." *NBC News*, November 30, worldnews.nbcnews.com/_news/2012/11/30 /15571149-killings-of-white-farmers-highlight-toxic-apartheid-legacy-in-south -africa.

"Revised White Paper on Arts, Culture and Heritage." 2013. South African Department of Arts and Culture, June 4, www.dac.gov.za/sites/default/files/REVISEDWHITE PAPER04062013.pdf.

Roediger, David. 1994. *Towards the Abolition of Whiteness*. London: Verso.

Rushkoff, Douglas. 2005. *The Merchants of Cool*. DVD. Directed by Barak Goodman. Boston, Massachusetts. WGBH Educational Foundation, PBS Home Video.

Russell, Alec. 2007. "Boer Roar: A Rock Song Celebrating an Historic Afrikaner Guerrilla Hero Has Become a Huge Hit in South Africa." *Financial Times*, July 21.

Russell, Diane E. H. 1993. "The Divine Right of the Father: Incest in the White Afrikaner Tribe." *Off Our Backs* 23, no. 3 (March): 10–11.

Sannar, Torsten. 2011. "Playing Sun City: The Politics of Entertainment at a South African Mega-Resort." PhD diss., University of California, Santa Barbara.

Sarup, Madan. 1993. *An Introductory Guide to Post-Structuralism and Postmodernism*. Athens: University of Georgia Press.

Schaffer, Brad. Filmmaker's website. www.bradshawschaffer.com.

———. 2006. *Bok*. www.erf81.co.za/bok_movie.htm.

———. 2004. *So is 'n os gemaak*. www.erf81.co.za/os.htm.

———. N.d. *Peter Van Heerden: Performance Artist*. www.erf81.co.za/compilation.htm.

Schechner, Richard. 2013. *Performance Studies: An Introduction*. 3rd ed. New York: Routledge.

Scott, Claire. 2012. "Die Antwoord and a Delegitimised South African Whiteness: A Potential Counter-narrative?" *Critical Arts* 26, no. 5: 745–761.

Sedgwick, Eve Kosofsky. 2002. "Paranoid Reading and Reparative Reading: or, You're So Paranoid, You Probably Think This Essay Is about You." In *Touching Feeling: Affect, Pedagogy, Performativity*, edited by Eve Kosofsky Sedgwick, Michèle Aina Barale, Jonathan Goldberg, and Michael Moon, 123–151. Durham, NC: Duke University Press.

Semien, Robyn, Miki Meek, and Sean Cole. 2015. "Cops See It Differently, Part Two." *This American Life*, February 13, www.thisamericanlife.org/radio-archives/episode /548/cops-see-it-differently-part-two.

Senelick, Laurence. 2000. *The Changing Room: Sex, Drag and Theatre*. London: Routledge.

Shafto, Michael. 1992. "Fuss over Bestseller Fazes Frank Marita." *Johannesburg Star*, September 7.

Shapiro, Joseph. 2014. "In Ferguson, Court Fines and Fees Fuel Anger." NPR, All

Things Considered, August 25, www.npr.org/2014/08/25/343143937/in-ferguson
-court-fines-and-fees-fuel-anger.

Shear, Keith. 2012. "Tested Loyalties: Police and Politics in South Africa, 1939–63."
Journal of African History 53: 173–193.

Sinha, Smriti. 2014. "Oscar Pistorius Didn't Get Away with Murder, But He Did Get
Off Easy." *Vice Sports*, October 22, sports.vice.com/article/oscar-pistorius-didnt
-get-away-with-murder-but-he-did-get-off-easy.

Smith, David. 2010. "Is Afrikaans Cooler as Engels?" *Mail and Guardian Thought Leader*,
February 3.

Socialite, The. 2010. "Jack Parow: Die Pirate of the Caravan Park." May 10, http://
thesocialite.co.za/2010/05/jack-parow-die-pirate-of-the-caravan-park/.

Sommer, Doris. 1991. *Foundational Fictions: The National Romances of Latin America*.
Berkeley: University of California Press.

Sonderling, Stefan. 1998. "The Politics of a Cultural Controversy: Langenhoven and
Pornography in 1930." *Journal of Literary Studies* 14, nos. 3–4: 322–347.

South Africa. 1989. *Guidebook to the Voortrekker Monument*. Pretoria: Official Government
Publication.

South Africa.info. N.d. "South Africa's Population." www.southafrica.info/about
/people/population.htm#.VQngHmbZc-8.

Southern, Neil. 2008. "The Freedom Front Plus: An Analysis of Afrikaner Politics and
Ethnic Identity in the New South Africa." *Contemporary Politics* 14, no. 4 (December):
463–478.

Spanierman, Lisa B., Nathan R. Todd, and Carolyn J. Anderson. 2009. "Psychosocial
Costs of Racism to Whites: Understanding Patterns among University Students."
Journal of Counseling Psychology 56, no. 2 (April): 239–252.

Steinberg, Jonny. 2013. "How SA Fell Out of love with Oscar Pistorius." *Mail and
Guardian*, May 27, mg.co.za/article/2013-05-27-how-oscar-pistorius-fell-off-track
-with-sa.

Stephens, Jimbo. 2013. *AKA: The Lives of Waddy Tudor Jones*. YouTube video, posted March
27. Part 1: Die Vraag: www.youtube.com/watch?v=cgRUlVZbpcg; Part II: Die
Antwoord: www.youtube.com/watch?v=zEd7WTqv4DA. Includes a transcript of
the documentary.

Steyn, Melissa. 2013. Plenary panel discussion. Whitewash Conference. March 19.
———. 2005. "White Talk." In *Postcolonial Whiteness: A Critical Reader on Race and Empire*,
edited by Alfred J. Lopez, 119–136. Albany: SUNY University Press.
———. 2004a. "Rehabilitating a Whiteness Disgraced: Afrikaner *White Talk* in Post-
Apartheid South Africa." *Communication Quarterly* 52, no. 2 (Spring): 143–169.
———. 2004b. "Rehybridising the Creole: New South African Afrikaners." In *Under
Construction: "Race" and Identity in South Africa Today*, edited by Natasha Distiller and
Melissa Steyn, 70–85. Johannesburg: Heinemann.
———. 2001. *"Whiteness Just Isn't What It Used to Be": White Identity in a Changing South
Africa*. Albany: SUNY Press.

Sue, Derald Wing. 2015. *Race Talk and the Conspiracy of Silence: Understanding and Facilitating Difficult Dialogues on Race.* Indianapolis: Wiley.

Sutton, Jennie. 2007. "'Transvaal Spectacles': South African Visions at the 1904 St. Louis World's Fair." *Safundi* 8, no. 3: 271–287.

Szechenyi, Christopher A. 1995. "A Segregated Town Survives in South Africa." *Chicago Tribune*, March 30.

Taylor, Diana. 2003. *The Archive and the Repertoire: Performing Cultural Memory in the Americas.* Durham, NC: Duke University Press.

Templin, J. Alton. 1984. *Ideology on a Frontier: The Theological Foundation of Afrikaner Nationalism, 1652–1910.* London: Greenwood.

Theal, George McCall. 1886. *Boers and Bantu: A History of the Wanderings and Wars of the Emigrant Farmers from Their Leaving the Cape Colony to the Overthrow of Dingan.* Cape Town: Saul Solomon.

Tolsi, Niren. 2013. "Pistorius 'Absolutely Mortified' at Loss of Steenkamp." *Mail and Guardian*, February 19, mg.co.za/article/2013-02-19-pistorius-absolutely-mortified-at-loss-of-steenkamp.

Trillin, Calvin. 2004. "The Satirist Pieter-Dirk Uys Adjusts to the New South Africa." *New Yorker*, May 10.

"Two Kindly, Jovial Fellows." 2011. *City Press*, August 20, www.citypress.co.za/news/two-kindly-jovial-fellows-20110820/.

Turner, Victor. 1969. "Liminality and Communitas." In *The Ritual Process: Structure and Anti-Structure.* Chicago: Aldine.

Unrepresented Nations and Peoples Organization (UNPO). 2013. Official website. www.unpo.org.

Uys, Pieter-Dirk. 2015. Official website. pdu.co.za.

———. 2013a. "All That Freedom—Where's the Speech?" *South African*, June 24.

———. 2013b. "Citizens of South Africa Deserve What They Get." *Cape Times*, June 13.

———. 2013c. Evita Bezuidenhout / Darling. Official website. www.evita.co.za.

———. 2013d. "Mý Suid-Afrika is nie Europa nie." *Die Burger*, September 7. English version: "My South Africa." *South African*, September 2.

———. 2013e. "You Have a Voice. You Have a Vote." *Cape Times*, September 18.

———. 2010. *Between the Devil and the Deep: A Memoir of Acting and Reacting.* Cape Town: Zebra Press.

———. 2004. "The Way We Were . . . and the Fear We Live With." *Independent*, June 20, pdu.co.za/freedom%202004.html.

———. 2002. *Elections and Erections: A Memoir of Fear and Fun.* Cape Town: Zebra Press.

———. 2001. Evita Bezuidenout Website. Defunct. www.millennia.co.za/evita.

———. 1999. "My Best Teacher." *TES Magazine*, October 1, pdu.co.za/articles%20by%201999.html.

———. 1995. *Funigalore: Evita's Real-Life Adventures in Wonderland.* Johannesburg: Penguin Books.

———. 1990. *A Part Love a Part Hate: The Biography of Evita Bezuidenhout.* Cape Town: Random House Century.

————. 1986. *No One's Died Laughing*. Johannesburg: Penguin.

————. 1985. *Skating on Thin Uys*. DVD. Directed by Bromley Cawood. Screenplay by Pieter-Dirk Uys. Brigadiers-Bapetikosweti Marketing Enterprises.

————. 1983. *Farce about Uys*. London: Jonathan Ball and Ad. Donker.

————. 1982. *Adapt or Dye*. DVD. Written and directed by Pieter-Dirk Uys. Johannesburg, South Africa. PD Uys Productions CC.

————. 1979. *Die van Aardes van Grootoor: 'n epiese Boeredrama in 780 episodes, vyf bedrywe en twee landstale*. Cape Town: Taurus.

van Bosch, Cobus. 2008. "Laat die Afrikaner met homself praat." *Rapport*, March 29.

van den Berghe, P. 1960. "Miscegenation in South Africa." *Cahiers d'études africaines* 1, no. 4: 68–84.

van der Merwe, Floris. 2007. *Frank Fillis: The Story of a Circus Legend*. Stellenbosch: F. J. G. Publikasies.

————. 1998. "Die 'Boeresirkus' van St. Louis, V.S.A. 1904." *South African Journal of Cultural History* 12, no. 2: 85–99.

van der Merwe, Hendrik W., and Thomas J. Johnson. 1997. "Restitution in South Africa and the Accommodation of an Afrikaner Ethnic Minority." *International Journal of Peace Studies* 2, no. 2 (July). http://www.gmu.edu/programs/icar/ijps /vol2_2/merwe.htm.

van der Vyver, Marita. 1994. *Griet Skryf 'n Sprokie*. Cape Town: Tafelberg, 1992. Available in English translation as *Entertaining Angels*. Translated by Catherine Knox. Cape Town: Penguin.

Van Der Watt, Liese. 2004. "Imagining Alternative White Masculinities: Steven Cohen's Living Art." In *Under Construction: "Race" and Identity in South Africa Today*, edited by Natasha Distiller and Melissa Steyn. Sandton: Heinemann.

————. 2003. "The Many Hearts of Whiteness: Dis/Investing in Whiteness through South African Visual Culture." PhD diss., SUNY Stony Brook.

van der Westhuizen, Christi. 2013a. "The Problem with Whiteness." *City Press*, March 31, www.citypress.co.za/columnists/the-problem-with-whiteness-christi-van-der -westhuizen/.

————. 2013b. "The White Angst of Red October." *Thought Leader*, October 14, www .thoughtleader.co.za/christivanderwesthuizen/2013/10/14/the-white-angst-of-red -october/.

van Gelder, Elles. 2011. "Survival of the Whitest: Inside an Afrikaner Boot Camp." *The Telegraph*, November 18, www.telegraph.co.uk/news/worldnews/africaandindian ocean/southafrica/8891519/Survival-of-the-whitest-inside-an-Afrikaner-boot -camp.html.

van Graan, Mike. 2014. "Towards a Policy and Strategies for the Growth of South African Theatre." December 16, https://mikevangraan.wordpress.com/2014/12/16 /towards-a-policy-and-strategies-for-the-growth-of-south-african-theatre/.

Van Heerden, Peter. 2010. Personal conversation with author, January 20.

————. 2008. Personal conversation with author, March 21–29.

————. 2004. "Trekker Manifesto." MA thesis, University of Cape Town.

Van Heerden, Peter, and André Laubscher. 2008a. "Kakstorm." Unpublished journal entry.

———. 2008b. "Kunstenaars besin oor hewige reaksie op fees-installasie: Kwiste en kwaste." *Die Burger*, April 28.

———. 2008c. *Preke en gebede*. Unpublished script.

van Heyningen, Elizabeth. 2013. *The Concentration Camps of the Anglo-Boer War: A Social History*. Johannesburg: Jacana.

van Jaarsfeld, Anthea, and Hendrik Petrus Van Coller. N.d. "The Footprints of Raka: On Rewriting and Canonisation." *International Journal of the Book* 5, no. 3: 89–96.

van Jaarsfeld, Floris. 1961. *The Awakening of Afrikaner Nationalism: 1868–1881*. Cape Town: Human & Rousseau.

van Niekerk, Marlene. 1994. *Triomf*. London: Abacus, Little, Brown.

van Wyk Louw, N. P. 1968. "Raka." English translation by Antony Dawes. Cape Town: Nasionale Boekhandel.

Vermeulen, Irma. 1999. *Man en Monument: Die Lewe en Werk van Gerard Moerdijk*. Pretoria: J. L. van Schaik.

Verwoerd, Hendrik. 1961. "April 14, 1961 Speech in Parliament." Pretoria. hendrikver woerd.blogspot.ca/2010/12/april-14-1961-speech-by-dr-verwoerd-in.html.

Verwoerd, Wilhelm. 1999. "Individual and/or Social Justice after Apartheid: The South African Truth and Reconciliation Commission." *European Journal of Developmental Research* 11, no. 2: 115–140.

Vice, Samantha. 2010. "How Do I Live in This Strange Place?" *Journal of Social Philosophy* 41, no. 3 (Fall): 323–342.

Walder, Dennis. 2011. *Postcolonial Nostalgias: Writing, Representation and Memory*. New York: Routledge.

Warren, John T., and Deanna L. Fasset. 2004. "Subverting Whiteness: Pedagogy at the Crossroads of Performance, Culture, and Politics." *Theatre Topics* 14, no. 2 (September): 411–430.

Warren, John T., and Amy Heuman. 2008. "Performing Parody: Towards a Politics of Variation in Whiteness." In *Whiteness, Pedagogy, Performance: Dis/Placing Race*, edited by Leda Cooks and Jennifer Simpson, 215–232. Lanham, MD: Lexington Books.

Wat Kyk Jy. Zef 2013. Website. www.watkykjy.co.za.

Watts, Derek, producer. 2008. "Ons vir Jou." *Carte Blanche Television Programme*. beta.mnet .co.za/carteblanche/Article.aspx?Id=3570.

Wicomb, Zoë. 2001. "Five Afrikaner Texts and the Rehabilitation of Whiteness." In *Culture in the New South Africa: After Apartheid*, edited by R. Kriger and A. Zegeye, 159–182. Cape Town: Kwela Books.

Wilshire, Bruce. 1982. *Role Playing and Identity: The Limits of Theater as Metaphor*. Bloomington: Indiana University Press.

Wines, Michael. 2014. "Reaction to Ferguson Decision Shows Racial Divide Remains over Views of Justice." *New York Times*, November 25, nyti.ms/1rfD3d5.

Wise, Tim. 2014. "Racism, White Denial and Criminal Justice: Ferguson and Beyond." Keynote speech, MOSAIIC conference, Lexington, KY, December 5, www.timwise

.org/2014/12/tim-wise-speech-racism-white-denial-and-criminal-justice
-ferguson-and-beyond-1252014-lexington-ky/.

Witz, Leslie. 2003. *Apartheid's Festival: Contesting South Africa's National Pasts.*
Bloomington: Indiana University Press.

Woods, Janee. 2014. "12 Things White People Can Do Now Because of Ferguson."
Alternet.com, August 18, www.alternet.org/news-amp-politics/12-things-white
-people-can-do-now-because-ferguson.

Yancy, George, and Noam Chomsky. 2015. "Noam Chomsky on the Roots of American
Racism." *New York Times*, Opinionator/The Stone forum, March 18, opinionator
.blogs.nytimes.com/2015/03/18/noam-chomsky-on-the-roots-of-american
-racism/?smid=nytnow-share&smprod=nytnow&_r=0.

Young, James E. 2000. *At Memory's Edge: After-Images of the Holocaust in Contemporary Art
and Architecture.* New Haven, CT: Yale University Press.

———. 1994. *The Art of Memory: Holocaust Memorials in History.* New York: Prestel.

Zaal, F. Noel. 2005. "First Attempts to Use Legislation for Social Engineering in South
Africa: An Analysis of the Seventeenth Century Cape Miscegenation Plakaten."
Fundamina: A Journal of Legal History 11: 200–217.

Exhibition of 1904, 52–53; reenactment of Battle of Colenso, 52–53, 57; reenactment of Battle of Paardeberg, 52–53, 55, 57, 202n10; reenactment of Christiaan De Wet's escape, 52, 57–58; Roberts, Lord, Cronjé's surrender to, 52–53, 55, 201n6; Sonja Loots novel, 202n7; St. Louis, MO, 15, 19, 48, 52–53, 58, 202n8; Transvaal Spectacle, 19, 48, 52, 55, 57–58, 202n17

boerekitsch (kitsch), 21, 163, 168, 191, 213n26; and Jack Parow, 21, 181–85; and Pieter-Dirk Uys, 21, 186–87; *Serial Kitschers*, 186–87. *See also* irony

Boere Nauseum/Museum, 21, 102, 163, 185–87. *See also* Uys, Pieter-Dirk

Boer(s). *See* Afrikaner(s)

Boetman Debate, between Willem de Klerk and Chris Louw, 79, 206n1

Border Wars, 20, 32, 69, 78, 69, 88–93, 205n21, 210n13. *See also* Freedom Park; post-traumatic stress disorder (PTSD); trauma

Botha, Pik, minister of defense, 114, 127, 129, 208n39

Botha, P. W., former prime minister, 3, 14–15, 63, 104, 107, 110, 113, 185–86, 196n20, 206n9, 208n3

Bou van 'n Nasie (1938). *See under* film

Bourdieu, Pierre, on symbolic capital, 37, 82

braaivleis (barbecue), 39, 87, 147, 183, 211n28–29

brandewyn bastards, reaction to *Totanderkuntuit*, 152, 156

Brewer, Mary F., on whiteness, 12, 16, 198n7

British: 15–17, 58, 62, 117; Afrikaans names for, 26, 78; and America, 53; author's ancestry, 4, 141, 153; colonization by, 198n2, 198n5, 198n8; competition with Boers, 26–27, 35, 38, 40, 50, 52, 55–57, 59, 66, 142, 200n29,

201n3, 202n16, 202n20, 204n10, 210n16, 211n34; imperialism, 24, 29–30. *See also* Anglo–Boer War; White English Speaking South Africans

Broederbond, 17, 34, 36, 76, 96, 107, 168, 196n26, 199n17, 200n25, 206n3

Brown, Michael (killed by officer Darren Wilson), xi

bruin Afrikaners. *See* Coloured(s)

Butler, Judith, on gender performativity, 13, 145, 196n19

Calvinism, 3, 16–17, 27, 46, 48, 75, 87, 104, 110, 118, 120, 121, 139–40, 142, 145–46, 148, 155, 168, 174, 196n27, 199n17, 210n18, 210n25. *See also* covenant; Dutch Reformed Church

Cape Colony, 3, 30, 73, 100, 195n12, 199n14

catharsis, and Deon Opperman, 65, 89; and Peter Van Heerden, 136, 148

cenotaph, of Piet Retief, 44–45, 201n3

censorship, under apartheid, 20, 89, 103, 106–7, 110, 112, 121–22, 204n5; Censor Board, 104–5, 186; contemporary, 208n40; Publications Act of 1974, 105–6

Chaudhuri, Una, on nation staged as museum, 13

chora, as theorized by Julia Kristeva, 149–51, 160

Chosen People: and Afrikaner covenant, 25, 35, 65, 75, 104, 119, 145, 197n27, 198n6, 200n24; Ninja as the Chosen One, 166, 170–71, 212n11

Christianity, 32, 42, 110, 139, 142, 179, 196n26. *See also* Calvinism

Cilliers, Sarel, Voortrekker leader, 32, 35, 45, 200n24

colonialism, xv, 193n5, 194n8, 210n25. *See also* settler(s)

Coloured(s), bruin Afrikaners, 27, 70, 83, 115, 117, 131, 146, 155, 157, 164–65,

168, 171, 175, 177, 180, 182–84, 187, 190, 193n3, 193n1, 194n1, 196n21, 197n1, 211n39

communitas, as theorized by Victor Turner, 51, 158

concentration camps. *See* Anglo–Boer War

Coney Island. *See* Boer Circus

conservatives, 6, 20, 38, 60, 65, 68, 70, 79–80, 108, 110, 121, 128, 140, 145–46, 148, 155, 163, 167, 179, 199n11, 207n14, 211n34; Conservative Party, 112, 114

covenant, 30, 32–33, 35, 39, 197n27. *See also* Day of the Vow/Covenant; Chosen People

Crapanzano, Vincent: on whiteness, 5, 196n6

critical race studies, whiteness studies, 1, 6–7, 11, 16, 189–90, 202n12

Cronjé, General Piet. *See under* Boer Circus

crucifixion, 139

Cruywagen, Riaan, SABC newscaster, 112, 207n22

Day of the Vow/Covenant, Geloftedag, 30, 142, 200n24. *See also* Blood River, Battle of; covenant; December 16

de Certeau, Michel, historicity, 25

de Klerk, F. W., former prime minster, 1, 72, 79, 112, 206n36

de Klerk, Willem. *See* Boetman Debate

de la Rey, General Koos, Boer War general, 19, 48, 50–51, 58–59, 61, 63–64, 88. *See also* Opperman, Deon; *Ons vir Jou*

"De La Rey," (pop song), 59, 64–66, 81, 202n19. *See also* van Blerk, Bok

de Lille, Patricia, Pan Africanist congresswoman, 114–15, 127

De Voortrekkers (1916). *See under* film; Shaw, Harold

de Wet, Christiaan, the Boer Pimpernel. *See* Boer Circus

de Witt family, characters in *Donkerland*, 71–88, 204n10

December 16. *See* Day of the Vow/Covenant, Geloftedag

Die Antwoord, 21, 163–80; abjection of whiteness, 169, 171–72, 175; African Gothic, 174–75; Anri du Toit (pseud. Yo-Landi Vi$$er), 164–66, 169–75, 176–80, 213n12; cultural appropriation, 168–69, 191; funk, funkiness, 173–74; Justin De Nobrega (pseud. DJ Hi–Tek), 164; Tudor Watkins Jones (pseud. Ninja), 164–66, 169–75, 176–80, 212n3, 212n11, 212n14. *See also* zef

Die Antwoord, works of: "Baby's On Fire," 21, 163, 176–77; "Enter the Ninja," 21, 163, 165, 170–71; "Fatty Boom Boom," 166, 172, 178; "I Fink U Freeky," 21, 163, 171–75; "Rich Bitch," 21, 163, 171; "Wat kyk jy?" 178, 213n3

"Die Stem," apartheid anthem, 40, 45, 50, 61, 89, 107, 201n31

Dingane, Zulu chief, 30, 34–35, 98, 200n23–24

dirt, 137, 144, 148–49, 171–74; dirty laundry, 70, 83, 151; and whiteness, 3, 85, 111, 178, 181, 212n16

Dolan, Jill, on theatre as field of play, 12, 137, 196n19

dominee, 139–40, 147, 153, 210n22

Donkerland, 19–20, 67–68, 73–75, 83–88, 203n1, 203n2, 203n5, 204n6

Du Bois, W. E. B., 9

Du Preez, Max, on Afrikaners, 61, 64, 168–69, 190

Dutch: colonization of South Africa, 2, 24, 26, 28, 40, 73, 146, 154, 198n2, 198n5, 199n13, 199n14, 210n14; language, 139, 196n21, 199n15–16

Dutch East India Company, 26, 198n8, 199n14, 209n10. *See also* van Riebeeck, Jan

Dutch Reformed Church, Nederduitse

language. *See* Afrikaans, language
Language Movements, 26, 199n15,
  205n17. *See also* Hofmeyr, Isabel
Laubscher, André, activist, 139–40, 145–
  49, 152–53, 157, 180, 209n6, 209n8,
  210n21, 210n22, 211n33. *See also* erf
  (81) cultural collective; Van Heerden,
  Peter
Lefebvre, Henri, on space, 37, 198n4
Leipoldt, C. Louis, Afrikaans poet, 82,
  205n17
Lekota, Terror, premier of the Free State,
  114, 127–28
Leon, Tony, leader of the Democratic
  Party, 114, 127
Lethal Weapon 2, film, 1–5
liminality, 12, 93, 137, 158
Louisiana Purchase Exhibition of 1904.
  See under Boer Circus
Louw, Chris. *See* Boetman Debate

Maharaj, Mac, political activist, 127, 130
Maingard, Jacqueline, on South African
  film, 30, 33, 38–39, 41, 117, 199n21
Malan, D. F., prime minister, 25, 41–42,
  61, 72–73, 104, 186, 199n10
Malema, Julius, leader of Economic Freedom Fighters (EFF), 60, 62, 66
Mandela, Nelson, 1, 26, 70, 72–73, 81,
  108, 114–15, 121, 126–27, 161
Martin, Trayvon (killed by George
  Zimmerman), xi
Martinot, Steve, on whiteness as a machine, xiii, 9
Marx, Hannelie, on zef kultcha, 165, 169.
  See also Milton, Viola Candice
masculinity: Afrikaner, 15, 68, 92, 116–
  17, 145–46, 197n30, 208n27; alternative, 20, 95, 116, 133, 206n2; and
  disability, xiv; phallic, 175; and rugby,
  103, 116–17, 147, 208n38; and whiteness, xiii, 21, 139; and vulnerability,
  162. *See also* Die Antwoord; Opperman,

Deon; phallus; Uys, Pieter-Dirk; Van
  Heerden, Peter
Mbembé, Achille, on the postcolony, xv,
  193n5
McClintock, Anne, on nation and gender, 35, 38, 76, 96–99, 200n29
McKaiser, Eusebius, on uncritical
  whiteness, 4
Meidjie, character in *Donkerland*, 76, 80,
  82, 86
melodrama, 30, 33, 59, 65–67, 77, 88,
  93, 118, 153, 184
Miller, Henry, on sacrilege of the new,
  151
Milton, Viola Candice, on zef kultcha,
  165, 169. *See also* Marx, Hannelie
minority: identity, 54, 70; rule, 4, 6,
  8, 18, 172; status, 8, 29, 34, 48, 56,
  66–67, 68, 74, 81–82, 85–86, 152–53,
  175, 203n24–26
miscegenation, 68, 83–84, 123, 177,
  195n12
Moodie, T. Dunbar, on Afrikaner ascendency, 16, 42, 196n26, 198n5
Morrison, Toni, on whiteness, 9, 32
Mulder, Connie, minister of information, 206n9, 207n25
Muldergate, Information Scandal, 103–4,
  110, 119, 123, 206n9
museum: Boere Museum/Nauseum,
  102, 163, 185–87; nation staged as
  (Una Chaudhuri), 13; Patricia Davidson theory, 13–14; Voortrekker Monument, 42–45

'n Nasie Hou Koers (1940). *See under* film
nation: and gender, 95–101, 129; and
  narration, 13–16, 24, 34, 37, 42–44,
  49, 55, 61,65, 72–75, 87, 92, 114, 126,
  135, 145, 150, 169–70, 180, 186, 188,
  197n1, 197n28, 199n9, 199n18; nation-
  building era, 42, 76, 196n26, 198n2;
  nation-building theatrics, 3, 15, 23, 38,

nation, 20, 44, 95–97, 206n5, 208n28; as national icon, 16, 39–40; and zefness, 181–182

Vrouemonument, Women's Monument, 97, 208n29

Warren, John T. and Heuman, Amy, on whiteness, 13, 195

Wat kyk jy?, 178, 212n3

white: Africans, xiv, 1, 17–18, 29, 151, 158, 194n7; allies/allyship, 6–7, 189; bodies performing, 69, 88, 93; femininity, 41, 77, 98–99, 144; masculinity, xiii–xiv, 21, 92, 135, 139, 150, 209n1; privilege, xiv, 5–8, 49, 112, 140, 142, 145, 151, 188, 191, 195n13, 202n12; psychosocial costs of racism to whites (PCRW), 206n22; -sight, 11, 13, 152, 175, 195n17; supremacy, xii, 7–10, 21, 46, 59, 133, 164, 174, 189, 191, 195n12, 199n17; talk (Melissa Steyn), 17, 168; trash, 21, 163–64, 169, 191; tribe (Marq de Villiers), 17, 173, 196n26, 197n28, 213n17; values, 9–10; washing, 122, 124, 173

White English Speaking South Africans (WESSAs), 11, 29, 64, 74, 193n3. See also British

whitely, whiteliness, 10–11, 94, 190, 192, 195n13; Vice, Samantha

whiteness: and amnesia, 8, 10, 14, 42, 45; and blackness, 9, 29, 31–32, 187, 193n3, 205n18; as contingent and situational (Thomas Blaser), 12; and deflated privilege, 8, 18, 21, 136; dismantling of, 7, 11, 13, 64, 134, 189; and empire, 7–8, 16, 18, 192; and epistemologies of ignorance (Melissa Steyn), 11; as fiction of racial difference, 9, 31, 98; as guilt-etched (Louise Bethlehem), 7; and indigestibility, 179, 185, 191; as inherently theatrical (Mary F. Brewer), 12; as interdisciplinary, 9; in inverted commas (Alistair Bonnett), 13, 192; and iterative performance, 12, 16, 24, 48, 158, 195n18; matters, 11; and navel-gazing, 6; and performance, xiv, 11–12, 20, 188; in Peter Van Heerden's *Bok*, 42–43, 210n19, 211n31; postcolonial remains (Alfred Lopez), 9, 11; and poverty, 3, 27, 30, 171–72, 204n7; as racial category, 1, 7, 8–11; reoriented and transnationalized (Boucher, Carey, and Ellinghaus), 8–9, 16, 151; and South African context (Nicky Falkof), 6, 17, 85, 195n10, 203n26, 205n19; troubling, 6; under erasure (Louise Bethlehem), 7, 195n11; as unmarked norm, 10. *See also* abjection

whitewash, 122, 124, 173

Whitewash Conference, 1, 6–7, 10, 21, 163, 188, 190

wiggers. *See* Kitwana, Bakari

Wise, Tim, on whiteness, xii

wit (white) kaffir, 139, 143, 177

Xhosa, 92, 126, 148, 157, 160, 165, 196n21, 197n28, 199n13, 208n38

Zef, zefness, or zef kultcha (referring to white Afrikaner working-class culture of 1960s, 1970s), 21, 163–70, 178–79, 181–87, 212n8

Zulu, 30–33, 40, 45, 57, 73, 76–77, 80, 98–99, 123, 126, 159, 165, 197n28, 199n13, 200n23, 200n24, 202n8, 208n38, 212n45

STUDIES IN THEATRE HISTORY AND CULTURE